THE GERALDINE CONSPIRACY

Grant-aided by the
Arts Council

First published in 1995 by
Marino Books
An imprint of Mercier Press
16 Hume Street Dublin 2
Paperback edition published in 1997

Trade enquiries to CMD Distribution
55A Spruce Park Stillorgan Industrial
Park Blackrock County Dublin
Published in the U.S. and Canada by
the Irish American Book Company,
6309 Monarch Park Place,
Niwot, Colorado, 80503.
Telephone (303) 530-1352,
(800) 452-7115.
Fax (303) 530-4488, (800) 401-9705.

ISBN 1 86023 034 2

10 9 8 7 6 5 4 3 2

A CIP record for this title is available
from the British Library

Cover painting courtesy of the
National Gallery, Dublin
Set by Richard Parfrey in Caslon
Regular 9.5/15

Printed in Ireland by ColourBooks,
Baldoyle Industrial Estate, Dublin 13.

THE GERALDINE CONSPIRACY

ANNE CHAMBERS

THE GERALDINE CONSPIRACY

ANNE CHAMBERS

For Tony

THE EARLS OF KILDARE

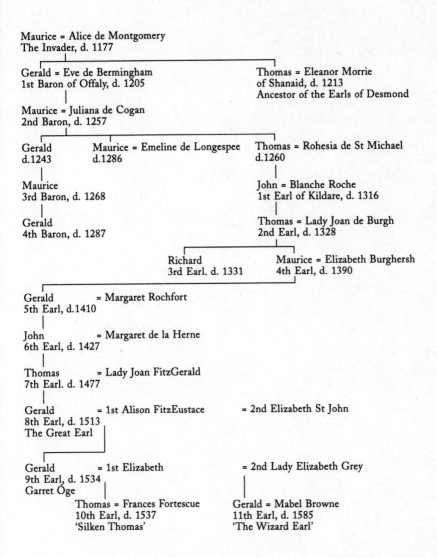

Maurice = Alice de Montgomery
The Invader, d. 1177

Gerald = Eve de Bermingham
1st Baron of Offaly, d. 1205

Thomas = Eleanor Morrie
of Shanaid, d. 1213
Ancestor of the Earls of Desmond

Maurice = Juliana de Cogan
2nd Baron, d. 1257

Gerald
d.1243

Maurice = Emeline de Longespee
d.1286

Thomas = Rohesia de St Michael
d.1260

Maurice
3rd Baron, d. 1268

John = Blanche Roche
1st Earl of Kildare, d. 1316

Gerald
4th Baron, d. 1287

Thomas = Lady Joan de Burgh
2nd Earl, d. 1328

Richard
3rd Earl. d. 1331

Maurice = Elizabeth Burghersh
4th Earl, d. 1390

Gerald   = Margaret Rochfort
5th Earl, d.1410

John   = Margaret de la Herne
6th Earl, d. 1427

Thomas   = Lady Joan FitzGerald
7th Earl. d. 1477

Gerald   = 1st Alison FitzEustace   = 2nd Elizabeth St John
8th Earl, d. 1513
The Great Earl

Gerald   = 1st Elizabeth   = 2nd Lady Elizabeth Grey
9th Earl, d. 1534
Garret Óge

Thomas = Frances Fortescue
10th Earl, d. 1537
'Silken Thomas'

Gerald = Mabel Browne
11th Earl, d. 1585
'The Wizard Earl'

GLOSSARY

a h-Uaisle: your excellencies (nobles)

Aithníonn ciaróg ciaróg eile: One beetle [villain] recognises another.

angel: English coin bearing the figure of an angel

aonach samhraidh: summer fair

arquebuse: a hand-gun

a stór: my treasure (term of endearment)

Bachall Íosa: bishops's crozier greatly revered in Dublin

bawn (*bábhun*): fortification around a dwelling or an enclosure for cattle

bata: stick

betagh (*biatach*): labourer who must provide food for his lord and the lord's retinue

bodach: churl

bonnaght (*buannacht*): billeted soldiers, billet

booleying (*buailtíocht*): custom of transferring herds to uplands for summer grazing

bothy: a small cottage or hut

brehon (*breitheamh*): a judge in the Gaelic legal system

cailín: girl

cailleach: old hag

caiseal: stone fortification, often ecclesiastical, as in *Caiseal Mumhan* (of Munster)

carrack: a large cargo ship that was also fitted out for fighting

cin comhfhocuis: kinship group, bearing joint responsibility in law for the crime of a group member

clachán: cluster of cabins

coshering: the ancient right of an Irish chief to quarter himself and his retainers on his tenantry

9

creaght: cattle drover

cuid oíche: provision for the night, stipulated food and lodging to be provided to a chieftain by a sub-chieftain

culverin: type of long cannon

deoch an dorais: lit. drink of the door=departing drink

derbhfine: family group, extended ruling family unit

demi-lance: short light spear frequently used in the 16th century

Dia dhuit/Dia dhibh: God be with you (ye)

Diarmuid Gallda: Dermot of the English

Dubhdara: lit. black oak (personal name)

eric (*eiric*): fine or compensation

gallowglasses (*gallóglaigh*): foreign warriors, usual mercenary soldiers from the Scottish Isles and Highlands

glib: fringe of hair

hauberk: long coat of chain-mail

prisage: the right of the king or overlord to a certain percentage of wine imported on ships

In ainm an diabhail: in the name of the devil

Is túisce deoch ná scéal: (have a) drink before the story is told

keening (*caoineadh*): custom of crying loudly around a corpse

kern (*ceithearn*): band of lightly armed footsoldiers

mallacht air: curse him!

mallacht go deo air: curse him for ever!

mallacht Dé ar a anam dubh: God's curse on his black soul

maor: steward or bailiff

marbhfháisce air: band of death on him (linen band which bound the jaws of a corpse)

meadar: wooden drinking vessel

morion: open helmet without visor

ollave (*ollamh*): a scholar, poet, bard (also ollave dána)

oireachtas: assembly

piseog: superstition

rath: prehistoric mound

rising out: compulsory provision of military assistance to overlord

Sasanach: English

Sean-Ghall: Old English, Anglo-Normans

skean (*scia*n): knife

sláinte: health (a toast)

sláinte 'gus saol agat: health and life to you

slantyaght (*slánaíocht*): custom of minor chieftain buying the protection of a stronger chieftain

spré: bride's dowry

T'anam 'on diabhal: your soul to the devil (a curse but sometimes used lightly)

tanist (*tánaiste*): successor-elect to chieftain

taoiseach : chieftain

tuarastal: gift from a greater to a lesser chieftain, which made the latter honour bound to the former's service

uisce beatha: Irish whiskey or spirits (lit. water of life)

urragh (uir-rí): sub-king, tributary chieftain

Introduction

For four hundred years, one family held centre stage in the convoluted history of Ireland, from their arrival in the van of the Anglo-Norman conquerors in the twelfth century to the destruction of the Gaelic world of their adoption by the Tudor monarchs in the sixteenth century. Originating in Italy, their ancestors had made their way, via Normandy, in the army of William the Conqueror, to England and via Wales to Ireland.

The English knew them as the FitzGeralds or later as the earls of Kildare and Desmond, denoting the two branches of the dynasty they established in Ireland. To the Irish, however, they were always known and will ever be known as the Geraldines.

> Ye Geraldines, ye Geraldines, how royally ye
> reigned
> O'er Desmond broad, and rich Kildare and English
> arts disdained.
> Your sword made knights, your banner waved, free
> bugle call
> By Glyn's green slopes, and Dingle's tide, from
> Barrow's banks to Youghal.
> What gorgeous shrines, what Brehon lore, what
> minstrel feasts there were.
> In and around Maynooth's strong keep and palace-
> filled Adare

But not for rite nor feast ye stayed, when friend or
                    kin were pressed
And foemen fled, when 'Crom-a-boo', bespoke your
                    lance in rest.
                                        Thomas Davis

PROLOGUE

BEAUCHAMP TOWER, TOWER OF LONDON, FEBRUARY 1537

The wind from the Thames buffeted the lattice window in the upper chamber of Beauchamp Tower and with a mournful wail reverberated through the passages and down the spiral steps. Crouched along by the wall, the lone figure took little notice, absorbed in the task he had commenced at first light. The handle of the pewter spoon had become sharply pointed as he scraped away the stone particles to shape the letters on the cell wall. The task had taken longer than he had anticipated. A pewter spoon was a poor substitute for a mason's chisel and the hard stone of the tower resisted his efforts. It would take him another day to finish. But even as he scraped the dust from the groove of the G of his name, the hollow echo of marching feet signalled that his time had run out.

For months he had dreaded this moment. Long days when the sweat streamed from every pore in his body as he lay on the straw pallet and thought of the agony before him. Long nights when he desperately fought to control the fear, the panic, that swelled within him and which threatened to spill forth from his mouth in a despairing cry into the black silence. Carving his name on the wall of his tower prison served to distract his mind from the torment that lay ahead. Calmly he continued to fashion the letter G as the iron-studded door swung open. As if in final farewell to himself, he ran his fingers briefly over the letters of his incomplete name, placed the misshapen spoon on the table and turned to stare at the door of his cell.

Framed by the doorway, the Lieutenant of the Tower drew a parchment roll from a leather belt at his waist and, with apparent detachment, read aloud his orders:

> *In the name of God and of his sovereign Majesty King Henry VIII, you have been adjudged guilty of the charge of high treason for your crime of rebellion against the King. You will be taken from hence to the place of execution at Tyburn where you will be hanged from the neck and while you are alive your body will be taken down, disembowelled and quartered so that no part of your person will remain intact as an affront to his Majesty the King and to the Realm.*
> *Given under Our seal and signet this third day of February 1537*
> *Henry Rex*

'God save the King,' the Lieutenant concluded crisply.

Silence, broken only by the crackling sound of the parchment as it snapped back to its cylindrical shape, greeted the grim details of the King's justice. The Lieutenant turned quickly on his heel and disappeared through the doorway. An armed guard of six halberdiers remained in the passage outside. The captain entered the cell and signalled to the prisoner who, in tattered hose and shirt, stood transfixed in the centre of the spartan chamber. Slowly the prisoner crossed to the window and from a ledge reached for a doublet of dark green velvet. A silken fringe lay limply along the length of the sleeves, the silken fringe that had become synonymous with his name.

As he stooped to retrieve the doublet from the window ledge of his prison, he remembered how vainly he had flaunted it in the tumultuous march through the streets of Dublin, with the shouts of the mercurial citizens inciting him further in rebellion; in the vaulted chamber of St Mary's Abbey, where he had flung the sword of state at the feet of the King's Council and boasted of his intention to rebel.

The captain of the halberdiers shifted impatiently. The prisoner slowly put on his doublet. He glanced through the window to the Green below and his heart lurched at the sight of his five uncles, standing in line between two rows of guards. Convulsively, his hands tightened into fists of compressed hatred and frustration at his sense of helplessness to avert the fate intended for them all. But despairingly he knew that it was he and he alone who had presented the king and his enemies at court with the opportunity they had long awaited, the annihilation of the House of Kildare and its ambition to rule over a unified Ireland, independently of the crown of England. The grand design, nourished by generations of Geraldines, had evaporated into the hot air of his intemperate actions. With a final look at his unfinished epitaph on the bare wall, he joined the soldiers in the passage.

They stepped briskly through the passageway, down the winding stairway and outside into the cold February air. A crowd of onlookers, residents and workers in the Tower were gathered in a loose-knit bunch to witness another deputation being prepared for Tyburn. Since the king's break with Rome, it had become a frequent occurrence. Roman Catholic clerics, nobles with vague claims to the crown, anyone who wittingly or unwittingly invoked the king's anger. Irish rebels were a novelty.

He joined his uncles and embraced each in turn. James, Walter, Richard, Oliver and John. There was nothing to say in answer to the silent agony in each pallid countenance. It had been a fearful wait as their fate swung like a pendulum in the hands of the volatile king. Pardon or execution. The long-feared answer was finally beyond doubt. Standing in line with his uncles, he thought of his father, and his gaze was momentarily drawn to the nearby outline of the chapel of St Peter, where the ninth earl lay with More, Fisher, Anne

17

Boleyn and the many victims of the king's vengeance.

God's mercy that he has been spared this day, he thought, and closed his eyes in silent thanksgiving.

The sound of hoofs and the clatter of wooden hurdles on the cobblestones heralded the arrival of their transportation to Tyburn. On the captain's curt order, the prisoners were spreadeagled and bound hand and foot. The portcullis of the Byward Tower was raised and the cortège issued forth over the muddied waters of the moat through the Lion Tower and into the city of London. The hurdles with the doomed cargo attached bumped over the ruts and cobblestones.

The air of expectation among the onlookers increased as the procession dragged its way up Tower Street into Cheapside, past St Paul's and into the Shambles. Through laneways and narrow streets, bordered by wooden-framed houses, taverns and shops, windows were thrown open and the contents of human and household waste were emptied down upon the stretched bodies on the hurdles.

'Death to the rebels.'

'Pox on ye, Irish traitors.'

As hounds to the kill, the shouts of the excited citizenry increased at every corner in anticipation of the sordid spectacle.

Leaving the city through Newgate, the cortège moved slowly up Snow Hill, crossing the bridge over the Fleet river and on through the gardens and fields of Holborn. As it arrived at Tyburn, a loud roar of approval issued from the mob assembled on the gallows field. Young and old, men and women, jostled for position and a closer look at the victims being dragged through the crowd. Hundreds of faces, eyes feverish with expectation, mouths wide open, spewed forth a stream of venom. The hurdles halted beside a platform dominated by a roughly hewn butcher's block. Alongside the platform was a gallows, the hempen noose swinging ominously in the wind against the leaden sky.

The guards unhitched the hurdles and laid them side by

18

side on the muddied grass. The crowd grew hushed as the hooded figure mounted the platform. From a box beneath the block the executioner removed the sinister tools of his trade.

A shudder ran through the youngest prisoner and a fearful trembling made his body shake uncontrollably. 'Jesus Christ, help me,' he whispered.

He felt a touch on his shoulder. The eyes of his Uncle Walter smiled into his. 'Courage, Thomas. It will soon be over.'

Great emotion welled inside him and, despite his efforts, tears rolled down his face. 'Forgive me, Uncle.'

With a smile, his uncle nodded his head and wearily closed his eyes.

The crowd was becoming restive, but as the first victim was unbound and led to the scaffold, an exultant roar of approval rose. Sir John FitzGerald was hoisted by the neck until his body jerked convulsively. The noose was removed with difficulty and he was placed on the block. A knife flashed and the executioner began his foul task.

The young prisoner closed his eyes as if he could block out the hideous sound. The frenzied wails of pain rose and fell as the sharp knife cut through flesh and sinew. The executioner held aloft the first trophy, to howls of delight from the crowd. A larger knife was then employed and, as it cut deep across the victim's abdomen, the agonising cries mercifully ceased. The dismembered body was flung piece by piece into a large wooden receptacle under the platform until, with a final flourish, the head was severed clean from the trunk. The executioner held high the grim proof of the completion of his task.

'God save the king,' he shouted.

'God save the king,' his audience howled in appreciation.

Five times the hooded royal butcher held a Geraldine head aloft. By the time it was the turn of the youngest prisoner to mount the scaffold, a strange numbness had spread through his body. The searing screams of his kinsmen, mingled with the clamour of the mob, had become remote. As the rough hemp rope cut into his neck and the breath was summarily ejected from his body, he was vaguely conscious of the pain and of his gasping efforts for air. The rope was jerked loose and he crumpled on to the wet boards. Hands seized him roughly and lifted him on to the execution block. Through a red haze, he saw a hooded face looming over him, the hood with slanted slits, through which black eyes stared impassively into his. A flicker of pity seemed to pass quickly across the eyes but the young man could not be certain. For a moment, the hand that held the knife hesitated. The victim closed his eyes.

Shielding the knife from the eager eyes of the crowd below him, the executioner inserted the lethal tool under the breastbone of the trembling body beneath him and with a sharp upward movement sent his twenty-three-year old victim to a swifter and more humane death than that intended by the king.

The executioner went through the motions of the execution ritual for the sixth and final time. The intoxicated crowd roared approval at every stroke. 'God save the king.'

The golden-haired head of Thomas FitzGerald, eldest son of Earl of Kildare, tumbled into the wooden receptacle in full and final retribution for the crime of rebellion against the king of England.

SPRING

1
—

DONORE CASTLE
LORDSHIP OF KILDARE

Thomas Leverous watched the boy's fitful breathing as he
tossed, murmuring incoherently, in the dishevelled bed.
Before he fled with the castle guard, the physician intimated
that the fever would soon reach a climax. Leverous held a
damp linen cloth to Gerald's burning brow. The outward
signs of the disease scarred the boy's sallow skin. The angry
oozing pustules distorted his face and gave him an appearance
older than his eleven years. Gradually Gerald's restless
movements lessened and he sank into a fretful sleep.

Leverous eased his tall frame from the chair. His body
ached from sitting in the same position. The day seemed
interminable and an equally long and solitary night beckoned.
From an oak chest at the end of the bed, he took a woollen
mantle with a deeply fringed collar and wrapped himself
within the warm folds. It was cold and damp in the castle's
bedchamber. The chill seeped from the flagged floor, despite
the covering of dry rushes. Leverous could never remember
Donore as being other than cheerless, even in summer. Ever
the least comfortable of the earl's castles, it was considered
no more than a garrison outpost, built by the first Anglo-
Norman Geraldines, four hundred years previously, to protect
their territory from the ravages of the Gaelic clans whom

they had dispossessed. But the protection afforded now by its very isolation made it as good a place as any to give sanctuary to the earl's son, time for him to recover from the fever of the smallpox and to hide from his enemies.

Leverous peered through the low recessed window into the gloom outside. It was a raw evening. The easterly wind which moaned around the high keep had ice in its sting. There will be snow before the winter is done, he thought. From the high vantage-point he looked beyond the curtain walls towards the desolate moorlands and bogs that surrounded the castle. All was strangely still. In the bowels of the castle a door rattled loosely. There was no light nor sign of movement among the thatched cabins that clustered like beehives around the outer walls. Everyone had fled – tenants, servants, retainers. Even the gallowglass, who recklessly risked life and limb in battle for their Geraldine masters, had succumbed to the fear of the smallpox. The son of the once omnipotent Earl of Kildare had been abandoned by the traditional guardians of his house and been left to the protection of his English tutor.

A slim protection, Leverous mused, against the combined might of the king of England, his deputy and council in Dublin, the Ormonds, and the pox.

For a fleeting moment he wondered should he have run with the rest. But he knew that he could no more abandon the boy than if he were his own flesh and blood. And he would like to have such a son as Gerald and should have, if the indecision that marked the course of his life had not inhibited him from committing himself to either woman or God, or both, he thought ruefully, as Gaelic Ireland allowed and Tudor England more recently permitted. He sighed with the annoyance and regret of self-accusation. For all the experience his upbringing in England and Italy had given him, neither God nor woman had been able to fill the aching void within him, a void fuelled by a memory and a friendship, which in truth, he realised, could never have been more and which he should have long since forgotten. Instead, it gnawed a black hole within him, leaving him unfulfilled. Nurturing his vain desire, he used it as a shield for the loneliness, that most feared legacy, that at times beset him and as an excuse for his reluctance to commit his emotions.

He turned from the bleak landscape and shivered within the folds of his Irish mantle. The approaching night brought an added chill in its wake.

Dark enough to light a fire, he thought.

Curious eyes would hardly detect the smoke in the black shroud that was slowly engulfing the remaining daylight. He busied himself at the open hearth and piled a mound of twigs and moss, topped by white ash logs, in the dark recess. His black hair fell in strands onto his broad forehead. High above his head the wind whistled shrilly in the cavernous chimney-piece.

He had lost count of the weeks since he had taken refuge in the remote castle on the fringes of the Pale. This bleak stone keep had become yet another temporary refuge, since the seizure of the boy's stepbrother and uncles and their incarceration in the Tower of London, to enable them to keep on the move and baffle their pursuers as to the whereabouts of the only Kildare Geraldine still at liberty. He had received offers of refuge from allies of the House of Kildare, from Old English lords of the Pale and Gaelic chieftains alike. But he could trust no one. The Earl of Kildare might well have enjoyed the loyalty of these lords and chieftains while he was alive but Leverous knew enough about the vacillating nature of Irish politics to recognise that circumstances had dramatically changed since his death. For in the absence of a centralising power structure in Ireland, which the earl had sought to establish, political loyalty was based on the concept of dependence and protection: the weaker lord or chieftain dependent on a stronger overlord for protection from his enemies. The Earl of Kildare was dead and no longer able to fulfil his part of this contractual alliance. Consequently his former client lords, Leverous knew, would seek protection from someone else, even and most likely, he thought ruefully, from the earl's adversaries, who, since his death in the Tower and the failure of his son's rebellion, were now in control in Ireland. As a result, yesterday's friends could become today's enemies.

Silken Thomas discovered that reality to his cost, Leverous reflected as he watched the flame creep through the crackling twigs.

The loyalty which the earl had carefully cultivated among the leaders of the two traditions in Ireland had not been forthcoming to his son. And, Leverous thought, he could scarcely blame them. For Silken Thomas's rebellion had been ill-timed and foolish, disastrous both to himself and to the House of Kildare. Leverous was convinced that it had brought about the sudden death of the earl in the Tower of London. For whether death had come by poison at the hand of the king, as many in England and in Ireland contended, or through grief at the folly of his son, Leverous was convinced that Silken Thomas's rebellion had caused the premature death of Garret FitzGerald, the ninth Earl of Kildare, his friend and foster brother.

The flames rose high in the chimney and the warmth from the fire slowly permeated the chill. From a window recess Leverous took a pair of black hide saddlebags and extracted a folded piece of parchment with the remains of a broken seal adhering. Garret's familiar handwriting covered the topmost part. Leverous read the words that by now he knew by rote:

Well-beloved friend and foster brother,
We greet you well with these lines written in haste from here, this place of Our confinement and we fear of Our execution. If you have ever loved Me and Mine as I have loved you I this day charge you to take unto your care and protection the son of My body Gerald your pupil and be

unto him a father as I have been a friend unto thee. Entrust his care and keeping to no other. Our enemies are all around us and seek to strike at us even from within Our own House.

The bearer Robert Walshe is to France to determine the King's mind regarding Our son's future welfare there. He will inform you more of My intent. I know not who be My friend in My shame and agony but We trust that you yet remain so.

I bid thee farewell, dear Leverous. From this Tower of London this 30th day of August in the year of Our Saviour 1536
Kildare

Leverous folded the parchment carefully. Garret's words imposed a first and final obligation on a friendship that spanned almost three decades. Fired by his father's service as legal counsel to Garret's father, the Great Earl of Kildare, at the royal court, it had been nurtured by the kindness of the Great Earl to him on the death of his parents.

The stench and the horror of the Black Death which had devastated London and his childhood were a vivid nightmare still, as was the gripping terror which enveloped him as he watched the death cart with the diseased bodies of his parents trundle out of sight. Every family had been visited by death that dreadful summer and the future of a ten-year-old orphan was of little consequence. But the Irish earl had adopted his lawyer's son, taken him to Ireland and reared him as one of his own.

His friendship with his adopted Irish family had been further soldered by the brotherly affection that had grown between himself and Garret, son and heir of the Great Earl. His friendship with his foster brother flew in the face of the exploitative egotistical spirit of Tudor England or the opportunistic code of Gaelic Ireland. Both cultures were intolerant of a friendship based on a lack of ulterior motive.

27

But it was their friendship that had made them equal, he recalled, and their equality bred the affection and respect they had for each other, which in turn was the cornerstone of the unbreachable trust between them.

He had become Garret's confidant and confessor, privy to the earl's innermost secrets and ambitions, particularly his clandestine aspiration to mould a Geraldine confederacy out of the political disunity in Ireland. Ireland unified under Geraldine rule: such an ambition could be entrusted only to a friend, to be whispered in confidence and in dread of the Tudor dragon across the sea. And now the circle of friendship had turned. Garret had entrusted him with his son and had presented him with an opportunity to repay the debt he owed him.

As a boy growing up in London, Leverous knew little about Ireland, and anything he learned had not encouraged him to know more. Even his father, albeit the Earl of Kildare's lawyer, had never set foot in Ireland and privately subscribed to the commonly held English view that Ireland was a barbarous, backward country, of savage, ungovernable people. The truth that had confronted him on coming to Ireland, Leverous recalled, was something entirely different. Dublin seemed but a less noisy and smaller edition of London. Maynooth, a sentinel on a fertile plain of waving green grass and golden corn, became the actual castle home of his boyhood fantasies. Its large, boisterous family became his family. The long-haired Irish chieftains who came to pay their respects to the Great Earl, the savages of his English mind, changed over the subsequent years of familiarity, into shrewd, quick-witted, if somewhat over-indulgent friends.

The flames threw darts of light across the boy's pale face. A film of sweat glistened on his forehead. Leverous dipped the linen cloth into the pewter bowl and held it to Gerald's brow. His breathing was shallow but regular. Leverous lifted the heavy oak armchair, with the wild boar crest of the House

28

of Kildare carved in heavy relief on the back support, and set it close to the fire.

It was the Great Earl who had encouraged him to study law at Cambridge, in the hope that he would take his father's place and become his legal advisor in England. But to leave Ireland and his adopted family, to live again in England, which seemed bereft of the spontaneous Irish warmth to which he had become accustomed, was unbearable. He returned to Maynooth instead, where the Great Earl sent him to serve an apprenticeship with the Irish brehon, MacEgan, to become versed in the tenets of Irish law.

Based on ancient texts, Irish law, he discovered, was a complex amalgam of Roman and feudal maxims and rules. It was administered by families of hereditary jurists like the MacEgans. One of the most striking differences between it and English law, he found, was the absence of a definable system of criminal law. Murder, thefts, arson, the common crimes of man, were by Irish law punishable by the payment of erics for damages to the injured party, his overlord or to his kin. Recalling that in England even a crime of theft was liable to be punished by death, Leverous had voiced his astonishment to the elderly brehon.

'And of what use is a dead man to his victim or to the victim's kin?' MacEgan had answered him. 'Is it not better that he remain alive and make restitution to them for his crime?'

To his initial dismay that he would never understand the complexities of Irish legal customs, MacEgan had replied that he would, when he understood Ireland. He accompanied the brehon to many of the Irish courts of arbitration, invariably held on an ancient prehistoric fort or hill. There the chieftains and their followers flocked to seek legal redress for crimes committed, to ratify treaties or to divide the clan lands on the death of a leader. Seated near MacEgan on the grassy mound, surrounded by the chieftains and their clansmen, each waiting his turn to have his case heard,

Leverous felt part of some ancient prehistoric ritual. He listened as the brehon delivered his verdict on each case and slowly began to realise that the laws catered adequately for the needs of a tribal people whose society was based on a system of exactions and payments. While never becoming an expert, like his tutor MacEgan, Leverous had become sufficiently versed to apply his knowledge of Irish law for the earl's benefit.

But when Garret succeeded the Great Earl to the earldom of Kildare, Leverous's tenure as lawyer ended abruptly. The new earl sent him to Italy to present his greetings to Piero Gherardino, Consul of the Republic of Florence. Descended from this Italian patrician family, the Irish Geraldines maintained contact with their Italian kinsmen. Before his death, the Great Earl had entertained a young scion of the Gherardini at Maynooth, much to the displeasure of the English council in Dublin, Leverous recalled, ever suspicious of the contacts of the powerful Irish earl with the Continent. Anxious to repay the hospitality shown to his son in Ireland, Piero Gherardino had been solicitous of Leverous's welfare in Florence.

To the Great Earl of Kildare and his son, the evolution of the Italian Gherardini from their patrician roots into progressive merchant rulers of the new Florentine republic had become an absorbing fascination. Both had visited the place of their origins to experience at first hand the republicanism espoused by Florence, with its roots in the Roman classical tradition. It had added a further dimension to the separatist cause they pursued in Ireland. A government chosen by its people and ruled by representatives elected by them might well be a system that could be applied in Ireland, particularly where election was the customary method whereby leaders were chosen in the Gaelic-ruled lordships.

Overwhelmed by the vibrancy of Italy, then in its Renaissance maturity, Leverous was bewitched like so many foreigners who thronged its pulsating northern cities. Cradle of the most spectacular rebirth of philosophy, art and literature, Florence held him spellbound. Under the wealthy patronage of the Medicis, the city's artistic tradition had reached perfection with Leonardo, Michelangelo and Raphael. With the multitude of other awestruck pilgrims to the shrine of artistic achievement, he had raised his eyes to wonder at the cathedral dome of Brunelleschi and had stood in mute admiration of Michelangelo's statue of David. When the Gherardino offered to become his sponsor at the University of Padua, Leverous sped a message to Garret in Ireland and accepted the consul's generosity without a second thought.

Padua, what memories the name invoked! The graceful curves of its stone and marble buildings, great arcaded houses, its innumerable stone bridges. Then under the patronage of Venice, Padua had become the Athens of Europe. Thither students from all over the world flocked to sip at the fountains of knowledge, erudition and eloquence. Here the great names in philosophy, literature, art and music dispensed their learning, their thought-provoking disputations. He remembered the rectors in their togas, the Capitan and their officers, trying vainly to keep in check the students in their multi-coloured attire, intent with flashing swords on upholding the tradition of broils with Padua's citizenry. The great Prata della Valle, scene of games, pageants, dramas and tournaments in which both town and gown participated. The exotic costumes of the Carnival, the haunting strain of lute, the sweet notes of the madrigal. The images and sounds were still vivid in his mind.

In the house of the renowned humanist, poet and diplomat, Pietro Bembo, Leverous had met professors and scholars, many foreigners like himself. An honoured guest in the Bembo household was the English nobleman Reginald Pole, whose scholarly reputation had preceded him to Padua. His status as cousin of the king of England further enhanced his standing amongst the Italians.

The Englishman was also a friend of the Great Earl of Kildare and had shown Leverous every kindness during his sojourn in Padua, including him in his company, to which many aspired but few were admitted. Pole's abhorrence of the religious confusion which Martin Luther's reforms had loosed on the world was evident in his opinions and writings. But his belief was tempered by his acknowledgement that the Church was in need of reform, but from within. His erudite defence of the Church, his appeal for unity, brilliantly expounded in the elegant simplicity of his Latin treatises, affected many within his circle, including himself, Leverous recalled. For it was Pole's twin pleas for Church unity and reform that eventually sent Leverous to seek the fulfilment that had eluded him at the University of Louvain.

A career in the Church had seemed to be his destiny, had not more human feelings intervened. He was certain Garret had been aware that his pursuit of scholarship was no more than an escape to fill some deeper need within him, a need which he chose not to reveal. His friend's suspicions had been correct. And the reason was the one secret Leverous could not share with him, for revelation meant the betrayal of the trust on which their friendship rested.

His gaze was drawn deep into the burning amber of the ash logs. Eleanor's hair had glowed with such intensity, that first night in Dublin. A night that had witnessed one act of deception and one sublime act of love, which, like the Lotus Eaters, he was doomed to crave forever. That was his punishment for his betrayal of his benefactor. A fire had flamed in her bedchamber at Thomas Court on the night he had won and lost: won her love yet lost her forever to the elderly MacCarthy chieftain and to the machinations of Irish political expediency, in which he, a commoner and a foreigner, had no part to play.

The staccato of approaching hoofbeats roused Leverous from his reverie. Friend or foe, a harbinger of ill tidings, he thought with premonition.

Swiftly he eased the iron bar from the door and entered the dark corridor. A wave of damp air engulfed him as he descended the steep steps. He removed the heavy wooden beam from the iron cups on either side of the doorway and emerged into the courtyard. The wind gusted around the inner confines of the castle and sent particles of dust eddying in spirals. He entered the ground level of the barbican.

The rider dismounted and approached the portcullis. Leverous recognised the square-cut figure of Robert, Lord Dunsany, father-in-law of Walter FitzGerald, Garret's brother, lately imprisoned with his brothers and nephew in the Tower of London.

'Over here, my Lord,' Leverous called out.

Dunsany started and looked suspiciously about him.

'The barbican,' Leverous directed him.

A florid figure of late middle age, dressed in a crimson riding cloak above mud-splattered riding boots, a flat hat covering his cropped grey hair, hurried towards the barbican. He peered into the archery loop in the wall.

'Leverous, 'tis I, Dunsany, let me in,' he called impatiently.

'I fear 'tis impossible, my lord. There is smallpox here.'

Dunsany involuntarily recoiled.

'Not I, my lord,' Leverous assured him.

'The boy?'

Leverous nodded. 'The fever may break tonight.'

'The physician attends him?'

Leverous shook his head. 'We are alone. Even the guard has fled.'

'God's blood but misfortune seems to strike the Gerald-ines in battalions!' Dunsany looked at Leverous with tired eyes. 'And, I fear, there is more. I came without respite from Howth. I was with St Lawrence when a ship called this evening from Beaumaris. St Lawrence elicited the news from the captain. Walter and . . . ' he swallowed hard and in a heavy voice continued. 'Walter, John, James, Richard and

33

Oliver . . . ' His voice seemed to caress each name. ' . . . were executed at Tyburn, by orders of the king, some three weeks past.'

Despite the icy wind that seered through the aperture, Leverous felt his forehead burn.

'Silken Thomas?'

Dunsany inclined his head in affirmation.

There was silence as they both absorbed the words and each allowed his mind to register the enormity of the grim news. Tyburn: the word was fraught with fear and revulsion. Leverous had once witnessed the bloody spectacle and had stumbled away to vomit his abhorrence into a London street. Silken Thomas, the hot-tempered dashing Geraldine, Garret's hope and pride, so unlike his wise and able father, but so beloved by him. A wave of memories, brimming with the flotsam and jetsam of unrelated incidents, washed over Leverous: Garret's great joy at the birth of his first-born son which together they had celebrated among the pipe staves in the cool cellars of Maynooth; his last meeting with Silken Thomas, his young face framed in annoyance at his plea for caution and his impatient dismissal of his suggestion to check the validity of his father's death in the Tower before embarking on his ill-fated rebellion.

'My father loved you as a brother, Leverous. He would expect you to avenge his murder.'

But Leverous knew better what Garret would have expected. He had taken passage to England and through his contacts in London discovered that the Earl of Kildare was indeed alive and secreted within the Tower. The rumour of his death had been deliberately fabricated by the king to inflame his hot-blooded heir into rebellion and thereby ensure that the vast Kildare estates would be forfeited to the crown. In haste Leverous had returned to Ireland, but he was too late. The flames of rebellion were already ignited and Silken Thomas had put himself and his house beyond the Pale.

'Leverous!' Dunsany's voice jerked him back from the past. 'The ship brought further news. The king orders Grey to have Gerald sent into England forthwith. 'Twill go hard with him, being the boy's uncle, for he knows as well as you or me that he sends him to his death, as assuredly as he sent his brother and his uncles before him. But . . .' he shrugged his shoulders, '. . . being the king's deputy he must do his duty.'

Still benumbed by the shock of Dunsany's revelations, Leverous stared at him uncomprehendingly.

'Leverous, listen to me.' Dunsany's voice was intense. 'The boy is the sole surviving Kildare. The king has much to gain by his death. Heir to the greatest lordship in these islands, vast acres, strategic castles, power and privilege. Mark me, 'tis the age of confiscations, and a helpless child will make an easier quarry than a wily cleric. How many child prisoners have mysteriously disappeared under Tudor 'protection' in the Tower? You can be assured that the king, the devil take him, will stop at nothing to seize the last Kildare Geraldine, now that he has gone to such public lengths to destroy the rest of his family.'

The implications of the plot that Dunsany outlined were beginning to register in Leverous's mind.

'I dare not offer him sanctuary,' he heard Dunsany continue. 'Mine will be the first likely refuge to be suspected. You must take him to his cousin O'Neill. The woods and bogs of Ulster may afford him better protection than the open pasturelands of the Pale. Or to his aunt in MacCarthy's country in Munster. For mark me, Leverous, there will be few safe places for him when the news breaks. The king will not be penny-pinching when it comes to a reward. And money will buy information now, even about a Geraldine.'

'The earl entrusted the boy to my care, my lord. Rest assured I will not betray him.'

'Your loyalty is above question,' Dunsany assured him. 'But who else can you trust? The earl is dead, and so the alliances he forged within the Pale and beyond are now void. The chiefs and lords once allied to him will seek their own keeping by whatever means they can. And, believe me, they will not spare Gerald in their considerations. For the heir of Kildare will make a worthy sop for any chieftain wishing to appease the king's anger and stay his hand from their territory.'

Leverous knew that his words made sense.

Dunsany sighed deeply. 'I must go to my daughter and break the news of Walter to her. It will go hard with her. It was a happy union. God's mercy on them all.'

'Amen,' Leverous answered softly.

'God go with you, Thomas. You have inherited an unenviable responsibility.' Dunsany stretched his hand through the aperture.

'The pox, my lord,' Leverous reminded him.

Dunsany let his hand fall dispiritedly to his side, turned on his heel and disappeared into the darkness. Leverous remained within the barbican until the sound of the hoofbeats receded.

In the upper chamber he found Gerald tossing restlessly and bathed in sweat. The following hours would be crucial in deciding the fate of the Kildare heir. Leverous wiped the beads of sweat from his gashed face and marvelled that the survival of such an ancient dynasty should rest in the fevered body of an eleven-year-old boy. The destiny of the mighty Geraldines whose roots were embedded beneath the ruins of Troy, in Latium and Etruria, in the great Florentine republic of Italy, in Normandy, with conquering William to England. They had come from there to Ireland, where for four hundred years they had reigned as virtual kings, and now seemed destined to be extinguished by the pox or by the revenge of a common usurper, the assassin of his family. Centuries of proud genealogy to be snuffed out by the vindictive breath of the Tudor parvenu. Leverous tightened his grip on the roughly hewn bedpost. 'It will not be.' His whispered words sounded loud in the silence.

The wind whistled high in the chimney-piece and with a downward swirl whipped the dying embers into a fiery glow. He piled more wood on the fire and resumed his vigil. Tiredness pressed upon him like a lead weight and his drooping eyelids lured him into an exhausted sleep. To banish the temptation, he took a book from the window ledge. His hand caressed the soft morocco cover, one of the few surviving volumes from the great library of Maynooth castle, now levelled and pillaged, the fine books and manuscripts trodden into the mud under the heels of the marauding English soldiers. He opened the volume at the title page. *Orlando Furioso* by Ludovico Ariosto. Beneath the title in bold calligraphy he read the inscription. 'From your kinsman Piero Gherardini, Consul of Florence, to Garret FitzGerald, Earl of Kildare, anno domini, 1519.'

It seemed not a year since he had been received by the consul at the Gherardini palazzo near the Ponte Vecchio on the eve of his departure from Florence. Among the gifts the Gherardini had entrusted to him for the earl was this book with its special significance for the two branches of the Geraldines in Ireland, the Kildares and the Desmonds. Leverous turned the fine pages until he came to stanza eighty-six of the famous poem.

Or guarda gl' Ibernesi appreso il piano
Sono due squadre: e il conte di Childera
Mena la prima: e il conte di Desmonda
Da fieri monti ha tratta la seconda
Nello stendardo, il primo ha un pino ardente.
L'altro nel bianco una vermiglia banda.

2

DUBLIN CASTLE

The persistent knocking finally roused the sleeping figure in the curtained bed.

'God's blood! Am I to have no rest, day or night, in this accursed country?'

He raised himself up on an elbow, dragged back the heavy damask curtains and shouted in the general direction of the disturbance. 'Who goes?'

'Dispatches from the king, my lord. I have orders to deliver them into your hands.'

Lord Leonard Grey, the king's deputy in Ireland, cursed under his breath. He threw aside the bed coverings and groped for his cloak. Shivering in the cold night air, he cursed his sovereign for the intrusion on his sleep and as his bare foot came into contact with the bedpost, he cursed him again for appointing him to such a thankless office in such a god-forsaken kingdom.

Three days he had spent in the mountain recesses of Wicklow searching in vain for the barbarous O'Byrnes to recover the spoil of cattle which they had plundered from the Pale. Over treacherous mountain passes, that soared dizzily skywards, to become lost in swirling mists which penetrated and chilled to the very marrow, and that descended vertical slopes into chasms and ravines from which there seemed no escape, he had led his weary soldiers in search of an enemy that remained elusive. Across sucking tracts of bog, their heavy English armour and weapons causing men and horses to sink to their knees, he had doggedly done his duty. On his return emptyhanded to Dublin, he had been compelled to ride to Dalkey. In his absence, the O'Tooles had descended from their mountain retreats and had looted the fishing village. Both clans had become more audacious in their attacks on the Pale since the death of the Earl of Kildare, with whom they had been allied, and since the rebellion of his foolish son.

Grey's temporary appointment as deputy, in succession to his brother-in-law Kildare, did not deter them from pillaging up to the very walls of Dublin. The mayor and burghers of the city had a path beaten to his door with a ceaseless litany of complaints and demands for action. He would not put it past that conniving mayor, urged on by Ormond and his overbearing wife, to complain of him to the king, who in any event expected the impossible: to rule Ireland without providing him with the necessary means. His army comprised the dregs of the back streets of London, raw labourers and landless country rustics. Sullen and mutinous, to a man they detested the Irish posting. The situation was aggravated because he had insufficient monies to pay them. But then, he thought, as he fumbled his way to the door, he cared little any more. His sole ambition was to be relieved of his post and return to England as quickly as possible.

The torchlight flickered in the draughty corridor.

'Pardon, my lord, but my orders . . .'

Grey waved aside the emissary's apology. 'What hour is it?'

'Past ten o'clock, my lord. We landed at Howth from Beaumaris some two hours past.'

Grey dismissed the messenger and lit a taper from the torch on the wall bracket in the corridor. He returned to the bedchamber and lit the stump of candle remaining in the gilt candlestick. The castle was quiet except for the soft slapping of the water of the moat against the outer walls. Using a pearl-handled dagger, he slit open the folded parchment, breaking the crimson seal. With red-rimmed eyes he read the opening pleasantries in Thomas Cromwell's neat hand. Then in disbelief he reread the second sentence.

'Cross of Christ!' His whispered words rent the silence. As his mind absorbed the details of the king's dispatch, he felt the blood drain from his body. His hand trembled and the parchment rustled in protest as he read of the fate of the victims whom he had sent to their end.

'Thomas, traitor son of the Earl of Kildare and the five brothers of the said earl . . . high treason . . . rebellion . . . Tyburn . . .' The parchment fell from his fingers. 'May God in his mercy forgive me,' he whispered.

His hand fumbled with the key of the cedarwood press where he kept the state dispatches and from it he removed a small pewter flask. Taking a goblet from the table, he poured a large measure of the colourless liquid. Like lava, the liquid coursed through his body, the fiery warmth bringing instant relief to the gnawing pain in his abdomen. The native aqua vitae, or *uisce beatha* as the Irish called it, he had come to realise, was the only recompense for soldiering in Ireland.

Fragments of the painful episode came tumbling back, making him wince. His protracted negotiations with his sister's stepson, to bring the rash youth to his senses and his ill-advised revolt to an end. How with patience he had succeeded in building a bridge of trust between himself and Silken Thomas which had resulted in the youth's surrender on promise of life and eventual restoration, which he in turn he had been told by Cromwell was the king's intent. It was on that understanding that he had conducted Thomas and his uncles to England. A heavy fine and a short stay in the Tower to cool the heels of the latter-day Hotspur was the outcome the king had led him to expect. Instead, he had led them to their execution, just as much as if he had pulled them on the hurdles to Tyburn.

'Tyburn.'

The dreaded word sounded more sinister in the gloom of Dublin Castle. As a soldier Grey had been trained to fight and to kill, and sixteenth-century warfare was bloody and uncompromising. But as a soldier, the premeditated human butchery perpetrated on the block at Tyburn repelled him. He poured another measure from the flask.

From the very beginning he had loathed his appointment to this troubled land. Ireland was as alien to him as the far-off Americas. Acquaintance with the country and its unruly natives had done little to dispel the sense of foreboding he experienced the day he had disembarked at Wood Quay. Over subsequent months he had traversed some of this land of primeval forests, of bleak moor and bog, an island battered by Atlantic seas and buffeted by fierce tempests, shrouded in mists which lifted occasionally to allow sunlight to reveal the moist green mantle of its pasturelands and the dark purple mystery of its soaring mountains. He found it a land of few towns or villages but where wood and wattle dwellings and indiscernible mountain tracks proclaimed the outmoded pastoral lifestyle of the population.

The political process by which the vast Irish world outside Dublin and the Pale was ruled was an anathema to his English belief in monarchy and centralised government. To his cost, he knew that the country was divided into a myriad petty independent chieftaincies which the Irish called nations; that the head of each nation was elected by members of a ruling family and did not inherit by primogeniture, as was customary in the rest of the civilised world; so that a brother could succeed a brother, or a nephew an uncle. Leaders of these individual nations strove to have as many sub-lords under their control as possible through a practice of clientship. Dominion over people rather than of land was the hallmark of power for the Irish lords. Each client or vassal lord was forced to make onerous payments to his overlord and was bound to fulfil specific duties, most notably to provide a specified number of fully equipped and provisioned fighting men in the inter-tribal wars which, in the absence of a centralised authority, were incessant.

The native chieftains shared power with Anglo-Norman magnates like the earls of Kildare, Desmond and Ormond, who ruled their vast estates by a mixture of native and feudal laws, which gave them powers and privileges unthinkable in England. Grey tried to imagine the Earl of Surrey, with a private army, waging war on another lord and exacting tributes from him, or being the sole arbiter and dispenser of justice within his earldom. Grey almost choked on his goblet at the thought. The king would have his neck before he could utter a single verdict.

The English crown claimed an unenforceable sovereignty over all Ireland, even the Irish-ruled territories in Ulster, Connacht and Munster and, as the king's representative, it was his duty to enforce and extend this tenuous claim. Given the insufficient military means at his disposal, he knew that if the Irish united behind one leader, the English enclave in Dublin would be overwhelmed and the absurdity of the crown's claim to Ireland revealed. His brother-in law had plotted to do so but Tudor vigilance had nipped his scheme ruthlessly in the bud.

Grey cursed himself silently for his ramblings. He picked up the king's parchment and held it close to the candlelight.

'It is Our further command,' he read, 'that you will take into your custody Gerald FitzGerald, second son of the late Earl, and send him to Us where he might stay under Our protection for his safe and better keeping.'

'Safe and better keeping.' The words, Grey knew, rang as hollow as the king's promise to Silken Thomas.

He read on: 'We know that your concern for the welfare of your nephew will ensure his apprehension and speedy conduct to this Our Realm of England.'

Cromwell's crafty hand. Grey threw away the parchment in disgust. They had him in a vice. As the king's deputy, he was bound to implement the king's order. Not to do so was treason. As the orphan's uncle, his natural instinct was to save him from the Tudor murder-lust, if only in memory of his sister Elizabeth, whose untimely death at the boy's birth seemed to have removed any remaining control over the independent posturings of his brother-in-law. Grey's Yorkist blood had made him a target for the king's obsessional suspicion in the past. To survive, he had adapted to the reversed fortunes of the White Rose, and accepted the inevitability of Tudor rule in England. The battlefield became his escape. But his brother-in-law, Kildare, could not be reconciled and had paid the ultimate penalty.

He glanced at the remaining lines of the dispatch. They merely confirmed the king's pleasure to extend his tenure as deputy in Ireland, indefinitely.

'A plague on the Tudor tyrant.' With difficulty Grey stifled the treasonable feelings that threatened to overwhelm him. He rose from the table and stared through the window into the grey night outside. The narrow lanes of Dublin, with their jumble of houses, stretched in rows of darkness to a black pool in the distance where the river Liffey met the incoming tide at Wood Quay. To his left, the square tower of Christ Church jutted into the sky, solid but uninspiring, built more to withstand attack than to stimulate sanctity.

Dublin was a city under siege within its own country, he thought, alien and removed from the indigenous population outside its walls that it purported to govern in the name of a foreign king.

What if, he wondered, Ireland were left to its own devices, to develop, as England had, or to stagnate and die at its own hand? Either way, he was certain, from England's perspective, it would prove less hazardous and certainly less expensive than subjugation.

But the conquering essence of his soldier's mind, the superiority instilled in him by his Englishness and the pragmatism of his office, made Grey dismiss such a premise. For he knew that however much England had neglected her neighbouring island in the past, she would never voluntarily relinquish her claim to rule over it. England would continue to tolerate Ireland's antique ways and outmoded practices so long as her claim over Ireland was not put at risk. The Earl of Kildare and his son had challenged the English claim and the gruesome outcome was testimony to the power of the hitherto sleeping English lion, who, once offended, sought total retribution. An eleven-year-old boy was the sole remaining salve to heal the lion's wounded pride and appease his anger. And he, at once uncle and king's deputy, had been chosen to spring the trap.

The candle on the table flickered wildly and was extinguished. In the darkness, Grey made his way back to bed and drew the covers over his head. But sleep would not come and, as the first glimmer of dawn pierced the grey sky over the bay of Dublin, he rose.

3

NEAR DUNGANNON CASTLE,
LORDSHIP OF TYRONE, ULSTER

The winter moon cast a silver hue over the dark oak trees, whose skeletal branches twisted upwards in supplication to the sky. The outline of the forest and the distant drumlins appeared in stark relief in the ethereal light. The sound of hooves, the crank of wagon axles, the intermittent apprehensive lowing of herded cattle and the muffled curses of the *creaghts* sounded ghostly in the stillness. From within the dark depths of the forest, a lone wolf howled in defiance at the moon.

At the head of a band of horsemen, Conn Bacach O'Neill, chief of his nation, Lord of Ulster, drew the folds of his woollen mantle tightly around him and sunk his chin deep into the warmth of the fringed collar at his throat. It had been a successful raid; he was well satisfied with the spoil. But the night trek back to Dungannon Castle made him uneasy. Slowed down by the cattle, he was vulnerable to a retaliatory attack by his urragh O'Hagan, or more likely from his enemy O'Donel, whose territory lay close by to the west. He was sufficient in number and in arms to defend himself, but the cattle, the black gold, pay dirt of the day's enterprise, would surely stampede into the darkness. Yet he had risked the march rather than endure another night in the open.

The winter chill played havoc with the wound in his left thigh, the legacy of an O'Donel dart in one of their many border wars. The pain jarred with every movement of his mount over the rough terrain. But O'Neill allowed no outward sign of his discomfort to show on his inscrutable features. It was unwise for a chieftain to appear weak in body since it might well give his competitors within the clan and his enemies without the impression that he was unable to defend himself. But the thought of the roaring fire in the great hall at Dungannon, the raw warmth of the *uisce beatha* and the soothing soft body of his concubine, urged him on through the night.

O'Neill turned around in the high stirrupless saddle. Some two hundred cattle and four wagonloads of spoil, he reckoned.

'A fine haul,' Devlin, the captain of his kern observed. 'O'Hagan will rue his pride when he counts the costs, *mallacht air!*'

'Better that he had paid his dues on All Hallows, as he is bound.' O'Neill's clipped tones conveyed little elation at the success of the raid. His sharp eyes darted over the bobbing heads of cattle. O'Hagan's dues to him amounted merely to fifty cattle, two horses and ten sacks of corn. He was well compensated for the expense he had been incurred to extract them from him by force.

'I never thought the bastard had it in him, to defy The O'Neill,' Devlin muttered.

'Nor does he,' O'Neill responded. 'You can be certain O'Donel's hand lies behind O'Hagan's defiance. The last sting of the dying serpent.'

'Aye!' Devlin looked up with a mixture of fear and admiration at the enigmatic face of his overlord. ''Tis said he will last but days. *Mallacht Dé ar a anam dubh.* His tanist, they say, is not Irish at all but a mongrel mix of English and French.'

'No matter. His O'Donel blood will wash away his foreign

ways. He will be, as every O'Donel has been, an enemy of O'Neill.'

O'Neill's words were emphatic. Slightly built and of medium height, his brown hair fell in tresses to his shoulders. A glib hung over his forehead, almost covering his eyes. A short beard marked the thin line of his mouth. His face was remote and brooked little familiarity. A cautious leader, he ruled his vast territory with a tight rein, jealously guarding his title and privileges as the premier chieftain in Ulster.

From the outset, he had known that O'Hagan did not act on his own initiative in withholding his yearly tribute to him as his overlord. It was O'Donel who had seduced his urragh from him with promises of protection so that he might weaken O'Neill's position in Ulster. To hold his liege lords loyal and dependent upon him was a chieftain's only guarantee of survival in the unceasing fight for power. O'Neill's retaliatory raid on O'Hagan had a twofold purpose: to reinstate his hold over his urragh and to demonstrate O'Donel's inability to protect him. For, despite O'Donel's promises, he had not dared to intervene in O'Neill's chastisement of O'Hagan which had brought his urragh firmly under his control once more. The cattle and spoil were merely a bonus. They had driven them from the bawn of O'Hagan's castle where they were herded for the night. The thatched cabins surrounding the castle he had torched. The wretched churls within offered little resistance, but plentiful reward in corn and supplies, enough to keep his own kern content with booty. He had scarcely required the service of the four score gallowglass in his train, he thought. His lightly armed and mobile kern, with their darts, spears and short swords, would have been sufficient.

Yet as he looked down at the disciplined, menacing lines of tall mercenaries, their jerkins of chainmail glistening in the moonlight, the two-handed axe, the hallmark of their trade, which they wielded with such terrible ferocity in battle, slung across their shoulders, he felt secure. They were worth the English angels and nobles he had paid for them. This batch came from the Scottish Highlands, with their captain Randall MacDonald. The remainder, which he had left to guard Dungannon, came from the Isles. They mixed little but did his bidding, were fed and housed by his betaghs, would receive the sum agreed in payment for their service at the end of their hire and return to their homeland in Scotland. Next year they might be hired by his enemy O'Donel or by a Sean-Ghall lord like Desmond in the south. Whatever chieftain or lord offered the best terms bought their fighting strength and loyalty for the allotted time. He would speak with MacDonald about extending their contract for another year, for he was well pleased with their service. With a share of tonight's spoil and sufficient *uisce beatha* inside him, MacDonald might prove amenable to his terms.

O'Neill's gaze alighted on his Irish kern and with a flash of annoyance he noted the undisciplined ranks, spears and darts trailing the ground, as they whispered animatedly amongst themselves. But they too had their value. Their loyalty to him was as deep-rooted as the great oak forests of Ulster. Born to serve their hereditary master, their only expectation was a share of the spoils and his protection. And on the boglands and moors, militarily, they were superior to the heavily encumbered gallowglass. Their speed and agility could out-run and out-manoeuvre even enemy horsemen.

'The kern must learn to use the new firearms, Devlin. See the constable at Dungannon. A score of arquebuses brought in from Scotland lie idle in the cellars. It is time they were put to use.'

'The men will make good shots,' Devlin promised, 'if the accuracy with which they throw the dart is any yardstick.'

'I will have a demonstration in one month. See to it.'

O'Neill was sorely in need of the additional power the new muskets would provide, especially now on the death of his cousin Kildare and the uprising of Silken Thomas. For the alliances the earl had forged in Ulster among the Irish chieftains would surely snap. Old feuds would recommence as each sought to gain advantage from the new situation. O'Donel's connivance with his urragh O'Hagan was but the start.

And what of the English in Dublin? O'Neill spat in irritation. The smirking servants of the English king, who looked at him in disdain on the rare appearances, encouraged by his cousin Kildare, he reluctantly made at their council in Dublin. They might not be content merely with the lands of Kildare, but, flushed with victory, might seek to extend their power further afield. To Ulster, perhaps, to Tyrone. A snarl momentarily flitted across O'Neill's set features.

Let them come, he prayed, as he thought of his lordship and its god-given protection of lake, river, forest and bog, a greater impediment to would-be intruders than a host of gallowglass. Let Grey and his town soldiers, on their heavy-set horses, attempt to ford the Great River, probe a course through the impenetrable tangled forests of Clanbrassil and Glankankoyne, negotiate the high mountains, cross unending tracts of bog and marsh, horses sinking to the houghs in the oozing mud and peat. Let them come. They would make easy pickings for his swift-footed kern. Those arrogant English hirelings knew nothing of his ancestry, of the essence of the ancient heritage, which both bred and bound him.

O'Neill's lineage stretched back into oblivion. His blood was the blood of princes and kings. His great ancestor, Niall of the Nine Hostages, had enriched his palace at Tara with the spoils of Rome. The Welsh upstart king in England had offered to confer on him, The O'Neill, a fancy English title if he agreed to rule the ancient patrimony of his ancestors by the laws of England. O'Neill allowed a brief smile to touch his face. There was one law in Ulster which had been there for so long that no one could authenticate when it had been introduced. But it was there when his ancestors had built the great rath of Emhain Macha near Armagh over three thousand years before. With a genealogical foot in each camp, an English title might have sat easily on the shoulders of his cousin Kildare but he, The O'Neill, carried the dignity of the most notable title in Ireland. And that was all he desired.

Once his ancestors had ruled as high kings over all Ireland before the coming of the Sean-Ghall. Since then the Irish had been divided among themselves and no one of sufficient strength had emerged to rule over all of Ireland again, until his cousin Kildare, by sword and by subterfuge, almost succeeded in moulding Gael and Sean-Ghall under his leadership. Kildare had even hammered out a treaty between himself and O'Donel, O'Neill reflected in astonishment. But only on the basis that he had been designated him the premier chieftain in Ulster and Kildare had taken O'Donel's son hostage to secure that fact. And regardless of Kildare's ambition to be ruler of all Ireland, his cousin had been careful not to impinge on O'Neill's authority over his urraghs. He would countenance no interference in his god-given rights as The O'Neill, not even from the great Earl of Kildare.

O'Neill had long suspected his cousin's design to rule like a high king in Ireland. He shrugged his shoulders under the folds of his mantle. It mattered little to him who ruled Ireland provided he, The O'Neill, ruled absolute in Ulster. That he was a kin of the earl made the possibility of Geraldine, rather than Tudor, dominance in Ireland more palatable. But it was all no more than a dream now. The Earl of Kildare was dead and his successor, Silken Thomas, was a different matter. O'Neill's warlord's mentality saw little to recommend in the immaturity of his cousin's son and, despite his relationship with and respect for Garret, he would never agree to be ruled by such an impetuous youth whose rash rebellion had simply played into the hands of the English king and his collaborators in Ireland.

The lights of Dungannon Castle beckoned in the distance. O'Neill felt the exhaustion and pain lift from his body. Set high on a steep rise, overlooking an undulating hinterland of hills and meadows, interspaced with diminutive lakes, Dungannon looked every inch the inviolate citadel, protector and keeper of the antique heritage that had bred and sustained its owners from time immemorial. The solid tower, encompassed by high embattled walls, ten feet deep at the base, its bulk resting on the three-thousand-year old rath of his remote ancestors, exuded a sense of timelessness and indestructibility. History and mythology, of valorous kings and warlords, epic exploits of godlike Celtic warriors, oozed from its ancient stones and enhanced the atmosphere redolent with immortality which enveloped it. And as The O'Neill, he was its champion, the custodian of the ancient way of life that it embodied.

The sentries heard his arrival and a golden glow of welcoming light spilled out through the open doorway. The deep-throated bay of the hounds signalled their master's return. A shadow flitted through the shaft of light. O'Neill reined his horse to a standstill and waited as his constable, Ross MacMahon, galloped towards him and in a single swift movement brought his mount to a sudden stop, leaping expertly from its back.

'What news?' O'Neill asked.

MacMahon hesitated.

'Well?' O'Neill waited with some impatience.

'Your cousins, Silken Thomas and his uncles, were executed by the English in London.'

No trace of emotion appeared on the immobile face of O'Neill as his mind digested the dramatic tidings. Behind him the kern and drovers whispered excitedly. He had marvelled at the foolhardiness of his Geraldine kinsmen, upon the failure of the rebellion, to allow themselves to be lured to London, like geese into the fox's den, on a vague promise of pardon and restitution of their lands. He knew better than to trust the smile or the word of the *Sasanach*.

As MacMahon outlined the details of the execution, O'Neill's agile mind analysed the implications of the decimation of the House of Kildare for his lordship. He issued his orders precisely and with assurance.

'Take the guard from Dungannon and double the garrisons at the passes to the Pale, Newry, Strabane and Armagh. Send notice to the O'Neill urraghs of a hosting here at Dungannon, one week from this day.'

MacMahon galloped back to organise the messengers and speed his master's orders to his liege lords throughout the far-flung lordship. The kern drove the cattle and the wagons towards the bawn at the rear and the gallowglass made towards the *clachán*, in the shadow of the high castle walls.

Riding up the rough winding track towards Dungannon, O'Neill wondered at the retribution the English might seek against him, as ally and kinsman of the Earl of Kildare. They would never penetrate to Dungannon, of that he was certain. But the outposts guarding his territories bordering the Pale would be most vulnerable. He must be certain of the fealty of his urraghs, lest O'Donel, as well as the English, seek to take advantage of him.

For a moment the demise of his Kildare relations flashed through his mind and he wondered about the fate of his young cousin Gerald. But as he entered Dungannon, O'Neill's preoccupation once more was centred on Ulster.

4
—

HAMPTON COURT PALACE, LONDON

The king awoke with a shudder and a shout which sounded like the echo of a thunderclap to his still somnolent mind. As he willed himself into consciousness, the echo seemed to reverberate in the vacuum of his dark bedchamber. He felt the sweat flow down the ample proportions of his body and the fine cambric of his nightgown was sodden against his skin. Henry shivered in the cold of his own sweat and groped the yawning space beside him. He needed the reassurance of human contact in the awakening panic of the nightmare. But as consciousness slowly righted itself, he remembered that Jane, at his insistence, now slept alone. He could take no chances, not even to satisfy his passion for the still supple body of his new wife, to achieve the ultimate ecstasy, the safe deliverance of the heir for which he had schemed, killed and lusted. But the aftershock of the nightmare almost impelled him now to seek comfort with his queen and expurgate the sense of guilt that, irritably, it had left in its wake.

He pounded the soft pillows with a clenched fist. Guilt had no place in the mind of a king, Henry told himself. The traitors had received a traitor's punishment, according to the law. But the stock reply sounded trite. For he knew that behind it lay decades of suspicion and fear which like a festering wound had erupted in rebellion and culminated in execution. The animosity towards the Tudors from the House of Kildare in Ireland was established long before his birth. From the start, the Tudors had ever to be on their guard against the Kildares in Ireland. As it had been for his father, so too it had been for him. But he was determined to ensure that it would not be so for his son, which, God willing, this time Jane would give him.

It had been a long and dangerous path to the English throne for the Welsh Tudors. From the very beginning the chief threat to their ambitions to the crown of England had come from the Kildares in Ireland. Even after his father had salvaged England from anarchy at Bosworth Field, it had been the Kildares who had persisted in the futile cause of the White Rose. With treasonable contempt, the Great Earl of Kildare had personally placed a crown on the head of the Yorkist pretender, Perkin Warbeck in Dublin, and proclaimed him King of England and Ireland. It was an affront no monarch should have tolerated. But ever conscious of the insecurity that dogged his claim to the crown, as well as the expense of all-out warfare against his powerful subject, his father had little option but to countenance Kildare's disloyalty until a more conducive opportunity presented itself.

'Stir no sleeping dogs in Ireland,' his father had counselled him, 'until a staff can be found to chastise them.'

And when Henry had come to the throne, he had been content to continue his father's toleration of Kildare. In the early days of his kingship to flex his muscles on the bright stage of Europe was his priority, not to wallow in petty warfare in a medieval outpost as Ireland. Irresistibly, he had been drawn to the European stage, where he dazzled François and the Emperor into acknowledging that he was a force to be reckoned with in their power-jousts, from which they sought to exclude him. But he had shown them, in the only way those haughty foreigners understood, by English steel, at Tournai and the Battle of the Spurs, that he was the absolute ruler of a powerful and united country.

Grudgingly he had to admit his then chancellor, the conniving priest, had diplomatically paved England's way in Europe. And it was Wolsey who also redirected his attention to the unfinished business with Kildare in Ireland. Even then, Henry recalled, he had little inclination to become embroiled. For deep down he knew that behind Kildare lurked the unattractive and long-neglected problem of Ireland itself. But Wolsey had his dagger in the Irish earl. For at every chance, Kildare sought to score points off the lowborn prelate, much to the delight of the English lords, who considered that Wolsey had flown too high, but were too cowardly themselves to risk his anger. But not Kildare, Henry recalled, who with his Irish wit and frankness never ceased to ridicule the pretensions of the lord cardinal at every opportunity. Wolsey in turn had persistently drawn his attention to Kildare's indiscretions in Ireland.

'Kildare employs Irish enemies to oppress Your Grace's loyal subject, the Earl of Ormond. Was Your Grace aware that my Lord Kildare is in league with the traitors, O'Neill and O'Connor; that he aids his rebel kinsman, the Earl of Desmond, in his treasonable intrigues with Your Grace's enemy, the Emperor? Kildare speaks the Irish tongue, governs his territory by the abhorred Irish practices, which your Grace outlawed. Does Your Grace realise that Kildare seeks to set himself up as king in Ireland?'

Yes, yes, yes, Henry thought; he well suspected Kildare's ambitions and intrigues and might have been content to countenance them yet further but for Wolsey's doggedness, which hinted at his inability to rule effectively.

His marriage to Anne distanced him further from Kildare. In the aftermath of their passion when, as she well realised, he was at his most amenable, she seductively poisoned his ear against Kildare in preference to her cousin Ormond, Kildare's bitter rival in Ireland. And Henry was wont to listen to Anne in those early days of infatuation and expectancy.

Slowly his mind began to harden against the Irish earl and the latent Tudor antagonism to the House of Kildare surfaced. And when the time was ripe for revenge on his disloyal subject, Henry needed neither the machinations of Wolsey nor Anne's sly prompting. For he too had changed, matured, secure in his kingship, supreme in his power, confident to unleash his anger on an enemy. Kildare perished in the Tower, by what means he had not closely enquired, while the butcher of Tyburn ensured the end of almost all his traitorous stock.

The bed creaked loudly as the king lifted his bulky frame.

The cursed nightmares had become a regular occurrence. Nightly the deathly faces flitted grotesquely through his dreams: Wolsey, Anne, More, Fisher, Ashe and, tonight, Kildare.

This nightmare was particularly vivid. The place was the tiltyard at Eltham on the wide expanse of Blackheath where in his youth Henry had often jousted with Kildare. There had been no rancour between them then, he recalled, only an intense and good-natured rivalry, as each sought to outdo the other and play the shining knight to the applause of the court and the admiration of the court ladies. Each had unseated the other on countless occasions and extended a hand to hoist his opponent up from the dust of the tiltyard. The Irish earl was the one noble on whom Henry could depend to provide a real challenge. The others, fearful that to topple the king might result in their displacement at court, preferred to allow him the advantage.

Henry opened the door of his bedchamber. The yeomen jerked to attention, surprised by the king's nocturnal prowl. He hurried down the length of the gallery, lined on either side by the immense tapestries from the looms of Flanders, some of the treasures amassed by Wolsey in his efforts to create a mansion to outshine the palaces of his sovereign. And he had admirably succeeded, Henry reflected, but had merely laboured on the red brick splendour of Hampton

Court for the pleasure of his king who was now the owner, and the proud prelate was in his grave.

Henry halted at a low recessed door in the long hallway and entered Wolsey's private closet. Ironically, here within the compact serenity of the small office where his cardinal chancellor had once plotted and intrigued, Henry felt secure and at peace. The walls were oak-panelled and covered by an arras of silk and gold. The Venetian carpet of crimson and gold felt rich and comforting underfoot. But it was to the ceiling high above his head that the king's eyes were automatically drawn.

Taking a candle from the holder on the hall outside, he lit the remainder in the silver candelabra on the desk. Overhead, the moulded ornate gilt gesso ceiling, bearing the Tudor rose and feathers of the Prince of Wales, glowed in the light. Midway above the panelling were vivid-coloured paintings of scenes from the passion of Christ with Wolsey's motto, *Dominus Mihi Adjutor* beneath. Before the brilliant illustrations the Defender of the Faith and now more lately Christ's self-appointed vicar in England felt strangely elevated. The realism of the paintings, combined with the sheer beauty of the ornate ceiling, evoked a sense of quiet contemplation.

Henry held the candelabra high. Yes, the face of the soldier with the cudgel raised to strike the stumbling Christ was the face in his nightmare. Wolsey had enshrined his hatred of the Earl of Kildare for posterity in the mural of his design. He studied the depiction of the soldier. The full face, crowned by a crop of gold-tinted auburn hair, trim beard, deep-set blue eyes, almost hidden by the heavy brows, was indeed the face of the dead earl. But Wolsey had given the full lips a twisted, cruel look, which defiled the otherwise handsome features.

It was the same face, but blood-streaked and with wild bloodshot eyes, of his dream. The face of the figure who had stood over him as he lay prostrate and unarmed on the ground of the tiltyard. With upraised sword, the figure slowly lowered the point closer and ever closer to his bared throat, until the tip loomed so large within his sight that it blocked out the leering face above. He shivered in remembrance. Kildare was destined to haunt him in death as he had done alive.

'Pox on that cankered breed,' Henry muttered.

The recent Yorkist uprising against the suppression of the monasteries in the north raised again the spectre of feudal anarchy in England. The diverse forces in England and abroad who continued to oppose and conspire against him could, he realised, as they had done before, find a catalyst in Ireland, behind the Kildare saltire. If Jane's child was to be the son he craved, he would make certain that he would inherit a kingdom secure from such threats. And if the danger to Tudor sovereignty in England emanated from an eleven-year-old boy in Ireland, then he would ruthlessly ensure that the last of the Kildares would be disposed of like his kin. Once the Kildare threat had been obliterated, the likelihood of renewed revolt in Ireland would be removed. The remnants of the Geraldines, headed by that bumpkin imposter Earl of Desmond, would soon succumb to the divide and conquer policy pursued there so successfully by English monarchs since the time of the Conquest. He would speak to Cromwell in the morning.

Beneath the vivid mural, the King stared with hooded eyes at the upraised arm of Wolsey's Kildare. Then abruptly he left the closet and retraced his steps along the gallery. Nearing his bedchamber, he paused briefly and strode in the direction of the queen's apartments.

5

KILBRITIN CASTLE, LORDSHIP OF CARBURY

Eleanor FitzGerald MacCarthy listened intently as she tried to identify the noise that had disturbed her sleep. Alone in the vaulted bedchamber, from force of habit she lay on the left side of the spacious bed, as if Donal was returning to fill the emptiness beside her. Since his death, the luxury of unbroken sleep seemed to have eluded her. Now the slightest noise in the night rent the slender veil of slumber. One needed less sleep as one got older, it was said, and in her thirty-sixth year, she could soon claim that excuse, she thought ruefully.

Donal's death, followed so closely by that of her brother, had rocked her world, leaving it bereft of the two stable supports on which it had depended. Her husband's death had been forewarned and with sadness she watched his life sift inevitably away. But Garret's end had been abrupt and unheralded. Lying awake in the small hours, her mind juggled the possible reasons for his inexplicable end in London. The MacCarthy women said as they superstitiously crossed themselves that her sorrow would not be appeased until death visited for the third time. Eleanor shivered in the cold air and pulled the covers close. She was becoming as bad as they with their piseogs she thought.

Because Kilbritin Castle was situated close to the sea,

the night sounds around it were magnified, except when the fierce southwesterly gales blew in from the ocean. Only then could she sleep undisturbed, lulled by the high winds that propelled the sheets of rain against the tightly shuttered windows and drowned the more irritating night noises. The stout fortress had been her home for almost twenty years since the summer of 1517 when she had come there as bride to Donal MacCarthy, chieftain of the Lordship of Carbury.

She could still recall her fear as she embarked that summer on the long journey south. Leaving the familiarity of her home in Kildare, she journeyed for days with her brother and their retinue, along wild mountain tracks and through deep forests, sinister in the summer light, until she thought that they must surely have come to the end of the world. Despite Garret's assurances, she knew that the life chosen for her would cut her off from her home, family and friends

But she had been reared for this separation from the day of her birth. Political and financial considerations alone dictated her matrimonial lot. The emotional aspects of the union had been of little concern to her father and his legal advisors as they haggled and argued over her worth with MacCarthy and his brehons. Few of her class expected or received happiness in marriage. But there was some redress. For marriage under Irish law was adjudged to be a secular matter, and divorce was widely accepted as part of the secular practice. It was a blessing for a woman who wished to rid herself of a promiscuous or violent husband, as well as a safeguard for the restitution of her *spré* (dowry) should her husband seek to rid himself of her.

Eleanor had been born, reared and guarded to fulfil the political designs of the House of Kildare. As the daughter of the Great Earl, her political value in the matrimonial stakes was substantial and her husband chosen for her solely for the political advantage that would accrue to her father. She had been given as a pledge on a political alliance contracted by her father with The MacCarthy, by which the powerful chieftain in turn agreed to become an ally of Kildare. A stipulation in her marriage contract, insisted on by her father, was that the eldest son of their union would succeed his father as chieftain according to the law of primogeniture and not at the whim of the Irish custom of tanistry. The MacCarthy elders at first had baulked at this departure, their brehons quivering with rage at the earl's intrusive deviation from one of the fundamentals of the Irish legal code. But her father had persisted and won.

The MacCarthys were not slow to realise the worth of the Great Earl's daughter as a bulwark against their powerful neighbour, the Earl of Desmond. In turn for her *spré* of five hundred cattle, twenty brood mares, ten riding horses, two gold drinking cups, five silver and gilt ewers, a chess board, wrought in ivory, and a substantial amount of household implements and furnishings, including her own rich trousseau, Donal MacCarthy had pledged certain lands with accompanying benefits in kind, in Carbury, as surety for its repayment, should the marriage be dissolved or, in the event of Eleanor's widowhood, for her future maintenance.

Marriage to a man whom she had never met, some twenty-five years her senior, living the crude life of an Irish warlord, had both frightened and repelled her. In vain she had pleaded, but her father would not be moved.

'Look to your duty, daughter, as did your sister Margaret,' he had told her brusquely.

Eleanor's anger and rebellion against her fate had found consolation in the arms of her childhood friend with consequences which, had they become apparent, would have spelled disaster for her and her lover. For, despite the promiscuity of the Irish aristocracy, many of whom had a plurality of marriages, lived openly with their concubines and entered into marriages inside the prohibited degrees of blood relationship, they prized highly their genealogy, which was jealously recorded for posterity by the clan bards, to be lauded at every clan gathering. Donal, kind and trusting, had little deserved the genealogical deceit she had practised upon him. And Leverous?

Dear Leverous, she thought. She had used his affection in a desperate final attempt to experience a natural love that, as the daughter of the Earl of Kildare, she was to be denied. She had been naive and green then in the ways of woman-hood. Her only sexual encounter had been to defend herself from the aggressive advances of her father's hostage, Manus O'Donel, whose sojourn at Maynooth had blighted her growing years.

With a subtle calculation that she was amazed to discover lay within her, she had enticed Leverous to reveal the attraction he felt towards her and which he had concealed from her and everyone else. But then she discovered how badly she had miscalculated her emotions. For Leverous's love had washed away the base desires of revenge, incited by wounded pride and spiteful deviousness that lay within her. In the sweeping tenderness in which he had enfolded her, the love that lay locked within her streamed forth.

The joy of her womanhood, awakened by such a passion, dominated her life, consuming her every moment. Every-thing else became irrelevant in her heightened state. Her betrothal, her family, the ordinary pattern of daily life, the danger, became subject to her desires. It was as if she lived in a permanent state of intoxicated anticipation. In his arms her body was tuned to a fine point, responsive to every sensation of his lovemaking. Her feelings fed on every tender touch of his hands, his lips, his words of love. As each day dawned on their ecstasy, it left her stunned by the feelings and sensations he aroused within her and to which she sought only to return.

But in the end the snatched trysts with her foster brother had left something else in their wake; the bitter taste of deception. In a blind panic she had betrayed herself, Leverous, Donal and her family. She had fallen in love with

Thomas Leverous in the certain knowledge that she could never marry him, whom her father and society deemed her social inferior. She had betrayed him and with selfish disregard had encouraged and responded to his love.

Her father had charged her brother Garret to escort her to Carbury for her marriage with MacCarthy. And it was Garret who had soothed her tears, which he imagined were caused by her removal from her family. He strove to quell the panic that assailed her, each mile of the trek, which brought her away from Leverous and nearer her uncompromising fate. He sought to ensure in his initial meeting with The MacCarthy that the political necessity of his sister's marriage might not be at the expense of her happiness. His fears had been unfounded. For Donal MacCarthy had not required her brother's promptings to stimulate the respect he bestowed on his young bride. Eleanor had found a warmhearted and loving partner in the mature, quietly spoken chieftain.

Her husband's Gaelic world warmed to her and cosseted her beyond belief. Initially accepted as the wife of their chieftain, the daughter of the Great Earl of Kildare, they came to accept her for herself. And eventually the love that had consumed her at Thomas Court was gradually by the affection of her husband relegated to a hidden recess within her, close to her heart, buried deep with the secret she dared not even think on. And Leverous . . .

The excited barking of the hounds in the courtyard broke into her thoughts and confirmed her initial suspicion. The shouts of the ward and the cranking of the barbican gate echoed loudly in the night. Eleanor sped to the window and looked down into the courtyard. The messengers she had sent to her sister in Offaly must be the bearers of urgent tidings if they dared to risk her son's ire by rousing the castle in the middle of the night.

She hastily buttoned the bodice of her long sleeveless day dress which she had slipped over her linen nightrobe.

With a silver bodkin she piled high her dark hair, snatched a cloak from the closet, and hurried into the dimly lit corridor. As she rounded the corner from her apartments, she collided with her son.

'By the Holy Virgin, Cormac, you frightened the life out of me. The messengers have returned. I must have their news.'

Her son had to stretch his legs to keep pace with her speeding form.

'Mother,' he started to protest, but she continued on her way unheedingly. Reluctantly he followed her fleeting shadow down the spiral stairway and through the narrow arched doorway that led into the great hall.

A wave of warm air enveloped her as she entered. A fire glowed in the iron brazier in the centre. Trestle tables and benches stretched in rows the full length of the spacious room towards the top, which was dominated by a raised dais. The lime-washed walls were hung with skins and antlers, while two Flemish tapestries, marriage gifts from her kinsman, the Earl of Desmond, hung on either side of the wide recessed window at the back of the dais.

A few hours previously, the room had resounded with feasting and music as her son entertained some Spanish sea captains, come to negotiate their yearly licence to fish the fertile sea off Carbury. The debris of the evening's entertainment had been cleared away, but the aroma of the mutton and venison and the stale tang of ale and *uisce beatha* still hung in the air.

A group of household retainers, speaking animatedly in Gaelic, were clustered in a group close by the dais. They fell silent at her approach. The castle steward shuffled towards her, his hands outstretched as if to discourage her from coming further.

'My Lady, 'tis bad news, I fear . . . ' His eyes looked in silent appeal to her son. ' . . . that, in truth, might be better told to you by The MacCarthy himself.'

Eleanor felt the first stab of fear. Placing her hand on the steward's thin shoulder, she gently moved him aside. 'Nay, Owen, 'tis best that I hear it directly.'

The old man dropped his head. The dry rushes rustled under Eleanor's feet as she crossed the hall. At her approach, the group moved aside to reveal two kern, their tight trews and fringed mantles mud-splattered, their faces pale with exhaustion.

'You have a message from the Lady O'Carroll?'

Furtively they looked at one another. Eleanor waited expectantly. As if cornered into an odious dilemma, the smaller of the two kern reluctantly divulged his message.

'We saw the Lady O'Carroll, as your ladyship ordered. She had news from the Pale.' The kern cleared his throat. 'Your brothers, the Lords Kildare, were murdered by the English king, three weeks past, at a place they call Tyburn, so 'tis said . . .' His voice trailed away.

The tall figure of his mistress, who had looked so determined and strong one second before, now appeared to shrink and pale before his eyes. Impulsively the kern reached out his hand to prevent her fall. With an effort Eleanor righted herself as the face of the messenger came into focus once more. She felt Cormac's grip on her arm.

'First Garret, now the rest, at one fell swoop,' she whispered.

Her head whirled in a kaleidoscope of flashed remembrances. A spring day at Maynooth, a room overlooking the inner courtyard, through a latticed window, together they watched their father, the Great Earl, resplendent in his fine apparel, setting off for England to confer with the king; the faces of her brothers, Garret, Walter, John, Richard and Oliver, and her sisters, the youngest, Mary, asleep in her mother's arms, Eustacia, soon to marry with the loathsome Ulick Burke, Elizabeth, like herself awaiting her matrimonial fate and, outside the happy circle clustered around the fire, the ponderous figure of her eldest sister, Margaret.

65

Dimly the hum of voices permeated Eleanor's swirling thoughts as her son conferred in urgent tones with the messengers. She heard them mention the name of her nephew.

'Silken Thomas?' she asked in vain hope.

Her son's bowed head answered her anguished question. Cormac stretched his arm around her shoulders.

'Enough bad news for one night, Mother,' he said gently, as he attempted to lead her away.

But despite the shock waves that careered through her body, she sensed that the litany of agony was not yet complete.

'There is more?'

The second kern nodded his head. 'Your nephew, the young Lord Gerald: the king sent orders that he is to be taken into England.'

Eleanor felt a surge of hope rush through her pain.

'Where is my nephew now? '

'It is said that he is at Donore. That the Lord Gerald is ill . . . with the pox.' The messenger crossed himself quickly, as did most of his listeners.

'How came you by this news?' Cormac interjected.

'The Lord Dunsany spoke with the Geraldine's tutor, Leverous, at Donore before coming to the Lady O'Carroll.'

Leverous. The name pricked her benumbed mind with darts of emotion and vague fear. The fate of her nephew pushed them aside.

'Gerald alone? But the Kildare gallowglass, the kern, the servants?'

'All fled, my lady; the pox makes mice of men.'

Eleanor whirled around to face her son. 'But Donore lies close to the Pale, Cormac. To the enemies within and without, not least my sister, for whom the execution of her own flesh and blood will bring unbridled joy. God in heaven, but my nephew is the only Kildare living.' There was a note of astonishment in her voice.

'And the easiest Kildare target yet for the king,' Cormac added.

The full extent of the tragedy made Eleanor shudder convulsively. 'God's mercy, how could he cut them all down so cruelly?' she pleaded to her son. 'A foolish rising by a headstrong youth. Doomed to failure. It was never a threat to the king, as well he knew. God's curse on that Tudor monster.'

The anguish which threatened to suffocate her broke now from her lips in an angry tirade which was just as suddenly replaced by heartbreaking sobs which wracked her body. Eleanor covered her face in a futile effort to stem the flow of tears that spilled through her fingers and to hide her sorrow and vulnerability from the sympathetic, staring faces of the MacCarthy retainers. Silently her son dismissed them and led her from the hall. The cold air in the corridor combined with the chill induced by her tearful outburst served to compose her mind and she fought to assert a logical reaction to the destruction of her family. Her mind focused on the one member still alive.

'Gerald must be saved.' The intensity of her voice stopped her son in his tracks.

'Mother, let it rest until the morning. I can scarcely comprehend the consequences of all this.'

'I comprehend, Cormac, only too well. And I tell you this: I will risk all to deny Henry Tudor the ultimate victory over the Geraldines. He will never have Gerald, dead or alive. On that, Cormac, I now swear my oath and you are my witness.'

Cormac had seldom seen his mother moved by such fierce resolution. In her marriage to his father she possessed the stronger character with an acute and accurate sense of people and events. But she never flaunted her ability or her position as the daughter of the Great Earl at his father's expense. She imparted her counsel quietly with a certain charisma that did not appear to undermine his father's authority. But he suspected that it was his mother's advice that often became official clan policy. His parents had complemented each other well and therein lay the success of their union. But the potential of his mother's true capacity lay exposed now in the face of her bereavement.

As she neared the door of her bedchamber, Eleanor turned to face him. Cormac was a Geraldine in looks, but possessed the same characteristics as his father and for that Eleanor was thankful. There was an intemperate streak in the Geraldines, epitomised by the rash revolt of her nephew and in the obsessional hatred of her elder sister, Margaret, that she was glad she had not passed on to her son. Deliberate and thoughtful, Cormac had an air of maturity that denied his nineteen years. For a moment the contrast between her son and her nephew, Silken Thomas, flashed through her mind. She could never imagine her cautious son flinging himself impulsively into a conflict motivated solely by rumour. Cormac would weigh the pros and cons with care but, once convinced of the course he must take, he would be committed.

At the election for Donal's successor, in fulfilment of the terms of her marriage contract, Cormac had been elected to succeed Donal, to the resentment of his uncle, who had been elected his tanist. People said that Cormac had inherited his father's character and she did all she could to encourage that belief. Donal had been a strong and able chieftain and had successfully steered the clan away from conflict without losing face. And his people had been grateful, except for the bonnaghts, to whom the absence of war meant no work for their arms and no booty as reward. Ireland was too flush with hot-headed lords ready to fly to arms over a difference of opinion with a neighbour over cattle, over succession or to continue some ancient dispute. The MacCarthys were no exception and for generations feuded with their neighbours, the Earls of Desmond. Despite her marriage to Donal, memories of past wrongs were evergreen. The election of her son as chieftain, at the behest of a contract made with a kinsman of their traditional enemy, still rankled deep with some septs of the MacCarthys. She knew she must tread warily for fear her request might place her son's position as chieftain in jeopardy.

'Cormac, I am the only Geraldine who can help my nephew. My sister is too close to the Pale. Your aunt, the Countess of Ormond, will be Gerald's most vengeful enemy. You know what my father and brother sought to achieve in Ireland. Their plan was supported by your father. I ask you now, as his successor and my son, to save Gerald and give him refuge here with us at Kilbritin.'

Cormac looked in silence at his mother. In the semi-gloom her eyes were luminous in her pale face. Strands of hair curled around the high prominence of her cheekbones. She looked suddenly young and vulnerable, and Cormac choose his words with care.

'Mother, I understand your great sorrow, your concern for Gerald's safety. But I must think of Carbury. If I shelter the Geraldine, it could revive bitter memories, reopen old grudges in the clan. Should the king hear that he is hidden here, his deputy may try to seize him by force. Remember my uncle's shadow is never absent from my shoulder. He and his supporters would gladly seek any way to overthrow me. And they have little sympathy for the Geraldines or their cause.'

'Cormac, the Geraldine cause lies buried in my brother's grave in the Tower of London. My cause is simply to save a child's life.'

'But Gerald is the heir to the lordship of Kildare.'

'Gerald is but an eleven-year-old child.'

'Aye, Mother,' Cormac said quietly, 'and I am but eight years older and chieftain of Carbury.'

His words hung between them in the darkness. Eleanor looked on his face and saw the determined jawline and steady look of his father. Their son, the MacCarthy chieftain, weighed with responsibility outside his birthright. She now asked the very thing that could destroy him by bringing him face to face with the secret she had hidden so deeply. But Gerald was Garret's surviving son and she owed her brother the right to his genealogy. She touched her son's arm.

'Just one month. By the time news of his being here is transmitted to Dublin, I will have found him an alternative refuge. I promise, Cormac. One month to save your cousin's life. It is little to ask.'

She could see the struggle within him and silently prayed that she would breach his obstinacy.

'*T'anam 'on diabhal*, mother, but you do it every time. What you should not have by logic, you will get by emotion. One month, no more.'

'God bless you.' She raised herself on her toes and kissed her son's broad forehead. 'Now I must to bed. I am weary beyond endurance.'

Cormac opened the door and closed it gently behind her. From within his mother's chamber the sound of muffled crying sounded forlorn in the night.

6

CATHEDRAL OF NOTRE DAME, PARIS

The flickering lights merged in a golden glow before his concentrated gaze. Robert Walshe averted his eyes from the hypnotic effect of the tapered candles that pierced the darkness before the altar of the side chapel. He looked anxiously in the direction of the unobtrusive door near the confessional. In the gloomy vastness of Notre Dame it was difficult to focus clearly, but he was sure it was through there that the abbé, who had conducted him across the river to the Île de la Cité from his lodgings on the rue St Denis, had disappeared. All of an hour since, he thought uneasily. He had begun to wonder if he was the victim of a dupe. But he had little option but to explore every possibility. After three months, his mission to France showed little result, despite his daily attendance at the royal court at Les Tournelles, where the clerk to the king's minister fobbed him off regarding the king's answer.

He had arrived in Paris from London the previous November, to carry out the Earl of Kildare's order and present his letter, requesting sanctuary for his son, to the king. For three frustrating months he had trailed the royal court from Paris to Fontainebleau, to Blois and back again to Paris, badgering petty court officials. Their lukewarm smiles had, he thought, turned more frosty of late. He was beginning to fear the outcome of the French reply. For all he knew, the English king might well have captured the earl's son and incarcerated him in the Tower, with his stepbrother and uncles. He had paid a contact at St Malo to forward him news of the Geraldine heir, elicited from ships arriving from Ireland. But there had been nothing.

His money was almost expended on lodgings, subsistence and in greasing the ever-open palms of court officials. Without hesitation, he had agreed to accompany the abbé to the cathedral on the latter's unexpected appearance at his lodgings that morning.

A door creaked loudly and disturbed the turgid silence. A figure emerged from the doorway and beckoned to him. Robert Walshe rose stiffly from the hard pew. The abbé motioned him up steep stone steps. Higher and higher they climbed, the blood pounding in his head from the exertion. At last the abbé stopped at a landing and Robert Walshe followed the swinging habit and sandalled feet through an arched doorway and into a long brightly lit corridor with many windows along its length, which looked out over the roof of the cathedral on the city below. His guide stopped outside a door and knocked gently.

A muffled *'Entrez'* emanated from within.

The abbé opened the door, motioned Robert Walshe inside and withdrew, closing the door behind.

'Father Walshe, is it not?'

The modulated English voice took him by surprise. An imposing figure, dressed in a flowing crimson soutane, stood behind a desk in a corner of the room. From a cleanshaven, somewhat angular, face, pale blue eyes observed him and smiled at his puzzled look.

'I see that the somewhat voluminous robes of my recent elevation conceal my identity,' the tall cleric said. 'Let me see if I can revive your memory?'

He sat behind the desk and motioned the Irishman to a high-backed chair. 'We first met, I do believe, at the fair

72

castle of Maynooth. And most recently at Hampton Court, when a brother cardinal sought to impeach your master. Irish wit and humour won that day, as I recall, and defeated Wolsey's plan. But sadly not, as I hear, that of his master.'

Recognition flashed like a beacon on the face of the Irish chaplain. 'My Lord Pole . . . forgive me, my Lord Cardinal, but it has been a long time and so much has passed . . .'

'There is no need to apologise, my friend. I heard of the afflictions that have befallen the House of Kildare. News of the earl's death reached me in Venice. It shocked me greatly.'

Robert Walshe's mind reeled at this unlikely meeting with Lord Reginald Pole, cousin of Henry VIII, last of the Plantagenets still at liberty, regarded by many as the legitimate claimant to the throne of England. Within the spare frame of this English noble remained traces of the distant War of the Roses, Plantagenet versus Tudor claims to the Crown and Tudor paranoia, brutally demonstrated by the execution and imprisonment of almost every descendant of Edward IV. Of his ill-fated family, Reginald Pole alone had escaped the Tudor wrath, Robert Walshe recalled, by opting for an academic career on the Continent, at the Sorbonne and later at Padua. But Pole's Plantagenet blood had finally brought him into direct conflict with the king over the Reformation. Henry's execution of Bishop Fisher and Sir Thomas More had elicited from Pole an acerbic theological treatise. And when he had accepted the cardinal's hat, intended for Fisher, his breach with the king was complete.

Robert Walshe recalled the visit of the young Plantagenet to Maynooth in the early peaceful years, when the Earl of Kildare had been at the height of his powers. The two had remained cloistered for long hours within the Earl's study, he recalled, emerging now and then to walk along the long oak-lined approach to the castle. There were rumours then that Pole was to secretly marry the king's daughter, Mary, and that her cousin, the Emperor, allied with the Pope, would overthrow Henry and install Pole as King of England. Walshe had not been privy to their discussions that summer, but it was plain to everyone at Maynooth that Plantagenet ambitions in England had an ally in the Geraldines in Ireland and a common enemy in Henry Tudor. But Tudor spies abounded and whatever intrigues they had plotted at Maynooth had been snuffed out by the vigilant Tudor network.

The cardinal sighed deeply and rose from the table, his face troubled. Robert Walshe experienced a sense of foreboding. The cardinal placed a comforting hand on his shoulder.

'My dear Father Walshe, I fear I am the harbinger of further sorrowful tidings. My friends at court inform me that the king has again vented his ungodly spleen on the House of Kildare. On the earl's eldest son and brothers, at Tyburn.'

'Tyburn.' Walshe repeated the fateful name and slowly crossed himself. 'All of them?'

The Cardinal inclined his head. 'God's pity on them all.'

'Amen,' the chaplain answered, his mind numbed of emotion. He thought the cardinal's news concerned perhaps his mission to the French court. He had scarcely thought about the earl's eldest son and brothers, temporarily incarcerated in the Tower by the king, until, it was believed, they had made good the cost of the rebellion in full from their estates. Silken Thomas and his uncles had been promised indemnity by the king and it was on that under-standing that they had surrendered to Grey. One of the earl's brothers, Richard FitzGerald, Walshe recalled, had not supported his nephew's rebellion. But it had obviously made little difference to the king's insatiable lust for confiscated lands and his determination to destroy the House of Kildare.

'The earl's youngest son is now the sole survivor of the Kildare Geraldines and the earl's heir.' Reginald Pole looked at the chaplain. 'The young Geraldine is the cause of your

74

mission to France, I hear.'

With difficulty Robert Walshe brought his mind to bear on the cardinal's question.

'It was the earl's last wish, your eminence. He expected the worst at the hands of Henry Tudor. He sent me to elicit the help of the King of France for his remaining son still at liberty.' Walshe shook his head dejectedly. 'Sadly, I fear with little success. With no influence or means, it has been impossible to obtain the king's ear to remind him of his promise to the earl?'

The cardinal smiled. 'Do not despair, my good Father. Look at me, a cardinal, a papal legate, with means and influence, yet my mission too has fallen foul of French self-interest. Think little of it. For François merely plays the game of politics. He must be seen to pander to Henry, to prevent an alliance between him and the Emperor. The pope's legate and a Plantagenet to boot at his court, as he well knows, would rouse Tudor ire and send Henry hotfoot in search of Spanish succour. And so, my dear Father, I must bide my time, hidden here among the rafters of Notre Dame, and you must waste your energies on petty court officials.'

'But I merely seek sanctuary for an eleven-year-old boy.'

'Ah, but the son and heir of the Earl of Kildare is considered as much a threat to the king as me. Henry's ambassador, Gardiner, knows of your presence here and demands that François have you gaoled or extradited to England.'

Robert Walshe felt the cold hand of fear clutch at his heart. He had been more careful than ever this time, sailing from London to Antwerp in the guise of an English cloth merchant and from there to Paris in the robes of an itinerant friar. He lowered his head.

'Then I have failed the earl most miserably.'

The cardinal observed the distress on his face. 'But the earl's son is still at liberty, is that not so?'

Robert Walshe shook his head. 'At the time of my coming

to France, the boy was in hiding in Ireland, in the keeping of his tutor, Thomas Leverous. That is all I know.'

'Thomas Leverous,' the Cardinal exclaimed. 'The earl's foster brother. I knew him at Padua. He is in holy orders.'

The chaplain looked with some surprise at the cardinal.

'No, my lord. Lawyer, confidant to the late earl, lately tutor to his son. Leverous never entered holy orders.'

'Strange.' The cardinal's brow creased in thought. 'I had presumed that was his destiny.' He shrugged his lean shoulders. 'No matter. The boy is in good hands. Leverous knows the devious designs of the Tudors and will be alert.'

'The earl greatly feared for his son's safety in Ireland.' Robert Walshe shook his head sadly. 'Alack, it seems that this unnatural alliance between England and France will now put an end to any chance the boy has of sanctuary in France.'

'The word of kings,' the Cardinal smiled ruefully and leaned towards him across the polished surface of the desk.

'Allow me to restore your faith in the word, if not of a king, then of a friend. The reason I sought this meeting is twofold. As legate of the pope but also on my own behalf. As a friend of the Geraldines, and, let us say, a fellow casualty of Tudor lust for power.'

Robert Walshe felt the first stirring of hope since his arrival in France. This influential prelate might yet find refuge for the earl's son where he had failed.

'The Geraldines and the Plantagenets have much in common, Father,' the Cardinal continued, 'especially a common enemy. Both have suffered at the hands of the Tudors. In my exigency, of all the lords of the realm, it was the Earl of Kildare alone who offered to assist me. I will not forget it. Relations, friends, secret opponents of Henry, fell away, one by one, all consumed by fear. All save my Irish friend. That my plans came to naught does not diminish the debt I owe him. And since he has perished at the hands of my cousin, I deem myself doubly indebted to his heir. Please understand . . . ' he lowered his voice, ' . . . regardless of what may later transpire, the earl's son will have refuge and protection with me.'

Robert Walshe felt the relief seep through his body. If he could not fulfil the earl's wish, at least an alternative plan had emerged which he instinctively knew would have met with the earl's approval.

'The earl praised you highly, both as friend and confidant,' he heard the cardinal say. 'His trust in you was absolute.'

''Twas easy to serve him, my lord. He inspired one to give of themselves. I miss him sorely.'

'Then perhaps in death he still inspires,' the cardinal said reflectively. 'Inspires me at least to repay a debt, long overdue. Listen carefully, my friend. There is little time. I will arrange for you, the boy and Leverous to be brought from Ireland to St Malo. Once in France, the boy will be under my protection. Should François in the meantime ally with Henry, he will not interfere with the diplomatic immunity of the pope's legate. Does my plan meet with your approval?'

'It is the answer to my prayers, your eminence.'

'Good.' The cardinal fell silent and his pale blue eyes searched the chaplain's face as if he seeking to reassure himself that he could trust him with what he was about to disclose. 'But now I must doff my cap as friend and don my hat as papal legate,' he sighed deeply. 'Not a part I would voluntarily choose, but . . . he shrugged, 'it was deemed my role by the Holy Father. It seems that England stirs at last against the Tudor yoke. There has been an uprising in the north, in Yorkshire, Lincolnshire, Lancashire, against the heresies and confiscations of the king. A pilgrimage of grace the people call it. The pope seeks to expand the English pilgrimage into an international crusade against Henry's reformation. An alliance between France and the Emperor, with Scotland to aid the English lords of the north. The greatest alliance of Catholic power since the Crusades.'

'François and Charles, allies?' Robert Walshe could not contain his incredulity, remembering the most recent bitter war between the two kings over Savoy.

Cardinal Pole smiled wryly at his reaction. 'My own thoughts precisely. But then power makes strange bedfellows. Especially under the flag of religion . . .' his face creased in anxiety, ' . . . which, I believe, serves only to unleash the inherent prejudices and cruelties of man. The fires of the Inquisition burn as foully as those of Smithfield. But . . .' he spread his hands apologetically. '. . . it is my duty to elicit support for this new campaign against my cousin.'

The Irish chaplain remained silent and waited with some anxiety as the cardinal rose from the table and moved to the window. Pole motioned him to join him. Together they looked out over Paris, past the Seine as it coiled an arm around the Île, southwards along the ancient rue St Jacques, street of Roman legions, of merchants and ambassadors, where pilgrims congregated each year for the start of the long trek to the shrine of Santiago de Compostella in far-off Galicia, up a steep incline and past the scattered buildings of the Sorbonne and on upwards towards the Hill of St Genevieve, over the rooftops of the huddled houses, shops and narrow streets.

The cardinal broke the silence. 'I could show you such a sight, Father, in every city in Europe, from Naples to Hamburg. Thousands of souls, men, women and children, different in race, language, dress and customs, but all with a single common denominator which binds and strengthens them into one race. God's race, Father, bound in faith together, in the strong embrace of His Church. From this strength comes order, progress and ultimately salvation. Remove it and there is chaos and darkness. Hell on earth.' He fingered the golden cross which hung around his neck. 'But as guardians of God's faith, we must also share the blame for the heresies that have spread amongst us. For we have been neglectful of our duty to God, allowed the faith he entrusted to our care to be defiled by human avarice and greed, encouraged division to grow within to be exploited for political and material gain.' He glanced at his companion. 'Do my revelations shock you?'

'No, your eminence,' the Irishman replied with conviction. 'You merely express the reservations I have hidden within me. Afraid to admit them even to myself. In my travels I have seen such evil done in the name of God, that it makes me shudder to recall it.'

'Then be assured, Father, you are not alone. There are many to whom the abuses that choke the Church are an anathema. I seek reformation from within, not the schism Luther thrusts upon us. But enough of this heresy,' the Cardinal said, turning away from the window. He sat at the table, indicating the Irishman to a chair facing him. 'Despite my personal reservations, I am bound to serve the Vicar of Christ and entice François and the Emperor back to Rome. It is the holy father's wish that Ireland should also partake in this crusade. He sends an envoy to carry his message to the principal lords of your country, to encourage them to revolt against England. The Earl of Kildare's ambition to free Ireland from England was known in Rome. His death has left a vacuum which the holy father hopes may be filled by another. His kinsman Desmond perhaps?' The cardinal looked enquiringly at his companion.

Robert Walshe returned his look with amazement. 'I fear that the holy father little understands the situation in Ireland,' he replied. The cardinal waited for him to continue. 'There is constant animosity among the Irish lords, some of whom would gladly side with the English or anyone else if it benefited them against a neighbour. True, the Earl of Kildare won their allegiance, but only over the space of many years and because, by force and stratagem, he became stronger than any of them. Since his demise there is no one of sufficient strength, I know of no one there who might command the same allegiance. Even the Earl of Desmond.'

The cardinal nodded. 'It is as much as I had suspected, although I know little of Irish matters. But surely to defend the Church, the Irish lords might agree to unite?'

The Irish chaplain fumbled for a reply. He could hardly reveal to the cardinal that the aspirations of the Church of Rome had ceased to have any relevance in Ireland. For centuries the Irish church had drifted, independently of Rome, back to its Celtic origins. The liturgy was but randomly celebrated. Churches and monasteries were legitimate targets in the inter-tribal warfare of the chieftains. Abbots and bishops, often unconsecrated and unlearned, depended on secular lords for advancement to holy office, which was the hereditary preserve of influential families. Clerics had long succumbed to the desires of the flesh and lay with wife or concubine. The reformation practices of Henry and Luther, Robert Walshe concluded, might appear trivial to the cardinal, if he knew the present state of the Church in Ireland.

'I fear, your eminence, the lofty ideals of the holy father's crusade may find little understanding in my country.'

'Strange that your fellow countryman should paint such a different picture to the holy father.'

Robert Walshe looked at the cardinal in puzzlement.

'The Holy Father's special envoy to Ireland,' Pole explained, 'who is to bear dispatches to the Irish lords,' he lowered his voice, 'and one to whom my pledge to the earl's son should remain secret. You understand?'

'Most certainly, your eminence.'

The cardinal rang a silver bell on the desk and, in response, the abbé appeared at the door accompanied by a Franciscan friar, his face shrouded by the sloping cowl of his habit. He made a low bow towards the cardinal and with a swift movement of his hand swept the cowl from his face. Robert Walshe gasped in surprise. There was no mistaking the sardonic, handsome face, topped by the clipped, golden hair. The blue eyes that both defied and taunted, smiled briefly at him.

'We are a long way from Maynooth, Father Walshe.'

Observing the Irish priest's continued bewilderment, the cardinal presumed that he did not recognise the stranger.

'Manus O'Donel, Prince of Tirconel.'

'The chaplain and I are well acquainted, believe me,' O'Donel replied. 'Perhaps it is my unlikely disguise that renders the good father speechless. I am not surprised. 'Tis the one garb for which he knows I am least suited.'

The cardinal smiled weakly.

Memories of Maynooth and of O'Donel's son, taken as hostage by the Great Earl to ensure his father's loyalty in Ulster, once more darted through the priest's mind. The earl had raised the boy with kindness with his own at Maynooth. O'Donel had been a precocious, even brazen, youth, Robert Walshe remembered, with the uncanny ability to extricate himself from trouble, invariably of his own creation and having others take the blame. Both Garret and Leverous had borne the brunt of the Great Earl's anger for O'Donel's misdemeanours on many occasions. A lusty youth, he had matured more quickly than the others and had developed a passion for the earl's daughter, Eleanor. Whether it had been reciprocated, Robert Walshe did not know. But the earl had nipped any development of the affair by taking O'Donel with him to the court. The king welcomed the sons of Irish chieftains in the hope that the civilising environment of his court might lure them from their native ways. O'Donel had lapped up his royal host's hospitality for two years, until the earl's imprisonment, when he had disappeared from court without trace.

'My lord O'Donel returns as chieftain in place of his father, recently passed away.' Cardinal Pole explained to the chaplain. 'He bears messages for the Irish lords from the holy father. Except for one, I believe. Is that not so, my lord?' The cardinal looked coolly at O'Donel.

'As you say, your eminence,' O'Donel replied withdrawing from the folds of his brown habit a square of parchment to which a large wax seal adhered. 'And should I be the bearer of this dispatch, then, I fear, the pope's crusade would be doomed from the start. With the benefit of your diplomacy, you, Father, might have a better chance of luring old wooden foot from his lair,' he laughed mockingly and extended the parchment towards Robert Walshe.

The chaplain took it and glanced at the name written in an elaborate hand. 'The Lord O'Neill, Prince of Tyrone.' So well might O'Donel decline to deliver. O'Neill would kill O'Donel sooner than allow him set foot in his lordship. Robert Walshe saw the keys and mitre of the papal seal impressed on the wax.

The cardinal extended his hand to him, his eyes holding him to silence. 'Safe passage back to Ireland, my friend. A ship awaits you at St Malo. Remember my pledge.' He turned towards O'Donel. 'You have much work before you. God go with you.'

Robert Walshe bowed towards the cardinal. O'Donel covered his head with the cowl and in silence they followed the abbé down the steep twisting steps and into the gloom of the cathedral.

7

DONORE CASTLE, LORDSHIP OF KILDARE

The unusual brightness of the normally gloomy chamber roused Leverous. He hurried to the window. Before him his prediction lay unquestionably confirmed. A blanket of snow covered the castle outbuildings and extended across the countryside as far as he could see. He looked upwards. The clouds hung low and ominous.

'What are you looking at, Leverous?'

'Snow fell during the night.'

Gerald struggled to raise himself from the bed. 'We had snow the winter my father went to England. My foster brother rolled me in it at Dangan. But I hit him a bullseye. My father said . . .' Gerald's voice trailed off into the silence that usually accompanied his every reminiscence of his father. With a sad face, he sank back into the bolster.

'I know,' Leverous told him cheerily, 'we will ambush the gallowglass with snowballs when they return. They will make easy targets from the parapets above.'

The idea roused Gerald once more. He broke into an impish grin which gave a grotesque appearance to his pale face. He threw aside the bed coverings and made to rise. 'A good plan, Leverous. Let us practise our shots before they return.'

Leverous moved quickly towards the bed and drew the

covers over the boy once more. 'Patience, Gerald. When you are stronger. The snow will be here for a some time yet, I fear.' He crossed to the fireplace. 'Food is ready. It makes me hungry.' He winked at his young charge, who looked doubtfully at the steaming pot.

'I wish I could have some venison or mutton. Or some almond pasties, like at Maynooth,' Gerard said wistfully.

Leverous stirred the rabbit stew and gingerly tasted it. Gerald's appetite had revived over the past few days, a welcome sign of his recovery.

'There now. So good, a gallowglass would give his best battle-axe for a taste.'

Gerald pulled a face. 'Not I, Thomas.'

Leverous smiled encouragingly at the boy but inwardly agreed. Five successive days of rabbit stew was bound to pall on even the most healthy appetite. With a wooden ladle he poured a portion into a deep pewter dish and handed it to Gerald. The boy showed signs of improvement daily. The characteristic pustules of the pox were still evident on his face, but a scab was forming on the lesions. If he was lucky, they would fall away and leave his face unblemished. Leverous had seen all too many victims of the pox who were doomed to bear the outward manifestations of the dreaded disease to their graves.

He had not yet told Gerald about the execution of his stepbrother and uncles. All in good time, he thought, for a boy barely come to terms with the death of his father.

The times were harsh on children, and especially so in Ireland. Gerald had been only five years old when he had been sent for fosterage to The O'Connor of Offaly, a tributary chieftain of his father. He had been reared in the O'Connor household, O'Connor becoming his protector and father figure, the chieftain's wife taking the place of his natural mother, which in Gerald's case was even more necessary, for she had died when he was four years old.

Elizabeth Grey was the earl's second wife. Leverous

remembered her with affection. Daughter of the Marquess of Dorset, lady-in-waiting to Queen Catherine, granddaughter of King Edward IV, her Yorkist pedigree made her a most suitable consort for a Geraldine and, as cousin of King Henry, a buffer for her husband against growing royal antagonism. Garret had been inconsolable at her death, and with good reason. Not only did he lose a loving wife, but Elizabeth's death removed the final restraint on the king's vengeance against the Earl of Kildare.

It was with Gerald's foster father, O'Connor, that Leverous intended to seek refuge once Gerald was fit to travel. Irish law regarding fosterage was unequivocal. O'Connor was bound to protect the life of his foster son, even at the expense of his own. His territory would be far enough out of reach of the English in Dublin to give them respite until he could find a more remote sanctuary, in Ulster or Munster, as Dunsany had suggested.

'Ulster,' Leverous had convinced himself. For Munster meant Eleanor, longing and vulnerability, which he dared not consider and, for Gerald's safety, could not risk.

Leverous half listened to Gerald's chatter and considered their situation. It was imperative that they should leave Donore at the first opportunity. Sooner or later their presence would be detected; but it would take almost two days for Grey or his captains to make the journey from Dublin. Their present proximity to the Earldom of Ormond worried him more. It was ironic that the greatest threat to Gerald's life should come from his own flesh and blood, from his aunt, the Countess of Ormond.

A loud banging interrupted his thoughts. Gerald looked at him in wide-eyed fear. Leverous strained his ears to listen but, except for the keening of the wind, all was silent again. Cautiously he moved to the window and surveyed the scene below. Tracks heading in the direction of the barbican were clearly visible in the snow outside, but he could see no sign of life outside the walls or in the part of the courtyard visible.

Whoever sought access had either retraced his steps or had gained entry to the castle from an entrance hidden from view.

With a word of reassurance to Gerald, Leverous withdrew a short sword from the leather scabbard that hung from a peg at the back of the door and descended the spiral steps. He drew back the heavy bolts of the outer door and stepped into the courtyard. No mark or footprint disturbed the virginal covering of snow. He felt the tension ease. Nobody, it seemed, had penetrated the castle. Leverous hurried across to the barbican, snow crunching under his feet. Through the archery loop where he had spoken to Dunsany, he had a clear view of the entrance. The footprints stretched from there to a clump of scrub bushes, some fifty yards from the outer perimeter. As he peered through the aperture, his eye was caught by a square of parchment impaled on the iron-studded outer door.

But where was the messenger? Was it a ruse to get him to open the door? Motionless, Leverous waited. A horse in the stables whinnied shrilly. An answering neigh emanated from the bushes outside. Stark against the white landscape, a horse and rider suddenly broke from the cover and disappeared into the distance. Leverous removed the oak beams from the iron cups, pulled the heavy door ajar and, leaning out, snatched the parchment, which was fixed to the door by a small dagger. He replaced the beams and, in the light of the courtyard, broke the seal and read the message.

It is the command of the King that Gerald FitzGerald, son of the late Earl of Kildare, be delivered to the King's Council in Dublin and from there to be sent to London for his better keeping. The Earl and Countess of Ormond are left Dublin this day to further the King's command.

The letter was unsigned and Leverous noted that the seal was blank. He examined the dagger. The ivory handle was engraved with swirls and flourishes which culminated in the letter G. He had seen the dagger before. His mind retrieved a memory of Lord Leonard Grey receiving the master-crafted tool, from Garret, as a momento of his visit to Maynooth. Was it Grey who had now put him on his guard in an attempt to save Garret's son? It hardly mattered. He had been forewarned and had the advantage, however slim. But if Grey's messenger had reached Donore, the Countess of Ormond would not be far behind. He must take Gerald away from Donore without delay. He would make a run for O'Connor's castle at Dangan and take his chance across the wild wastes of the Bog of Allen.

As Leverous ran across the courtyard, flakes of powder-dry snow started to fall gently from the darkening sky.

8

LORDSHIP OF KILDARE

Menacingly stark against the incandescent snow-covered background, a band of cavalry cantered into view. Three white pennants, with the red cross of St George, fluttered among the forest of hooked bills held upright by each mail-clad rider. A scabbard, from which a sword hilt protruded, rested alongside each stirruped thigh boot. Faces with short-trimmed beards looked grimly out from under iron morions, worn low over the forehead. Despite the snow, the horsemen had covered the distance of forty miles from Dublin without respite. The hot pace set by their leader had never slackened. The coats of the horses glistened and their breath was laboured in the stillness of the afternoon. Clouds of steam rose from riders and horses alike.

'The men grumble that you set too fast a pace.' Piers Butler, Earl of Ormond, kneed his horse alongside the figure at the head.

'I have little use for those who cannot keep the pace.' The deep voice of his wife was uncompromising. Ormond felt himself included in the disdainful remark. His body ached all over. God's death, she must be made of iron, he thought darkly. Aloud he said, 'Kildare country is hardly the place for an Ormond to be caught with an exhausted escort.'

A sneer stretched across his wife's thin lips. 'What frightens you, my brave husband? I see little evidence of Kildare power. Their gallowglass and kern lie skulking in the undergrowth, afraid of their shadows. We could beat a thousand Geraldine kern. They are beaten, in mind and in body. And remember, you are under the protection of a Geraldine.' Her short laugh was humourless.

Ormond looked at the masculine profile of his countess with a mixture of admiration and aversion. Her copious black velvet riding cloak, trimmed with a band of ermine at the throat, scarcely concealed her enormous girth. Her excessive appetite for food mirrored the excesses of her character. She made a better friend than a foe, as he had discovered on his marriage to the daughter of his enemy, Kildare. The hatred she bore her family needed no Ormond spur to goad her to provoke the age-old Ormond-Kildare feud, which ironically their marriage had been intended to heal. But the killing of their eldest son by a Geraldine dart, five years before, had deepened her hatred. The malevolent intensity with which she pursued her vendetta against her own flesh and blood at times repelled him, but Ormond did not remonstrate. It was futile, he had come to realise, to try to contain her obsession and besides it was to his political advantage that she should succeed and fulfil his ambition to become the king's deputy in Ireland. His only contribution in realising that ambition was his willingness to acknowledge his wife's unique, if repellent, qualities and the undeniable fact that it was she who ruled Ormond and himself. Many times he thanked God it was the Geraldines and not he who were the object of his wife's vengeance.

Approaching her forty-third year, Margaret FitzGerald, Countess of Ormond, cut an impressive figure. Standing almost six feet tall, her large-boned body had fallen into flesh. Her formidable physique accentuated the sense of power and strength she exuded, intimidating all who came into contact with her.

'God's blood, but my Lord of Ormond hath neither place in his bed nor in his kingdom with such a mate,' the king had joked when the Earl of Ormond first presented his new wife at court. But the king's levity was replaced by degrees by respect for the political acumen of the Irish countess. 'This woman could singly rule the realm,' he confided to Thomas Cromwell and instructed his chief counsellor to ensure that the countess had whatever support she sought at court to fulfil her ambitions against the Geraldines in Ireland. And while the earldom of Ormond might not be the realm, the countess vindicated the King's opinion of her and ruled it with an iron will.

No trace of emotion appeared now on her heavy face as she surveyed the destruction of her family's lordship of Kildare. The rebellion of her rash nephew, which she had provoked, had made it a wasteland. The army of the king had burned and plundered, while her Ormond hordes had completed the denudation of what she remembered as the most fertile land in Ireland. The blanket of snow could not conceal the blackened shell of villages, the acrid smell of burned flesh and the decay. Across the rolling plains nothing stirred. There were no cattle, no people. The once fertile grasslands had been scorched black and bare by the incendiary torches of the crown, picked as clean as the skeletal corpses that swung from the branches of the great oak trees.

The countess sat erect in the saddle, her black hair drawn severely back to reveal a pale fleshy face and a strong chin. Her dark violet eyes dispassionately surveyed the desolation from under a sapphire velvet cap with a white plume. She knew every acre of this country. She had travelled every rutted road and grassy track as a young girl with her father, the Great Earl, long before her marriage and banishment to Ormond, long before the hatred had overwhelmed her. She had been happy then. Kildare was her kingdom and the Great Earl her shining knight and she . . . What had she become?.

Her youthful pride in her Geraldine ancestry, the love

that she had locked deep inside her, so deep that she could not give it expression, so intense that it had consumed itself, had been suffocated by humiliation and neglect and been supplanted by a profound emotional reversal. Love did not come easy to her. She felt awkward when emotions tugged, when feelings surfaced. By silence and by scowl, she suppressed the threatening sensations. Her height, her grossness, the veil of sullen broodiness that she espoused became her defence and confined her to the outside where she pretended to want to be, but silently she cried out for admittance to the warmth of their company.

But they never heard, those brothers and sisters who had mocked and sneered, smug and secure in the inner light of the close-knit family fold. The cruel tricks and jibes of childhood gave way to abrupt silence and winking collusion on her intrusion into their youthful conversations. But by then it mattered little. She had progressed beyond their childish games to become the trusted confidant, loving daughter and companion of the Great Earl. With him she felt secure, loved and responsive, no longer the unwanted outsider. Her trust in him was complete. He was her mentor, protector, the recipient of whatever love she could expend. It was he who directed and nurtured her ability, encouraged her interest in the world around her, in government and politics and in the administration of his lordship. He rewarded her devotion by introducing her to the complexities of his office as the king's deputy and as overlord of a vast estate. She became a familiar figure at the council meetings in Dublin. She mastered the complex amalgam of Irish and English laws whereby the Kildare estates were ministered. Rents, payments in kind, tributes owed to the earl by his tributary lords and chieftains, she recorded with precision in the leather-bound ledgers at Maynooth. The earl was loud in his admiration and boasted of his daughter's rare abilities, declaring that it would take an intrepid man to woo her from him.

'You will make a fine wife, Margaret,' he had teased her,

'for some wild chieftain or not so wild Palesman. But by St Bride they will pay dearly for the privilege.'

Her scowling silence served only to make him laugh more loudly. But despite her political worth in the matrimonial market, to her relief, few Irish chieftains or lords from the Pale inclined to offer for her hand.

But then her brother Garret returned from fosterage and so began the slow but persistent process of her replacement. Gradually her proven abilities of negotiation and administration were deemed unseemly. Her presence in the male preserve became a source of embarrassment to her father and a threat to her brother. The Great Earl's attention became focused on his eldest son and heir. His English foster son, Thomas Leverous, displaced her as the earl's administrator. Her assistance was at first mocked and discouraged, then finally forbidden. Alone on the fringe once more, she smarted at the slight to her intelligence and the rebuff of her love.

Her love became finally twisted into the black thorn of hatred when her father sacrificed her as a sop to his hereditary enemy, the Earl of Ormond. The arrangement was concluded before she became aware that she was to marry her father's avowed rival. As long as she could remember, mention of the name of Ormond in the Kildare household had been accompanied by a curse. The origins of the feud lay in the dim past, a century after the Conquest, when both houses had vied for power in Ireland, and it had continued uninterrupted since. Rejected and humiliated, she turned her back on her family and plotted her revenge from within the Ormond lordship and at the English court, where, she discovered, the real power lay. Her husband made a token resistance to her intervention at first, but soon realised the advantages he could gain by her antipathy towards Kildare. She was content then in the early years of her marriage in her ambition to make Ormond a powerful rival to Kildare. The murder of her son in a skirmish with her brother's kern had changed the depth of her revenge. The cataract of hate seething within her finally burst open and, over the still body of her son, she had vowed destruction on the House of Kildare.

And in the event it had been easy, she mused as she surveyed the desolation around her. A whisper here, a promise there, rumour, subterfuge, court intrigues, a Machiavellian mix that had proved lethal. First her brother, then her rash nephew and now the runt of the litter. She would be supreme and not merely in Ormond, where her husband was too old and indifferent, but with the annihilation of the Geraldines, supreme over Kildare as well. If only her father had lived to see the fruits of his rejection.

Her ultimate ambition was not confined within the boundaries of Ormond and Kildare but soared beyond to the most coveted office of all, the deputyship of all Ireland. While acknowledging her capability, since her brother's treason, the king, reluctant to entrust the position to an Irishman again, had appointed Grey. She knew how to restore the king's trust and by the same token to discredit his English deputy. For she was about to deliver to the king what he most desired and what Grey seemed treasonably intent on denying him.

The boy would be the last and easiest mark, for Tyburn had removed any real Geraldine threat. Her sisters did not feature in her tapestry of revenge. Her sister Eleanor, married to MacCarthy, was cut off from the centre of power by the woods and mountains of Munster. Eustacia, brow-beaten and abused by her unbalanced husband, was a virtual prisoner in the far west. Her frivolous youngest sister Mary, in Offaly, mattered even less. The capture of the sole surviving Geraldine would seal her plan to ensure the ascendancy of the House of Ormond in Ireland and she, Margaret FitzGerald, as *de facto* head. She had made it possible and she alone would now make its conclusion certain.

Grey had dragged his feet about the boy for too long, a

fact she would yet use against him to her own advantage. An English deputy reluctant to fulfil the orders of his king would survive for an even briefer period than an Irish one and might make the king agreeable once more to appoint a loyal and dependable Irish subject as his deputy. Grey stubbornly denied knowledge of his nephew's whereabouts, but the silver pennies dropped into the hand of a Kildare servant, reduced by his masters' downfall to begging his bread in the gutter of a Dublin street, had told her all she required.

'Leverous should have stuck to his books. His choice of Donore smacks of lunacy.'

'The snow doubtless forced the choice upon him,' her husband offered lamely.

'Pah, a light scattering, no more. Had I the keeping of the boy, I would be in Ulster with O'Neill by now.'

Ormond looked at the determined line of his wife's jaw and knew that she spoke the truth. He shivered, silently cursed the lightness of his English clothes, mandatory for a loyal earl but inappropriate for the Irish climate, and with unease thought of the forthcoming encounter at Donore.

9

THE BOG OF ALLEN, LORDSHIP OF KILDARE

The open cart creaked slowly over the white landscape. Leverous held the leather reins firmly and, with clucking sounds, urged the hesitant horses forward. Behind him a large willow wicker basket balanced precariously. In the hasty retreat from Donore, it had seemed the only way to transport the sick boy. Provided Leverous could steer the horses on an even course across the treacherous terrain, Gerald was safe enough in the basket beneath the feather quilt. It was snowing as they fled from the castle and Leverous prayed that it would conceal the telltale tracks of their hurried departure. To his relief, the snow had stopped. Any prolonged fall would make impossible the already hazardous journey across the wild expanse of the Bog of Allen to O'Connor's territory. Already Leverous found it difficult to differentiate between the vague lines of the narrow causeway and the snow-covered vastness which concealed the seeping boggy morass around them. Any slight divergence would mean death.

The snow played tricks on his eyes, making it difficult to gauge distance or to discern shapes. It lay everywhere and covered everything in its track. Hedgerows and bushes, every familiar landmark was enveloped, planed to an anonymous sameness within its enveloping embrace. Where the wind had caused drifting, virginal layers were sculptured into voluptuous, undulating mounds. Concave and convex, the shapes were moulded smoother than the most skilful tool could emulate. There was something feminine, almost sensuous, he thought, about the way the snow curved and entwined around hedges and tree trunks, gradually to taper away and merge with the lower-lying cover. But out on the wastelands of the blanket bog, the snow lost its intangible appeal and Leverous shivered as he surveyed the white ocean that threatened to engulf them.

Southwards, in the distance, the soft contour of Slieve Bloom beckoned. He had set his compass to keep north of the mountain to avoid contact with the boundaries of Ormond, which since the destruction of Kildare, stretched its tentacles further and further northwards. He must reach an O'Connor outpost before nightfall. Otherwise, the elements would fulfil the wishes of the Tudor king and his Ormond allies.

The clouds which had threatened were beginning to disband and a spectral sun flitted behind a veil of swirling mist that hung low towards the west. A breeze gusted and blew a shower of snow powder across his face. He half closed his eyes against the sting and peered ahead. On the horizon, a group of figures stood motionless, stark against the opaque landscape.

Leverous reined the horses to a halt. There was nowhere to hide, nowhere to run. If it was an Ormond scouting party, the game was over. If they were outlawed Geraldine kern, old loyalty to the House of Kildare might buy them safe passage. He felt in his belt for Grey's dagger and from the scabbard that lay at his feet, withdrew a short sword and laid it across his knees.

'Gerald, keep calm, we have company.' There was no response from within the basket.

Leverous watched them approach at a measured pace.

About eight horsemen and a dozen foot he reckoned. As they drew closer, he noticed the stirrupless pillions of the Irish horsemen. The group halted some yards distant from the cart. The captain nudged his mount forward. A wooden shield, criss-crossed with bands of metal, encased his arm. From a leather scabbard the hilt of a short sword protruded.

'Who are you?' His eyes swept the cart and came to rest on the basket.

'I am making for O'Connor's country in Offaly,' Leverous answered evasively.

'From where?' The rider circled the cart.

'From Kildare.'

'You are not a soldier. By dress and accent not Irish?'

'I am a tutor.'

A murmur issued from the group. The rider moved closer to the cart. 'Your name?'

Something in the earnest approach of his inquisitor prompted Leverous to take a chance. 'Thomas Leverous.'

The effect was instant. Horsemen and footmen milled around the cart. 'The Geraldine. Where is the Geraldine?'

Leverous stood up, withdrew the dagger and held the sword threateningly forward.

The captain called out, 'Stay your hand, Thomas Leverous. We are O'Connor's men, sent to find the Geraldine, to bring him to Dangan.'

Leverous felt his knees buckle with relief.

'The O'Connor sent bands to scour the countryside, not knowing where you might seek refuge, north or south. We took the way across Allen.' The captain's eyes fixed on the basket.

Leverous lifted the lid. Inside Gerald appeared to be sleeping, but with mounting disquiet Leverous noted the damp strands of hair on the boy's brow. He beckoned to the leader, who looked long and hard at the upturned mottled face.

'The Lord Gerald recovers from the pox,' Leverous told

97

him, 'but I fear that the fever has returned. We fled Donore in haste. The Countess of Ormond may well be on our trail.'

The captain swore loudly. 'How far back?'

''Tis difficult to say. She could have reached Donore shortly after our departure. Perhaps the snow covered our tracks.'

'Not from the countess's eyes.' The captain's words were emphatic. He spoke rapidly to one of the kern, who set off with loping strides across the snow-covered expanse.

'God grant he finds help before the Countess of Ormond finds us,' the captain muttered fervently and motioned Leverous to drive on.

On either side, the kern pushed the cart with willing arms. The pace quickened. Leverous looked anxiously behind at the basket, which teetered as they hurried westward.

The evening sun broke through from behind a dark cloud. The pristine brilliance of the white landscape was streaked by arcs of pink gold which gave shadow and depth to the snow's ethereal beauty. They journeyed in silence for more than an hour when, with a loud cry, a kern at the back of the group pointed dramatically. Behind them in the distance a closely bunched group of horsemen stood outlined against the skyline.

The captain shouted hoarsely. The cart jolted crazily over the uneven surface propelled by the kern on either side.

'Keep going,' the captain shouted as he wheeled his horse around to face the oncoming threat, and formed his small party into a forlorn line of resistance. Leather shields were hastily unfastened and buckled on to arms. With spears held aloft and swords at the ready, O'Connor's soldiers awaited their adversaries. The English cavalry stopped some fifty paces away. In silence each group took stock of the other.

Suddenly the air was rent by a bloodcurdling roar as the age old warcry of the Kildares, 'Crom aboo' issued from Irish throats as they flung themselves with ferocity on the English.

Behind him Leverous heard the familiar warcry followed

by shouts and the clash of metal on metal. Intent on keeping the cart on the narrow track, he dared not look behind. The kerns shouted to keep going and ran back to help their companions. The horses were exhausted and struggled to keep their footing on the slippery surface. The sounds of fighting were gradually replaced by an eerie silence. Leverous pulled on the reins as a dozen English horsemen surrounded him. Silently they motioned him to turn the cart around.

The scene of the battle was made more grotesque by the white surface on which the mutilated bodies of the fallen lay moulded. Rivulets of blood seeped in angry weals through the snow. The entire O'Connor force had been annihilated, their brave challenge contemptuously hurled aside by the superior armed English cavalry who had wreaked havoc among them with lance and bill. Many of the bodies were decapitated. As Leverous stepped down from the cart, the eyes of the O'Connor captain stared sightlessly into his. He stooped and closed the lids.

'Had your tutor's head ruled your Geraldine heart, Thomas Leverous, this slaughter might well have been avoided.' The Countess of Ormond picked her way through the carnage.

'Nay, my lady, 'tis your lust for vengeance that caused this butchery, and more besides,' he retorted, his fear momentarily overcome by a loathing that had less to do with the dead bodies of O'Connor's men than with a deeper previous antagonism.

'Still the same Leverous, bound slavishly to a doomed cause. I had hoped that your English birthright might have cured your Geraldine addiction. But unfortunately not. The boy?' she asked, pointing to the basket.

Leverous remained silent.

'What inventiveness!' the countess mocked.

Still the same ogre of old, Leverous thought, remembering Maynooth and the slights he had endured from her barbed tongue. He had feared her then, a threat to his world, and he feared her now.

One of her escort opened the lid on the basket and with a look of horror sprang down from the cart.

'Cock's blood. He is riddled with the pox.'

The countess edged her horse from the cart. 'Is this true?' She rounded angrily on Leverous. He looked away from the fixed stare of her violet eyes.

Ormond whispered in urgent tones to his wife.

'Pox or no, I have not endured all this to return to Ormond empty-handed,' she upbraided him. 'Well, Leverous,' she nudged her horse forward, 'it appears that your rare qualities make you more immune than lesser mortals. You will accompany the boy to Ormond and care for him until he is fit to be placed under the king's protection.'

Leverous picked up the reins. He was trapped. Inside the basket Gerald lay motionless under the folds of the quilt. Leverous felt his fevered brow. The pox might yet deny the countess and the king their final victory over the Geraldines.

The cortège moved slowly southwards towards Ormond. In desperation, Leverous looked back in the direction of Offaly, but nothing stirred on the empty terrain. The English soldiers rode warily at a distance from the cart, followed by the earl and countess. The dark mass of Colaughtrim forest on the boundary of the lordships of Ormond and Kildare loomed before them. Once inside the borders of Ormond, Leverous knew their fate was sealed. The countess would have them in England before anyone was aware of their capture. Gerald would fall victim to the king's vengeance, as surely as had his father, uncles and stepbrother, while he, by virtue of his English blood, would be executed as a traitor.

Primeval oak, with snow-encrusted branches, rose high above the dense undergrowth. They made towards a clearing bordered by trees on both sides.

Suddenly like spectres, from behind each massive tree trunk, armed kern emerged, steel-tipped darts held threateningly aloft, and barred their way. Behind them a line of horsemen with spears drawn, materialised from nowhere. On each side, tall gallowglass, covered from neck to heel in coats of chain mail, iron conical helmets covering each head, leaned on their axes. The Countess of Ormond whirled her horse around to face the line of riders who blocked the rear, her face blotched red with anger.

With a surge of relief, Leverous let the reins rest in his hands and looked over his shoulder at the leader of the Irish horsemen who sat in the pillion, solid and powerfully built. A leather morion, bound with bands of metal, partially concealed his cleanshaven face. He appeared quite young, no more than twenty. A short mantle, rolled back at the neck, revealed a fine leather jacket, reaching to mid-calf and richly decorated with chevrons, circles and squares. With quiet authority the rider studied the Ormond group. The countess barged her way through her startled soldiers who wheeled around in disarray.

'How dare you draw arms and block our way. You court disaster, whoever you are.'

The youth looked pointedly at the milling English horsemen and smiled with composure. 'I fear disaster has already struck . . . at you, Aunt.'

The countess looked intently at the face before her. 'Who are you?' Her violet eyes narrowed.

'I would hardly expect you to recognise one of your blood, since you have shed almost every drop,' a woman's voice answered from behind the line of Irish cavalry. Enveloped in an Irish mantle, the russet fringes high around her neck, auburn hair coiled around her head, Eleanor FitzGerald MacCarthy rode into the company and drew rein in front of her sister.

Leverous felt his heart contract, the blood surge through his veins, as his initial disbelief was replaced by a feeling of rediscovery, of a memory, a face, an emotion, long desired but, until this moment, unobtainable. The face that had haunted and pursued his dreams and daytime reverie, that

101

had placed barriers on his emotions, like a mirage appeared now from the suppressed past. Like a bemused spectator at a pageant in which he had no role to play, he watched the drama unfold.

Without a trace of emotion, even of surprise, the hard eyes of the countess raked the lithe figure of her younger sister whom she had not seen for almost twenty years.

'Then, sister, I advise you to return to the safety of your backwoods in Munster, if you value yours,' she sneered.

Eleanor shook her head more in regret than in anger. 'What devil drives you to such foul deeds against your own? Have we not suffered enough? First Garret . . . our brothers . . . Silken Thomas. Now an eleven-year-old child! What in God's name can you hope to achieve by his execution? For mark me well, sister, that is what the king intends, the moment you hand our nephew to him. How can you rest easy with a child's blood on your hands?'

The countess moved her horse nearer her sister. Her voice was low and laden with a fury that made the jowls of her heavy face shake. 'As easy as our brother rested with the blood of my son on his.'

'Your son fell in battle, an accident of war,' her sister pleaded. 'But you purposely plot our nephew's execution.'

Impatiently the countess tossed her head and contemptuously turned her back.

'Then be warned, sister,' Eleanor called after her. 'Geraldine blood is infused in others who are able and willing to wreck your evil scheme.'

The Earl of Ormond leaned slightly in the saddle behind his wife the better to observe his sister-in-law. Through the line of English horsemen, Leverous gazed at the face that had haunted him, to his sight, unchanged. The luminous hazel eyes, locked in anger with the countess, had not looked in his direction.

'This then is your army of retribution . . . ' the countess pointed a finger contemptuously towards the MacCarthy forces, 'and this callow youth no doubt your champion?' She looked dismissively at her nephew.

'Perhaps a demonstration might serve to quell your doubts.' The youthful leader's voice was soft but menacing and was echoed by a low murmur from the gallowglass, ranged on either side, who with drilled precision, in a single coordinated movement, raised their axes from the ground and advanced on the outmanoeuvered English cavalry. The Earl of Ormond surreptitiously retreated into the ranks of English horsemen. Eleanor's son issued a curt order. Four of his men made towards the cart and motioned Leverous to descend. Leverous stood up, but remained where he was. At that moment his eyes met Eleanor's in a brief moment of recognition and he saw her speak quickly to her son. MacCarthy called out an order to his men, who moved in a protective circle around the cart, reinforced by the kern who unnoticed had slipped from their position at the forest opening.

'I have come for my nephew and intend to leave with him. Whether you wish to fight or release him peacefully, the decision is yours,' Leverous heard Eleanor say.

'Let it lie for now,' the Earl of Ormond cautioned his wife as he viewed the advancing gallowglass with alarm.

'You are a fool to think you can hold back the tide of change,' the countess shouted with fury at her sister. 'If I do not have the boy, Grey or some enterprising chieftain will take him to curry favour with the king. You merely postpone the inevitable by this futile display.'

The sisters stared long at one another, as if they were strangers. Eleanor broke the silence first, her words heavy with suppressed emotion.

'I promise you this. While Gerald lives, the deaths of my brothers and nephew that you callously plotted will be vindicated and your spiteful ambition thwarted. For as long as Garret's son is alive, you will never have legal right to his inheritance. And . . . ' she leaned forward in the pillion towards her sister, '. . . mark me, I will see to it that my nephew will long outlive you.'

Determinedly she turned her back on her sister. On a signal from her son, the gallowglass and kern backed the Ormond cavalry into the forest and stood resolutely until they had retreated among the dark oak. Her face drained of colour after the confrontation, Eleanor dismounted and approached Leverous. His eyes met hers and a brief smile lit her face. She seemed to be searching for words to say.

'We must make straight for Kilbritin, Mother,' her son interjected. 'Dangan is too close. My aunt will not be deprived of her prey as easily as this.'

She looked quickly at her son and back at Leverous. Somewhat disconcerted, Leverous thought, she introduced them. MacCarthy's greeting was terse. In silence they appraised each other. Leverous recognised the high cheek-bones and square-cut jaw of the Geraldines in her son. The grey-blue eyes held his steadily in a reserved though not unfriendly stare.

Eleanor broke the silence. 'My nephew?' she asked.

Leverous removed the cover from the basket. Gerald had regained consciousness. Leverous lifted his head and gave him a drink of water from a flask. Eleanor looked down at the scarred face.

Gerald smiled weakly, his eyes feverish. 'Are you my mother?'

'I am your aunt. I have come to take care of you.' Eleanor reached out to stroke the tousled hair. Leverous stopped her hand, shaking his head.

'And Leverous?' Gerald asked.

Her gaze remained fixed on the boy. Leverous waited for her answer. But there was none.

'Can he make it to Munster?' MacCarthy asked.

'He is yet with fever. But I would rather take a chance with the pox than with the Countess of Ormond.'

A wry smile crossed MacCarthy's face. 'Are you to

accompany us?'

Leverous looked at Eleanor, expecting her approval, but instead caught an anxious look that for a moment clouded her face, a look that urged him to decline. He felt a pinprick of pain.

'As Gerald's guardian, I am bound by oath to your uncle,' he replied.

'Then let us make all haste to Kilbritin,' MacCarthy said, remounting.

'And may God protect us,' Eleanor said softly.

'Amen' Leverous echoed and for a brief moment they exchanged a glance of apprehension and familiarity across the wicker basket.

10

Kilbritin Castle,
Lordship of Carbury

The journey south was long and arduous. The MacCarthy maintained a steady pace until they had forded the Blackwater at Lismore. With the deep waters of the river to shield them from a rear attack, the pace slackened. They crossed the territory of Muskerry, whose chieftain, The MacCarthy's urragh, provided them with the *cuid oiche*. Skirting the unfriendly walls of Cork city, they crossed the Lee upriver into Carbury and turned south again towards the sea and Kilbritin.

Here in the far south, washed by the warm waters of the Gulf Stream, the climate was milder and the snow confined to the uplands and mountain ranges. The land was fertile and wooded but petered out into mountain scrublands to the west.

From the mud cabins, the betaghs and creaghts everywhere emerged to greet their chieftain. Occupying the lowest rung in the structured order of Gaelic society, this exploited class was the backbone of every lordship. They herded the cattle herds, tilled the soil, and were compelled to sustain and accommodate the chieftain's fighting men and hangers-on, who constantly preyed upon them. Prohibited from bearing arms, they were bound to their chieftain by a blind loyalty and fear. They expected and received little in return for their labour except his protection. 'MacCarthy aboo,' they shouted from the doors of the cabins as their chieftain and his party passed by.

Eleanor and her son were welcomed with obvious affection when they finally reached Kilbritin Castle. It seemed to Leverous that a less than total welcome was reserved for Gerald and himself. Gerald had coped with the rigours of the long journey better than Leverous had hoped. After a week's rest and nourishment at Kilbritin, he was well on the way to recovery. Isolated in rooms at the topmost part of the castle, until all contagion had passed, Leverous continued the final lap of his solitary vigil. Donore seemed but a memory, part of an unreal experience, culminating in his unlikely reunion with Eleanor.

For the duration of the journey from Ormond to Carbury and within the confines of Kilbritin Castle, he had little opportunity to assess her reaction to him. Surrounded by her son and their escort and with Gerald's safety uppermost, there was little time to appraise her reaction to their meeting. The memory of a youthful infatuation may not have survived nineteen years of apparent marital harmony and motherhood. For all he knew, she might resent his inadvertent intrusion into her life, of which he knew so little. He had noticed her reluctance that he should accompany Gerald to Kilbritin, and to a degree it was understandable. For this was her world which the strong arm of political necessity had forced her to accept all those years before and, from the brief time he had spent with her, it was obviously a life to which she had grown accustomed. But most of all, it was a world in which she seemed to prefer that he did not tarry. And yet, the look they had exchanged across the wicker basket encouraged him to hope. For what, he could not think, because the only tangible bond between them now was their Geraldine background.

Had she been happy with her chieftain in this remote

stronghold, he wondered, as he looked out over the white-flecked waves that tumbled in lines against the castle keep? Or had she pined for the comfort and familiarity of Maynooth? Had she thought of him? He knew so little about her life since she had left his. It would be difficult for either of them to breach the emotional chasm that the passage of time had created between them. Why even try, he asked himself? For the basic impediments to their relationship still existed. Though an adopted brother, he had no status in the elitist society of which she was part. She would always be a Geraldine.

His gaze was drawn to the courtyard below. Idly he wondered at the unusual level of activity; from daylight groups of horsemen and kern had been streaming through the castle gate. The bawn was full of horses, some one hundred he reckoned, while in huddled groups around the perimeter the long-haired warriors, shrouded in their woollen mantles, talked among themselves. Occasionally faces looked up in the direction of the room where Gerald lay.

A knock, low and urgent, sounded on the door. From the dim corridor Eleanor stepped inside, closing the door quickly behind her.

He backed away from her. 'My lady . . .'

'Nay Thomas, I fear not contagion . . . nor gossip,' she said noticing his concern. 'There is news which I fear cannot await either Gerald's recovery or social propriety.'

Leverous felt a pang of disappointment. What had he expected, he asked himself? He had lived in apprehension, mingled with hope at the prospect of their first meeting alone. Afraid of having his dream evaporate, yet anxious to be close, to see, to touch, to what end he did not dare to think.

Eleanor held the gaze of Leverous in a long silence. From his grey eyes emanated the same air of quiet trust and confidence that had always attracted her. His straight black hair was clipped short in the English fashion. He had matured, as she had imagined, when on occasions she had thought of him, through the long years since Maynooth, since Thomas Court. She felt as drawn to him now as she had ever been, in a deep bond of affection that had always existed between them. They were content and at peace in each other's company, even as children, she recalled. But she had used and betrayed his trust and had broken their special bond, unselfish and rare, knocked it from a pedestal of friendship, to the lowly ground of sexual gratification. In panic, she had willed him not to accompany her to Carbury, to the world to which she had fled with the secret that irrevocably bound them, a secret that she could never divulge.

Yet from the very moment she had seen him at Colaughtrim wood, instinctively she knew that the affinity which like a magnet had drawn them towards each other before, was still there. It would take but one unguarded look, a single touch, to fire emotions into the passion they had once shared. It was ironic, she thought, that for the first time in her life when she was free to choose whom she might love, that the consequence of their past love stood between them as decisively as had the Great Earl. As before, she needed Leverous's trust and friendship, but this time she would make certain that she did not betray him. She would allow no emotional lapse on her part to mar their renewed friendship and their endeavours to protect her nephew's life. This much she had vowed. It was the least she owed Leverous.

The silence between them was heavy with expectation, with memories which they both realised were now intrusive and embarrassing. Eleanor kissed him hurriedly, a brief warm touch of friendship. The movement broke the air of suppressed emotion and the moment of danger passed.

'It seems that the Geraldines are ever to be in your debt, Thomas.'

Leverous felt uncomfortable and searched for a reply to preserve the formality she had introduced between them.

'It is but an opportunity to fulfil a promise . . . to Garret, a chance to repay a debt, long overdue.'

'Gerald?' she pointed to the inside room.

He nodded and opened the door. Together they looked in on the boy peacefully asleep on the canopied bed.

'The pox has been kinder to him than most,' she whispered, observing the unblemished face on the pillow.

'Yes, he has recovered well. A few days' rest and nourishment and he will be fit to go hunting as Cormac promised him and for which he has not ceased to badger me.'

She smiled. 'Yes, it would be a happy sight.'

'Your son and nephew. MacCarthy and Geraldine.' He hoped his voice did not reveal the bitterness that crept into his mind, stung by her wistful expression at the mention of her son. The son that might have been his own.

She turned her face from him, lest her eyes betray the mixture of fear and desire that assailed her. 'The stag must wait for Gerald another time,' she said quickly. 'I fear there are more urgent matters. Some of Cormac's followers are unhappy that he is sheltering the Geraldine heir. Rumours abound that Grey and Ormond will attack Carbury. Cormac has tried to stifle such talk but the fear is exploited by others anxious to use his protection of the Geraldine as an opportunity to unseat him as chieftain. His uncle incites the people further, invoking memories of the old Desmond-MacCarthy feud, which my marriage...' her voice trailed away as if she sensed where such memories might lead them. She turned towards him. 'I must not compromise Cormac further, Thomas. He is young, vulnerable to the plots of those who wish him ill and who even now converge on Kilbritin.'

'I wondered at the activity below, ' he said as they left Gerald's room. 'Do not worry. Kilbritin is but a temporary refuge until Robert Walshe returns from France. Now that Gerald is on the mend, I shall seek another sanctuary. Perhaps in Connacht or in Ulster with O'Neill. One way or another, I intend to keep Gerald safe. That was Garret's wish.'

'And mine.' Her voice was intense. 'And unlike my son, I have nothing to lose.'

'Except your life,' he reminded her. 'The king will not spare women in his lust for revenge.'

'Nor faithful friends as you,' she said softly. 'But it would be unnatural, if no one of Gerald's own blood came to his assistance, if only to balance the evil intent of my sister.' She was silent for a moment. 'I sent messengers to my kinsman, the Earl of Desmond. He agrees to give Gerald sanctuary.'

Leverous looked at her in surprise but she continued quickly. 'He has immense power and bears a deep hatred towards the Tudors. The Ormonds and the king will be wary of attacking him. He offers to meet Gerald at the borders of Carbury and take him, and you,' she added hurriedly, 'to Askeaton Castle.'

Eleanor's determination to remove Gerald from Carbury surprised Leverous. Despite her worries, it seemed to him that her son was much respected and in absolute control within his lordship. For a moment he felt manipulated, outmanoeuvered. Since Garret's imprisonment in the Tower of London, he had had sole responsibility for Gerald. Every decision regarding him, his safety and security, he had made alone.

'Can Desmond be trusted? Why his sudden interest in Gerald's welfare?'

'I really cannot say. Perhaps it lies in his hostility to the king. Or in his kinship to Gerald. Remember Garret backed him against the claims of his cousin to the earldom. Either way, Thomas, he can be a powerful buffer against the king and my sister.'

She imagined that he must hear her heart thump, that her eyes might betray her anxiety. It was the only way she knew to alleviate the danger to Cormac's position as chieftain, posed, not by the presence of Gerald in Carbury, but by Leverous himself.

111

God forgive me, she prayed silently. It is the price I must pay. She saw that he was not as yet convinced. 'Let us put Desmond's offer to the test,' she said, seeking to reassure him. 'We will both accompany Gerald. You to fulfil your promise to my brother, I as guarantor of Desmond's intent.'

Leverous hardly knew what to say. He had seen the struggle she had waged with herself before offering to accompany him. Her real intent was, he suspected, to be rid of him. It was obvious that his presence in Kilbritin embarrassed her. Perhaps she had another suitor. He felt a stab of loss, but quickly hardened his heart against it and against her.

'Our enemies are all about us and seek to strike at us even within our own House.'

Garret's words from the Tower burned in his head. Did his warning include his sister Eleanor? And yet he knew, on face value, her offer made sense. It was even essential, if, as she had said, the MacCarthy's internal wrangling placed Gerald's safety in jeopardy in Carbury.

The Earl of Desmond, head of the Munster Geraldines and kinsman of the Kildares, was an unknown quantity to Leverous. Isolated by the wide expanse of moorland, forests and river from the centre of English power in Dublin and alienated over the centuries from the English crown, the Munster Geraldines had become more Irish than the Irish. Unlike their Kildare kinsmen, they had cut themselves adrift from England. They refused to attend court or to appear at the council in Dublin and openly intrigued with England's continental enemies. For generations they had ruled their vast estates by Irish custom which endowed them with great riches and powers. Every native chieftain in Munster, including MacCarthy, owed them fealty. Ties of common ancestry, and a deep-seated hatred of the Tudors, made the present Earl of Desmond a willing, if unpredictable, ally of Garret, against the king and a willing abettor of Silken Thomas in his rebellion.

'Well, Thomas. The decision is yours.'

Eleanor's voice jerked him out of his reflections. Leverous felt her hand touch his shoulder. The warmth seemed to burn a hole through his doublet. He knew that if he turned to face her, looked once into her eyes, touched even her hand, he would succumb to the desire that here in the half-light of his chamber might be as easily realised as it had been at Thomas Court or just as easily rebuffed. He dared not take a chance. He needed to dream, to hope a little longer. He moved away from her towards the slit defensive window, through which a shaft of pale winter sun filtered.

'Let it be to Desmond then.' His voice sounded hollow.

His back seemed as a barrier, stiff and unyielding between them. Eleanor sensed his coolness and guessed the cause and inwardly mourned her loss, her inability to comfort him within the friendship that had been theirs before Thomas Court.

11

DUBLIN CASTLE

The temporal and spiritual lords of the king's Irish parliament, in their crimson robes, together with officials, clerks and administrators, streamed out of the council chamber. It had been a stormy session. In the foyer a babble of voices continued the acrimonious argument that had dominated the proceedings for an entire week. Strident English tones mingled with the soft intonations of the Irish-born Pale lords. But the parliament that claimed to legislate for the entire country was strangely bereft of the throaty burr of the Gaelic tongue. No bemantled chieftain nor gaelicised Anglo-Norman lord were among the doublet-and-hosed throng. For this was an English parliament, rooted in English custom, governed by English rules, conducted in a foreign tongue, its edicts neither of interest nor relevance to the Irish world outside the Pale, which it purported to govern in the name of the English king.

The session had brought to the fore the antagonism that existed even among loyal adherents of the crown in Ireland. At issue was a matter guaranteed to reduce loyalty and principle to the common denominator of the human condition. Human greed surfaced in bishop, lord and official alike. Hot words flew across the velvet-covered pews, as God and Mammon vied for the spoils of the Irish monasteries and the lands of the earldom of Kildare, which were about to be officially declared forfeited to the crown, once their eleven-year-old heir had been captured and dispatched like the rest of his kin.

At the stroke of a pen these vast estates could then be declared forfeited to the king, who, in his bounty, might be inclined to dole them out to his temporal and spiritual Irish supporters in lieu of rent and loyalty. But the loyal Irish lords and bishops faced stiff competition for the spoils from a new and disturbing quarter. For at the first scent of the dissolution of the Irish monasteries and the Kildare confiscations, English officials in the Irish service saw their way to personal fortunes and added their voice to the clamour for the escheated estates. These were joined by new arrivals from England, where news of the El Dorado in Ireland made the once repugnant Irish service a more attractive proposition to second-rate clerks and lawyers and the disenchanted younger sons of English landed and merchant classes. Amid the clamour, the claim of the rightful heir to the Kildare estates was pushed aside, for it was presumed that his capture was imminent and his demise certain.

Lord Deputy Grey steadfastly ignored the calls and tugs on his cloak, as he hurried through the raucous throng. Reaching his office gratefully, he closed the heavy door on the tumult outside. He fell into the chair at his desk, closed his eyes and savoured the silence. His excursions against the O'Byrnes in their wild Wicklow fastness seemed heavenly now compared to the parliamentary inferno. Greed, avarice, subterfuge and malice were but part of the baseness displayed as crozier and sword fought over the Irish spoils. Grey belonged in the field, where the issue of life and death was clear cut. Parchment and quill, the devious stratagems of lawyer and entrepreneur, the temporising and double-talk of political administration, left him weakened, sick in his stomach.

His eyes alighted on the parchment deeds on his desk.

With some satisfaction he noted his small but significant success in the ignoble wrangling. He had secured Maynooth and a thousand acres, snatched them from the avaricious maw of the competing Brabazon, his ambitious under-treasurer. Why he had bothered he could not really say. He had been but once inside the great fortress, on the marriage of his sister to the earl. The next time he had seen it was as a ruin, roofless and forlorn among the splendour of the great oaks that lined the approach and dotted the surrounding parklands. He had no ambition to own anything in Ireland. His intention was to quit the afflicted country at the earliest opportunity, before he died of the ague or of frustration. The notion to salvage Maynooth from the base scramble had come upon him on impulse as he watched the vultures in the Chamber pick the Kildare carcass clean.

Perhaps his action sprang from contrition, remorse at the shameful fate he had inflicted on his step-nephew and his uncles. Or perhaps he had been thinking of his young nephew, Elizabeth's child, now a wretched fugitive, heir to nothing but an empty shell and a blighted ancestry, a victim of the rashness of his family and the avarice of his enemies. Maynooth might be a shell but it would be ever the symbol of the Kildares and, he thought, perhaps a symbol of hope to an innocent orphan when kinder times prevailed and royal anger had been assuaged.

But perhaps his spontaneous gesture was in vain. Grey fingered the parchment on the desk. The king would never rest until the last of the Kildares was under lock and key in the Tower, and there, by some devious conspiracy, to be assassinated like his family. Marauding dogs like his under-treasurer Brabazon would seek to ensure the latter. For until the heir to the Kildare estates was dead, their grip on the escheated estates would not be assured, particularly when Henry's successor was still his daughter Mary, who might well look with more sympathy on the victims of her father's scourge. But the boy's fate, despite his warning, might already be sealed at the hand of the Countess of Ormond. Grey's face creased in thought.

A furtive knock on the door signalled the end of his musing. He busied himself at the desk.

'Enter,' he called out brusquely. His eyes narrowed with dislike as the black-caped figure of his chief clerk, Crowley, sidled with assumed meekness into the room. 'Well?' he enquired. With a feigned mixture of apology and reproach, Crowley's eyes slid towards the ledger he was carrying. 'The army musters, my lord, as you requested.'

Gray sighed with annoyance and directed Crowley to the desk. Since the ending of the rebellion, the privy council in England had systematically reduced army numbers in Ireland. In theory Grey was supposed to have a complement of seven hundred trained soldiers, but the king was reluctant to maintain a sufficient army in the Irish service or to make monies available to maintain it. The king's policy, coupled by desertion and illness, had reduced the numbers to a dangerously low level. Grey looked more closely at the figures in the ledger. He held Dublin and the Pale with less than five hundred men. And further desertions had occurred since the king had introduced debased groats to pay the soldiers. It was an imbecilic move, a recipe for mutiny. Grey had seen the soldiers fling the new 'coin of the harp' at the feet of the paymaster in the castle yard, and he could only sympathise with them. Despite his pleas to Cromwell and, in desperation, directly to the king, there had been no improvement. Now that the danger of further rebellion had receded, the king simply rejected any proposal in Ireland which cost him money, and Grey was expected to make up the shortfall by impounding men and supplies from the lords of the Pale, not always willing to pay the price of loyalty.

Grey examined the rows of figures in Crowley's neat hand: men, arms, last payment and station. Two hundred men in Dublin, excluding the castle guard, the rest stretched thinly in border fortresses along the boundary of the Pale. A slim line of defence against the unknown might of the Irish-held territory beyond. Thank God, he thought, the Irish preferred to fight one another. For if they ever combined and directed their might against the fragile English enclave, it would simply be overrun. Divide and conquer must be England's essential alternative to military conquest, if England's toehold in Ireland was to be preserved.

'If I may suggest, my lord . . . ' Crowley's voice intervened. 'You could move the garrison at Leighlinbridge to perhaps the fortress of Donore and thereby give protection against O'Connor in Offaly.'

Grey did not raise his head from the ledger. Crowley's words hung in the air. Why should his clerk mention Donore? 'And, pray, what will protect us to the south?' he asked quietly.

'My Lord of Ormond can easily garrison the route south and save both money and men,' the clerk replied.

Crowley's advise sounded plausible, and even sensible, except that Grey knew that he was in the pay of the Countess of Ormond. He had seen him and Brabazon cloistered with Ormond and his countess. The countess had her spies everywhere, even within his own administration. The ambitions of his under-treasurer and clerk fed on Ormond aspirations to the deputyship, of that Grey had no doubt. What had occurred at Donore he could but guess. Had the Ormonds discovered his hasty warning to Leverous? There was little concrete evidence to implicate him if his message had fallen into their hands. The ornate dagger had been given to him by his brother-in-law in the presence of Thomas Leverous. The countess might have her suspicions but she could have no hard evidence to implicate him.

'The garrison remains at Leighlinbridge. The remnants of the Kildare kern may yet regroup and attack.'

Crowley directed him a side look. 'With respect, my lord, such an occurrence is unlikely. The Kildare kern skulk like starving wolves in the marshes and woods.'

'Wolves must eat.' Grey's voice brooked no continuation of the conversation.

Crowley's lips tightened perceptibly. He dipped the quill in the silver inkstand and awaited Grey's instructions.

The lord deputy turned a page in the ledger. Rows of columned figures showed the composition of the private armies of the Pale lords. He frowned in irritation. He detested this Irish practice. Many such private armies scattered the length and breath of the country were the main cause of the state of constant unrest.

In the past the crown had tried to convert the situation to its advantage, by using the private forces of the Pale lords to augment the king's inadequate army. Although bound by allegiance to provide a specific number of armed and provisioned fighting men out of their own resources, the Pale lords did so reluctantly, motivated more from a sense of self-advancement than loyalty. Since most of them out of loyalty or fear or both, he mused, were once allies of the Earl of Kildare, their support of the crown, despite his death, was still indifferent. And when he did succeed in extricating from them a rising-out, it was he and not the king who was at the receiving end of their incessant demands for favours in return. If he offended the sensibilities of any of them, they were likely to plead illness, poverty or some such excuse to evade their military commitment.

Grey's frown deepened at the name which headed the list: the Earl of Ormond with one thousand fully equipped men. An increase of four hundred since the last muster, he noted with unease. As well as building his account with the king in England, Ormond, or more likely his countess, had been busy since Kildare's fall from grace. There was nothing more certain to secure the fealty of one's neighbours in Ireland than to impress them by numbers and force of arms, and by these figures the Ormonds were impressive indeed.

With a telepathic sense of timing, the door of his chamber was thrown open and the formidable figure of the Countess of Ormond strode towards him.

'Madam, I protest.' Grey rose in anger from his seat. 'You intrude on the king's business.'

'King's business. Hah! Little you care about the king's business when you, his deputy, seek purposely to obstruct it.'

Grey felt a pulse of fear. 'By God's grace, you talk treason. Madam, have a care, I warn you.'

'Nay, my lord, 'tis you who will account to the king on that charge, believe me.'

The countess spat her words across the table. Crowley moved aside as if his proximity to the deputy might be interpreted as support for him.

Still in her mud-spattered riding attire, the countess leaned her arms on Grey's desk. Her eyes fastened on him with gimlet intensity. Grey felt a stab of fear as if faced by unsurmountable odds. Her sheer physical bulk was intimidatory and, combined with her mental aptitude, she exuded a sense of indestructibility. They had clashed from the first day they had met. Even as his ship pulled close to the dock at Wood Quay, Grey had noticed her large, menacing figure garbed in black among the reception party. At their introduction, her cold, calculating eyes and unfriendly disposition warned him that he had met an implacable foe.

'Our nephew,' her tone was sarcastic, 'has been spirited into Munster, forewarned no doubt by those still in sympathy with the Geraldines. A friend, a follower, a relation . . . ?' Her eyes bored accusingly into his. 'We have been ambushed by MacCarthy of Carbury, attacked, carrying the king's banner, doing the king's duty.'

Grey felt the first glow of relief. Leverous had received his warning and had taken flight.

'A hazard, madam, that unfortunately seems inescapable in Ireland. But surely your nephew intended you no harm?' He could not keep the sarcasm from his voice.

'God's blood, Grey, have you forgotten your duty?' Her

large body shook in anger. 'You are the king's deputy, bound to avenge this attack on his honour.'

'Bound to do so many things with, alack, insufficient means.' Grey turned the pages of the ledger and avoided her eyes. 'From these accounts it appears that I have an army of less than five hundred to defend the king's interest, aye and the king's loyal subjects.'

'I need not your defence. I could provide the king with a thousand, nay thousands if I were . . .' The countess checked her words abruptly.

'If you were in my office? Lord, would that you were.'

A flush of anger spread like a stain across the swollen face. 'I am not here to bandy words of sarcasm. I know the king's commands to apprehend my nephew and I also suspect your intent to obstruct them. I am as close in blood to the boy as you, yet my duty to the king overrides such ties. If I should forget my duty as the boy's aunt, it would be forgiven as an understandable lapse.' She leaned threateningly across the table. ' But should you forget yours, the king will deem it treason.'

There was silence. Behind him Crowley coughed affectedly. Grey felt the anger rise within him at her provocation. His hands clenched the sides of the table.

'My duty to the king rests accountable on my record,' he heard himself shout. 'Have a care, madam, that your desire to do duty to the king is not a screen that hides a deeper lust.'

The countess's breath hissed sharply through her teeth. She straightened her spectacular height and glanced at Crowley, before fixing her eyes on Grey once more.

'The Geraldine fugitive is still at large, removed by MacCarthy to Munster, in open defiance of the king. So the king's government in Ireland is still threatened by a Geraldine. As the king's deputy, you have completed but half your duty. I demand, and Mr Clerk here is witness, that you retrieve your nephew from MacCarthy and dispatch him to England, as the king commands you.'

Grey felt a throbbing in his head. 'Madam, despite your aspiration to the same, you little understand the constraints of my office. I do not have the king's writ to invade Mac Carthy's country.' Almost involuntarily he brought his fist down on the table with a bang. 'And even if I had, I have not sufficient means to effect such a costly and, most likely, fruitless exercise.'

A sneer distorted the countess's features. She picked up her riding-stick from the desk and pointed at the open ledger. Grey looked at the point of the stick which rested on the Ormond entry.

'There is your means; I will see to it that you get your writ.'

Despite her bulk, the countess turned agilely on her heel and disappeared in a shadow of black velvet through the door.

Grey sank back into his chair. The pain shot like firebrands through his belly. Wearily he dismissed Crowley and reached into the bottom drawer of the desk for the only potion he knew that would bring him relief.

Outside in the congested hall, the countess was joined by her husband and a younger, stockily built man, whose lack of height was compensated for by an air of aggressive confidence. Dark-haired, with a neat pointed beard accentuated by a long nose, his restless eyes narrowed in anticipation at the countess's approach. A gold chain was arranged around his shoulders, the interconnecting links glowing against a crimson doublet of fine silk. William Brabazon was one of the new breed of English adventurers lately come to Ireland, determined on a lucrative career in the Irish service. His position as under-treasurer owed more to Ormond favouritism than to his knowledge of Irish affairs. There were rich pickings to be had in the Irish service and Brabazon intended to harvest his share. As a younger son of minor gentry, his prospects for advancement were not encouraging in England. Many of his ilk had joined expeditions westwards towards the Americas. Lack of stomach for sea life had made him choose Ireland to seek his fortune under the Ormond banner.

'Well?' the Earl of Ormond asked his wife as they entered the courtyard.

The wide cobbled expanse was cleared of snow, which lay piled in soiled mounds along the base of the high crenellated walls and was bustling with activity. The mail-clad, sober attire of horseman and foot soldier contrasted with the multi-coloured livery of the servants of the lords, bishops and of the castle retainers. Horseboys darted back and forth to the stables at the far side of the courtyard, leading their masters' mounts.

'As I suspected, Grey is in it up to his neck. What game he plays remains to be seen but I warrant that he somehow got a warning to Leverous.'

'Is he to give chase?' Brabazon asked.

'He pleads lack of men and the king's writ to invade Carbury.' She gave a short laugh. 'I have promised him assistance. You will ensure that he is beset in the council until our return.'

'Return?' her husband asked wearily.

'We go to England . . . to the court. There is nothing more to be gained here. Grey is a mule and there is only one stick with which to move him. The prize is too great and so nearly within grasp, for all of us to back away now. One last effort is all that is required to push him into the abyss.'

Brabazon fingered the gold chain of his office. 'Be assured, my lady, that the deputy will not know on which elbow to lean in your absence.' He coughed affectedly behind his hand. 'The scent of spoil proved too strong for him today in the chamber.'

The countess looked sharply at the under-treasurer. 'What do you mean?'

'The deputy snatched Maynooth and a thousand acres.'

The countess's face blanched noticeably. Maynooth was to have been her ultimate triumph, the symbolic conclusion of her crusade of vengeance against Kildare. She slapped her hand with her riding-crop in irritation.

'A temporary ownership, I will see to that. His greed can yet be worked to our advantage.' She would kill rather than see Grey installed in Maynooth Castle, the pinnacle of her retribution.

Two horseboys dressed in the blue and silver livery of Ormond assisted her to mount. With a nod to Brabazon, she rode across the courtyard in the direction of the gatehouse, the earl and the Ormond retinue following in her wake. Through the portcullis and gateway, where the shrivelled heads of Geraldine kern grimaced hideously above them, they crossed the bridge over the moat into the busy streets of Dublin.

'Butler aboo.'

With a caustic smile and a slight inclination of her head, the countess acknowledged the shouts of the mercurial citizens, clustered around the castle gate. A short time before, they had similarly cheered her brother Kildare.

They countess and her party turned into Fishamble Street, bustling with people and traffic, its narrow confines lined on either side by steeply roofed houses. A herald cleared the way for the Ormond train.

Outside a dingy tavern a large crowd had gathered, spilling into the street. Despite the best endeavours of the Ormond front riders, the Ormond entourage was brought to a halt. The crowd's attention was centred on the innkeeper, large and red-faced, who held a shabby bearded figure by the heels and, to the merriment of the onlookers, shook him like a rug.

'You pay for your ale in this town, minstrel,' he roared.

'You'll get little change out of them trews, landlord,' a wag in the crowd shouted to more laughter. Nearby a small harp lay splattered by the slush and mud.

'Move along there,' the Earl of Ormond shouted. He was weary, hungry and cold, and longed for the comfort of his rooms in St Mary's Abbey across the river.

The crowd moved aside and the landlord saluted the noble party, at the same time absent-mindedly dropping the harper, who fell with a thud to the ground.

'What is this disturbance, landlord?' Ormond called testily.

'With respect, my lord,' he replied bowing, 'the kern here is a thief.'

The harper, who by now had regained his feet and his harp, rounded sullenly on the innkeeper.

'You lie,' he said. Turning to the Ormond party, he continued, 'I am no kern. I am a harper. I offered to pay with my music, as is customary.'

'Not in this city,' the landlord retorted angrily.

The countess moved her mount forward. 'Your name?' she asked the harper, who was wrapping himself in a mud-streaked mantle. His face was thin and hungry.

'MacGrath.'

'To whose house do you belong?'

The harper looked fearfully around the perimeter of the crowd as if to seek a space through which to escape. But there was no way through the tightly bunched citizens.

He swallowed nervously. 'The O'Byrne.'

An angry murmur greeted his remark. Memories of O'Byrne raids on the city rankled deep.

'A rebel as well as a thief,' the landlord shouted triumphantly. The crowd moved ominously closer. The countess put her horse between the now cowering harper and the menacing citizens.

'I will see to him.' Her cold voice brooked no questions. She motioned to a horseman in her party, who took the harper by the arm. The crowd gaped in silence after her as she led her retinue towards the bridge.

125

12

BORDER OF THE LORDSHIPS
OF CARBURY AND DESMOND

The small cavalcade crossed the partially submerged stone causeway. The river was in winter spate, the brown swirling waters swollen by the melting snows high up at its source. Skirting the great forest of Kilmore to the right, they rode west for some miles before turning north again to enter the narrow pass between Kilmore and the dense woods of Clonish, which stretched westwards towards the high ridges of the Paps and beyond towards the Lordship of Desmond. The day was overcast and silent. A breeze sighed occasionally through the brittle branches of the outlying string of birch and alder which lined the pass between the darker mass of oak, ash and yew that stretched into the distance. Overhead a goshawk circled. There was a chill in the air. The mountain peaks were snow-streaked but the track through which Eleanor's group rode was muddied by a spring thaw.

Eleanor and Leverous had left Kilbritin two days previously. The MacCarthy had given them an escort to conduct them safely across Munster to their rendezvous with the Earl of Desmond. The escort was small enough to evade attention, but well-armed and horsed to resist attack or outrun pursuit. Yet the impediments they encountered on the journey sprang not from human adversaries, rather from the wild and inhospitable environment. To lessen the risk of discovery, they had skirted all signs of human habitation and had encamped at night hidden deep within the woodland fastness. Despite their copious Irish mantles and a campfire, which through the night cast some warmth on the sleeping forms stretched within its light and deterred the wolves that foraged in the undergrowth, they felt the full misery of the woodlands in winter. They were obliged to cross streams swollen with winter deluges without the aid of a ford, the icy water swirling waist high. Gratefully they supped the *uisce beatha* and felt the fiery liquid restore life to their frozen limbs.

Gerald seemed not to have suffered any ill-effects from the unseasonal journey and after an exhausting day in the saddle, his energy was amazing. Riding between Eleanor and Leverous on his hardy Irish cob, the young Geraldine maintained a constant flow of conversation, punctuated by endless questions. 'Why must he leave Carbury? Would Cormac send the young red deer to Desmond, the one he had hand-fed and which followed him around the bawn? How old was his kinsman, the Earl of Desmond? Did he have many gallowglass? As many as his father? Did he have sons?'

The inquisitive mind of the eleven-year-old never rested. It was to both Leverous's and Eleanor's relief when Gerald took to the company of one of the MacCarthy horsemen and directed his questions to him.

Riding a few paces behind, Leverous glanced at Eleanor, her face wan under the turban style head-dress. Despite her fatigue, she sat erect in the saddle, her eyes alert. They had resumed their earlier easy amicability that had faltered for that brief moment in his rooms at Kilbritin. Gerald had become the bond between them now, displacing the deeper one that they had pushed into the hidden recesses of the past, afraid to trust each other's emotions. They were reunited again, this time in the cause of Gerald's safety.

127

Leverous eased his horse alongside. Eleanor's hazel eyes smiled a welcome which lit the paleness of her face.

'We can stop and rest for an hour if you wish.' He tried to make his concern for her comfort as impersonal as he could.

She shook her head. 'We had best ride on and keep our rendezvous with Desmond. The thought of another night in the open holds little appeal to this aching body,' she laughed lightly and then suddenly blushed, as if her statement contained some innuendo. She was so tense and taut in her conversation with him and chided herself silently for her fatuousness. 'We must think of Gerald,' she added, once more in control.

Leverous appeared unaware of her discomfort and eased his weight in the soft pillion.

'I pray Robert Walshe did not perish on the way to France.'

'Murdered more likely by Cromwell's assassins,' she said decisively.

'He had safe passage from the French king.'

'I hold little faith in the word of kings, Thomas – English or French.' Eleanor's voice had a bitter ring. 'They play with lives as with the dice. François's promise to my brother was perhaps well-intentioned at the moment of its giving but paled as circumstances changed and was worthless by the day of his death in the Tower. The king will keep his promise to my brother only if it is to his benefit. And,' she added reflectively, 'I am not sure that I wish him to.'

Her disclosure took Leverous by surprise. He looked at her sharply. 'Gerald's life depends on the French offer of asylum.'

'Does it?' She looked at him with troubled eyes. 'I would rather my life in the hands of the lowliest Irish kern than a foreign king.'

'Alack, my lady,' he rebuked her, ''tis not the kern who dictate. Would you place such trust in their masters? I fear the Irish chieftains could teach François a sharp lesson in duplicity. Irish, French or English . . . ' he shrugged his shoulders under the folds of his mantle, ' . . . 'tis all the same. Trust is the utopia of the human condition. Ever hoped for but seldom realised.' His voice was cold and emphatic.

The silence weighed heavily between them. Her face was half-hidden from his view by the deep fringe of her woollen mantle but Leverous fancied he saw a crimson tint touch her pale cheeks. Inwardly he cursed himself for his premeditated insensitivity. Making her atone. For what? For his loneliness, the aching emptiness that since their unexpected reunion had begun to consume his soul again, turning him bitter against himself, against her. Blaming her for the barrenness of his life, for his own weakness that still craved her body and soul, so that he might be whole within himself. There was a base selfishness to his reasoning.

'Perhaps we are both right,' he conceded lamely. 'Native or foreign, loyalty is for hire to the highest bidder. But with us,' he smiled reassuringly at her, 'at least Gerald will be certain of that.'

For a moment he thought she would not reply. She raised her head from the high fringe at her throat. The hazel eyes looked somewhat speculatively at him as if she was appraising him or even seeing him for the first time. He subdued the longing that he feared would shine like a beacon from his eyes and turned away.

Eleanor looked on the finely shaped features, the high forehead, the deep intensity of the dark blue eyes, the masculinity combined with refinement, intelligence, that rare combination that she had found so compelling in him. The strong lean body had ripened with the years. There was an attractive substance to his broad shoulders. The traces of grey that highlighted the fine dark hair at his temples seemed to complement the impression of mellow confidence that he exuded. She had heard intermittently of his accomplished record at Cambridge and Padua. There had been talk of the church after his return from Louvain. It was said that Garret had earmarked the rich diocese of Meath for him but, in the event, Leverous was apparently content to serve the Geraldines as Garret's advisor and friend, and now protector of his son.

She had thought of him often. The memory of their passionate lovemaking had encroached on the early days of her marriage. Hidden deep in some recess of her mind, it was the face and body of Leverous who lay above her, consuming her with passion, to which she eagerly responded. But she had reaped in full the bitter cost of their brief liaison and the web of deceit and lies in which it had entangled her. Her husband had been loving and unsuspecting and she had responded to his kindness, initially from a sense of atonement, shame and fear of the legacy of her relationship with Leverous. But the Great Earl of Kildare's daughter was above suspicion and the birth of her son had been celebrated throughout the MacCarthy lordship.

Gradually the memory of her consuming intimacy with Leverous became relegated to the edges of her mind and had waned in relevance over the years. It was with a shamed sense of relief that she heard of his departure to the Continent. The distance between them released her further from the disturbing memory of their love and from the fear of discovery. Determinedly, she suppressed emotion and regret and forced his memory from her mind, for her son's security, she told herself, for her own sanity. Her son was now the legally elected chieftain of the MacCarthys, an uncankered branch in the all-important genealogical tree of the once royal house of Munster. She would never allow any hint of suspicion to taint his birthright.

It was perhaps inevitable that they would meet again. But she had refused to prepare herself for that eventuality. She suspected their reunion aroused emotions in both of them. Emotions that simmered below a very thin surface and which for all their sakes must be denied, buried with the memory of their love.

'Gerald's safety is paramount.' She made her voice sound practical, unconcerned with Leverous's previous innuendo. 'You can rely on me to do everything in my power to ensure that, and . . .' she looked away from his disturbing eyes, ' . . . that I will not compromise you, this time.'

She kicked her horse forward and joined her nephew and the captain of the horsemen at the head of the escort.

Leverous cursed himself under his breath. The gap created by Eleanor's departure from his side reflected the emotional gulf his careless words created between them. He had let his mask slip and she was now on her guard.

They emerged from a narrow pass between the foothills of the Mullaghareirk mountains to the left and the distant Galtees on their right and moved downwards towards the swollen waters of the Blackwater. They drew to a halt before the deep flowing river. An agitated conference was taking place between the captain and his men. Eleanor moved her horse forward. Leverous followed at a distance. The men's voices carried in the quietness of the rapidly darkening evening.

''Tis madness,' the leader of the MacCarthy escort said emphatically. 'I would scarcely chance it with the men. With the boy and, with respect, yourself, Lady Eleanor, it would be sheer madness.'

Leverous moved closer. 'What is the matter?'

Without replying, the captain of the escort looked towards Eleanor. Leverous turned towards her. She avoided his look.

'The captain says it is too dangerous to cross. We should go downstream, to the ford at Mallow Castle. But this way,' she said, indicating the river, 'we can avoid being seen and, once across, we are safe in Desmond's territory.'

The captain threw a twig into the river and in a thrice it was borne swiftly out of sight. He shook his head. 'Even without the boy and you, my lady, it is inviting death.'

131

To risk capture when they were so near safety was unthinkable but to attempt to cross the wide river, in full winter spate, without a ford, was sheer madness. Leverous grimly contemplated the dark swirling water.

'I'm not afraid.'

The boyish shout caught them by surprise and before anyone could stop him, the small figure on the light hob cantered past them straight into the river. For a moment they stood rooted to the spot and stared in disbelief as the waters rose higher and higher until the pillion was barely visible. With an anguished cry, using her feet and hands as spurs, Eleanor urged her reluctant horse into the river. The stronger horse overtook the hob and she grasped Gerald's reins in her left hand. For a second it seemed that both might make the opposite bank as her horse held his feet against the surging current. But suddenly he stumbled and threw her into the flood. The current carried her horse rapidly downstream out of sight.

Leverous felt his blood freeze and in a second he was in the water, shouting at the men to move downriver. They needed little telling. Eleanor's head was visible above the water. She still held on to the reins of Gerald's horse. It would prevent her from being swept away, Leverous thought but, just as quickly realised, that it put her in danger from the threshing hoofs of the hob, which was being swung helplessly around and around in the whirlpool. Gerald held grimly onto its mane. Leverous shouted his frightened horse into the current and felt the water surge past him.

'Hold on, Gerald,' he shouted.

Dimly Eleanor heard his voice and lifted her head. The icy wetness of the river seeped into her bones. Except for the pain from the wet leather reins which bit deeply into her wrist, she was numb all over. Through a watery haze, the face of Leverous loomed above her as in her past fantasy. She felt a sharp jolt as if someone had pulled her back from a precipice, then silence and darkness.

Leverous seized the mane of the frightened hob and, leaning precariously across, managed to attach his belt to the bridle, which he wrapped around the pommel of his saddle. Silently he thanked God for his English saddle with stirrups which freed his hands, while controlling the animal with his knees. He shouted words of encouragement to Gerald before reaching down again into the flood to grasp Eleanor's cloak which streamed behind her. She seemed unconscious and frantically he hauled her closer and closer until she lay alongside. He slipped from the saddle into the icy water and cushioned her head in the crook of his arm while he held fast the reins with the other. Reassured by the presence of the other horse, the hob ceased threshing and the current carried them, almost leisurely now, towards the line of horsemen, who formed in a fan shape downstream. Willing hands propelled them towards the bank, where the exhausted horses scrambled to safety.

The captain lifted Gerald from the saddle. White-faced with shock, he shivered in his wet clothes. One of the men quickly wrapped a woollen mantle around him. Leverous carried the still form of Eleanor from the water and laid her on the wet bank. The MacCarthy men stood silently in a circle around them, their faces grim. Leverous that saw she was breathing, but shallowly, her face a blue tinge against the darkness of her wet hair. Gently he undid the leather reins which had eaten an angry weal into her wrist and rubbed her ice cold hands. At last, she opened her eyes and looked wonderingly into his. Like a magnet her eyes drew him towards her and as he lowered his head towards her, her gaze shifted away from his face over his shoulder and her forehead creased in surprise. Leverous looked behind and slowly rose to his feet.

Around them a force of mounted men silently appraised the bedraggled band. Their leader, a small, elderly man, with stooping shoulders, smothered from top to toe in the folds of a dark green mantle, a look of sardonic amusement on his wrinkled face, addressed Eleanor in slightly mocking tones.

'Well, cousin, it seems I am too late to render you assistance. But no matter, I see you are already well served.'

Leverous stooped down to assist Eleanor, who was attempting to rise to her feet. She swayed against him. Her long hair streamed in lank wet lengths down her shoulders. Her sodden linen dress clung to her body. The black eyes of the stranger took in every detail.

Regaining her composure, Eleanor eased away from Leverous. She felt foolish before the intrusive stare of her kinsman.

'Cousin Desmond, I scarcely thought we would meet like this.'

'Nor I cousin, nor I,' the rasping voice mocked. 'Are you fit to travel?'

Eleanor nodded in response. The Earl of Desmond moved to where Gerald stood, almost invisible within the folds of the captain's mantle. He looked down at the boy. The small shrewd eyes searched every detail of his face as if committing it to memory. Noticing the voluminous mantle which fell in untidy folds around him, the earl remarked. 'It seems my Geraldine kinsman has not yet mastered the wearing of the Irish mantle. But no matter, it is a start.' He smiled down at Gerald. 'I see we have much to teach you in Desmond.'

He returned to where Eleanor stood with Leverous. His eyes swept them both before settling on Leverous. 'You are the boy's tutor?'

'And guardian.' Leverous saw the earl's eyebrows shoot inquisitively upwards. 'By written command of the late Earl of Kildare.'

'You have proof of this?' Desmond's small eyes narrowed suspiciously

'I have proof,' Leverous replied with quiet conviction.

The earl turned from him and addressed Eleanor. 'The night draws in. We will make for Kilmallock and tomorrow, if you are able . . .' he inclined his head towards her, ' . . . to Askeaton.'

He barked orders in Gaelic to his men, one of whom dismounted and led his horse towards Eleanor. Leverous helped her mount. She looked dazed and pale.

'Are you able?'

She smiled reassuringly down at him. One of Desmond's men handed each of them a heavy mantle and they wrapped themselves within the comforting warmth. Bidding farewell to the captain of the MacCarthy escort, they remounted and, surrounded by Desmond horsemen, continued on their journey.

13

WHITEHALL PALACE, LONDON

The spring sunlight penetrated the casement window and flooded the interior with a glaring brilliance. The king squinted his hooded eyes against the light and with feline intensity watched his chief secretary and vicar general scratch his commands onto the parchment with a quill.

Henry contemplated the dark, corpulent form of Thomas Cromwell, self-made solicitor from Putney, avid student of Machiavelli, now most feared and, next to himself, most powerful man in the realm. Some thought him, like his former master, Wolsey, more powerful than the king. Henry laughed silently to himself. There would never be another Wolsey. He would make certain of that. Never again would he allow his God-given power to be usurped by another. With Wolsey he had learned a sharp lesson and a Tudor needed but one warning to be ever on his guard. Where now the great cardinal who once held England in the hollow of his hand? The king allowed a satisfied smile to play over his jowled countenance.

At present Cromwell's star shone brilliantly, but confined, within the orbit of his king's necessity, to implement the policies of his reformation, especially the dissolution of the monasteries. In this task, Cromwell scored handsomely over his predecessor. Where Wolsey had been a priest, Cromwell was a priest-hating layman. A most suited scapegoat, Henry thought, should the murmur of public disquiet against the monastic seizures become more strident. The common classes already blamed Cromwell, not the king, for depriving them of the source of their traditional succour and employment, while to the aristocratic lords of the realm, the appointment of a commoner in ascendancy over them guaranteed their hatred of Cromwell from the start. Yes, Henry thought, with smug satisfaction, he had laid his plans well to ensure that he would reap the benefits and Cromwell the antagonism.

The silence eased the king from his reverie. With quill suspended above the parchment page, Cromwell awaited his pleasure. Henry lifted the paper and read the contents. His eyes narrowed in concentration. He dipped the quill in the silver inkstand and signed, *Henry Rex*, in his artistic hand.

'A timely reminder to old Norfolk. If this does not propel him against the rebels in the north, God's blood, We swear he will become shorter by a head. We have never trusted that Rome-loving Howard breed.'

'His reluctance to punish the rebels, seems . . . foolhardy, your grace.' Cromwell's tones held malice in every syllable.

Henry well knew that there was little love lost between the haughty Duke of Norfolk and his secretary. But from the outset of his reign, to dilute the influence of powerful aristocrats like Norfolk, he had purposely introduced capable commoners like Cromwell to posts of influence within his administration.

'Foolhardy? By my oath, it smacks of treason.' Henry watched Cromwell make ready the wax and tip a dollop of the pungent liquid onto the parchment. He removed a ring from his little finger and made his royal imprint on the hot wax.

'He blows hot and cold over a rising by a few Lincolnshire rustics. A Pilgrimage of Grace. Pah, no more than a fire of straw, easily kindled and soon spent.' Henry threw the signed parchment across the table.

Cromwell folded it neatly into a square. 'By your leave, your grace, 'tis the wind that fans the fire that makes it more suspect.'

'Scotland, with the connivance of France. A cabal, Cromwell, as predictable as yesterday's weather,' the king replied contemptuously.

Cromwell sifted through the dispatches piled beside him on the table. He coughed apologetically and handed the king a document, 'From Gardiner at the French court, Your Grace.'

Henry glanced at the deciphered message and as his eyes scanned the lines his face creased into lines of anger.

'Pole.' He uttered the solitary word with a mixture of venom and fear. The parchment shook in his grasp. 'That cursed Plantagenet hydra. How many heads must be chopped before We are rid of it?'

'My Lord Cardinal,' Cromwell said the title with deep sarcasm, 'it appears, is secreted within Notre Dame. The French king will not receive him, openly at least, while there is hope of an alliance with Your Grace against the Emperor.'

'Let him hope,' Henry snarled. ''Tis like a juggling act, playing these foreign eels one against another. We will continue Our policy of backing both and so confuse them. But Pole must be crushed, Cromwell, like the rest of his traitorous brood.' Henry brought his clenched fist down on the table.

A blob of ink erupted from the inkstand. With a linen handkerchief Cromwell calmly mopped the widening black pool.

'It seems Pole has been active within his sanctuary,' he continued unperturbed. 'A servant of the late Earl of Kildare . . .'

At the mention of the Irish earl, the king rose abruptly and limped across to the window. Cromwell remained silent, familiar with the signs of an imminent eruption of the king's anger, which of late simmered below a very thin surface.

The ulcer in his leg seemed to trouble him more than he cared to admit, and the queen's pregnancy placed an added strain on him. Henry gripped the heavy brocade curtains. His knuckles showed white against the wine-coloured fabric.

'Must I be for ever damned, night and day, with reminders of that cankered breed?' He thought of the leering face of his recent nightmare but subdued the tide of anger that rose within him. 'What of Kildare's servant?'

'His chaplain, Your Grace, one Robert Walshe, visited Pole in Paris.' Cromwell hesitated.

The king swung from the window, anger spreading like a stain across his bloated features. Cromwell hurriedly rose to his feet and continued.

'With Kildare's heir still at large in Ireland,' he spread his hands, 'it is not outside the bounds of possibility that Pole may use the situation, allied with the uprising in the north, to extend the Roman plot against Your Grace.'

'Plantagenet and Geraldine.' The king uttered the words as if for the first time. He looked down on the courtyard of Whitehall, bustling with activity of state. The sore in his leg shot an arrow of pain through his body.

Ireland, that cursed cloud to the west, lay as threatening and troublesome as always. Like a young wench, with the green sickness, he thought, wayward and brazen from want of occupying. Sooner or later he knew he must grasp the nettle lest its wild, disorderly state be used against him by his enemies.

Not for the first time had whispers of a conspiracy between Plantagenet and Geraldine abounded. But he had scuttled their foul attempts before and must do so again, to ensure the safety of the Tudor dynasty which would continue to rule England, if Jane provided him with a son and heir.

'Has Grey apprehended Kildare's son in Ireland?'

Thoughts of the son he craved reminded him of his unfinished business with the remaining son of the traitorous Irish earl. The birth of one would of necessity sound the death knell of the other. He was determined that no Kildare would live to become a threat to his son, as he had been threatened.

Cromwell shook his head. 'I fear not, Your Grace. My Lord Grey stays singularly quiet about the whereabouts of his nephew. Perhaps he needs an incentive to do his duty.'

The king glanced at his secretary with narrowed eyes. Trust Cromwell to have Grey's measure, he thought.

'The Earl and Countess of Ormond are hotfoot from Ireland and beg an audience with Your Grace.'

A brief smile flitted across the Henry's heavy features. 'The Irish virago. By Christ's cross, Cromwell, an admirable choice. It may well take a Geraldine to catch a Geraldine. Have her brought to Us.'

Cromwell bowed, well pleased with his suggestion, and padded noiselessly towards the door.

The king eased his weight on to a high-backed chair and rested his aching leg on an embroidered footstool. Despite his best efforts, his cousin Reginald Pole had slipped through the net in which he had entrapped the rest of his brood. The *bête noire* of the Tudors had ever been the numerous shoots of the blighted white rose of York. His father had commenced the cull and by the Tower and the axe had cut most of them off. But yet remaining were the descendants of the Duke of Clarence, through his daughter, Margaret Pole. Initially he had treated her and her son with kindness, he recalled. And how had they reciprocated? Henry shifted his leg on the cushion and cursed in painful remembrance. By plotting to oust him from the throne so that Reginald Pole might marry his daughter Mary and rule in his place. But he had outsmarted their damned conspiracy. Pole had fled to Europe to continue his studies. To continue his treason, more likely, succoured by the pope and the emperor. His cousin's provocative acceptance of the cardinal's hat and his virulent opposition to his reforms were proof enough of his continuing treason. Cromwell's suspicions were well-founded and timely, he acknowledged. Pole's personal vendetta, if allied to the growing opposition to his religious reforms, could spread and engulf England.

Within England, even within his own administration, silent but dedicated opponents to his reformation, in league with his enemies abroad, lurked ready to strike at him when their evil plot was in readiness. But he was determined to seek out and destroy each participant in the conspiracy which sought to topple him. Make Norfolk do the dirty work of punishing the northern rebels and thereby isolate him from their cause, of which, if Cromwell's intelligence could be believed, he covertly supported. Cromwell and his network of spies would see to his cousin Pole, the Countess of Ormond could be used to eliminate the remaining Geraldine threat in Ireland and counter any disloyal activity by his deputy Grey, while like a skilful puppeteer, he would manipulate the strings of all.

A muffled knock heralded Cromwell's return, followed by a tall, large-boned woman, of enormous girth, and a red-haired sprightly nobleman of late years.

'The Earl and Countess of Ormond, Your Grace.'

The woman curtsied as low as her ponderous girth allowed, while her husband made his leg well enough, Henry observed. Smiling broadly, he rose with difficulty to greet them. He had little doubt as to where the real power in this unlikely union lay and concentrated his attention on the countess. It was hard to imagine this unfeminine woman as the daughter of the Great Earl of Kildare, the handsome charmer he remembered from his youth. But he knew that the earl's unlikely daughter had nonetheless inherited his cunning, which the Earl had used to plot against him. Henry was determined to use that cunning now to his advantage.

'My Lady of Ormond, We have long missed your presence. Have attractions in Ireland made our poor court lose its allure?' he scolded her in jest.

The countess curtsied again. 'On the contrary, we have

long pined to bathe in Your Majesty's gracious presence but, alack, to protect Your Majesty's interests in Ireland seemed the more urgent course to follow.'

He smiled benignly and led the countess towards a casement seat which overlooked the courtyard below.

'Strange,' he turned towards her, 'Our deputy there has not advised us of any difficulties, other than the usual turmoil which Ireland seems to breed. She is well named, Our other kingdom, is she not Cromwell? *Ire*-land. What say you, Ormond?'

Henry laughed with gusto and a smile crossed the sullen features of his secretary. Ormond cleared his throat nervously and seemed about to reply but his wife cut across him.

'I fear that in the present situation, such is the case. For Your Grace's deputy seems incapable or reluctant to govern there in Your Grace's interest.'

The king looked with feigned surprise towards Cromwell.

'That, my dear countess, is a serious charge to lay against Our deputy.'

'My wife does not insinuate any deliberate disloyalty on Lord Grey's part, Your Grace,' Ormond hurriedly intervened.

'I do.' The stark statement was barked out and caught the three men by surprise. 'In the matter of Your Grace's commands for the apprehension of the Geraldine heir.'

The air of jocularity evaporated. The King's face grew cold and remote. 'Then the boy is still at large?'

The violet eyes of the countess held his. 'The boy has been abducted into Munster, Your Grace. For what reason is not yet apparent. But I have my suspicions.'

The king looked at Cromwell and back again at the Irish countess, as if making up his mind as to the next move. The countess made it for him.

'With deepest respect, Your Grace, as one familiar with Irish affairs, I may have a solution to deliver the Geraldine into your protection, as you ordained, and at the same time remove the possibility of future conspiracy against Your

Grace in Ireland.'

Henry feigned surprise at the countess's offer, which he had anticipated. He took his seat beside her at the window, his large body filling the remaining space.

The countess shifted surreptitiously away from the king and glancing sideways at the heavy-set features, noticed how the fair hair had thinned and the bull-like neck and torso had thickened considerably. But the animal magnetism which the king exuded, from the protuberance of his codpiece to the exaggerated expanse of his broad chest, was accentuated by the sheer opulence of the royal attire: a full-skirted slashed doublet of ivory satin, encrusted with rubies, surmounted in gold, under a crimson cloak, lined with ermine, the puffed sleeves embroidered in gold and pointed with more rubies. She wondered what her father, the Great Earl, would say, if he could see her now, about to become the indispensable ally of his enduring enemy.

'My Lady of Ormond . . .' The king raised her hand to his lips and with calculated amusement, watched a blush spread across her features. '. . . your loyalty and that of your house' he nodded in the direction of her husband, ' to Us is noted and appreciated. We will be glad to hear your design to protect and extend Our rule in Ireland. Perhaps while We talk, some refreshment.'

He motioned to Cromwell and then turned expectantly towards the countess.

14

ASKEATON CASTLE,
LORDSHIP OF DESMOND

From his perch on the wall-walk below the ramparts, Thomas Leverous surveyed the countryside beyond the high curtain walls which linked the four angle towers of Askeaton Castle. Strategically situated on an island in the river Deel, the ancient seat of the Earls of Desmond commanded a view over the rolling fertile plains to the east and south, to where the dark shadow of Kylemore forest stretched for miles into the distance towards the Galtee mountains. The castle was an immense sprawling enclosure, encompassing towers, living accommodation, stores, kitchens, bakehouses, out-offices, stables, workshops, a self-sufficient unit, the largest in the defensive chain of castles that protected the vast Desmond lordship.

The stone walls rose up from the river, encircling the angle towers and the square keep, situated on the west side. Alongside was the largest banqueting hall in the country. Even Maynooth did not possess such a fine example of medieval craftsmanship, Leverous mused, as he looked across the courtyard towards the great building with its carved windows and vaulted, lead-covered roof. Inside the castle walls, part of the bawn was laid out in gardens, while outside, an orchard stretched down to the water's edge. Across the river on the mainland, a *clachan* of thatched mud and stone cabins clustered together near the arched bridge that spanned the Deel.

A north-westerly wind blew in from the broad expanse of the Shannon, flecking white the choppy waters. It carried the fresh scent of spring to his nostrils. Leverous inhaled the slightly tangy aroma, filling his lungs until they could hold no more. The April air was like an elixir. The sentry nearby rested his cumbersome arquebus on the parapet, stomped his feet and looked on indifferently at Leverous's moment of pleasure. After an eight-hour watch in this unprotected position, he could hardly be expected to have a similar sense of appreciation, Leverous thought, as he continued his stroll around the walls, his every step watched by the sentries stationed fifty paces apart.

Leverous had been conscious of the watchful suspicion directed at him since his arrival at Askeaton. It had been instigated by the cool reception he had received from the earl, who made little effort to conceal his irritation that Leverous remained. His English apparel and accent seemed to disturb the Desmond followers. Although English had been the household language of the Earl of Kildare, Leverous was fluent in the Gaelic tongue. He had found the language difficult to conquer but the pleasing cadences had encouraged him to persevere. Here in Desmond, the Gaelic tongue was the only language spoken, with the occasional lapse into Latin. The brooding looks directed at him by the earl's retainers were initially accompanied by uncomplimentary remarks which were reduced to muted whispers when it became obvious that the Englishman understood.

Leverous had yet to find the measure of the omnipotent twelfth Earl of Desmond. That he was a much-feared ruler, dominating the myriad urraghs, retainers and swordsmen who swarmed around Askeaton was plain. A week previously, Leverous had watched from his chamber, as Desmond, looking every inch the medieval warlord, from the plume on his iron morion to the silver rowels on his square-toed boots, led his army from the castle. Swathed in an Irish mantle, which spread behind him over the flanks of a black stallion, the white and red banner of Desmond was hoisted over his head as he shouted the traditional warcry of his house. The echoing reply, 'Shanid Abu', erupted from five hundred throats and reverberated around the deserted courtyard, long after the earl's army had disappeared towards his town of Tralee to the west. The scene, Leverous thought, belonged more to a medieval age and he tried to imagine such an occurrence in an English shire. There, time, aided by the strong arm of the Tudors, had overpowered Desmond's counterparts long decades past. But in Ireland, time, for the moment, was on Desmond's side.

In his palatine court in Tralee, the Earl of Desmond was supreme: 'All law belongs to God and to Desmond.' The local saying, Leverous suspected, did not exaggerate.

By the chance of history the earl was the sole arbiter and dispenser of justice within his jurisdiction, a power, which in England, Leverous reminded himself, was deemed the God-given right of kings. But a foolish English monarch, had, in the past, bestowed palatine status on one of the earl's ancestors. While successive English kings lived to regret their predecessor's largesse, the earls of Desmond refused to relinquish the power over life and death that their palatine powers conferred on them.

Leverous descended the narrow flight of steps to the courtyard. It was past time for Gerald's Latin lessons. Since their arrival at Askeaton there had been little time for scholarship. Desmond was adamant that the boy should continue his military training and, since this had been Garret's wish, Leverous did not object. But he had been equally insistent to fulfil Garret's wish that his son should have an adequate time for schooling and to this the earl had reluctantly agreed.

Leverous sighed as he descended the last few steps.

146

Warfare was the predominant topic in Irish society. It dominated life from the womb to the tomb. To retain his position, a chieftain must continuously demonstrate his warlike ability. Garret too, he recalled, had been firstly trained in the hard school of the Irish warrior class, before being sent to England, at the express command of Henry VII, who had feared that the heir to the premier earldom in Ireland might become completely Irish.

But in true renaissance style, Garret's military prowess was tempered by an appreciation of learning. A fine orator in Irish, English and French, he wrote with a clear hand, and was well versed in the classics. His library at Maynooth was the envy of his contemporaries. From France, Italy and England he had collected rare and beautifully tooled volumes. He employed learned scribes to translate the ancient heroic sagas and legends of Ireland from Gaelic and Latin into English. It was Garret's intention, Leverous recalled, that Gerald would have access to knowledge and learning and had entrusted his tuition to him. Gerald was an eager and receptive pupil, already proficient in Gaelic, English and Latin. He could write an acceptable hand and possessed an enquiring mind. If circumstances permitted, Gerald would become an accomplished scholar.

Leverous emerged into the bright light of the rectangular courtyard. He spied his charge astride the tough Irish hob that the Earl of Desmond had given him. In his right hand Gerald held aloft an Irish spear, its iron tip pointed towards a stake fifty yards distant, on which hung a straw figure. Minus his habitual hauberk, MacSheehy, the captain of Desmond's gallowglass, stood nearby, shouting instructions. A dozen Desmond kern lounged along the wall, while some of the castle servants had abandoned their chores to watch.

Gerald kicked his heels into the sides of the hob and with the spear held above his head, galloped in the direction of the straw target and inexpertly threw the weapon, which sailed harmlessly above it. MacSheehy said something inaudible to the watching kern and there were general guffaws. Shamefacedly Gerald dismounted.

'Where are you off to, my lad?' MacSheehy shouted. 'Back on that horse. That pitiful effort would have left you dangling high on an Ormond lance.' He threw the boy a spear.

'I have not practised with the spear before,' Gerald earnestly explained, his cheeks aflame.

'Hear that, lads,' MacSheehy turned to his audience. 'Some Geraldine this one. Too much Sasanach blood.'

Leverous saw Gerald raise the spear threateningly above his head and aim at his tormentor. Leverous walked quickly towards the group, who watched his approach with ill-concealed hostility. MacSheehy spat into the ground. 'And too close attention by Sasanach hirelings.'

Leverous ignored the taunt. 'How can the boy be expected to learn if he is not taught?'

MacSheehy turned away from him and with a leer addressed his audience. 'Come to make us as foppish as he has the Geraldine.'

Ignoring the jeers, Leverous mounted the cob and took the long spear from Gerald, who looked wonderingly at him. 'Like this, Gerald,' he said.

The hob surged forward towards the target. Keeping his body erect and steady with his knees, Leverous threw the spear at the straw target as he galloped past. Gerald ran excitedly after him and retrieved the weapon which was fixed in the exact centre of the target.

'Bullseye,' the boy shouted triumphantly towards the group of stony-faced kern. He handed Leverous the dart. 'Again Leverous.'

'Enough for today, Gerald,' Leverous said, taking the weapon from him. He rode back towards the group. 'Besides, there are others who may need the practice.'

As he came abreast of the now silent gallowglass captain, Leverous raised the spear above his head. For a moment a flicker of fear flashed across the scared face. Expertly

Leverous hurled it at the ground where it landed, the point embedded in the dirt, inches from the leather-thonged feet.

'Not bad for an English hireling?' he said to MacSheehy as he dismounted.

The sound of a slow handclap disturbed the tension. Leverous looked up towards the wall-walk. Sentries stood motionless, watching the drama below. The slightly croaking voice of the Earl of Desmond spoke from the shadows.

'Perhaps MacSheehy should teach Latin and Leverous become a gallowglass.'

MacSheehy's face turned red at the laughter of his companions.

Leverous searched the high ramparts to locate the earl's slight figure. He sensed that the gallowglass captain was on the point of retaliation but had been forestalled by the earl's intervention. Leverous cursed his own impetuosity for allowing himself to be drawn into an incident that might well have ended in disaster. A gallowglass was bred for war. Killing was all he knew. One did not needlessly arouse the blood lust that seethed below the thin veneer of restraint.

Emerging from the shadows, Desmond beckoned. Telling Gerald to await his return in his chamber, Leverous dismounted. He had been expecting such a summons. Since his arrival at Askeaton, he had scarcely set eyes on the earl, who seemed immersed with the administration of his vast lordship. When not cloistered with his brehons and seneschal, he was in his town of Tralee or leading punitive raids against an enemy or a recalcitrant vassal. The earl had not asked further about his guardianship of Gerald, nor had he asked to see Garret's letter, which lay safely concealed inside Leverous's doublet.

Eleanor, too, was as elusive as the earl and seemed intent on avoiding him. When they did meet at dinner or in the castle grounds, it was never alone. Whether her avoidance of him was at the earl's instigation or her own preference, Leverous could not be certain.

Dressed in tight woollen trews, a quilted jacket of fine leather, studded with gold fastenings and buttoned high to the neck, around which hung a heavy gold chain, Desmond watched him approach.

'For an Englishman, you throw the spear well enough.'

'My lord,' Leverous bowed in acknowledgement of the backhanded compliment, 'I am long enough in Ireland to have had ample practice.'

'I thought my cousin Kildare had dispensed with such Irish practices in the English Pale.'

'My Lord Kildare's authority extended far beyond the Pale, my lord.'

A thin smile played around the corners of the tight-lipped mouth. 'Aye, my cousin Kildare's ambition knew no bounds.' Desmond pulled the folds of his mantle close around his spare frame. 'We did what we could in Desmond, aye and beyond, to help him against the English.' He threw Leverous a sidelong glance to observe his reaction. 'We Geraldines have reaped a bitter harvest from the English, you know. Before even the cursed Tudors grasped the rod of power. Imprisonment, torture, confiscation, execution. A poor reward for conquering this wild land for the crown, do you not agree?'

Leverous remained silent. He had heard the rumours of the earl's intrigue with the French and Spanish kings, offering both support against Henry Tudor. Unlike Kildare, the Earl of Desmond's hatred of the English was open and defiant. But while it was possible that Desmond had inherited part of his antipathy towards the English kings from his antecedents, Leverous suspected that a far more personal reason was the spur to his present vendetta against Henry.

For it was common knowledge that the king nurtured within his court one James FitzMaurice FitzGerald, considered by many to be the rightful ruler of Desmond. But the present earl had used Irish law to gain the earldom by force from his cousin.

James FitzMaurice FitzGerald had fled to Henry for succour, but because of Desmond's power, there was little the king could do. So well might Desmond support any conspiracy against the patron of his rival.

It begged the question, Leverous thought silently, as he kept pace with the earl on the wall-walk, if Garret had been successful in his bid to unite Ireland under his rule, where would the powerful Earl of Desmond have fitted into his plan? As his kinsman's loyal liegeman? Leverous glanced at the earl's enigmatic face. Somehow he could not imagine this gaelicised, vainglorious and proud warlord, master of 500,000 acres of land with a revenue of almost £7,000, leader of an army of a thousand warriors, recipient of privileges and tributes due a king, playing second fiddle to anyone. 'The Geraldines will always be grateful to you,' the rasping voice cut across his speculations, 'for your care of the Kildare heir. It must be trying for a Gall to defy his king. As you know, it comes easier to a Geraldine.'

What was the wily earl getting at, Leverous wondered? 'I have much to be grateful for to the House of Kildare,' he replied.

The earl did not answer for a moment. 'The Lady MacCarthy speaks highly of you. How well you have done your duty.' Desmond threw him a speculative look.

Leverous felt the unease rise within him. ''Tis more than duty, I assure you, my lord. 'Tis a debt I owe my foster family. And one which I mean to repay in full.'

Desmond stopped short and faced him. The black eyes turned cold. The wind blew the long strands of grey hair across his sharp features.

'And I hereby relieve you of your debt. The boy is safe. Among his kin. Protected and cared for. Your obligation to the House of Kildare is fully discharged.'

So the earl's purpose unfolds a little more, Leverous thought. He was encouraging him to go, to leave Gerald behind in Askeaton. For what reason he could not yet ascertain. Idly he wondered if Eleanor was party to the earl's scheme?

'Alack, my lord, I fear both my duty and debt still remain unpaid. I pledged my word to the earl to protect his son until his chaplain secured his safety at the French court and that I intend to do.'

The earl moved closer and grasped Leverous by the arm. The black eyes seared uncompromisingly into his. Leverous could see that Desmond did not like having his wishes denied.

'You are out of touch, Leverous.' His voice held a warning. 'The French do not give a cuckoo's spit about the boy. Their king is hand-in-glove with Henry Tudor. Leave the boy's future in the hands of those who know best.' The earl's strong grip tightened on his arm. 'Much has changed since Kildare's death. His hopes for his son can no longer be realised. The boy's future is in Ireland.'

'What future?' Leverous asked him. 'To be hunted like a wild animal across the country. Run to ground in the derelict towers of his family. To be pursued and harassed from pillar to post, even by his own family. No, my lord, it was his father's wish that he should be taken out of Ireland until English policy changes and he can be restored to his inheritance. The king cannot live forever.'

'Pah,' the earl barked derisively, 'the Shannon beyond has as much likelihood of changing its course as the boy has of being restored. His future, I tell you, is here. Among his own. Not as a pawn in the political games of foreign princes.'

'Perhaps as a pawn in the games of Irish princes.'

A flicker of surprise passed across the wrinkled visage. Leverous realised that he had hit the target for a second time that day. The earl cleared his throat.

'The boy stays in Desmond. That is final. There is too much at stake. For him. For us all. His future will be made clear shortly,' he added ominously.

'His future was entrusted to my care,' Leverous protested

angrily, 'by the express command of the Earl of Kildare.' He withdrew Garret's letter from inside his doublet.

A slow sardonic smile spread across Desmond's face as he glanced dismissively at the folded parchment which Leverous extended towards him.

'I fear, sirrah, 'tis Desmond's writ that runs here. But no matter. So that there may be no doubts. You say you await the return from France of Robert Walshe. Then wait no longer.'

The earl turned towards a recessed arched doorway, from which a hooded figure emerged. The figure stood motionless for a moment, as if undecided which one of them to acknowledge. The cowl slipped down to reveal the face of Robert Walshe. He smiled a greeting and after a brief hesitation hurried forward to embrace Leverous. Shared memories of Garret, Maynooth and the Tower rendered them both speechless. But as he grasped his hand, Leverous saw the tears of remembrance and sadness welling in the priest's tired eyes.

'Father Walshe, I fear, brings little solace from the French Court, Leverous, but he does bring orders from a higher authority.' Desmond's dry voice broke into their shared memories. Leverous looked enquiringly at the chaplain but before he could speak, Desmond grasped Walshe firmly by the arm. 'All will be revealed in due course,' he said briskly, drawing him back towards the doorway. 'Father Walshe's mission is not as yet complete. Is that not so, Father?'

Before he could reply, the earl hustled the chaplain through the door, which closed determinedly behind them.

With a distinct feeling that events were rushing out of his control, Leverous replaced Garret's letter inside his doublet. The hostility he had experienced since his arrival in Desmond was not imaginary. He had been deliberately kept at a distance while Desmond hatched his plot. His promise to Garret was no longer the straightforward mission he had set out to accomplish, but was rapidly becoming embroiled in something more sinister that had yet to reveal itself. For as well as being under threat from the king, the Ormonds and the English in Dublin, the boy's life was being endangered by his erstwhile protectors, even by Robert Walshe, it seemed, Garret's confidant, whom he would have trusted with his life. Leverous wondered what part Eleanor was playing in the web of intrigue. It was she who had suggested coming to Desmond and had deliberately avoided him since. Did she keep her distance out of the embarrassment that clearly his reappearance had caused her or was she part of this conspiracy that flew in the face of her brother's last wish?

From the wall-walk Leverous saw the earl escort Robert Walshe across the courtyard. The chaplain mounted a horse and, accompanied by three of Desmond's men, disappeared through the barbican. Leverous retraced his steps in the direction of Gerald's apartment. There was little he could do but await Desmond's scheme to unfold further before making his play. He knew he had little option.

15

St Patrick's Cathedral, Dublin

With a flat wide-brimmed hat shielding his face from the inquisitive stares of the occasional citizen hurrying homewards before the curfew, Lord Leonard Grey walked quickly through the deepening gloom. The stench of sewage and household waste wafted towards him from the Pool. He picked his steps with care on the narrow dirt causeway between the deep ditch that encircled the city walls and the river Poddle, before turning sharply down Bride Street.

To avoid detection, he had left the castle through the Ship Street tower, slipping through unnoticed, he hoped, into the alleyway. But he had also left himself little time before curfew. His indecision whether to ignore the message or not, which, on reflection, might well have been the wiser course, had cost him precious time. It was sheer madness for the king's deputy to risk being found in breach of the city curfew, on a clandestine mission that was not conducive to his office but, Grey suspected, totally adverse to it. How the Countess of Ormond and Brabazon would crow should he be caught by the city constables! With malevolent glee they would relay his indiscretion to the king, to add to his already overdrawn account at court.

The message had been unsigned and that in itself should have been a sufficient deterrent. But in a single moment he had thrown caution aside, lured by the reference to his nephew and the promise of foreign tidings that the message said would be to his advantage. He knew that the Countess of Ormond must soon return from court, armed, most likely, with a stinging rebuke from the king on his failure to apprehend the Geraldine heir. Grey had gleaned knowledge of her flight to England only when her ship had been well on its way to Beaumaris.

His deliberate delay in effecting the king's command to capture his nephew had, he fervently hoped, allowed the boy to make good his escape to the Continent, where, perhaps, he might find sanctuary among the Catholic princes and kings. Henry could not live forever, and given his proclivity for excess, his end might be precipitated. His heir was still Catherine's Mary who might be more kindly disposed to the young dispossessed Geraldine on her succession.

Such a theory, Grey realised, depended on unknown contingencies. Was the boy still alive? Was he in Ireland or had his tutor succeeded in fleeing with him abroad? And what of English foreign policy and the consequence for his nephew's future, Grey wondered, as he hurried down Bride Street. With little influence and few friends at court, Grey knew he lacked an insight into the king's present political manoeuvres against his continental adversaries, the King of France, the Emperor Charles V and Pope Clement VII. To which of the wily foreigners did Henry now proffer support? His reformation policies and his break with Rome, of necessity, must have led to a reassessment and realigning of English alliances.

On Grey's departure from England, Henry had been openly allied with the Emperor. If the king's allegiance now inclined towards France, then Grey knew his nephew would find little welcome there. Depending on how much he needed Henry's support against the Emperor, the fickle French king might be induced to pander further to Henry and deliver the fugitive Geraldine heir to England as a gesture of his goodwill .

The Countess of Ormond was due from England, well-primed, Grey expected, to the current flow of the king's foreign intrigues. Her political advantage over him would thereby be further enhanced. Grey could not allow her to erode his authority, especially now when it seemed that he was to be damned to another term of office in Ireland. The message from the mysterious stranger promised to give him the latest intelligence and was the reason he was risking the clandestine meeting.

The massive limestone tower of St Patrick's Cathedral loomed menacingly above him. Grey skirted the north transept and entered the iron-studded door of the entrance porch on the south transept. The great nave, with its high groined roof, pointed arches and black marble columns, was singularly silent. He paused for a moment in the shadows. Nothing stirred within the impressive vastness. Keeping close to the outer walls of the aisle, he made his way towards the chapter house. As he was about to push in the heavy oak portal, a hand emerged through an incongruously cut hole in the door and a voice whispered, 'A hand, to chop or to shake, as your Lordship desires.'

Grey started in surprise and then remembered the popular story about the origin of the hole in the chapter house door, when the Great Earl of Kildare had pursued his adversary, the Earl of Ormond, into the cathedral. Ormond had locked himself inside the chapter house and, despite Kildare's assurances that he would not harm him, had refused to budge. It was then suggested that a hole should be cut through the door so that the rivals might shake hands. Still Ormond smelled treachery. Might it not be a trick on Kildare's part to chop off his hand? To prove his good intent, Kildare 'chanced his arm' by putting it through the hole, whereupon Ormond emerged, embraced his rival and for a time, a very short time it was said, they were at peace.

'Who are you?' Grey's impatient whisper reverberated in the stillness.

The heavy door creaked open and a well-set figure emerged. Golden hair glinted under a fashionable velvet bonnet, set at an angle. A sleeveless cloak, trimmed with coney, revealed a slashed doublet of sapphire. A sword hung from a leather belt at his waist, and from an embroidered pouch, the hilt of a dagger protruded.

Grey moved his hand to his sword hilt and silently cursed himself for his rashness. With a mocking glance, the blue eyes of the stranger followed the stealthy movement of his hand. Grey felt his annoyance mount.

'Who are you?' he repeated brusquely.

The stranger made an elaborate bow, his sword swinging by his side. The gesture bore a suggestion of disdain.

'It seems I failed to make an impression at our last meeting.' The mocking voice held the soft ebb-and-flow tones of Ulster. 'Manus O'Donel, chieftain of Tirconel.'

Grey squinted in disbelief in the semi-light. This elegantly attired English-speaking peacock, an Irish chieftain! He looked again at the vaguely familiar countenance and recalled the young scion of the Tirconel chieftain, taken as hostage by the Great Earl of Kildare and reared in his household. Kildare had later presented him at court where he had become something of a novelty and a favourite, especially of the court ladies, Grey recalled. He had met him briefly at the marriage ceremony of his sister to Kildare, but had formed no opinion of him then.

'This covert meeting is hardly conducive to renewing acquaintances. The castle chamber is customary,' he said stiffly.

O'Donel smiled, showing a row of perfectly formed white teeth. 'Apologies, my lord. But having once endured the status of hostage, like the wild bird I am wary of confined spaces, no matter how well-appointed the cage.'

'We have a covenant with the Tirconel chieftain,' Grey said testily.

O'Donel shook his handsome head. 'Not any more, my lord. You see before you the new chieftain of Tirconel. My father made me wait my turn longer than I had anticipated. Still, doubtless it will prove worth the wait.'

O'Donel's composure irked the deputy. 'According to your Irish custom, I understand you must compete for the chieftaincy with others of your sept.'

O'Donel's smile was disdainful. 'My rivals will offer little competition,' he said with certitude. 'But should they, as your lordship is perhaps aware I am equally at ease with either the customs of Ireland or England. If I do not have the chieftaincy by native rite, I will have it courtesy of English expediency. Your king's policy is to reward true and loyal Irish subjects, is it not?'

In the distance the great bell of St Audeon's sounded the first warning of the curfew. Grey look anxiously around him. The cathedral seemed deserted. He turned towards O'Donel.

'You say in your message that you have news of interest about my nephew. I have little time to waste.'

'Alack, the bell binds us all, even the King of England's deputy,' O'Donel mocked. 'Never fear, my lord, I will be brief. I come from France, from one who has your welfare at heart as well as that of your nephew. France secretly aligns with England against the emperor. The French court is no longer safe for the Geraldine heir. I am commanded to put a proposition to you that will at once safeguard the Geraldine, until he is of age, and,' he paused dramatically, 'make you regent until he attains his majority.'

Grey heard his own voice explode in the silence and echo woodenly in the black space above them. 'Regent! What nonsense is this? Your words are treasonous.'

O'Donel placed a finger to his lips. Feeling foolish, Grey looked around the vaulted expanse, lest his outburst had been overheard.

'The very reason I choose such a sanctuary as this to sound them,' O'Donel whispered mockingly.

"Tis well you did. For were we in the Castle, an iron shackle would adorn your elegant neck. Who commands you to utter such treason?'

'A relation of your own. One who presumes your true allegiance reflects your shared pedigree. My Lord Cardinal Pole.'

'Cardinal Pole?'

O'Donel seemed to relish the effect his words had on the deputy, who stood open-mouthed before him.

'Aye. My Lord Pole was given the red hat intended for Bishop Fisher, most cruelly slaughtered by the Tudor Antichrist.'

Grey's hand moved towards his sword. O'Donel watched in amusement.

'Do not think of it, my lord. I have learned my swordcraft from the best in England and in France. Moreover, your royal master is not worth a scratch. I am merely a messenger for my Lord Cardinal, who gives me this as proof of the truth of my message.' O'Donel handed him a square of parchment. Inside lay a white rose, its petals almost withered.

With mounting alarm, Grey read the brief message:

Cousin
The bearer, my Lord of Tirconel, speaks my words to you
in the hope that you will play your part.
In God We Trust.
Pole

The bell from St Audeon's again disturbed the silence.

'I must away, my lord,' O'Donel said. 'There is little more to say, save that a crusade against the king is underway in Europe and in England. Your nephew is to be the rallying point of opposition against Henry Tudor in Ireland, a decoy for the conspiracy abroad. The principal chiefs are invited by the pope to ally with the Geraldine and unite behind him. You and the Earl of Desmond are to be appointed his

160

protectors and rule in his place until he reaches his majority. All Ireland will rise with you to be rid of the Tudor yoke.'

Grey felt his legs buckle as if he had received the blunt edge of a sword thrust. ''Tis madness. Plain and simple. I am a soldier, not a kingmaker. I serve my king, whosoever he may be, Lancaster or Plantagenet. But that we are in holy sanctuary, O'Donel, by God's truth, I would call the guard and have you imprisoned. A plague on you and your master cardinal. You compromise my position and make me suspect, although I am in truth an innocent victim of your intrigue.'

O'Donel stifled a yawn. 'And I am but a messenger. Both of us drawn into a conspiracy not of our making. But be warned, my lord, now that you are privy to the plot, it will be let slip at court that you are the prime mover, should you divulge it.' O'Donel settled his velvet cloak about his shoulders. 'And from what I hear, you have powerful adversaries there who may be inclined to believe your involvement, particularly when you fail to find your nephew. And there is also your shared ancestry of the White Rose.' He bowed mockingly. 'Now I must away, before the constables incarcerate me for breach of the curfew.'

Transfixed, Grey watched O'Donel swagger down the aisle and dissolve like a phantom into the shadows, leaving him to wonder if the encounter had been a dream. A nightmare. The cardinal's parchment reminded him that the meeting had been no illusion. Gathering his wits, Grey stuffed it inside his doublet. He hurried from the cathedral, leaving a trail of withered white petals behind. From behind one of the marble pillars, a hand picked them one by one from the ground.

16

Lordship of Tyrone, Ulster

The falcon swept off O'Neill's gloved arm and, with a piercing shriek of predatory anticipation, soared skywards to circle some several hundred feet above him. Drifting effortlessly on the wind currents, she waited for her prey to be flushed from the undergrowth below. O'Neill signalled to the beaters to unleash the hounds, who were straining at the leather thongs. With shrill yappings they darted into the mesh of briar and bush. Three snipe tumbled in terror into the clearing. O'Neill looked skywards in anticipation. He was not disappointed. His falcon had already sighted the prey and, with closed wings, talons stretched wide, was hurtling soundlessly groundward. The snipe lifted but a few feet into the air when, in a scattering of feathers, head askew, it was borne again to earth in the vice-like grip. The falcon began to pluck the feathers with her curved beak to feed on the flesh beneath. O'Neill dismounted and, making gentle clucking sounds, approached her cautiously. For a moment she flapped her wings in anger at his interruption. But he persisted and in a single fluid movement sliced the snipe's head and placed it on his gloved arm. The yellow-ringed eyes looked balefully into his and then the falcon hopped obediently on to his proffered arm and started to feed. He waited until she was done and, stroking the silken plumage, gently slipped on her hood and handed her back to his falconer.

'Enough for today,' he said in answer to the surprised look on the old man's face.

Both knew that the falcon could easily fly another time and there was still the new goshawk to try. But O'Neill was on edge, his mind still preoccupied with the events that had prompted the hawking session. There was no respite, however, not even in the tranquillity of the mirror waters of Lough Neagh, stretching like a great landlocked sea southwards farther than the eye could see. Normally the rustling of the golden reeds, which like a host of raised spears guarded the marshy shoreline, would have released his mind from the captive thongs of whatever problems beset his lordship. But today there was no such release. The pope's letter ensured that. Stiffly O'Neill remounted and beckoned to his followers who sensing their chief's disaffection followed him in deferential silence.

O'Neill had evinced no outward sign of surprise when Kildare's chaplain had presented himself at Dungannon. But inwardly his mind seethed with curiosity, while instinctively he felt a sense of foreboding at Walshe's unforeseen arrival.

Trouble, he had realised long since, invariably came from outside. If only he could hack off Ulster from the rest of Ireland and govern it his way, in glorious isolation from the intrusiveness of the outside world. If the cursed foreigners had not come from England four hundred years previously, he, like his forefathers, would be King of Ulster now. But even with the less powerful position of The O'Neill, he still retained many of the privileges of his royal ancestors: the tributes, dues and rents of his urraghs, the bedrock on which his status and control rested.

Birthright, he knew, was no guarantee of position in Ireland. His own sons would have to fight to establish their claim to the chieftaincy on his death, as he had had to do. Which of them would prove the strongest it was yet too early to tell. Shane, his eldest by his first wife, showed promise of the aggressiveness required. His favourite, Matthew, the son of his concubine, was still but a child. But then the right to succeed him was not confined to his own offspring but was open to all male members of the ruling O'Neill sept. His nephew might prove more acceptable to the clan's *derbhfine* than either of his own sons. O'Neill shrugged. It would matter little to him; he would be in his grave. But now he was in control and intended so to remain.

He nudged his horse forward to distance himself from his followers. From a leather pouch in his belt, he withdrew the parchment and read again the Latin words above the papal signature and seal: ' . . . a glorious crusade to liberate the faith of Christ and the people of Ireland from the tyranny of the English king.'

Even on a second reading, the pope's phrases and words meant little to him. There was nothing with which he could could come to grips in the empty-sounding, unfamiliar exhortations; nothing to warrant his risking the security of his lordship or his position as The O'Neill. 'To liberate the faith of Christ.' What did it mean? He could hardly be expected to hire gallowglass, issue a rising out to his urraghs, risk life and limb, so that the pope in Rome might retain the source of his wealth in England. His urraghs would rightly think him mad, more fit to rule over bedlam than Ulster. O'Neill owed no allegiance to the popes, who in matters relating to the Irish church had ever bowed to the will of England. Was it not the popes who at the behest of the English kings, had foisted English-born prelates on the sees within his jurisdiction? Even the most Irish of sees, the ancient see of St Patrick at Armagh, had been given to an Englishman. And now that it seemed that the pope was to be denied not only his Peter's Pence from the English but from the Irish church as well, he wished to change horses in mid-course and embrace those whom he had previously disdained.

Even if he agreed to assist the pope against the English monarch, O'Neill knew that he could not exhort his followers to wage war in the hope of some innate spiritual advantage. His urraghs expected more tangible reward than an indulgence for their efforts and his gallowglass expected to be paid. In any event, unlike the church in England, the Irish church had little relevance to the daily life of the people and confined itself to matters of a purely religious sphere. In state and social events, its rules and edicts hardly mattered. He had been inaugurated The O'Neill, not in a Christian place of worship, such as the cathedral at Armagh, but at the pagan rath at Tullahogue, the coronation place of his remote ancestors. On the question of matrimony, a marriage ceremony might receive the blessing of a priest, but it was considered to be primarily a civil matter, of political rather than religious significance, especially among the ruling class.

As it had been in his own case, O'Neill reflected. His first marriage, to the daughter of O'Neill of Clandeboy, had been a mere political necessity, appeasement proving more appropriate than coercion as a means to ensure Clandeboy's allegiance. His second to Honor O'Byrne had been arranged with the connivance of his cousin Kildare, anxious to strengthen ties with his neighbour, O'Byrne. That marriage had ended in divorce, for, regardless of his cousin's political preference, Honor O'Byrne had neither pleased him in his bed nor at his board. His present liaison with Alison O'Kelly suited him well enough. She kept him more than sexually satisfied and, unlike her predecessors, displayed little political acumen, which gratified him. He preferred his bed to be for pleasure and slumber than for a regurgitation of the troubles of his office.

He had found churchmen as eager and able as any to protect their lands, cattle herds or possessions by force of arms and just as likely to lie with wife or concubine as any man. He had appointed many favourites to clerical office within his lordship. Consequently, when a liege lord needed chastisement, monasteries and other religious establishments in his territory were the source of rich plunder.

In any event, the Irish had little inducement to assist the popes in Rome, O'Neill thought with some bitterness. Was it not a pope who had given Ireland to an English king in the first place? And when the Irish lords had reason to complain about the harassment and ill-treatment of the English, the support forthcoming from Rome was merely a stinging reaffirmation of England's right to rule over them. Now when the pope was at loggerheads with the King of England, he expected the Irish lords to help him.

O'Neill folded the parchment and put it inside his jerkin. The political ambitions of Pope Clement had little relevance to Ireland and none to the lordship of O'Neill.

Yet his instinct urged him to attend the assembly which, as Desmond implied in his letter, could affect the future of Ireland. His future. The lines across O'Neill's brow creased in vexation. Desmond, that crafty Sean-Ghall bastard, ever involved in outlandish plots with foreigners, for fear they had not brought enough trouble in their wake in the past. But then, O'Neill reminded himself, Desmond was one of them. The blood of Italy, England and Wales, mixed with Irish, ran in his thin veins. An unstable but lethal mix, he concluded. Yet he must know what Desmond was plotting. He could not afford to be left out, particularly if, as Robert Walshe had intimated, O'Donel was already implicated. He could not let his enemy think that he had scored a point over him lest it be translated into an admission of weakness on his part.

He had met the new O'Donel once before at Kildare's castle. He recalled the youth's vain threats and idle boasts as, with an immaturity that belied his looks, O'Donel sought to rile him, seeing him not only as the traditional enemy of his house but as the cause of his captivity in Kildare. Disdainfully O'Neill had refused to be drawn into O'Donel's patent trap. His uncle, the Great Earl, he had later heard,

166

had seen fit to shift his hot-blooded hostage to England and away from his daughter, for whom the brash youth had developed an attachment. Whatever the world had taught him since, O'Neill knew with certainty that O'Donel's antipathy to him was as ingrained as it had been in his ancestors.

Yes, O'Neill decided, he would go to Desmond's grand meeting and in the style that befitted his rank as the premier Irish prince. He would show Desmond and at the same time give clear warning to O'Donel that no matter what they connived together, he, The O'Neill, was powerful enough to stand aloof, or to resist, if what they planned threatened his status in Ulster.

He beckoned to his constable, Ross MacMahon. MacMahon came closest to what O'Neill would tolerate as a confidant and advisor and he would have liked to have MacMahon with him in Munster, but it was more imperative to ensure that his enemies in Ulster would not take advantage in his absence.

'Have the captain of the gallowglass prepare two hundred of his best men, armed and mailed with provisions for one month.'

MacMahon's eyes evinced surprise. 'One month?' he echoed in wonderment, knowing that it meant either a long trek or a difficult campaign, because his master was seldom absent from Dungannon for more than two weeks.

O'Neill ignored the question in his constable's voice. Not even MacMahon would know of his destination until the last minute. Idle gossip easily reached the ears of the enemy.

'Levy one hundred kern with provisions, armed with both darts and short swords from Maguire, O'Hanlon, Clandeboy . . . ' he hesitated, 'and from O'Hagan.'

That would make his recalcitrant urragh desist from contemplating any retaliatory action in his absence.

'Have the grooms ready thirty of the best hobs and sufficient pack horses with the usual horseboys.'

'Is it against O'Donel?'

O'Neill's face remained immobile.

'You promised me the privilege of spearing his black heart,' MacMahon persisted. 'It is my right.'

O'Neill glanced at his tall constable. MacMahon had cause to be bitter against O'Donel. The MacMahons were a minor clan, whose territory straddled the Tyrone border with O'Donel. They were traditional allies of The O'Neill and, because of their position habitually bore the brunt of O'Donel aggression. Ross MacMahon, had seen his father decapitated by O'Donel. On becoming O'Neill's constable, MacMahon had extracted from him the right of vengeance for the murder of his father. Now that O'Donel was dead, MacMahon would seek retribution from his son.

'Not O'Donel this time,' he told him. 'You will stay in Tyrone to ensure that he does not take advantage. Should he be so tempted, the head of this new Lord of Tirconel is yours.'

'*Mallacht go deo air*,' MacMahon muttered darkly and cast a grateful look at his chieftain.

His absence from Tyrone would, O'Neill knew, unleash the unquiet ambitions to the chieftainship that lurked among members of his extended family, especially the conniving and ambitious sons of his half-brother, a few of whom he suspected of being in league with O'Donel. He would take them to Munster, lest in his absence they too were tempted. His lordship would be safe with MacMahon, whom he trusted more than any of his kin.

'Take the pick of six kern trained with the arquebus. They will impress either friend or foe. And,' he added as an afterthought, 'I need a gift to bring with me.'

MacMahon looked perplexed.

'In case the object of my destination turns out to be a friend.' O'Neill liked the effect which his propensity for keeping his own counsel had on those close to him, never letting them know what might be turned and used against him. It was a policy that usually paid handsome dividends, for a secret could be both a friend and a foe.

'Perhaps the falcon,' he nodded towards the hooded bird perched on the falconer's arm.

If it is good enough for the Prince of Ulster, he thought, then it should be twice too good for the Earl of Desmond.

17

Askeaton Castle,
Lordship of Desmond

Since dawn from the window embrasure set high in the west tower, Eleanor had watched them converge on the castle: mounted chieftains with their urraghs, followed on foot by escorts of gallowglasses and kern, the size of a chieftain's retinue denoting his importance in the Gaelic hierarchy. Even at a distance, Eleanor recognised O'Neill's contingent by their sheer numbers as soon as they broke cover from Clonish forest. Over two hundred, she reckoned. She watched their leader dismount in the courtyard, carefully concealing his limp, as he hurried inside the castle, surrounded by his long-haired followers. She had known him as a girl, when on rare occasions he had accompanied his mother to Maynooth or later when, as The O'Neill, he came to confer with her father. Even as a youth, she recalled, O'Neill had always seemed older than his years. Though he was taciturn and aloof, Eleanor instinctively liked her Ulster cousin.

A clatter of hooves on the bridge, which linked the castle with the mainland, heralded the arrival of the Pale lords, their short English cloaks swirling about their shoulders. Unlike their Gaelic counterparts, they came unaccompanied, so that their absence from the Pale might be less easily detected by the English in Dublin. They cantered into the courtyard with an urgency that betrayed their anxiety to be gone. Desmond's invitation must have contained some secret allurement, Eleanor reckoned, to entice them into the heart of the Gaelic hinterland, far outside the protection of the Pale. Traditionally they had little in common with their Gaelic counterparts and, before their recent alliance with her father and brother, had been adherents of the crown of England. What promises or enticements Desmond offered them to identify with their Gaelic neighbours, she could not imagine.

Eleanor recognised among the dozen or so horsemen Robert Dunsany, whose daughter had been married to her brother Walter, and Lords Slane, Fingal and Howth. All were blood relations of her family and had been frequent visitors to Maynooth. She was at first suspicious when Desmond told her of his intention to summon the allies of Kildare to Askeaton, to ascertain their support for her nephew, he explained. She did not believe him, but for Gerald's sake did not question him further. Since the French king appeared to have reneged on his promise to her brother, Gerald needed all the support and protection that could be mustered on his behalf in Ireland.

Her gaze was drawn to a figure, the last to dismount, distinguished from the Pale lords by a long Irish mantle which swung from his shoulders. She watched him stride towards the castle with a swagger that seemed somehow familiar, taking off his gauntlets as he went. As if instinctively aware of her gaze, he glanced upwards towards the tower and his eyes found her at the window before she could withdraw. Even now, despite the distance of time which separated them, Eleanor felt uneasy under Manus O'Donel's arrogant scrutiny.

The memory of his strong persistent hands, pinning her helplessly among the shadows in the labyrinth of corridors in Maynooth, his breath harsh and hot in her face, made her recoil. She had been hardly more than a child then,

171

uncertain of her own sexuality and untutored in the ways of fending off unwanted advances. She did not wish to appear naive and was anxious to preserve the budding dignity of womanhood. O'Donel was two years older but seemed then to have had a lifetime's experience. The year he had lived with them at Maynooth had become her nightmare. She was ashamed to reveal the harassment she endured from the handsome young hostage, feeling in some illogical way that her body was responsible for attracting his advances, that this was a normal process of growing. It was Leverous, his face distorted with anger, who many times had torn her tormentor from her and thrown him to the ground and, with his knee in his chest, struck him repeatedly. Eventually, to her relief, her father had taken O'Donel with him to England. She suspected Leverous's hand behind his removal, but dared not question the reason for her improved fortune. She had met O'Donel once again in Dublin, at Thomas Court, but by then she was a woman in love and impervious to his presence. With a feeling of repulsion now replacing her adolescent fear, she watched, as with exaggerated ease, Manus O'Donel bowed low in her direction.

She turned sharply from the window as a knock sounded on her door. Leverous stood outside. Eleanor sought for some words to excuse her deliberate avoidance of him since coming to Askeaton, but no words would come. Leverous's company seemed even more desirable than before, after seeing O'Donel. She steeled herself against the longing within her.

'I came to ascertain your part in Desmond's plot, playing games with Gerald's safety.'

The coldness in his voice and the directness of his accusation took Leverous by surprise. She had never heard him speak in such a tone and felt as if she was being reprimanded by a stranger.

'Plot? Games? Whatever do you mean?'

'All this,' he pointed to the courtyard below. 'O'Neill,

172

'O'Brien, Burke, O'Connor, Pale lords, traditional foes, suddenly allies. Even O'Donel is expected to sit with O'Neill.'

She remained silent.

'It seems that Desmond plots more than Gerald's safety. This elaborate assembly smacks more of politics than protection. Do you not agree?'

'I know no more than you. Desmond says he must have their oaths in person to ensure Gerald's protection.'

She read the disbelief on his face and it cut her to the quick. There had been such a bond of trust between them once.

'I will give you my oath, Thomas, if you no longer believe my word', she told him and regretted her words the moment she had uttered them. They sounded prim and self-righteous.

'Christ's blood,' he swore softly. 'Is anybody what they seem in this country? Or is everyone as fickle as the Irish climate?'

Would she fail him a second time, he wondered. There was more than their emotions at stake now. Gerald's life depended on his assessment of this new development. There was some plot being hatched by Desmond, of that he was certain. Was Eleanor a party to it? Almost reluctantly he looked at her, knowing that to look was to remember and to imagine what might have been. She was visibly shaken by his outburst.

'Desmond as much as ordered me to leave. To abandon Gerald. Is that your wish too?'

His question caught her offguard. Initially she felt a sense of relief at the possibility that, inadvertently, Desmond might release her from the dilemma posed by Leverous's proximity and ensure that their dark secret would continue to remain sequestered and safe with her. But her relief was almost as quickly replaced by a profound sense of loss and anxiety at the possibility of losing him again and foregoing the stability which his presence had ever given her, a sense revived by

173

O'Donel's arrival at Askeaton. She hoped her face revealed nothing of her thoughts.

'But Garret appointed you Gerald's guardian.'

His eyes searched her face. 'You are doubtless aware, I presume, of the outcome of Robert Walshe's mission to France.'

She nodded. 'It is no more than I expected.'

'*Touché*,' he said, remembering her earlier reservation, his eyes cold and unfriendly. 'Your brother, however, did not share your scepticism. He expected the king to honour his commitment and made no allowance for any other course. So now Desmond may appoint himself Gerald's guardian and use him for whatever purpose he desires, a political pawn in whatever devious scheme he plots. And I am powerless to stop him. But he might be less inclined to go against the wishes of one of Gerald's own blood. Against you.'

Leverous stopped short. Eleanor was not listening but was looking at him such a mixture of sadness and concern that both perplexed and aroused him. A shaft of sunlight slanted through the archery loop. It brightened the dim confines of the draughty corridor and threw its fleeting radiance on her slim figure, crowned by the tresses of auburn hair that spilled around her shoulders. Her linen dress hung from her shoulders, unadorned but for a string of amber beads that glowed in the rise and fall of the outline of her breasts. He felt as if time had for a moment regressed and they were together alone before the glowing fire in her chamber at Thomas Court, facing each other for the first time in the discovery of their intense longing. She had looked at him then, as she did now, with the same tantalising mixture of apprehension and yearning that begged him to take the initiative.

In a moment he was beside her, drawing her into his arms, feeling the rigidity of her body slowly ease in response. He crushed her to him, every curve and bend of their bodies fusing instinctively as if they had never been apart. He kissed her lips until they opened and responded eagerly to his with a desire that both surprised and thrilled him. Hesitantly her arms encircled his neck and they clung together in the silent delight of rediscovery, fearful that to utter a single word might break the spell of the moment.

The derisive voice seemed to come from a distance and took a few moments to penetrate the emotional sanctuary into which their senses had retreated. Like barbs, the words eventually registered. As in a trance, they released each other, arms falling listlessly to their sides.

'This seems vaguely familiar. A few small but significant changes. Let me see: Kildare's castle instead of Desmond's. And I enjoying the lady's embrace and Leverous the envious onlooker.'

The words echoed tauntingly in the silence as they stared at the source of the intrusion. Leaning nonchalantly against the wall, arms folded across his chest, Manus O'Donel observed their surprise with ill-concealed pleasure.

'I thought to pay my respects, my lady,' he bowed in Eleanor's direction, 'never suspecting that you already entertained old friends.'

Eleanor felt Leverous's body stiffen. Her face flamed before O'Donel's provocative look.

'How is it with you, Leverous? Still chasing the Holy Grail?' O'Donel said, without taking his eyes from Eleanor's face.

Eleanor turned deliberately away from him, more in anger than embarrassment, that above anyone it should be O'Donel who witnessed the one moment when the barrier she had erected around her emotions had been breached.

Leverous's face was rigid. 'It seems the English and the French have failed as miserably as the Irish to teach you manners.'

'Rest assured, my friend,' O'Donel's bantering tones scarcely concealed his malice, 'my exile in England and France has not been in vain. I have acquired many talents.

Perhaps a demonstration of one?' O'Donel moved his hand with slow intent towards his sword.

Eleanor moved quickly between them. 'What do you want here?'

O'Donel's handsome face was lit by a dazzling smile, the smile that Eleanor knew from experience concealed the dark side of his nature. His eyes slid slowly over her body, making her recoil with distaste.

'What I have ever wanted, my lady.' The insinuation of his tone was clear.

With a shout of rage, Leverous leapt at O'Donel's throat and they grappled, feet spread apart, by the wall. Each was prevented by the other's hands from reaching for his sword or striking a blow. They grunted in their efforts to gain advantage over the other in the confined space.

A clatter of feet sounded on the spiral steps. Sword in hand, Cormac MacCarthy rounded the last bend and stared in amazement at the two men locked in combat and then at his mother standing transfixed in the doorway.

'What is going on here?' The soft burr of his Munster accent held the promise of threat.

Leverous and O'Donel broke away from each other and looked at the young chieftain. Their breath came in gasping gulps.

'Cormac!' Eleanor's voice sounded both relieved and apprehensive.

Leverous noticed Eleanor's embarrassment before her son and sought to make light of the situation.

'Tis nothing. A difference of opinion. No more.'

The MacCarthy seemed unconvinced. 'Are you all right, Mother?' His eyes held the two men with suspicion.

'It is as Leverous said,' Eleanor made her voice sound unconcerned, 'a difference of opinion between grown men who should know better.'

O'Donel smoothed the white ruff at his neck and shifted the leather scabbard into position at his waist. 'Are we not to be introduced?' he said, looking at The MacCarthy. 'Your son, my lady, did I hear correctly. Surely not a full grown man as this?'

A chill of alarm ran through Eleanor but she forced herself to remain composed under O'Donel's calculating scrutiny.

'I can only think of you as a young girl. Far too young to be the mother of such a man.' O'Donel held out his hand to Cormac. 'Manus O'Donel, of Tirconel. I regret we meet in such an unseemly way. I came to pay greetings to your mother, but that can wait for another day.'

Reluctantly MacCarthy took O'Donel's extended hand and then watched him disappear down the spiral stairway.

MacCarthy looked at Leverous, as if expecting an explanation for the fracas with O'Donel, but Leverous was not to be drawn.

'What brings you to Askeaton? I thought a MacCarthy would sooner die than be found in Desmond territory.'

Cormac smiled. 'The pope's letter. It makes for unlikely allies.' He turned to his mother. 'It arrived at Carbury after your departure. I thought it better to know what Desmond's plots.'

'But your uncle,' Eleanor protested, 'he will surely take advantage of your absence.'

Her son shook his head and smiled. 'Not when he is here also. I played to his intense curiosity and brought him with me.'

Eleanor seemed unconvinced and argued further with her son. Leverous watched Cormac as he soothed her fear and told her of his journey from Carbury. From their brief acquaintance, Leverous had grown to like this son of Eleanor and felt the youth's liking for him in return. Eleanor caught his glance and for a moment he imagined he saw a look of alarm flit through her eyes. Perhaps already she was regretting their brief embrace, that she had allowed her feelings for him to escape the wall of reserve she had built around herself.

Did she suspect that she had allowed him to hope again? If O'Donel had not intruded on their moment of rediscovery, Leverous wondered what might have been.

He made his voice sound lighthearted, to counteract the emotions that surged within.

'I must go to Gerald. He will be glad to hear of your arrival,' he told MacCarthy, 'so that he might badger you further about the deer he left behind in Carbury.'

MacCarthy smiled in response.

Leverous turned towards Eleanor. Her eyes were troubled and had lost the look of love that he had clearly seen when he had bent his head to kiss her. He took her cold hand and raised it to his lips.

'My lady, I will leave you with your son. Perhaps we might speak later.'

Without waiting for her answer, Leverous bowed briefly and left.

18

ASKEATON CASTLE

The sharp spring breeze blowing through the open doorway did little to assuage the discomfort of the cooks, kitchen boys and skivvies, who scurried in clouds of steam, sweating and cursing profusely in the stifling atmosphere of the Earl of Desmond's kitchens.

Quarters of red beef and carcases of pink, spring lamb turned slowly on iron spits in the yawning hearths, the aroma pungently overpowering, the heat intense. Iron pots, blackened by the flames of countless fires, simmered on hot coals, broiling fowl and wild game. Mounds of freshly baked oaten cakes, each a foot in diameter, were ladled from within the recessed ovens and packed into wicker baskets. From a pantry at one end of the kitchen, a steward, the keys of his hereditary profession hanging from an iron ring at his waist, counted pewter plates and goblets into the arms of the scullery boys. At intervals, yard men, with armfuls of ash and birch logs, replenished the inferno within. Everywhere people scurried; orders were given and as quickly counter-manded. Smoke, smells, knives, pots and pans, the floor slippery with entrails and bones, relished by the long-tailed hounds who, regardless of the kicks and curses, foraged determinedly under the wooden tables.

In contrast to the heat and turmoil above, all was cool

and calm in the spacious cellars below. From the great oaken casks that lined the walls, the sun-ripened sack of Andalusia and the rich ruby Gascony, carried across the sea in the earl's hulks, flowed into the pewter jugs held beneath the spigots. From a vat opposite, a spicy aroma emanated from the *uisce beatha*, flavoured with raisins and fennel seeds, as the colourless liquid was poured into earthenware flagons. Small flasks, garnished with silver gilt, were carefully lowered into a hogshead, perched high above the casks and the golden honey-based mead, nectar of the Celtic gods, was made ready to be served to the most favoured guests at the Earl of Desmond's table.

Outside, the day was rapidly melting into night, sustained momentarily by the lingering western twilight. Inside, under the vaulted oak beams of Desmond's great banqueting hall the shadows danced on the lime-washed walls, as the castle stewards escorted the guests to their allotted places. The rows of trestle tables and wooden benches, which stretched from one length of the hall to the other, gradually filled. A carpet of green rushes covered the expanse of the flagged floor. Shields, pikes, darts and swords, intermingled with antlers of Irish elk and deer and the skins of wild boar, adorned the high walls. From long wooden staves, protruding from the wallplates above the stone corbels, the banners of the visiting chieftains were displayed: O'Neill's red hand of Ulster, the oak tree of the O'Connors, the three lions of the O'Briens, the stag of MacCarthy, – symbols redolent of the pageantry and pride of fallen kings and vanished kingdoms. At the top of the long hall, the wild boar crest of the Earls of Desmond dominated. The hall, warmed by a brazier in the centre and lit by torches in iron wall brackets, reverberated with a mixture of Gaelic and English tongues.

Chieftains in worsted trews and quilted jackets of leather, their hair falling around their shoulders, lords from the Pale, in doublets of russet, ruby and olive green, speculated about the reason for the unlikely mingling. All had been summoned by the earl, urged to Askeaton to hear tidings of importance. Unused to participate in such a communal gathering, they had accepted Desmond's invitation with suspicion and reluctance. They sat uneasily at the board, their eyes darting in recognition or suspicion at friend or foe. Ties of blood, marriage, fosterage and clientship bound these Irish aristocrats, but did little to unite them in political cohesion. Despite decades of intermarriage between O'Neills and O'Donels, Desmonds and MacCarthys, O'Briens and MacWilliams, politically they remained apart, separate and disunited, protecting their independence and privileges, nurturing their age-old feuds.

Alert to the current grudges, the household stewards endeavoured to ensure that a chieftain did not find himself seated beside an enemy or placed in a position where his honour and status within the complex political ranking might be impugned. It required diplomatic wizardry on the part of the chief household steward, in consultation with the earl, to work out the appropriate seating arrangements.

On a raised dais at the top of the room, under an elaborate traceried window, flanked on either side by two candlestands, on which twelve wax candles glowed, a long table with ten high-backed oak chairs remained unoccupied. Richly carved in heavy relief, the table was dressed elaborately with silver-gilt goblets and plate. Behind the dais, seated on a backless stool, the Desmond harper held a harp close to his shoulder and with long fingernails plucked the brass strings in a plaintive tune.

The final guests were being seated. Ulick Burke, husband of the Great Earl of Kildare's daughter, chieftain of Galway, was directed to a bench well away from his avowed enemy, MacWilliam Burke of Mayo, but close enough to the top to reflect his political status as the most powerful chieftain in the province of Connacht. MacWilliam, with his ally O'Malley, chieftain of the notorious seafaring clan of the western seaboard, looked on with ill-concealed dislike, both their territories having recently been ravaged by their turbulent neighbour.

Manus O'Donel, chieftain of Tirconel, attired in the more traditional clothes of his new status, yet distinguishable from his Gaelic peers by his cropped hair, took his seat at the upper end of the table beside Burke. At a nearby table, Eleanor's son slipped quietly into his allotted place, while towards the lower end of the hall, Leverous was shown to his place beside the Earl of Desmond's brehon, the captain of his gallowglass and the earl's physician, his non-aristocratic origins barring him from a more exalted placement.

The harper ceased playing and silence gradually descended on the packed hall. The air bristled with expectation. Servants stopped filling the pewter goblets of the higher tables and the wooden meaders of the lower tables, with wine and ale, as the diminutive figure of the Earl of Desmond appeared at the top of the hall with his wife, the sister of his neighbour Conor O'Brien, and beside her, Eleanor. The two were the only women apparent in the huge hall. As the aunt of Gerald, representative of the House of Kildare, Eleanor's presence was deemed necessary. Courtesy required the presence of the earl's countess, as hostess and chatelaine of Askeaton Castle.

The earl stood in silence before the assembled throng, his eyes scanning the faces which stared expectantly back at him. He had every reason to feel satisfied. Not even the Kildares in the heyday of their power had managed to assemble under one roof the principal leaders of the two traditions of the fragmented country, *Gael* and Sean-Ghall. He had lured them from their lairs, from all corners of Ireland – even from under the noses of the English in Dublin, he noted with satisfaction, seeing Dunsany, St Lawrence and the rest of the lords of the Pale.

Desmond's glance fell on the vacant places at his table. For three days he had used all the wiles, diplomacy and subterfuge that had sustained him in his dubious power in Munster, to hammer out a semblance of accord between those who were about to fill the vacant places at his table. The most difficult, as he had expected, was the aloof warlord from the North. O'Neill had refused to countenance anything that remotely impinged on his supremacy in Ulster. The hatred he bore O'Donel seemed reciprocated in full measure. The smooth tongue and suavity of the new lord of Tirconel made little penetration in O'Neill's armour of mistrust and long memory. But Desmond had persevered. It was a significant triumph. He needed O'Neill's support at this delicate juncture to sway less powerful lords to his plan. Once his scheme was in motion, O'Neill would be expendable and O'Donel the natural choice to ensure his downfall.

Desmond's stooping shoulders straightened with an invigorating surge of power. Then no one would be strong enough in Ireland to oppose him. He looked around the smoky haze which enveloped the great hall. With the assistance of the Emperor Charles, and concealed behind the cause of the young Geraldine, his ambitions would at last be realised. He would be more powerful than his cousin Kildare had ever been. The Great Earl's daughter had indeed presented him with the way to achieve his goal when she had sought sanctuary for her nephew at Askeaton. In the guise of protecting and supporting the Geraldine heir, he would make Henry Tudor regret the protection he had given his rival.

'*A h-Uaisle*,' he addressed the assembly. 'I welcome you to Desmond. Askeaton Castle is honoured to host such a princely gathering. But our assembly is not yet complete.'

He turned expectantly towards the door.

A pleasant-faced man of middle years, his high colouring betraying his fondness for hunting and Spanish sack, lumbered towards Desmond. As he took his place at the table, all present recognised the earl's brother-in-law, Conor O'Brien, descendant of the kings of Munster.

Myles MacMurrough Kavanagh, descendant of the kings of Leinster followed.

'Diarmuid Gallda.'

The half-hushed taunt from the middle of the hall accompanied The MacMurrough to his allotted place, a perennial reminder of the treachery of his royal ancestor, on whose invitation the Anglo-Normans had invaded Ireland in the twelfth century. Irish chieftains had long and unforgiving memories.

A loose-limbed man of about thirty, his hair falling in curls to his shoulders, the glint of an antique torque of gold around his neck, brought a murmur of recognition from the western chieftains. Felim O'Connor, direct descendant of the last high king of Ireland, now reduced to the status of chieftain, took his place next to the Countess of Desmond.

There was a slight pause and Desmond held his breath until, eventually, the figure of Conn Bacach O'Neill emerged cautiously into view amid whispers of astonishment from the hall. Desmond's revelations must be of some consequence if they had lured the powerful descendant of the kings of Ulster south to sit with his enemy O'Donel.

The significance of the descendants of the four provincial kings of ancient Ireland, seated for the first time in peace at one board, was not lost on the assembled Irish chieftains, who murmured either their surprise or approval, it was difficult to ascertain which. The ploy had the effect desired by Desmond: it had concentrated the minds of all. The second remaining place at the table was taken, as was customary, by Finn O'Daly, the hereditary ollave dána of the House of Desmond and foremost in precedence in the earl's household. But the earl did not merely pander to tradition by seating O'Daly at his table. Like every Gaelic leader, he both revered and feared his ollave – and with good reason. O'Daly's satirical tongue could just as easily disparage as praise his patron. As keeper of the genealogical records of the Munster Geraldines, O'Daly had power over Desmond. His dubious claims to the earldom could ill afford to fall foul of the ollave's knowledge. O'Daly's grey hair was tossed back on his shoulders to reveal a high-browed hawk-like countenance. His eyes swept the assembled throng with a hauteur appropriate to his status.

At the end of the hall Leverous waited expectantly for Gerald to be seated in the remaining chair at the top table, but it was Robert Walshe who next appeared on the dais and was introduced by the earl as the 'murdered Earl of Kildare's chaplain and confidant, recently returned from the French Court.'

The initial ceremony completed, Desmond sat between O'Neill and O'Connor and signalled to his steward to commence feasting.

From his lowly seat at the end of the hall, Leverous saw Eleanor incline her head in conversation with her cousin O'Neill. What was being plotted? What was being said? Where did Gerald fit into the web of intrigue being woven by Desmond and into which he hoped to entice these disparate strands of Irish society? Was Eleanor privy to Desmond's plans? Was her embrace, importunately interr-upted by O'Donel's brashness, a mere sop to conceal the truth from him? From his peripheral seat, with no part to play in the drama unfolding, no contribution to make to the political machinations that simmered around him, Leverous felt an outsider, superfluous to the proceedings, his role as Gerald's guardian now usurped by the earl of Desmond.

Beside him the gallowglass captain MacSheehy turned pointedly away from him to converse with his other neighbour. The earl's brehon, noting the slight, sought to make amends and engaged Leverous in a discourse in Latin on the advantages of the Irish legal principal of *cin comh-fhocuis*. Half-heartedly Leverous strove to concentrate on the brehon's arguments, his thoughts elsewhere.

In huge pewter and wooden platters, the steaming joints of beef and lamb were carried into the hall. Quail, plover and partridge, salmon from the Shannon weirs, garnished with watercress and leeks, were laid in abundance on every table. With dagger and knife, chieftain and lord cut and ate their fill, tearing apart the oaten cakes to absorb the herbed juices from the meat and fowl. Wine, ale and *uisce beatha* flowed continuously into goblet and meader. Irish chieftains were measured by the hospitality of their table, and in this, like many of the customs of the Gaelic culture adopted by his antecedents, the Earl of Desmond was not found wanting.

Mellowed by the food and drink, voices grew louder and more raucous. Beneath glib and crop, eyes glowed feverishly in the candlelight, as the guests argued or agreed with their neighbour. Yet Desmond waited, his sharp eyes scanning the faces of his guests, his ears receptive to the ebb and flow of the discordant snatches of conversation around him. Soon the atmosphere would be right to unfold his grand design, or most of it.

At the earl's table, Conor O'Brien, his face flushed a deeper crimson, argued goodnaturedly with the ollave O'Daly over the Irish bardic schools' continued usage of the formal syllabic metre in love poetry.

'It is all right for the heroic sagas of Cu Chulainn and Finn Mac Cumhail. But not when I need a honeyed tongue to woo a *cailín* to my bed,' O'Brien teased the eminent ollave.

O'Daly sniffed the air in derision. 'Love poetry. Pah! The training ground for apprentices.'

O'Brien smiled unconcernedly at the ollave's curt dismissal.

The young O'Connor chieftain was paying gallant, if achohol-induced, compliments to the elderly Countess of Desmond. Beside him, Eleanor reminisced with her cousin O'Neill about the Great Earl and Maynooth. At the end of the table, The MacMurrough Kavanagh looked deep into his silver goblet and spoke to no one.

On an imperceptible movement of the earl's hand, his chief steward struck the oak table three times with his *bata*. A gradual hush descended. Despite the liberality of food and drink and the now oppressive heat of the hall, the faces of the assembled lords were alert with expectation.

The earl rose to his feet. The gold links around his neck gleamed on the rich silk of his quilted jacket. He moved forward to the edge of the dais. At the back of the great hall, Leverous could feel the air of palpable expectation, as chieftain, lord and retainer craned towards the slight figure. He could feel his own heart thump in anticipation.

Desmond seemed loath to dispel the air of anticipation he had created. In the silence his look lingered on each upturned face as if gauging the reaction of the guests to his awaited declaration. Finally he cleared his throat to speak.

'Friends, Gael and Sean-Ghall, Irishmen all. This day we are participants in a unique event: our coming together for the first time, in peace. The annals of Ireland will mark this day as the milestone that it most surely is. But our participation in this *oireachtas* is not merely to test the hospitality of Desmond. Though,' he smiled thinly, 'I hope it is to your liking.'

A polite murmur greeted his statement.

'Nay, you most surely know that some event of great significance compelled me to ask you here. And compelled you to journey from the furthest parts of the four provinces. You are right. And had you declined,' he paused, 'the curse of your descendants would have ever been on your heads.'

A hum of interest rumbled around the hall. Desmond held up his hand and continued. 'You have heard of the butchery of my Kildare kinsmen at Tyburn. 'Tis not the first time that Geraldine blood washed the streets of London, but I tell you this, on my oath, my friends,' his thin voice rose perceptibly, 'it will be the last. The murder of my Kildare kinsmen serves as a bloody reminder of the treachery of the Tudor tyrant across the sea. And believe me, his blood lust is not yet sated. My kinsmen Kildare yesterday, perhaps you MacWilliam, you MacCarthy, you O'Carroll . . .' He pointed his finger dramatically at each chieftain '. . . or any one of us tomorrow. My friends,' his voice fell to a whisper, 'do we simply await the king's pleasure to do with us as he has done with

187

Kildare? Or do we free ourselves once and for all from his oppression? Make certain that no Irishman will ever again be cut in pieces like a side of beef, torn asunder by an English mob, to sate the blood lust of a usurper. Vindicate the butchery of the House of Kildare. The dream of my kinsmen, for which they suffered the ultimate sacrifice, must not be in vain.' The high-pitched voice rose higher and higher. 'For only together, my friends, as one, can we be masters of our own destiny; be masters of Ireland. Divided as the English wish to have us, as we are now, we are doomed to become their slaves. But united in a common cause, under one leader, we are invincible.'

A hundred pairs of eyes stared impassively up at Desmond. There was no obvious indication of how his words were being received by chieftain and lord, friend and foe, as they sat and listened while Desmond led them slowly towards the kernel of his scheme.

Yet Desmond and everyone else present could hazard a guess. To the Gaelic chieftains, his words revived bitter memories of the invasion of his Anglo-Norman ancestors, which had put paid to the very idea of Irish unity Desmond now propounded. To the lords from the Pale, whose allegiance to the English crown, albeit a nominal one but one which was as much part of their heritage, as the high kingship was to the Gaelic chieftains, it smacked of treason. Straddling the divide were the two branches of the Gerald-ines, the Kildares and the Desmonds, whose blood, a mixture of both traditions, bridged the cultural chasm. The Kildares had had their chance and failed. Now it was the turn of the Desmonds. But the earl knew he must choose his words with care if he was to garner the support of the represent-atives of the varied traditions.

'As we are now, divided and at war one with the other, our blood makes fertile the ground for the English to sow the seeds of division amongst us. Divide and conquer: the winning ploy of the oppressor, the bitter harvest of the conquered, of which Ireland has reaped her share. Take a leaf from the English book. Once they were as divided and weak as we are, now they are unified and powerful.'

'Under the very tyrant you propose to rid us of,' Ulick Burke shouted from his seat below Desmond. 'Who, pray, is to become the tyrant of Ireland?'

A rumble of approval greeted his remarks. Desmond raised his hand and the tumult subsided. 'I speak to you merely as a messenger, a conduit for a revolution of mind and purpose that will make us all masters of our destiny, strong and able to defend ourselves from Tudor oppression.'

Desmond's words were greeted by silence. He had recaptured their attention. 'If we make a stand together, we shall not be alone. We,' he indicated those at the top table, 'have been invited to become part of a larger conspiracy against the Tudor king.'

'Invited,' a querulous voice interrupted, 'by whom?'

Desmond reached his hand inside his jacket and withdrew a parchment with a large seal adhering. 'Pope Clement in Rome.' He held the square of parchment high for all to see. 'An invitation to be part of a crusade against the English heretic king. It promises a plenary indulgence to all who participate. Each of us has received a similar summons,' he said, pointing to O'Neill, O'Connor, MacMurrough, O'Brien, 'and my Lord Dunsany.'

''Tis Rome who gave the English licence to invade Ireland in the first place,' O'Connor of Offaly shouted from the body of the hall.

'When his English ally has become his foe, the pope seeks Irish help,' another voice added.

'Then let us turn the pope's difficulty to our advantage,' Desmond responded.

But his suggestion received little support from the assembly. Irish distrust of the papacy was long and bitter.

'Who else is party to the crusade?' The MacWilliam of Mayo asked.

'France and Spain, the Papal States and Scotland.'

'France and Spain allied?' St Lawrence's scornful laugh emanated from near the dais. 'By Christ's cross, a shaky foundation on which to build a crusade.'

'The French king and the emperor are set to put their differences aside,' Desmond hurriedly continued, 'and to unite under the banner of the pope. Is it not time that we in Ireland united too?'

There was silence. From the back of the hall Leverous watched chieftain and lord struggle with the radical proposal Desmond had propounded. Unity might mean strength elsewhere but in Ireland it hinted at an erosion of the lord-client relationship on which individual power was based. Only the House of Kildare had been strong enough to challenge the traditional ethos and, under the implacable arm of both the Great Earl and Garret, it had united the fragmented leaders behind the banner of Kildare. Leverous waited to hear the question that he knew would surely come. The MacWilliam of Mayo asked it on behalf of all; the soft sounding brogue of the western chieftain sped the question across the rows of heads towards Desmond.

'Under whose banner?'

One hundred pairs of eyes were riveted on the Earl of Desmond. He turned sideways towards the table behind him. The eyes of the crowd slid in turn over the faces of the representatives of the ancient royal houses, past O'Brien, O'Connor, MacMurrough, to rest briefly on the impassive features of O'Neill. Was it to be under the Red Hand banner of O'Neill? They held their breath. At that moment Desmond motioned towards his steward, who disappeared through the door at the back of the dais, to reappear with a young boy, dressed in a quilted jack and long trews. In his hand, he held a wooden flagpole on which was affixed a furled banner. Desmond led the boy by the hand to the front of the dais. He then slowly unfurled the banner and shouted triumphantly, 'under the saltire of Kildare.'

Amidst a loud clatter of overturned goblets and meaders, chieftain, lord and retainer rose in unison and pushed forward to feast their eyes on the small figure before them.

'*A h-Uaisle*, Gerald FitzGerald, Earl of Kildare.'

Desmond's voice was submerged in the roar which erupted in the charged atmosphere. It reverberated off the lime-washed walls, rose upwards towards the vaulted ceiling to echo among the great oak beams high above the crowd.

'Crom aboo.'

The ancient war cry of the Kildare Geraldines issued from the throats of Gael and Sean-Ghall alike, as emotion replaced wariness. Allegiance to the House which had been their virtual rulers for decades past, for the moment superseded their independent posturing, overcame feuds and suspicion as, with one voice, they acclaimed the Kildare heir. They crowded round him as if he were the Messiah returned to walk among them. Gerald, his face pale and unsmiling, backed away from their wild eyes, their excited shouts, their rough grasp, as they reached out their hands to touch him, to satisfy themselves that he was flesh and blood. But Desmond's strong grasp on his arm made him stand his ground and endure their scrutiny and wild emotion.

As the cheering slowly subsided and the chieftains returned to their seats, the earl faced the frenzied gathering.

'Loyalty to the Geraldines still lives, despite Henry Tudor's cruel efforts. Let us put that loyalty into action. Here is the new leader of Ireland, his blood a mixture of Gael and Sean-Ghall. Call him king, call him *taoiseach*, the title is unimportant. What is important is that we this night pledge our allegiance to him, as we did to his father and his grandfather. Through him we shall rid ourselves of English power in Ireland. Allied with the international conspiracy against the Tudor king, our cause will triumph. Gerald FitzGerald from this night is the new Lord of Ireland, in place of the usurper, Henry Tudor.'

The cheer from the hall was loud and sustained.

'But he is but a boy. Too young to do battle,' a voice argued.

The cheering subsided. Desmond responded to the question he hoped would be asked. His darting eyes flicked over the upturned faces. He sensed he had them sufficiently interested to reveal the core of his plan.

'Tonight we shall form a league – the Geraldine League – to protect the young Geraldine and to fight his battles until he is of age.' He turned and smiled benignly down at Gerald, who stood still and solemn at the table, the crimson cross of the Geraldine saltire trailing behind him. 'And from the skill he shows with the dart and spear since coming to Desmond, my friends, I tell you it will not be long before he leads us himself. Until then, he will continue with his military training, as was his father's wish and as is our custom.'

'With whom?'

At the back of the hall, Leverous rose to his feet. His voice, clear and strong, sent heads turning until the concentrated gaze of the crowd was directed at the tall Englishman. He was aware of Eleanor looking sharply in his direction.

'With whom, my lord?', he repeated. 'By this declaration,' he held Garret's letter from the Tower high above his head for all to see, 'the Earl of Kildare entrusted his son to my care, until sanctuary could be found for him in France.'

A murmur of surprise emanated from the crowd.

'The Earl of Kildare is dead.' Desmond cut across the whispers, his anger concealed beneath an icy smile. Ignoring Leverous, he addressed the assembly. 'His wish to have his son sent for protection to France is no longer attainable, as his chaplain Robert Walshe will vouch. I know what my cousin would wish. That his son's life be entrusted to the protection of his Irish allies and kinsmen, not to fickle strangers. No Englishman,' he looked directly at Leverous, 'will divert us from the noble path we have chosen. Should he persist, he will be treated as a spy.'

Leverous felt the crowd's rising hostility. In front of him he saw Lord Dunsany rise to his feet but before he could open his mouth, the earl's gallowglass captain, MacSheehy, pushed Leverous roughly, so that he stumbled against the table, sending goblets and plate crashing to the floor. Leverous righted himself. Behind the earl, Eleanor had risen to her feet and across the distance that separated them, her eyes beseeched him to be silent. From the dais Gerald looked fearfully in his direction. A ripple of anticipation ran through the company as Leverous faced up to MacSheehy. The captain groped for the skean in his belt. Eleanor's son swiftly stepped between them.

'Don't waste your breath on dead embers,' MacCarthy muttered quickly in English to Leverous, 'at least not under Desmond's own roof.'

Leverous looked around at the faces, which stared back at him, some neutrally, others with dislike, but all eyes feverish with emotion, intoxicated by Desmond's hospitality and exhortations. He realised that MacCarthy was right. The atmosphere was like a tinderbox. With a last look in Eleanor's direction, Leverous left the hall.

All attention centred again on the dais. Behind the still standing figure of Desmond, a chair scraped loudly as O'Neill rose to his feet. Desmond half-turned his head and a flicker of annoyance flashed across his face. The crowd's attention was fixed on the Ulster chieftain.

'I hold no truck with foreign kings or popes. What do they care for us, save as a means to achieve their own ends? Let them pay for our support for their crusade against the English king. And with something more tangible, I say, than blessings and indulgences.'

Shouts of 'Aye, aye,' greeted O'Neill's remarks. Desmond's shrewd eyes picked up the seeds of doubt that O'Neill's intervention had sown among his guests. He knew he must retrieve the advantage.

'I agree with The O'Neill,' he told them. 'But unlike him,

I have had dealings with the emperor in the past and have more faith in his word than others.' He shrugged his narrow shoulders. 'However, to satisfy my lord O'Neill and anyone else among you, I will send an emissary to the emperor for assistance, for soldiers and weapons.'

'I propose that we send Robert Walshe.' Dunsany's suggestion was greeted with general approval.

The Earl of Desmond seemed to hesitate for a second. 'As you wish.' His thin lips were compressed in annoyance. 'Meanwhile, the Geraldine must be kept out of the clutches of the king and his Ormond cronies. We,' he indicated the four chieftains at his table, 'are agreed to become his guardians so that he will have sanctuary, at any time, in any of the provinces of Ireland. For the present, it is agreed that he will remain in Desmond. His enemies presume him to be with his aunt in Carbury. Each of the descendants of the provincial kings of Ireland, my Lord Dunsany to represent the interest of the Palesmen, and myself, as guardian and kinsman of the Geraldine, will form a council for his future protection.'

A mixture of muted approval greeted the plan. To take advantage of the response and to deter further intervention, Desmond continued quickly.

'Tonight is written a glorious chapter in our history. Tonight, my friends, the Geraldine League is born. To protect and free not only the Geraldine heir but all of us who value our freedom, our customs, our country. Together we are strong, able adversaries of the English king. Alone, we are but fodder for his evil designs. Let us toast, with the *uisce beatha* of our country, the life and success of this great enterprise.'

Benches and chairs scraped the floor, as chieftain and lord rose to their feet to toast Desmond's plan. Many did so half-heartedly, others with alcohol-induced gusto, some with determination.

'Let us toast the one, on whose young shoulders rests the destiny of Ireland: the Geraldine.'

Two hundred voices answered, loudly and in unison, 'The Geraldine!'

Desmond's ollave led Gerald to the front of the dais. O'Daly's bony hand gripped the boy's shoulder. He threw his haughty gaze over the excited throng. A deathly silence eased over the hall. The crowd seemed mesmerised by the spectre-like figure, enveloped in a mantle of tawny gold, the fringed neckline merging with his long hair, like the shaggy mane of a lion. From deep within his chest, a resonant sound, like the rumble of thunder, erupted in the first lines of his eulogy. The majestic metres of the Gaelic verse spilled out over the attentive audience, like unrelenting waves crashing on a rocky shoreline, as the ollave shaped and moulded with classical erudition his eulogy on the fate of the Geraldine dynasty. From Troy to Florence to Normandy to England and Ireland, the verses extolled their noble heritage, valiant deeds, liberality, greatness and learning. Angry growls erupted from his spellbound audience as he intoned the more recent sorrows inflicted on the Geraldines by the kings of England: the execution of an Earl of Desmond, the imprisonment of the Great Earl of Kildare. But the ollave concentrated most of his vocal passion on the recent carnage at Tyburn. The Earl Garret, Silken Thomas, Richard, Walter, John, Oliver, the names rolled off his tongue, every syllable caressed. Like an ocean his voice rushed unstoppable to a great crescendo, as he urged the company to deny the Tudor king the final victory and unite in the cause of the Geraldine.

The hall rose to its feet in a great climactic roar, a mixture of anger and triumph.

'Geraldine aboo!' the ollave's eulogy ended.

'Geraldine aboo!'

The answering roar of allegiance seemed to lift the great beams from the stone corbels. With his lionlike head thrown back, his energy spent, the ollave pushed the Geraldine forward into the massed outstretched arms of the crowd who carried him shoulder high around the great hall of Askeaton.

19

COURTYARD, ASKEATON CASTLE

After the oppressive cauldron of Desmond's hall, the night air was like an elixir, the silence of the courtyard a soothing balm to Leverous's throbbing head. The earl's brehon had a liberal hand with his master's aqua vitae and had replenished Leverous's meader after every sip. In the distance, he could hear the earl's thin voice bending his captive audience to his will. Desmond had put on an impressive show, he conceded as he sought the solitude of the shadows on the far side of the courtyard. Like an artful conjuror, the earl had manipulated his fellow conspirators and his audience with words, pageantry and the *coup de grâce* – the presentation of the Geraldine heir, presumed by most of his audience to be dead or imprisoned. In the heady atmosphere, the ploy was guaranteed success.

Leverous propped himself against the door of the smithy. Across the courtyard, long shafts of light spilled out from the lancet windows of the great hall. Except for the sentries above in the towers and guarding the barbican, the courtyard was deserted. Leverous tried to rationalise the night's events. It was obvious that the Earl of Desmond intended to capitalise on his offer of sanctuary to Gerald. It had taken time for the nature of the price he demanded to emerge. The League was either a genuine attempt to secure the safety of the defenceless boy or a ploy by Desmond to secure, through the boy, the power that had once belonged to Gerald's father. Leverous's instinct told him it was the latter. For under the guise of protector of Kildare's heir, the allegiance of the chieftains and lords, once allied to the Earl of Kildare, could be exploited by Desmond during the years of Gerald's minorship.

It was common knowledge that Desmond had attained his position at the expense of the legitimate heir to the title, now ensconced at Court. The present earl had sufficient enemies within his lordship who, given the chance, would intrigue with those who sought his downfall. Yes, Leverous thought, Desmond needed the league as a base from which to protect his claim and extend his power. Henry Tudor respected nothing as highly as a strong foe and if Desmond's strength was sufficient, the king would be reluctant to expend money on the restoration of a weaker rival.

Garret's letter crackled inside Leverous's doublet, as he eased his weight on to a nearby barrel. It seemed like a lifetime since Robert Walshe had thrust it into his hand, in the gloom of a dingy tavern in Bankside, opposite the Tower where Garret lay ill and in despair but determined that the last of his offspring would not suffer a similar fate. And now the earl's trusted chaplain and confidant seemed part of the conspiracy against his son. Or perhaps Walshe was just as much a prisoner of Desmond's ambition as were Gerald and himself.

And Eleanor. What part did she play in Desmond's charade, in the flagrant betrayal of her brother's last wish? Her presence at Desmond's table implied the approval of the House of Kildare for Desmond's scheme. And it was she, Leverous recalled, who had suggested Desmond as a refuge in the first place. Their impulsive embrace seemed now as imaginary as their lovemaking in Thomas Court. Of his feelings for her, Leverous had no doubt but, as before, they seemed about to be commandeered by events over which he had no control. Like a rudderless ship, he was being driven at the whim of the winds of political expediency. But even in his befuddled state, he realised that it had always been so. Since Maynooth, since Thomas Court, he had allowed his fate to be determined and planned by the House of Kildare. First the Great Earl, then Garret, Eleanor and now Gerald. From as far back as he could recall, he seemed to be always reacting to events, never the instigator of his own destiny. Perhaps it was time he began, he thought, by breaking free of the bonds of emotion and devotion which bound him to Eleanor and Gerald. Maybe, as Desmond said, he had paid his debt to the Kildares in full.

A stealthy footfall sounded loud in the darkness. Leverous fumbled around him, grasped a loose cask stave and crouched behind the barrel. He had seen the blood lust in MacSheehy's fevered eyes as they faced each other in the hall. His death would give Desmond a free rein to use Gerald as he wished. Well, he thought grimly, he would make the gallowglass fight hard for his victory. The footsteps shuffled closer. He grasped the stave firmly, his body tense and ready to strike. A figure loomed large before him. Leverous raised the stave above his head.

'Thomas, hold your hand. 'Tis I, Walshe.' The whisper cut through the darkness. 'Rest easy, my friend. Rest easy.'

Robert Walshe pushed him into the shadows under the curtain walls and, with a finger to his lips, pointed towards the nearby tower. They hunkered down, their backs to the wall. Walshe's thin face was outlined in the semi-gloom. Leverous had always liked this unassuming, quietly spoken cleric, but knew little about him. For Walshe seemed to flit like a shadow back and forth to England and the Continent. Leverous could not recall having seen the chaplain perform the duties of his cloth. He had never seen him read a breviary, officiate at Mass, marriages, christenings or burials. His life seemed devoted to secular activities. Secretary, emissary, confidant of Garret, he spent more time away from his master than with him. An aura of intrigue and secrecy seemed to envelop him. He was as economical with words as he was fastidious in his habits and dress. Leverous still did not know, nor indeed would he enquire of the enigmatic cleric, how he had penetrated the labyrinth of the Tower, what hand he had greased, what influence he had invoked, on what pretext he had gained access to Garret and smuggled his letter through the impenetrable security with which the Earl had been surrounded. Educated at Salamanca and Louvain, where Leverous's own indecisive footsteps once led him, Walshe was an intrepid traveller, more familiar with Paris, London and Antwerp than with Limerick, Cork and Galway. His linguistic talents and unobtrusive appearance made him pass as a native of any country to which the Earl of Kildare's business brought him. Where the earl would have attracted attention, his unobtrusive clerical emissary could pass undetected about his master's business.

But, Leverous wondered, as he stole a glance at the churchman, where did the chaplain's loyalty lie now in relation to the pope's crusade and the Earl of Desmond's intrigue? Had the chaplain's loyalty to Garret died with him in the Tower or would he transfer it to his son ?

'I greatly feared that your attempt to thwart the earl in his moment of glory might well have spelled your doom and served the young Geraldine ill,' he quietly rebuked Leverous.

Leverous inclined his head in acknowledgment of the censure. 'I felt as if a tide was bearing Gerald along like a piece of flotsam,' he whispered angrily. 'Desmond's interest in the boy is self-motivated. A short cut to power. Surely you must see that?'

Robert Walshe squinted into the darkness as if seeking an answer there. 'Believe me, Thomas, I am not blind to the earl's design. But answer me this. What alternative do you propose?'

The question was simple but its bluntness took Leverous by surprise. He had not thought of an alternative. From the time of his precipitate flight from Donore to Carbury and on to Desmond, he had had little time to plan. He had been borne along by a fast-moving current of events over which he had little control. To keep Gerald alive and at liberty until he could smuggle him to France had been his sole motivation. Now that the door to France was closed, he had no other to open. Leverous held his face in his hands, his mind befuddled with alcohol, fatigue and frustration.

Walshe watched Leverous struggle. 'Do not berate yourself,' he said kindly. 'There is simply nothing you or I can do . . . for the moment.'

Leverous raised his head from his hands and looked at the cleric. 'For the moment,' he repeated, searching the other's face in the semi-darkness for a sign, a plan which might give him some hope.

Robert Walshe spoke rapidly. 'I intend to take Desmond's proposals to the emperor at Toledo, to buy time for the Geraldine. The same reason that you must be patient here and not incur Desmond's anger.'

'We could smuggle Gerald to Spain and seek sanctuary with the Emperor.'

The chaplain shook his head. 'We could never spirit Gerald to Spain without Desmond's knowledge. Besides, I trust the emperor even less than the King of France. His adherence to this crusade is motivated, I suspect, more by human greed than by spiritual righteousness or by loyalty to the pope, whose city he sacked but a year ago.'

'Then why Toledo?'

'Despite the emperor's new-found piety, I am certain that in the end he will treat with Henry. They were allies once, you recall, against François, before the King divorced the emperor's aunt. Queen Catherine's death has removed the source of their estrangement. Besides, Charles's hatred of François runs too deep to be negated by the exhortations of the pope.'

'In that case he is less likely to support Desmond. Or to give sanctuary to the son of the enemy of his ally.' Leverous was perplexed.

'*Touché*, my friend, *touché*. And as Charles hides his ambition behind the banner of the pope, Desmond hides his behind the Geraldine banner. The emperor will never support the earl against Henry, as much as he might promise. He will waste no soldiers or arms on Desmond's lust for glory in Ireland. And with no Spanish army, Desmond will not be able to play the king. The smokescreen of the Geraldine League will be seen for what it is.'

'And what of Gerald? Where is he to find sanctuary when Desmond's league falls apart?'

The chaplain paused, a smile playing around his mouth. 'To wager is against my cloth. But if it were not, then my money would be on France.' He observed the troubled countenance of his younger companion and continued. 'It is possible that this league could do as Desmond promises: protect the boy from the king until he is of age.' He shook his head. 'I doubt it. Desmond is no Kildare. The lords and chieftains whom he seeks to rule will be swayed only by force. If Desmond fails to get an army and weapons from the emperor, his hopes of becoming the *de facto* leader in Ireland will evaporate like the dew. But for now, for us, for Gerald, there is no alternative but to play along with his scheme. The boy must be protected by somebody until we can find sanctuary for him abroad. And remember, Leverous, if Henry's expected child is female, then his legal heir is still Catherine's daughter, Mary, who may have sympathy for the victims of her father's ire. Gerald could yet be restored.'

'If the king has a male heir?' Leverous voice whispered back.

Robert Walshe looked at him. His eyes crinkled in a smile. 'You cannot think that I would risk Gerald's life on the vague possibility of Mary's succession. Nay, my friend, should Ireland and France fail Gerald, then he will have the protection of a man who is above either political or religious expediency.'

Leverous looked inquiringly at the priest. Walshe looked

towards the ground. For a moment, Leverous thought he would not divulge his contact. 'Cardinal Reginald Pole,' he said quietly.

'Cardinal!' Leverous's voice betrayed his astonishment.

Walshe inclined his head. 'In place of Fisher.'

Leverous silently contemplated the chaplain's revelation. Reginald Pole, cousin of the king, friend of Garret, his mentor at Padua. The very name gave him courage, made his spirits revive.

'He lies low in Paris until François declares against Henry and is as convinced as me that it will be so. Until that time we must endeavour to keep Gerald out of the clutches of the king and the Countess of Ormond.'

'And Grey?'

Walshe drew a deep breath. 'God's truth, I pity Grey. His is the most unenviable position of all. His Yorkist roots, his relationship to the boy, make him suspect to the king and the countess. As the king's deputy, few Irish will trust him. And besides, O'Donel has further implicated him, by making him privy to the pope's scheme.'

'O'Donel?' Leverous's voice betrayed both surprise and antagonism.

The chaplain looked sharply at him. 'Yes. Most strange. He came to Paris with Cardinal Pole from Venice. 'Twas he who prompted the cardinal to involve Grey.'

'Grey had already involved himself,' Leverous said, and explained about the warning he had received at Donore.

'God help him, should word of his collusion get to the king. And from what I hear, he has some determined enemies in his own camp. O'Donel's message has him trapped.'

'I do not trust O'Donel.'

The chaplain looked into the darkness. 'It brought back memories of Maynooth, to see the Lady Eleanor, you and O'Donel together. After all this time.'

'Bitter memories,' Leverous added. 'O'Donel has not changed.'

'And you, Thomas?' Walshe asked. 'I'm sure Lady Eleanor

has long forgotten O'Donel's rash immaturity. But you, my friend, seem more determined to cling to past obsessions. 'Tis bad to pine for what cannot be, Thomas. It cankers the present and extinguishes the future. O'Donel is conceited, I grant you. But he seems committed to Gerald's cause. Perhaps your . . . affection for the Lady MacCarthy colours your opinion of him. I recall your friendship with her at Maynooth. But she has her son to protect her now, if indeed she needs protection, from O'Donel or anyone. From what Desmond says, she appears as formidable in her own way as her sister. It seems that the Great Earl's blood runs as strong in his daughters as it did in his sons.' The chaplain smiled and rose to his feet. 'So, my friend, be patient, I beg you, until I return from Spain. As I seem to fall in with Desmond's schemes, you do likewise. Do not invoke his anger, for Gerald's sake.'

He held out his hand and Leverous took it. The chaplain turned to leave but suddenly stopped. 'If after two months I do not return, get word to Cardinal Pole at Notre Dame in Paris. He will know what to do.'

Leverous watched until the slight figure disappeared into the shadows. Across the courtyard the doors of the great hall were thrown open and through the yellow light the crowd spilled out. With loud shouts of 'Crom aboo', they carried the Geraldine high on their shoulders into the night.

20

ST MARY'S ABBEY, DUBLIN

Like a caged lioness, the Countess of Ormond paced the confines of the narrow anteroom in St Mary's Abbey. For three days Grey had kept her waiting. At first she had willed herself to be patient, the success of her mission to the king keeping her rising wrath at bay. Gradually her elation was displaced by an innate craving to confront Grey with the fruits of her success. But in a petty attempt to deny her victory, to preserve his tattered dignity, Grey had absconded again to the wilds of Wicklow. Yet another senseless foray against the O'Byrnes, who must laugh loudly, hidden deep in their mountain fastness, at the Englishman's folly. But sooner or later Grey would have to return to Dublin, she consoled herself grimly, and he would find her waiting. The stinging rebuke in the king's own hand, contained in the square parchment she had brought with her, would spur him to do his duty. Grey's childish reaction simply postponed the inevitable. But, the countess thought with mounting annoyance, every hour lost put a further distance between her and her quarry.

In retrospect it had been easy to manipulate them. She was disappointed at the relative ease with which the king and his supposedly Machiavellian secretary, Cromwell, had fallen for her scheme, which she had let them think was of their own creation. They were all the same these men, king, lord, administrator, down to the lowliest churl. Man's instinctive disdain for the female intellect was their inherent weakness, if it was used by woman to her advantage. But it took a singular woman to exploit this male weakness. She had to be willing to sacrifice on the high altar of personal achievement the desires of her sexuality, the emotional and material dependence on man, which both nature and society placed as diversions, barriers towards realising her real potential. But the countess had been trained by a man who was a master in duplicity and manipulation and she had been a receptive student, a credit to her tutor.

A discreet knock on the panelled door was followed by the compact figure of the under-treasurer, William Brabazon, pointed beard thrust forward aggressively. Impeccably dressed from the black velvet bonnet on his cropped curls to the square-capped shoes, Brabazon oozed the assurance of someone who never doubted his own potential. She disliked this conceited, ambitious, English adventurer. For despite the clothes and cultivated manner of the courtier, Brabazon's motivation was as base as that of any pirate or mercenary on the trail of plunder, and there were rich pickings to be had in Ireland. She detested his class, either crawling with feigned servility like Crowley, or puffed up with assumed arrogance like Brabazon. Both species were contemptible, but necessary to her scheme. And, like servants, they could be hired or fired, their loyalty bought, their 'friendship' tolerated.

'My lady,' Brabazon bowed low.

'Ah, Brabazon. Come to keep us company.' The violet eyes gleamed contemptuously down at the low-sized English-man.

'At your wish, my lady.' The suave reply did not fool her. Brabazon could scarcely contain his curiosity about the outcome of her mission to the court and to boast of his efforts on her behalf during her absence.

'So Grey has bolted like a rabbit.' She placed her heavy

bulk into a high-backed chair beside the window. 'So well he might, when he reads the king's writ.'

The under-treasurer's eyes slid towards the parchment on the table. 'Your mission was a success.' It was a statement rather than a question. 'My Lord Ormond remained at court?'

A look of disdain crossed the heavy features. 'My husband lies abed, retching what remains of his guts that has not fed the fish from Beaumaris to Howth.'

'I sympathise.' Brabazon's response was genuine.

'And you,' the violet eyes focused on him, 'what new spoils have fallen into your lap since our departure?'

Brabazon did not rise to the bait. 'As you instructed, my lady, I kept the fires stoked in parliament. Grey was under siege the greater part of the time. The distribution of church lands continues and the queue grows longer for the Kildare confiscations. So many claimants,' he laughed shortly, 'by God's truth, a new earldom of Kildare will need to be found to satisfy them all.'

Not least for yourself, the countess thought. 'Has Grey assigned himself more?'

Brabazon shook his head. 'Unless someone acts for him in secret. The ruins of Maynooth and a mere thousand acres are alone in his name. Strange, as deputy he could have had first choice of something of greater value.'

That Grey should seek such a seemingly worthless spoil as a ruined castle was beyond the Englishman's comprehension. As the king's deputy, Grey had the giving of countless Kildare castles, many untouched by the rebellion, thousands of fertile acres, rivers that teemed with salmon and trout, a myriad income-rich rights, like the prisage of wine at the Kildare ports of Drogheda and Waterford and rich monastic benefices, each worth a king's ransom.

But as a Geraldine, the countess knew the significance of Maynooth, heartland of the Geraldines, for generations the symbol of their proud dynasty. To her, it was the most coveted prize of all. Even roofless and despoiled, it could still invoke memories, inspire loyalty and in unloyal hands encourage hopes of restoration. She would demonstrate to the king just how ill-intentioned were the hands that held it now. Brabazon, the commoner and the foreigner, saw only the ruin. She, the aristocrat and a Geraldine, saw the significance of the ruin.

'Is that all?' she asked brusquely, anxious to be rid of him.

Brabazon smoothed the stiff ruff at his neck, a sign that he had some tidings of importance 'The Pale lords have disappeared.'

'Disappeared!' The countess's voice rose sharply in derision. 'By what conjuror's trick, pray, has this miracle been effected? Would that it could be forever.'

Brabazon blushed visibly under her sarcasm. For a fleeting instant his loathing of his mentor distorted his smug countenance, but the veil of attentiveness that he espoused towards her was quickly restored. Ambition made strange bedfellows and endured much in its achievement.

'Pardon, my lady. But My Lords Dunsany, Baltinglass, Howth, Gormanstown and Slane have departed their lordships two weeks past. They have not been sighted, either at parliament or anywhere within the Pale. I understand they held a council at my Lord Dunsany's in Meath, whence they immediately rode south, towards Munster. It is indeed as if a conjuror spirited them away.'

'Munster,' the countess's brow was ridged in thought. 'What escorts did they bring?'

Brabazon's face lifted in wonderment. 'None, it appears.'

'None,' her voice echoed around the room. 'They rode into Munster unescorted. God's blood, they must surely prefer to face an Irish javelin than the king's chastisement. Nay, Brabazon, there is more to this. And I swear an oath on St Brigid's grave that the whereabouts of my nephew lies at the heart of it.'

She rose and began to pace the floor. The wooden boards heaved under her weight. 'My sister and her boy champion. Huh, 'twould take more than that to entice these badgers from the safety of the Pale to go coshering to Carbury. And unescorted at that. They must have been given safe passage. Now who is strong enough to guarantee them passage through Munster?'

She stopped in her tracks. The violet eyes looked through Brabazon as if he were invisible. He could imagine the wheels of her agile brain whirring as she juggled with the permutations before arriving at her answer.

'Desmond.' She breathed the name, not as a question but with certitude. 'The Geraldine, my sister, the Pale lords and the Earl of Desmond. What strange company . . . or cabal. There is something afoot, Brabazon. My sister must be able to attract more than a wild chieftain if she has lured the wily Desmond to her side. I must know what is being plotted before I drag Grey into Carbury. If I fail to locate my nephew there, Grey will crow to the king, rant about spending money on wild excursions outside the Pale, gain face after all I have expended on his loss. The devil take him!'

The countess continued her pacing. Brabazon waited. Finally she stopped and faced him.

'Tell Grey I am unable to meet with him this evening. Plead fatigue. Nay, 'a gleam came into her eye, '. . . say I suffer from malady of the sea. Let him stew in dread of the contents of the king's letter another day. It will afford me time to plot a way through this.'

Brabazon waited expectantly for the countess to divulge her plans.

'Well?' she rounded on him. 'Better not to keep your master waiting.'

With a curt bow in her direction, Brabazon withdrew, the loud banging of the door behind him revealing his annoyance. The countess smiled in satisfaction at his disappointment and then looked bleakly through the narrow casement window which overlooked the fields of Oxmantown, stretching towards the mud flats of the Liffey, across the river to where the walls of Dublin Castle rose above the steeply pitched roofs.

A secret once spoken is no longer a secret. The advice of her father had ever fashioned her actions. Her father. The paragon and predator of her life. What would he say now if he knew she plotted his grandson's death? In her mind's eye she saw him, his broad back towards her, his arm around the shoulders of her brother Garret. Without a thought, he had turned from her, cut her off from the admiration and love that she needed to keep at bay the darker side of her mind, which compelled her to strike out, to eliminate anything that stood in her path. The Geraldine line would exist only through her. The life of her nephew for the life of her son, over whose still body she had vowed vengeance on Kildare. Yes, she thought grimly, her account with her father remained but half-settled.

She rang the bell on the table and her maid, Bessie Blount, entered quickly. A solid, dependable but unimaginative woman from Kent, she had been in her service since her marriage to Ormond. She kept her distance from her Irish peers, content to do her mistress's bidding and no more. She listened attentively to the countess's orders and disappeared, returning almost immediately, with a shabbily dressed kern, from whom the stench of ale and an unwashed body filled the small room. Her nose signifying her distaste, Mistress Blount gratefully departed.

With a strong heave, the countess threw open the casement window and turned to examine what she had saved from the gutter weeks earlier outside the tavern in Fishamble Street. The harper rubbed a dirty hand across his shaggy beard. His mouth twitched nervously before the baleful look of the huge woman confronting him and he seemed to wilt before her cold stare.

He knew of her by reputation. They said she could wield a sword as well as any man, that with her own hands she hanged her prisoners from a jutting stone in her tower of Ballyraggart. His hereditary master, The O'Byrne, had been an ardent ally of the Kildares and an active supporter in the rebellion of Silken Thomas. O'Byrne's animosity to the Ormonds had been as ingrained as his loyalty to the Kildares. Often to please his master, the harper now recalled with growing alarm, he had composed and sung derisive songs about the House of Ormond . . . about her. Now his fate lay in the hands of this changeling, a she-devil, if the stories about her were to be believed. Better to have run the gauntlet of the landlord of the Nag's Head and the Dublin mob, he thought, than to have fallen into her clutches. He clung to his harp tightly as if to gain courage from the feel of the familiar wood.

'You are minstrel to the rebel O'Byrne?' The question was like a whiplash. The harper flinched.

'I left Wicklow before the rebellion,' he stammered.

'How convenient for you,' the countess sneered disbelievingly. 'By birthright you are attached to that rebel house; whether you left before or after the rebellion is of no consequence. You are tarred with the same rebel brush as your master O'Byrne. The city constable will string you up on the gibbet. Dublin citizens have long memories where the O'Byrnes are concerned.'

Like a cornered animal, the harper looked frantically around the confined spaces.

'However,' the merciless voice continued, 'if you do my bidding, I may be inclined to save your neck. I have work for you, in Munster. In keeping with your profession,' she added, her gaze falling on the harp, half-hidden beneath the ragged mantle.

'Munster?' the harper asked, as if she had said the moon.

'Munster. To irritate ears there with your harping as you have doubtless done in Wicklow.'

210

MacGrath's mouth dropped open in anguish. An itinerant harper, belonging to no house, with no roots, no rights within the structured Irish society, was little better than a beggar, lower than the lowliest *bodach*. When The O'Byrne returned to his castle from hiding, his intention had been to go back to Wicklow and resume his hereditary position in his household. But this she-devil had other plans for his future.

The countess noted his hesitation. 'I hear no words of gratitude for saving your neck.'

With downcast eyes, the harper woodenly mumbled some platitude.

'But I must have some pledge that you will follow my instructions to the letter. Now what pledge can you offer?' The countess walked around the harper. 'Money? I think not. Possessions? I see none but that,' she pointed dramatically to the partly hidden harp.

The harper's grasp tightened on the wooden frame. His eyes stared at her in terror. 'But it is my . . . my life, my heritage. In my family's keeping since, since – '

'And it will continue to be, when you complete the task I set you. In the meantime, I will have a replacement given to you.' She held out her hand determinedly.

From the folds of his mantle, the harper slowly extracted the small wooden-framed harp and, as if she was about to chop off his arm, extended it towards the countess. The soundbox was carved with intricate designs. A row of mother-of-pearl inlay was worked along the neck; the smooth willow wood was polished with the shine of countless hands which had lovingly caressed it. It was a fine example of the traditional Irish harp but the emotive value of this hereditary heirloom to MacGrath, the countess knew, made the instrument priceless.

She placed it in a cupboard in the corner of the room and locked the door. 'Safe and secure until you complete your mission. Now to business.' She motioned the harper to a stool by the window.

211

21

ASKEATON CASTLE

The strain of being cooped up in her chamber at Askeaton had become almost unbearable. Ever since the Earl of Desmond had revealed his scheme for the formation of the league, Eleanor had avoided contact with the other guests and inhabitants of Desmond's sprawling castle. To Cormac's anxious enquiries, she had pleaded a vague indisposition. Only Gerald she admitted to her company.

Every evening he read stories to her from the parchment pages of the leather-bound book. Between the covers, in the scribe's clear hand, were his favourite tales of heroic feats, brave warriors, powerful kings, of cattle raids and swordplay, the legends of ancient Ireland, of Finn Mac Cumhail, Oisín, Oscar, Ferdia, and the Hound of Ulster, Cú Chulainn. The boy reminded her of her father and his absorption in scholastic as well as military pursuits. In his daily visits to her apartments, Gerald also brought her news of the happenings within the castle. Many of the earl's allies, he told her, stayed on at Askeaton, negotiating the numbers of fighting men, supplies and weapons they intended to pledge to the league.

For the present Desmond seemed anxious that she should remain too, her presence being of some intangible use to the wily earl. Perhaps, as Leverous had said, as a sheen of Kildare approval for the league. But whatever his reason, Eleanor knew for certain that it was not out of concern for Gerald's welfare. It was blatantly obvious that Desmond's welfare took precedence over everything else, and for that reason, she knew she must remain as a buffer between Desmond's ambition and her nephew's safety. She had given her word to Gerald and to Leverous.

To her dismay, Manus O'Donel also stayed and had made several attempts to meet her, which was the main reason for her self-imposed confinement within her chambers. But it was not the only reason. For Leverous also remained, stubborn in his determination to fulfil her brother's wishes, regardless of Desmond's unfriendly hints. She felt it was but a matter of time before the earl made his wishes plainer. He might well have dismissed Leverous before this if it were not for the undoubted reliance and affection that her nephew had for him. And Desmond would be reluctant to be seen to thwart the expressed wish of her brother, made public by Leverous at the meeting, lest it alienate support for the league. She shuddered when she recalled Leverous's brave, if foolhardy, interruption in Desmond's great hall. She thought that the earl had surely signalled Leverous's end when she saw the gallowglass captain go for his skean. Leverous would have proved easy prey for the professional warrior.

But Desmond was unscrupulous. What he could not have by persuasion, he might well seek by violence. Eleanor felt a stab of fear. She had avoided Leverous, afraid of where another encounter might lead them. Their brief embrace had roused memories and feelings that, despite their years apart, were still alive no matter how deeply they had buried them. But her feelings for him were further complicated by the continuing presence of her son.

For Cormac also remained, deciding to negotiate his biannual dues with Desmond, rather than incur the expense of a *cuid oiche* for his overlord and his vast retinue later in the year at Carbury. Gerald's chatter had confirmed her fears of his developing friendship with Leverous.

'Leverous and Cormac went boar-hunting. In the woods near the Maigue,' Gerald had told her. 'Both speared the boar at the same time,' he reported, his eyes bright with envy.

To Gerald, like any boy of his age, everything was a game. The moving from Donore to Carbury and from there to Askeaton. The attention of so many, from chieftain down to the lowliest kern, all anxious to have some hand in the protection, training or entertainment of the Earl of Kildare's son, the new high king in waiting of Ireland. Eleanor had tried to explain to him the political plotting being done in his name, in a way that did not create anxiety or fear. Her nephew had experienced little stability in his young life. The momentous political designs being woven around him were as well left to the weavers. That he was safe from the clutches of the butcher of his family and his agents in Ireland still remained her only concern. The fact that his safety and freedom now seemed destined to be intertwined in an international conspiracy, rendered her powerless to ensure her nephew's long-term welfare. But she had given Leverous her word as guarantor of Desmond's intent, and as long as her nephew remained in Desmond, so would she.

Gerald was still seven years from his majority and, as a minor, had no control over what was being plotted in his name. Eleanor had long enough experience of Irish politics to realise that her nephew's welfare, regardless of Desmond's high-sounding ideals, would be secondary to the earl's political aspirations. But there was little she could do. Her brother's last request to have his son sent to France was no longer attainable. In the present circumstances, the league seemed the only option. But it was now more imperative than ever that Gerald should have others to ensure that what was being plotted in his name would not be at the expense of his safety. And in this there was no one she could trust but Leverous. Each participant in the league, no matter how loudly they proclaimed their loyalty to her nephew, acted from a sense of self-preservation. To the Irish chieftains and lords, the league filled the void created by the fall of the House of Kildare, as a buffer between them and the English. The child's fosterer, her brother-in-law The O'Carroll, was also rendered powerless to effect his obligation to his foster son, by the proximity of his lordship to that of Gerald's most committed enemy, his aunt, the Countess of Ormond. Of all the participants, it would be to her taciturn cousin O'Neill, reluctant supporter of the league, to whom Eleanor would be inclined to turn, should Gerald's safety warrant it.

She felt cowardly to have isolated herself from the problems that beset her. It ran contrary to her nature. She had always preferred to face a problem squarely, believing that if nurtured, it grew. But in this there seemed no easy solution. As she had feared, Gerald's safety had become inextricably linked with the one secret she knew she could never face. She wished for Leverous to be gone far away out of her life and just as eagerly wanted him to stay, so that she could be near him, that his presence and the occasional glimpse she caught of him from the loop windows of her self-imposed prison might sustain her and fill the need his presence aroused in her. On the other hand, Gerald's casual remarks about his developing friendship with Cormac filled her with foreboding.

The friendship between Cormac and Leverous had been an instinctive happening. She had intercepted the look that had passed between them at their first encounter in the snow at Colaughtrim wood. A quizzical glance of recognition, as if they had met before. It had haunted her since. Perhaps if she spoke to Desmond and urged him to complete his negotiations with her son, Cormac might be inclined to return to Carbury sooner.

She sighed and opened the leather covers of the parchment pages in her lap. It told of the epic story of the *Táin*, the Great Cattle Raid of Cooley, the most popular of all

215

Irish sagas. She had promised Gerald that they would read it today, or part of it, she thought, as she leafed through the pages, idly glancing at the familiar passages.

It was early afternoon and warm sunshine poured through the south-facing window of her chamber. Eleanor stretched her back and basked in its rays, feeling the warmth on her face and shoulders, relieving her anxiety. The winters were long and cheerless. She was glad of the approach of summer.

She heard Gerald's steps climbing the spiral stairway leading to her chamber and she opened the door. The smile of welcome froze on her face. Behind her nephew stood Manus O'Donel.

'Look, the Lord of Tirconel picked these in the orchard for you,' Gerald said, extending a bunch of purple orchids towards her.

Absentmindedly she took the flowers, her eyes fixed on the handsome features of O'Donel whose blue eyes stared with brazen sensuality, making her skin crawl as it had in the days of torment at Maynooth. Involuntarily she backed away from him but he did not appear to notice.

'Why not look in the kitchens for a flagon for your aunt's flowers?' he said to Gerald, his eyes unmoving from her face.

Gerald looked towards her for permission. Before she could deny it, O'Donel's voice intervened. 'Let him go.' The words were spoken quietly with a clear undertone of intimidation that carried a promise of some hidden threat.

Gerald, perplexed by the strained, unfriendly atmosphere he detected between them, waited for her to speak. For a moment Eleanor felt the panic rise within her and wanted to pull Gerald inside and slam the door on the insolent face behind him. But with an effort she smiled at her nephew and bade him not to delay. Clutching the flowers, Gerald scampered down the steps.

O'Donel made towards her chamber. Resolutely Eleanor barred the way. 'What you have to say, you can say it here,' she told him in as steady a voice as she could muster.

He shrugged. 'As you wish. Though 'tis a shame to risk a secret that you have hidden so well for nineteen years.'

An iron band seemed to constrict her heart. Her lungs inwardly gasped for air. Outwardly no sign of the shock that made her reel within was immediately apparent. She steeled herself so that it might not transfer to her face. But for a fleeting moment, the turmoil within her escaped and flashed like a lighting bolt across her eyes and was exposed and registered instantly by the perceptive eyes of the Ulster chieftain. Like a hound to the scent, that glance of fear gave him the remaining proof that he had trapped his quarry.

Eleanor's heart hammered within her breast. For nineteen years, her secret had been concealed, Now in a single second it lay naked before the probing of this odious creature. Always at the back of her mind the spectre of discovery had haunted her mind, and she expected that someone, some day, would confront her with the truth. Who it would be and under what circumstances she had often speculated. Leverous, Cormac, one of the MacCarthys having stumbled across a hint of gossip, a loose comment, seemed the most likely. Manus O'Donel, the tormentor of her girlhood, she had never even thought to see again.

'You know nothing of me.' Her words sounded strident and forced.

'I know more about you than you can ever imagine.' O'Donel looked at her with a familiarity that both embarrassed and incensed her. 'I do not concede easily. As no doubt you recall.'

'I loathed you then, O'Donel. The years have not changed my preference.' The intensity of her words surprised even herself.

But O'Donel seemed indifferent, even amused. He stepped boldly past her into the chamber. His eyes took in every detail with a sweeping glance, coming to rest on the canopied bedstead, the curtains of sea-green damask drawn back. His eyes lingered on the bed before turning to look at

217

her as she stood outlined against the brightness of the sunlight that poured into the room.

The passing years had hardly touched her, he noted; if anything, they had made her more desirable, ripened and matured her in a way that made his pulses pound. He would have her this time, by God, and there would be no Great Earl nor lowly lawyer to stop him. Fate had led him to stalk the lovers' trysts at Thomas Court and had rewarded his persistence. He had made many conquests since the far-off youthful gropings in Maynooth. In England, France and Italy, he had set about tuning his natural sensuality, as another might enhance one's appreciation of art, of literature. He had been tutored by the best, from brothel to boudoir. His good looks, the raw magnetism his body exuded, his youth and agreeable charm, had brought to his bed virgin and widow, harlot and lady. Strange, he thought, that she, the only failure in his list of conquests, should still torment and entice him.

'My attempts for your affection in Maynooth were the clumsy efforts of youth, green and untutored in the ways of love. But, my lady, my desire was sincere. I swear it. As it is now.' His voice was heavy. His handsome face was flushed. The blue eyes burned with an arrogant desire. He laid his hand on her shoulder. Eleanor recoiled from his touch.

'And my aversion to you has also remained unchanged.' Her hazel eyes were bright with angry pride and a revulsion that both astonished and aroused him.

O'Donel had not realised the depth of her distaste. He presumed that she had repelled his advances before from a sense of immaturity, of inexperience, the shyness of youth. But it ran deeper than he thought. He had never been refused before and it made the anticipation of her submission to his will and her taking all the more pleasurable.

Eleanor turned her back and stared out of the window. She pressed her arms against the window ledge. The cold stone absorbed the moisture in her hands and composed her racing mind. What did he want? What did he know? She caught her breath as below her in the courtyard she saw Cormac and Leverous emerge from the shadows of the castle, talking easily together. In the bright sunlight they waited as the horseboys brought their hobs from the stables.

A hand was placed on her shoulder and an arm pinned her and prevented her from turning. She tried to avert her head, but O'Donel locked his face against hers and the hard stone. The harsh sound of his breath was loud in her ear. She felt his breath on her face. He followed her gaze to the men below.

'Father and son. What a pleasing picture. Reunited after all these years.'

She tried, but could not control the shudder that shook her body from head to toe. He had trapped her again. His half-whispered words made her ears flame.

'I long suspected your desire for the tutor. Whatever would the Great Earl have thought?' O'Donel mocked. 'The son of The O'Donel he deemed not good enough for his lovely daughter. What chance a humble tutor in the Kildare matrimonial market? Love will have its forward way but, alack, must pay the price. MacCarthy was old enough to be hoodwinked. Cuckolded. But not I, my sweet, not I. Thomas Court may have kept the secret of many trysts in its chequered past but happily not yours.'

She twisted out of his grasp. Her breath came in strangled gasps. 'What do you want of me? I have never harmed you.'

'Nor ever loved me, yet.' The blue eyes shone with taunting pleasure. He was enjoying her agony, her denigration, the power he commanded over her.

'Nor ever will.' Her reply was fierce.

He shrugged. 'Then it will be your loss. My time in France has not been wasted. I could bring you close to the very stars. Or further for certain than MacCarthy or Leverous have ever taken you,' he laughed softly. 'Like this.'

In a single catlike movement he held her face between

his hands in a vice and kissed her long and hard so that she struggled for breath as much as to escape. He pushed her against the wall, his breath rasped in her ear. She felt his hand move slowly down the length of her neck, her shoulders, to her breast. His body pressed urgently into hers. A rage swept over her and with a sudden heave she pushed him from her. Her hand lashed his face before she realised she had even raised it. A red welt spread slowly across his cheek. He stood and looked without expression at her. Calmly he caught her hand in his and raised it to his lips, his eyes never leaving her face. Suddenly he crushed her limp hand in his, making her cry out in agony. His voice hissed in her ear, all pretence of languid teasing gone.

'Listen well, my lady. I know your secret. Your son will exchange his chieftain's cloak for a woodkern's rags should the MacCarthys find out that he lacks an essential ingredient to be their chief: MacCarthy blood. And Leverous, he will hardly thank you for keeping his son from him all these years, while he mooned for you like a love-sick calf. The shame attaching to you, to have perpetrated such deceit, will be written into the annals to besmirch the name Kildare forever.' His hand intensified the pressure. 'Unless, of course, you accept my proposal.'

'No.' Her cry was a mixture of pain and revulsion.

O'Donel fell back a few paces in mock surprise. 'Do not flatter yourself, my lady. My proposal is of a business nature. There is no shortage of women to fill my bed, without coercion, I promise you. My proposal is of a union of mutual convenience. Like your marriage to MacCarthy,' he taunted, 'politically expedient for me, essential for you. As the new chieftain of Tirconel, my position needs a boost, preferably at the expense of O'Neill. Marriage with the Earl of Kildare's daughter bears some prestige yet. Enough at least to break O'Neill's stranglehold in Ulster. You know my loyalty to the Geraldines is total,' he mocked. 'I will be glad to entertain his daughter in Tirconel,' he pulled her roughly towards him, 'in like manner as your father entertained me in Kildare.'

She jerked away from his grasp. 'How dare you threaten me! I will have Desmond throw you out of Askeaton, as my father did from Maynooth.'

'Brave but idle words, my lady. Call it a threat if you will. The price of my silence about your son is your consent to become my wife. But do not despair. It may not be for long. Should the arrangement not be to my liking, after one year we can be divorced. Leverous has waited long enough. Another year will hardly matter.'

Feet sounded on the steps outside and Gerald came into view, holding an earthenware flagon full of the flowers.

'Good lad.' O'Donel's voice was full of light-hearted banter. 'Why not place them on the table, close by your aunt's bed? They will remind her of me,' he laughed, 'in case she may forget.'

He took Eleanor's limp hand and bowed low, his lips caressing her fingers. 'I will have your answer on the morrow.' His voice barely concealed the threat.

Eleanor closed the door quickly behind his departing shadow and leaned against it to regain her composure. Gerald sat by the bed already engrossed in the book of the *Táin*. Eleanor's eyes alighted on the flowers and in a second her hand sent them and the flagon crashing to the floor. Gerald started and looked at her in wide-eyed astonishment.

22

DUBLIN

As Grey entered the city through St Nicholas's gate, the tumult assailed his ears. A soldier drew his attention to a pall of smoke that hung like a noxious vapour in the distance above the tower of Christ Church. People were running from the houses on Rochel Street and Shoemaker's Lane, up the steep incline of Nicholas Street, in the direction of the cathedral. For a moment the possibility of an attack by the O'Tooles flashed across Grey's mind. But regardless of the source of the turmoil, the likelihood of a fire within the city sent a shiver of apprehension through him. Fire was the great hazard, the single most frequent nightmare of any citizenry. And in Dublin, houses, shops and taverns, every structure within the city walls, with the exception of the churches and the castle, were potential torches of timber, plaster and thatch.

Despite the weariness that beset him, Grey dug spurs into the flanks of his horse and cantered up Nicholas Street, his footsoldiers running hard behind to keep pace. His mounted escort shouted a way clear through the people running in the same direction. At the market cross, at the intersection of High Street and Skinner's Row, Grey drew rein sharply, his horse plunging in protest. Behind him his cavalry and infantry clattered to a halt and looked in amazement.

Outside the great iron-studded doors of Christ Church, a huge bonfire blazed. Angry flames of fire licked upwards. High above, the evening sky was darkened by a pall of smoke. The acrid smell of burning filled Grey's nostrils. In the shadows around the bonfire, long cassocked figures, like witches in a coven, cavorted, stooping now and then to throw extra combustibles into the fire, sending sparks skywards. It was like a scene from the *Inferno* of Dante, Grey thought. And as each object was flung into the flames, angry murmurs arose from the citizens who had formed in a circle around the conflagration.

Grey recognised the berobed figure standing on a stool in the light of the fire as that of George Browne, Bishop of Dublin and ardent advocate of the Reformation. His arm was raised high in admonishment; his staccato voice berated the crowd.

'True worship of Christ needs not idolatrous images. Heathen Romish relics do naught but liken you to the pagan. Into the fires of hell, I say, cast every false image that entices you from the path of true worship.'

A collective groan rose from the crowd and many onlookers fell to their knees, their heads bowed, as if they feared some sign of divine intervention. The bishop raised above his head a long bar-like object which glistened in the fireglow. Even Grey recognised the object which Browne was about to consign to the flames. The *Bachall Íosa*, the most revered relic of the city of Dublin. Over one thousand years old, the wooden staff, encrusted with gold and precious stones, was reputed to have been given by Christ to St Patrick in his mission to christianise Ireland. Venerated by generations of Dubliners, the staff was kept in Christ Church, where it was used as a pledge on which oaths were sworn and treaties were made. In times of attack, the citizens carried it as a talisman in procession through the streets.

Grey urged his horse through the crowd. He could not risk a riot, much less a fire within the city. Browne saw him approach and purposely threw the staff into the fire. The flames exploded under the impact. Grey's horse shied away. The mood of the crowd turned angry. They advanced on the bishop.

Grey positioned his horse between them. 'The spectacle is over,' he shouted above the din. 'Return to your homes. There will be no further burning.'

'There is nothing left to burn,' a voice from the crowd replied.

'Return to your homes,' Grey repeated and motioned to his retinue. They fanned out in a circle around the fire. 'Get water and douse that fire,' he ordered.

His determination seemed to quell the anger of the crowd, who slowly began to drift off into the shadows of the nearby streets.

Bishop Browne approached him, the fleshy jowls of his bulldog countenance quivering with rage. 'You hinder the work of the glorious Reformation. God's work is not yet complete,' he rebuked Grey, pointing to a small pile of wooden statues and some handsomely carved boxes. 'Images and relics, the tools of Satan.' His eyes burned feverishly in the light of the leaping flames.

'My lord bishop,' Grey could scarcely conceal his dislike, 'my concern is for the present world which, should your bonfire spread, will be of very short duration for all of us.

'It is the king's command to rid this city of all Romish images,' Browne screeched in reply.

'And I tell you, there will be no city left unless this fire is extinguished.' Grey turned away abruptly and signalled to his men.

A shower of sparks exploded into the night as the first stream of water hit the fire. Soon all that was left of the bishop's bonfire were smouldering embers. Grey left some soldiers to guard the blackened remains, in case the fire took hold again, either at the wind's or the bishop's volition.

'The king will hear of your interference, aye, and more

besides,' Browne hissed after him.

Grey ignored him and rode wearily towards the castle. The last person he needed in Dublin was an overzealous church reformer. The citizens should be encouraged to adopt the new reforms, not coerced by having their age-old customs burned before their eyes.

In time he knew Dublin would accept the changes wrought by the king's Reformation, just as London had done. For Dublin was an English city, in language, custom and by political affiliation. Governed by a mayor and corporation, by royal charters and bye-laws, with guilds, pageants, musters, it had all the trappings of an English metropolis. Its population were the descendants of alien stock. Established by the Viking invaders in the ninth century, Dublin had subsequently become the headquarters of the next wave of conquerors, the ambitious Anglo-Normans of the twelfth century. Regular influxes of immigrants, mainly merchants, tradesmen, craftsmen and labourers from England, Wales and, to a lesser degree from the Continent, had swelled its population over the centuries. The citizens of Ireland's capital had little common interest with the rest of the population outside the city walls. Their loyalty was to the crown, whence they derived their protection and livelihoods. But the religious reforms of the king in England had made little headway in the city and, by and large, the majority of the citizens still held to the old religion. But it was Thomas Cromwell's contention that if the citizens continued to share a common religion with the Irish outside the city gates, it could conceivably give rise to an alliance between them based on a shared religion. Whether Cromwell was right or wrong, Grey was certain that the only way to convert the citizens of Dublin was to ease them gradually away from the old beliefs and not, as Browne seemed intent on doing, by forcing the new concepts down their throats.

In any event, Grey had little truck with religion, reformed or otherwise. Priest or parson, the purveyors of salvation were all the one to him; they were, like the leech, to be avoided until unavoidably necessary, on one's deathbed. A convert to the new religion of the king, Browne's methods employed the convert's fanatical zeal. Grey had given the bishop a wide berth since Cromwell had appointed him to the see of Dublin, but he made a mental note to watch his conversion tactics more closely in the future lest they disturb the essential peace within the city. There was enough mischief brewing outside.

He dismounted in the castle courtyard and watched his soldiers lead two luckless kern to the dungeons below, the meagre success of yet another exhausting expedition into the wilds of Wicklow. With irritation Grey saw the stocky figure of his under-treasurer waiting for him at the entrance. He nodded curtly to him.

'I see my lord deputy's latest expedition to Wicklow has borne success at last.' Brabazon's voice was laced with sarcasm.

Grey pushed past him without reply. Exhaustion and hunger lay with equal weight upon him. Brabazon hurried after him down the draughty corridor.

'My lord, a moment please,' he called. Grey stopped in his tracks and, without turning, waited for Brabazon to reach him.

'The Countess of Ormond returned from England – three days past,' he emphasised. 'She bears urgent dispatches from the king.' The crafty eyes of the under-treasurer searched Grey's face for some reaction. Grey forced himself to show none.

'She awaits you now in your office,' Brabazon added and waited for his response.

'That will be all,' Grey told him and turned purposefully in the direction of his office. It was best to confront her now, he reckoned. His exhaustion and stomach would have to wait.

He found the countess in whispered conversation with

Crowley in the ante-room. Crowley rose at his entrance and with a mumbled apology excused himself and faded through the door, leaving the stale odour of conspiracy in his wake. Grey bowed briefly to the countess and continued through to his office.

'I understand you wish to see me.'

The countess followed him, filling the space before his desk like a malevolent colossus, her face displaying her dislike and annoyance.

'Yet another futile excursion against O'Byrne spectres,' she taunted him. 'While the rest of the country plots conspiracy and rebellion, you choose to chase shadows in the Wicklow glens. You seem hell-bent, my lord, on a course of self-destruction.' She lifted her heavy shoulders resignedly. 'But far be it from me to stop you,' she added with sarcasm, throwing a square of parchment on the desk between them.

Grey glanced at the seal which joined the edges. The royal signet was etched deep in the crimson wax. So she had got to the king's ear, as he had never doubted that she would and, from the vindictive look on her face, with some success. He made no move to open the dispatch. Let her wait for her victory, he thought.

She read his thoughts. 'It is to be opened in my presence. The king intends that you will be under no misconception as to your duty this time.' The violet eyes fastened intently on him. Grey knew he had little option but to concur.

The message was written in the king's own hand, an indication of his interest and anger, Grey thought ruefully. As he expected, it contained a stinging rebuke on his record as deputy. Henry's angry words accused him of alienating the Countess of Ormond and her husband, who 'unselfishly acted only to further Our interest in the troubled land of Ireland'. Grey laughed inwardly. Henry was not that stupid but was playing his own game with the unsuspecting countess. The king accused him of leniency towards those who conspired to obstruct his rule and who actively plotted

227

with his enemies in Europe against him.

'But,' the missive continued, 'Our singular disappointment in your stewardship of Our Irish affairs stems from your noted reluctance to execute the commands of Our last dispatch to you to apprehend the son of the late Earl of Kildare, whom We now understand has been spirited away to MacCarthy's country in Our province of Munster.'

The countess had brought him up to date with a vengeance, Grey noted silently.

'Lest there be any misunderstanding on your part, We hereby command that you proceed without delay to the said country of MacCarthy, retrieve the son of the late traitor Kildare and have the Countess of Ormond bring him to Us in England. In your recent dispatch you plead that insufficient men and arms have detained you from undertaking the aforesaid expedition. We are content to accept the offer of the Earl and Countess of Ormond, who at their own cost, will furnish you with a force of five hundred men, armed and provisioned. We trust that this loyal gesture will be fully reciprocated by you, Our Deputy, in the speedy apprehension of the Geraldine heir and prevent Our enemies at home and abroad from taking advantage of Us through him in Our lordship of Ireland.'

There was little ambiguity in Henry's orders. The countess had succeeded beyond all doubt. Grey had hoped that Henry's aversion to the relations of his executed queen, Anne Boleyn, might have prevented the Ormonds from gaining access to him. But Henry had readily submerged his antipathy in exchange for the countess's assistance. Five hundred provisioned soldiers, more than the entire English army in the Irish service! Grey's brow creased in thought. Had the king stopped to think what havoc such an army might do against the crown, should the Ormonds become his enemies? Knowing Henry's agile mind, Grey knew with certainty that he had. But for the moment, the Ormond army was a useful tool to be used to Henry's advantage.

The dispatch, however, left him under no illusion what the king expected of him. There was little more he could do to protect his nephew further from the king's vengeance. And if the countess or her minions got scent of O'Donel's proposal to him in St Patrick's, he would follow his Kildare relations to the scaffold at Tyburn. He hoped to hear no more from Reginald Pole or from his agents in Ireland. Perhaps they no longer needed him in their deranged conspiracy against the king. Perhaps O'Donel's proposal was no more than a trick to implicate him. But, either way, he knew that his Yorkist blood and Kildare connections made him already suspect. The Countess of Ormond's revelations had merely increased the king's mistrust of him.

'I trust the king's letter is as clear as his words were to me,' the countess's voice broke into his thoughts. 'Speed is of the essence now, lest the boy be taken from Carbury elsewhere. I smell the stench of a conspiracy in his abduction. And so does the king.' The countess was emphatic, her power in the ascendant.

'It will take a week to outfit my army for such an expedition,' Grey countered. He saw the countess raise her eyebrow in suspicion. 'But we should be in Munster in three weeks.'

Her eyes seared him as she weighed up his excuse. 'We shall meet at the borders of Ormond two weeks from today. And thence we will proceed without further delay, to Carbury.'

Grey choked on his reply. The damned woman planned to accompany him. 'There is nothing in the king's dispatch that warrants your presence in the expedition. I can assure you, madam, that I am well capable of leading an army without – '

'Capable perhaps, but willing . . . ?' The countess let her words hang in the air and turned on her heel to depart. As she reached the door, she spun around and faced him again.

'You will doubtless rejoice in the news that the king is to

229

become a father again in the autumn. The Tudor dynasty may yet be assured. God willing,' she added, a sardonic smile on her lips.

Grey cursed her softly but viciously under his breath.

SUMMER

23

LORDSHIP OF DESMOND

With shouts and curses, the outriders shepherded the stag away from Kilmore, but just as it seemed they had him faced once more towards open ground, he bolted between them into the outlying thickets and was lost from view within the forest. With bays of indignation, the hounds bounded after him and disappeared from sight amid the dense tangle of undergrowth. The pursuing hunt thundered to a halt at the forest edge. The horses milled about impatiently as the riders discussed tactics to raise the stag. It was decided that they would divide into two groups. The first, which included the Earl of Desmond and Manus O'Donel, elected to patrol the edge of the forest in case the stag broke from cover. The second group, which included Leverous and Cormac MacCarthy, fanned out and entered the forest in pursuit of the stag and hounds, whose excited barking emanated faintly from within the leafy depths.

Leverous was grateful for the brief respite. The stag had given them a hectic chase over the broad plain of the Maigue since they had first flushed it from the cover of a small wood to the east of Askeaton Castle. The blood seemed to course with a tingling energy through his body. He felt exhilarated and renewed. The weeks of confinement, the tense waiting and watching evaporated into the bright sunlight of the glorious summer morning. He needed little encouragement from The MacCarthy to join the hunt, the Earl of Desmond's final entertainment for his guests. Tomorrow, the remaining chieftains would disband, return to their territories and await the return of Robert Walshe from Spain. The chaplain had already sailed from Dingle, a reluctant emissary on the league's behalf to the emperor's court at Toledo.

Despite his continued suspicions of the Earl's motives, Leverous had to acknowledge that the threat to Gerald's safety had receded since their coming to Desmond. The Countess of Ormond had made no further attempt to seize her nephew, deterred most likely by Desmond's undoubted strength. The king's deputy posed a lesser threat. Grey's initial warning signified his reluctance to enforce the king's orders for his nephew's capture. And even if compelled to intensify the search for Gerald, Grey's army was no match for Desmond's, especially in his own territory. Robert Walshe was right: until some other opportunity presented itself, Gerald's safety was best guaranteed in Desmond.

Despite his antipathy to the Earl, Leverous was in awe of his undoubted powers of persuasion and organisation and with the rapidity with which he had managed to set events in motion. One day after the formation of the league, Robert Walshe was embarked on the earl's ship to Spain. The earl spared no expense or energy in entertaining his fellow conspirators at Askeaton, with the notable exception of O'Neill, who with his urraghs, gallowglass and kern had returned to Ulster. It was obvious that Desmond sought to retain the initiative he had won in the great hall of Askeaton and to capitalise on the emotion and enthusiasm the league had aroused. For the earl realised better than anyone that O'Neill's lukewarm response might influence the other participants should he fail to deliver the promises he made regarding Spanish arms and reinforcements. In his experience of the political ethos pertaining in Ireland, Leverous knew that if the earl was successful in eliciting Spanish assistance, he would be strong enough to persuade the sceptics and overawe his rivals. Then the wily earl would be in a position to take full advantage of O'Neill's reluctance, and assume the mantle of absolute leader in Ireland.

But then, Leverous concluded, almost everything about the Earl of Desmond and the hidden world over which he held undoubted sway, tended to astound. Perhaps it was the ease and regularity of the earl's contacts with the Continent, especially with Spain and France, that surprised Leverous more than anything else. He had never set foot inside Desmond's vast lordship before and expected to see a society backward and isolated from the rest of the world. Instead, he found a complex political structure, albeit as different from that pertaining in England as one could find, yet providing structures and laws whereby the people were governed, taxes paid in service and in kind, justice dispensed and, what amazed him most, a society as *au fait* with political happenings on the Continent as the royal court in England.

For at the Earl's harbours of Dingle and Youghal, Spanish, French and Venetian ships, as well as discharging their cargos, brought emissaries to Askeaton from the courts of the continental kings and princes, to confer with the powerful 'Prince of Desmond', as they styled him. If Garret had little inkling of the extent of his kinsman's contacts with Europe, then, Leverous deduced, the king and his Irish council had even less. The trade links between the lordship of Desmond and Europe appeared to be established and regular. The earl's castles and those of his vassals reflected the fashions, furnishings and flavours of Spain and France, paid for in woollen mantles, cask staves, hides, tallow, skins and fish, the produce of the 'Prince of Desmond's' kingdom.

Since Leverous's confrontation with MacSheehy, the Earl seemed inclined to overlook his presence at Askeaton. Perhaps it was Eleanor who had prevailed on Desmond to let him stay and kept him from countenancing more drastic measures against him, Leverous thought ruefully, remembering the dark looks directed at him by the earl's henchmen. But he knew that neither Eleanor nor Gerald's intercession would stay the earl's hand against him, should Spanish help arrive. For then the earl would be the indisputable leader in Ireland, more powerful than Kildare had ever been. He would fear no interference in his guardianship of Gerald, whom he would be free to use as he wished.

What Eleanor thought of Desmond's plot, Leverous had no inkling. She seemed determined to avoid him, remaining resolutely alone in her chambers, refusing his requests to meet. From Gerald, he learned that she was well and had asked often about him. She seemed intent on locking him out of her world and maintain the distance she had set between them, which for that single moment had been bridged in their brief embrace. He was a fool, he had told himself so many times since, to allow himself to become ensnared for a second time. But any intention he had of leaving had been postponed once more on Gerald's disclosure about O'Donel's visit to her chamber and the smashed flagon of flowers.

He had never liked O'Donel. With the Countess of Ormond, O'Donel had been the other blight on his otherwise contented youth at Maynooth. Before him, O'Donel had made no effort to conceal the ruthlessness that lay behind his mask of suave congeniality, the softly spoken voice and agreeable demeanour he adopted towards the Great Earl and his family. Even Garret had been hoodwinked, he remembered, reluctant to believe O'Donel's duplicity, even when confronted with the evidence. But with an arrogant contempt for Leverous's lowly origins, O'Donel allowed the mask to fall before him and bare his hatred of the Great Earl and his family. The Great Earl had presumed that Leverous's animosity to O'Donnel stemmed from some youthful rivalry between them.

But it was in O'Donel's lecherous pursuit of Eleanor that the depth of his passion for revenge over his captor had become apparent to Leverous. And his behaviour was not attributable to a youthful passion, Leverous recalled. For there was no affection in O'Donel's obsessive lust for Eleanor, more a depravity, coldly calculated to terrorise. And he had succeeded, compelling Eleanor to seek protection from his aggression. It was the only time Leverous had reason to be grateful to O'Donel. For out of her initial cry for help against O'Donel, their love had been born. But now O'Donel had returned with the antagonisms of his youth intact. Whether his fixation for Eleanor had also survived, Leverous intended to determine.

His horse picked its way through the undergrowth, densely tangled with fresh summer growth. The sun was high in the sky and pierced the leafy canopy above his head. Shafts of light filtered through the upper branches and dappled the dark moss-covered spaces between the trees. Birds flitted between the branches of oak and ash, their cries sounding loud and alarming. Twigs and bracken snapped underfoot as Leverous rode deeper through the trees. From time to time he caught a fleeting glimpse of his companions among the massive tree trunks. The MacCarthy was somewhere to his left, with The O'Brien and some of the chieftains from the west close by.

A companionable and easy friendship had developed between Leverous and the chieftain of Carbury. There was a maturity, a steadfastness about the young man that bridged their age difference. They were at ease in each other's company, as if they were contemporaries or long-time friends. Almost, Leverous thought, like his friendship with Eleanor, before it became complicated by emotions. He had satisfied Cormac's curiosity about his association with his mother but had felt a fleeting stab of annoyance that Eleanor had erased his memory so thoroughly that she had never even mentioned his name. With some mild prompting, he elicited enough from Cormac to fill in the missing years in her life since she had left him. To all appearances, her life had been happy with MacCarthy, of whom his son spoke with affection and pride.

Leverous ducked his head to avoid a low-lying branch of a huge oak tree in his path. At that precise second his head seemed to explode on his shoulders. He felt himself sliding from the saddle, the reins slipping from his powerless fingers. He lay prostrate among the undergrowth. Through a haze of pain and blurred vision, a large figure loomed above him, blocking out the light. The figure raised his arm which held a large implement. In his semi-conscious state, Leverous tried to cry out. But no sound came from his open mouth. He waited for the final blow. Suddenly there were shouts of alarm and sounds of a scuffle. Bodies crashed around him, accompanied by grunts and an occasional profanity. A shout of pain was followed by feet crashing through the undergrowth. The sound of horses, bits and spurs tinkling, voices, more voices which became fainter and fainter still, until there was silence.

Consciousness came in waves, ebbing and flowing in his mind, gradually making him aware of his surroundings. Someone's hand was laid on his brow. It was soft and cool to the touch and he wished it would remain. He heard muffled voices. The scent of fresh lavender pleased his senses. He drifted back into unconsciousness, into the darkness from which he had momentarily emerged.

It was dark when he opened his eyes. Not the impenetrable black from whence he had come. The soft soothing glow of candlelight pushed back the shadows. He knew it was night. He moved his head on the soft pillow. A thousand darts of pain ripped though his body. Something rustled outside the pool of light and Eleanor's face leaned above him. He stretched up his arms and drew her towards him. She made no resistance and for a moment she lay still on his breast. He closed his eyes. The sense of peace was complete, enclosing them in its embrace. His lips touched her face in a whispered caress. Through the soft linen of her night shift, he felt her heart race in step with his. He wished to fold her tightly to him but his arms seemed unable to respond to his wishes. He whispered her name. She raised herself abruptly from him, a coldness replacing the warm pressure of her body on his. Long strands of hair caressed his skin. Her eyes looked at him with a luminous intensity, revealing for an unguarded moment the look of love, passion and fear he had seen in them before.

'You are back with us, thank God.' Her voice seemed part of the shadows. 'You had us worried.' Her hand stroked his brow. He took it in his.

'Us?'

'Cormac and Gerald. Indeed, all the hunt.' Her hand sought release from his. He resisted and held on.

'And you? Did you not wish for my recovery?' His voice trailed away.

She read his meaning in his unfinished question.

'My God, Thomas, has it come to this? That you could think that I might wish you dead.' She shook her head in disbelief. 'It is as if I would wish myself dead. You are . . . have ever been part of me, body and soul.' Her voice faltered. 'You have never left me but have ever been as close as we are now. God forgive me, I tried to leave you behind at Maynooth but your memory would not leave me.'

She snatched her hand from his and covered her face, as if she could not bear his gaze. Leverous watched her struggle with herself, his love renewed by her disclosure, brought back from the cooling brink of memory to the warm fire of reality. These were the words he had her say when he conjured her memory in his mind, her face, her body, the eyes that mirrored the hidden secrets of her heart, every part of her, over the long years of separation. And now he had heard her speak them of her own accord. The empty vessel of his life was suddenly renewed to the brim. He felt elated, rejuvenated with expectation.

Heedless of the pain in his head, he struggled to rise in the bed, praying silently that in this moment, until now a fanciful illusion, his strength would not fail him. He drew her towards him again. His hand stroked the satin tresses of her hair. She lay against him, unresisting, as if her strength was spent, her resolve breached. Gently he laid her beside him. Her arms crept around his neck and, like children, they clung to one another in the silent wonderment of being together again, fearing that to move, to speak would break the spell. It was as if they lay once more behind the heavy brocaded curtains, under the high canopy of her bed in Thomas Court, shrouded from the troubles that awaited them outside and which for the moment their love kept at bay. Their union then when passion had enveloped them seemed but a physical manifestation of some more profound coupling of the very essence of their beings, a deep affinity of hearts and minds, conceived in friendship, born in love. Was it still there he wondered now, that elusive consummation, or was it the residue of some improbable unrequited desire that had shadowed his every footfall since they had parted?

She lay in his arms without speaking. His hand caressed her body, with a loving sense of rediscovery. Her loose linen nightgown slipped easily from her shoulders. He kissed her and felt the awakening response to his touch. His whisper broke the silence.

'I have imagined, rehearsed this moment. A thousand times in what seems as many years. And now, I feel that anything I might say will make you disappear, make me lose you again.'

Her eyes searched his. This time he saw no sign of indecision or fear, only the tantalising mixture of loving trust that shone from them when they had lain together at Thomas Court.

She placed a finger on his lips. 'Then say nothing,' she said.

240

He kissed her tentatively at first as if testing her response. Beneath his lips her passion answered his, making their breath come in strangled gasps. With the hunger of long denial, the frustration of pent-up sexuality, like a flood undammed, a passion coursed through him, swollen with the irrefutable knowledge that it was she, Eleanor, the spectral being of the imaginary reunions he had conjured during the years they were apart, whom at last he held to him. He wanted to be gentle, to prolong the ecstasy, to wait so that he might transport her with him to the heights above, where he knew instinctively his passion would carry him. But he could not hold back the flood. Beneath him her body melted into his, her lips whispered lovingly in his ear, her hands bound him to her and seemed to urge him on and on. A shuddering convulsion seized his body. From a distance he heard his voice cry out, a shout of triumph and elation.

'My love. Oh my love.' Her voice sounded somehow forlorn, even sad in his ear.

Bathed in sweat, Leverous moved a little to one side and lay still for a moment looking down at her, his passion expended. With a finger he traced the outline of her face and gently kissed her lips. A great tranquillity descended on him, born of fulfilment, the long years of emptiness repleted.

He looked on her face beside him on the pillow, her hair lay spread around her like a silken shawl. He entwined a tendril around his finger.

'I fear I should have been more patient. More gentle.'

She laid a finger again to his lips, her eyes smiled into his, the tantalising lustre of their depths shone in the soft candlelight.

'It was as if the years had stood still, that we were back in Thomas Court,' she sighed. 'Remember the curtains of the bed drawn tight to shut out the world outside. To enclose our love. To evade the parting, the sadness. What children we were then and now.'

He buried his face in her breast to blot out the flicker of

sadness he had seen in her eyes. His hand found hers and instinctively their fingers locked tightly. The warmth of their bodies as they lay together induced in him a most delicious repose.

She kissed his cheek as she might a child. 'So much I want to say to you. To share with you. The debt I owe you, my life . . . Gerald.'

'I do not keep accounts,' he murmured drowsily against her skin, 'except of the countless times I have thought of you.'

'My dearest. Sometimes love demands too high a price.' He heard a sob in her voice.

With an effort he willed himself awake. ''Tis time, my love, that we collected the interest that has accrued. There are no barriers, no appeasement, no bargains to be made, nothing to deter us now. You are free. I have no ties, except that which ties me to you.' He turned her face towards him. His eyes searched hers. Amidst the love that undoubtedly shone, fear lurked within their lustrous depths. He felt the first pinprick of unease.

'Gerald told me of O'Donel's visit to you. He did not . . .?' She shook her head.

'I truly feared you dead, when I saw them carry you in,' she said quickly. He felt his anxiety about O'Donel recede.

'I remember little after falling from my horse.'

'Your assailant escaped,' she whispered. 'You must be careful, Thomas; you have enemies here who resent your association with Gerald. They see you as a barrier to them and their desire to use him for their own means. Promise me you will not antagonise them.'

''Tis hard to be rid of me, as you should know.' His arms tightened around her. He felt drowsy, contented; the pain in his head had receded. 'Who saved me? I recall shouts. A struggle.'

She did not reply immediately and he was conscious of her body stiffening beside him.

242

'It was Cormac,' she said eventually.

Leverous smiled as drowsiness descended upon him. 'Somehow I knew it was.' His voice sounded strangely disembodied to his ear.

Her fingers caressed his head and her lips brushed his. He was vaguely aware of a rustle of clothes and the chill induced by her body moving away from his. He called out to her, deep within his subconscious mind, but he could not be certain that she answered him.

24

ASKEATON CASTLE

Since the first shaft of light speared the sky to the east, Eleanor had found neither relief nor answer to her torment. With a heavy heart she had left the warm shelter of Leverous's body and looked down on his face, pale against the linen covers. For a moment she faltered and almost succumbed to the overwhelming desire to return to his side, draw the bed curtains tightly against the troubles that awaited her outside and feel his arms draw her close. With Leverous lay the means to the happiness that life denied her and seemed set to deny her again. But she was as powerless now to avert the fate that lay in wait for her as she had been nineteen years before. O'Donel expected her answer this day. To become the wife of the loathsome ogre of her youth, to live in close proximity to him, to relive every day her dislike, her disgust, perhaps to share his bed . . . The reality of her plight made her heart pound with dread. How could she endure his touch, even more abhorrent now after Leverous, whose lovemaking had aroused in her emotions and responses that she knew she could never compromise again?

Her mind was in turmoil as she searched for an answer, for a key to unloose the shackles that fast-bound her to O'Donel. This time, unlike her first marriage, she would have greater control over the conditions of any contract. As a widow, it was her prerogative to instruct the brehons. She could have them insert a clause to ensure the termination of their marriage at the end of one year as O'Donel had suggested. But she did not trust O'Donel now and would trust him even less if she were to become his virtual prisoner in Tirconel. O'Donel could and would, she had little doubt, use and abuse her at will. And who would act as her guarantor should he renege on the contract and refuse to allow her a divorce, force her to his bed? Neither her father nor brother were alive to overawe him with Kildare power. Her son was not strong enough. Desmond's only concern was his own ambition and which, in view of O'Neill's apparent reluctance to back him, made O'Donel's support all the more necessary. For all she knew, Desmond might well have encouraged O'Donel to seek her hand to enhance his status in Ulster at O'Neill's expense. And having married his most bitter enemy, she could hardly expect her cousin O'Neill to come to her assistance.

She sat on the side of the bed and dressed her hair, braiding the long tresses. And Leverous, she thought, what in God's name could she say to him, when it would seem that she cast him aside, made a mockery of their love again? This time it would appear to be by her own choice, without the coercion of her father. What could he think but that she sought to demean him further, by marrying the person she purported to revile. And above all others, Leverous could never know the reason for which O'Donel now demanded the ultimate price.

She rose from the bed in agitation, her hair half-dressed, the silver comb falling from her senseless fingers. Last night had happened like the first time at Thomas Court. The same uncontrived attraction leading instinctively to its natural conclusion. She loved Leverous, had always loved him, of that she was no longer in any doubt. But the fruit of their love, which should have bound them further, ironically must now force them apart and force upon her a choice that, no matter which way she choose, could bring only heartbreak. Cormac or Leverous. She knew the choice Leverous would wish her to make. She knew him, the inner soul of him, as well as she knew herself. They were one, would always be one, and neither political necessity nor blackmail could ever change that fact. But the decision which O'Donel forced upon her would surely and irreparably shatter his love for her, a love that miraculously had survived one deception, but which must surely succumb to the second.

Yet even in her anguished state of mind, she realised that, regardless of O'Donel's blackmail, she had already compromised Leverous. She had deceived him from the very moment she concealed from him that she had borne him a child, whom she had raised as another's. The temptation to tell him was overpowering, to share the joy and the sorrow of Cormac's birth with him. He would be happy and proud that Cormac was his son and perhaps, from the instinctive affection she had seen develop between them, not overly surprised. But as O'Donel said, he would also feel duped and slighted that she had denied him the right to know his own son.

'Leverous, what have I done?' she whispered fearfully, as the full guilt of the double deception she had practised on him made her cringe with remorse.

She must see him alone before she gave her answer to O'Donel, before the tidings broke and Leverous might hear it from a stranger. She owed him that at least. Perhaps that instinctive knot that bound them to each other might make him understand that the appalling course of action she contemplated was necessary to protect some secret of their love. It was a forlorn hope, but in her agitated state of mind, she could not think of anything better.

Hastily she finished dressing her hair, pinning the braids around her head. In the silver hand-mirror her reflection stared back at her. Her eyes, tired and faintly puffed, were like coals in her pale face. If O'Donel could see her now, she thought ruefully, perhaps he might not want her. It was a vain hope, she knew, for O'Donel's aspirations for her hand sprang from more than a fanciful desire for her. As he had boasted, he could have his pick of women. But his designs on her sprang from a repressed sense of retribution for being taken hostage by her father and confined in Maynooth, of being deemed an unsuitable match for her, his pride further humbled when she had chosen Leverous in preference. But the tide had turned and she knew that through her he would take his revenge. O'Donel had ever sought to dominate her through fear, but Eleanor vowed silently, as she closed the door of her chamber, he would find her changed from the young girl he had terrorised in the dark shadows of Maynooth.

The castle courtyard teemed with activity, as the chieftains and their retinues prepared to depart to their far-flung lordships. Horseboys darted hither and thither with the mounts of their respective lords. Voices shouted orders and farewells. The chaos and numbers were augmented by those arriving to participate in the first outdoor festival of the season, the *aonach samhraidh*. Eleanor paused in the morning sunlight and scanned the milling throng for sight of Leverous. Behind her, footsteps sounded on the stairway that led from the castle to the courtyard. She turned hopefully. Conor O'Brien, chieftain of Thomond, emerged into the sunlight, followed by The MacWilliam of Mayo and the dark swarthy chieftain of the seafaring O'Malleys.

O'Brien's eyes lighted on seeing her. 'My lady, a vision to brighten this fine summer morning.'

The two chieftains from Mayo inclined their heads in her direction, their soft western brogues mingled in greeting.

'We were saddened in the west to hear of the Tudor king's butchery against your brothers. *Marbhfháisce air!*'

'Aye, and 'tis the like English savagery that creates such unholy alliances in Ireland,' O'Malley added, looking across the courtyard.

They followed his gaze to where Manus O'Donnell was in deep conversation with Ulick Burke.

Eleanor felt her blood run cold, as the reality of her plight confronted her once more.

'*Aithníonn ciaróg ciaróg eile*,' O'Brien intervened. 'Maybe the Earl of Desmond will whip them into shape.'

''Twill take more than Desmond to change these two, as we know in Mayo,' O'Malley replied.

MacWilliam nodded in agreement. 'If it is not Burke from the south,' he explained to Eleanor, 'it is O'Donel from the north. Like locusts they swarm over us and bleed us bare.'

'Perhaps the new O'Donel will be different,' O'Brien offered.

MacWilliam spat into the dust. 'What's in the marrow cannot be taken from the bone.'

Eleanor listened to their conversation, her eyes fixed in dread on O'Donel. She felt she was being observed and caught O'Malley's look. Brown eyes, crinkled against the sunlight, appraised her shrewdly. A burly man, his powerful physique reflected his nickname, *Dubhdara*, Black Oak. His craggy face seemed to have felt the lash of every wave over which he had sailed. The gold ring in his ear conjured the exotic seafaring world to which he belonged. Unfettered by the bonds that bound his landlocked contemporaries, the O'Malley chieftain showed the confidence and fearlessness of one accustomed to face perils greater than man's petty squabblings. Eleanor could imagine him at the helm of his galley, his eyes on the horizon, feet planted firmly on the deck above the heaving waves. She had heard her father speak with admiration of this pirate-trader from the remote west who acknowledged no overlord but who steered an independent course through the weft and warp of Irish dynastic struggles.

O'Malley shifted his gaze from her to O'Donel and Ulick Burke. 'Desmond must have some hold over them if he thinks he can mould them to his way. I'd sooner trust the devil than either of them. With no dishonour intended to you or yours.' He inclined his head towards her.

'None taken,' Eleanor replied truthfully. She had little inclination to defend Burke, cruel abuser of her sister, whom he had deserted after their marriage for his own first cousin, without the benefit of divorce or any provision for her welfare, until the Great Earl had, by laying siege to his castle, compelled him to fulfil his contractual obligation.

'Well what's done is done.' MacWilliam shrugged his shoulders beneath his chainmail jacket. 'We have pledged ourselves. 'Tis an opportunity, perhaps, to put our differences aside. Your brother's death,' he said to Eleanor, 'put paid to such hope before. The new Geraldine is but a boy, but he bears the same blood and he has my allegiance. But God speed the day when he is old enough to grasp the Geraldine saltire in his own hand.'

'Amen,' O'Malley said.

'Provided he stays free of the clutches of the Tudor dragon in the meantime,' O'Brien added.

'Well, he'll be in little danger in this pile, for sure,' MacWilliam said looking around the towering walls and towers of Askeaton.

'Provided there is no danger within,' O'Malley said under his breath and glanced quickly at Eleanor.

'Well, O'Malley,' MacWilliam slapped his companion affably on his broad back, "tis time we made a start, if that ship of yours can find its way back to Mayo?'

O'Malley smiled wryly at his companion as if well used to MacWilliam's banter.

O'Brien laughed. 'When O'Malley can ply Biscay and beyond, from Desmond to Mayo will be but a skip.'

They bid Eleanor farewell and sauntered away, but O'Malley suddenly retraced his steps. There was something about him that reminded her of her father, the Great Earl. The same sense of power, of indestructibility, she thought.

O'Malley regarded her in silence for a moment as if undecided what to say. 'These newfound allies of the young Geraldine . . . take care they do not use him badly. This league may be but a ruse to hide more devious ambitions. I have talked with your nephew's tutor.' He glanced around at the milling crowd in the courtyard. 'He seems to have the boy's welfare at heart. For unlike the others he has nothing to gain. Fortunately for him, your son was near him at the hunt.'

'It was provident,' Eleanor murmured in reply. There was silence but she sensed O'Malley had not finished.

He cleared his throat and looked beyond her into the distance. 'I admired your father and your brother, and what they tried to achieve. In my travels, I have seen their vision a reality in other countries. But alas, my lady, Ireland still bears the curse of Cain, brother against brother. And despite this league, I fear it will continue to be so. For Desmond is no Kildare, though they may be sprung from the same stock.' He looked at her keenly. 'I would have given my loyalty and my ships to your father and brother, you know.' He shrugged his massive shoulders. 'However 'tis water beneath the bow now. But perhaps some day I can be of help to their kin.'

From around his neck O'Malley took a chain, on which hung a silver horse, wrought in the most exquisite filigree Eleanor had ever seen. O'Malley placed it in her hand.

'Should you ever need a friend in the west, my lady, send this to me in Mayo.'

Eleanor thanked him softly and watched him disappear with swinging gait among the crowd. She looked at the delicate token in her hand.

'Thinking of life on the sea?'

She swung around. O'Donel's sardonic face was at her side.

'Not with a pirate, I hope.' His smiled mocked her. 'We have galleys aplenty in Tirconel. Should you fancy a trip on the brine, I will gladly be your mate. How goes it with your other mate? Has the blow to his head made him realise his station? Leverous has always had a tendency to fly too high.'

She turned on him furiously. 'You devil's spawn, O'Donel. You had a hand in it.'

He laughed in her face. 'Waste my time on such a lowly target! Come, come, my lady. Give me more credit. There are others who want your lover dead. Sad, but then the daughter of the Great Kildare should have known her place, even if her lover did not know his.'

She turned abruptly from him, but he caught her by the arm, his fingers biting deep into her flesh.

'I want your answer.' His voice was harsh.

'Unhand me.' She jerked her arm violently from his grasp. Like a bully thwarted, he was momentarily taken aback. 'You will have my answer in my time,' she said and stalked away.

'This day,' she heard him call after her.

The encounter fuelled her anxiety to find Leverous before O'Donel, with sadistic pleasure, could flaunt their imminent marriage before him. She hurried across the courtyard towards his chamber in the east tower, through the throng of chieftains, their tanists, gallowglass and kern. She was stopped by familiar faces in the crowd, who wished to talk of her father, Garret, Tyburn, of the league. She smiled, acknowledged their greetings and answered their questions as briefly as she could. She felt a hand tug her dress.

'I waited by the solar as you said. Are we not to go to the fair in the village. You promised.' Gerald's eyes looked up at her with reproach.

'*A stór.*' She forced her voice to sound unconcerned. 'I completely forgot. So many people, all wishing to talk of you.'

'I know none of them but you and Leverous. If Leverous dies, then all I know will be you and Cormac.'

'Leverous will not die,' she assured him quickly.

'But someone tried to kill him. I saw them carry him in.'

'Do not fret.' She hugged him. 'Leverous is recovering now.'

251

Engrossed in the problems that beset her, she had forgotten Gerald and the trauma that he had so grievously suffered. Without warning his world had been turned upside down. Leverous was the one semblance of normality he could cling to. All others were strangers to the boy, including herself, she realised.

'I know,' she said brightly. 'Let us find Leverous. Then we shall all go to the fair. Come along,' she said, continuing towards the tower.

'But he is not there,' Gerald called after her. 'I saw him leave with Cormac. Perhaps they went to the fair,' he added hopefully.

Eleanor's heart skipped a beat in apprehension. Wherever Leverous went, as if by a magnet, her son seemed drawn to his company. It was as if some genetic attraction was at work, forging an inexplicable bond between them. Impatiently, Gerald dragged her by the hand in the direction of the tower gate. Eleanor let herself be led, anxiously scanning the faces in the crowd.

They crossed the wooden drawbridge, amidst a logjam of mounted men, carts and wagons, a continuous stream of people on foot, entering and leaving the castle. They walked along the rutted track which led through a row of thatched cabins, stretching in a line like a string of amber beads.

On a green common, bordered by willows and larch trees, a blaze of exotic colour met their eyes. Awnings of azure blue, mad red, primrose yellow and russet brown, covered rows of stalls and tents from which an inner glow of colour radiated. Merchant and hawker, as colourfully garbed as the awnings that sheltered them, called out their wares in a babble of mixed tongues and accents. Around them the saffron shirts of the Irish milled about or pressed close to the stalls which displayed the more enticing wares.

The tangy aroma of ginger, cloves, pepper, spices from the Orient, assailed the nostrils. Great bolts of crimson satin, indigo velvet, translucent shades of raw silk, fringed lace and fine taffeta from Venice and Genoa, were measured for those lucky to afford them. Painted glass from the Low Countries vied with the peaked shoes of finest leather with points and laces of silver. Further down the line, less exotic merchandise was offered by the traders from Limerick, Cork and Waterford. Irish mantles and blankets of the finest wool, rolled ells of fine Irish linen and the finished cloth of England. The sound of harp and pipe lulled the customers into a festive spending mood.

Gerald whooped excitedly and went running towards the multicoloured booths. He beckoned Eleanor to a stall that had captured his attention. His eyes were affixed on the merchandise within, with the uninhibited delight of a boy. Within the booth the sallow-faced owner cajoled his customers with Spanish exclamations and much gesticulation. Nonchalantly he flexed the gleaming silver blade of a Toledo sword with a wonderfully curved hilt. With a rapid flick of the wrist, like a magician, he extracted from within wooden boxes, lined with pale tangerine satin, evil-looking daggers, their blades hooked in the Moorish style and hilts rich with silver filigree. Before his mesmerised audience he dangled silver spurs, rich inlaid harness, gilt jesses and bells, fit for the falcon of a king.

Gerald's eyes glowed in appreciation. 'Look, Aunt,' he said pointing to a fine leather bridle, 'for the hob my Lord of Desmond gave me.' His eyes pleaded.

She could not resist and indicated to the smiling Spaniard to give it to him. Gerald clutched his prize with unconcealed pleasure and skipped along by her side. She would have given much to have shared his pleasure, to have dallied and indulged him, but her mind was elsewhere. She urged him along, resisting his attempts to divert her towards the varied and colourful items that bewitched his eye at every step.

Their way back to the castle was blocked by a crowd who had gathered in a circle. As she scanned the faces for Leverous and her son, her eyes came to rest on a crouched figure in the centre. Seated on an large boulder, a harper played a merry tune, his long-nailed fingers plucking the wire strings with dexterity. The sound was pleasing, gay and carefree and she paused to listen. The itinerant harper raised his head from the strings and for an instant caught her eye, before letting his gaze alight on Gerald, who stood by her side. There was something familiar about the narrow face, but she forgot her fleeting perplexity and continued towards the castle, certain that neither Leverous nor Cormac were at the *aonach*.

In the courtyard, the visiting chieftains were mounted on their horses, waiting in a circle around the stairway leading from the main tower. Servants went among the horsemen with silver goblets, dispensing the *deoch an dorais*, the customary drink of departure. The Earl of Desmond, flanked by O'Connor, O'Brien, MacMurrough and Lord Dunsany, appeared on the platform above them. Just at that moment, Eleanor felt her arm being taken in a strong grasp and O'Donel's voice hissed in her ear.

'Our allies await to toast the Geraldine before they depart.'

He reached out towards Gerald, who sidestepped O'Donel's grasp and, with a look of dislike, stood his ground beside his aunt.

'Then you bring him,' O'Donel told her with a look of annoyance at Gerald and strode before them towards the platform.

'Ah, Lady MacCarthy,' the Earl of Desmond advanced to meet her and lead her up the steps, 'I believe we have cause for a double celebration today.'

She looked at him in bafflement and then beyond him to O'Donel, who smiled in smug satisfaction. In panic she realised what Desmond meant. But already the earl, his hand on Gerald's shoulder, had begun to address the crowd.

'*A h-Uaisle*. Before your departure from Desmond, it is meet that we renew our pledge to the Geraldine League.'

His words echoed off the high curtain walls. 'To protect the young Geraldine from the Tudor king, we are agreed to join in the pope's holy crusade against the heretic. When our allies abroad give us word to strike, let us be ready.' He stopped and indicated to O'Donel, who stepped forward to join him. 'There is no place in our ranks for those who do not give their full support. Despite O'Neill's reluctance, we are confident that behind O'Donel of Tirconel, Ulster will be at one with us.'

There was a murmur of surprise from among the riders grouped before him.

Desmond raised his hand for silence. 'To further solder the links that bind the new chieftain of Tirconel to our league, it is a fitting moment to announce that My Lady MacCarthy, daughter of the Great Earl of Kildare, aunt of the Geraldine, is to marry The O'Donel.'

The words seemed to echo off the high walls and mock and benumb her mind. Eleanor stared in disbelief at Desmond, who smiled wanly in her direction. She vaguely heard the murmur of surprise that rose from the assembled chieftains. The faces of Dunsany, St Lawrence, the allies of her father and brother, looked up in surprise. As if stricken with the palsy, she allowed O'Donel to take her hand and lead her to the edge of the stairway. She looked down and Cormac's face stared back at her in dismay. A movement at the back of the crowd caught her eye. Her heart cried out in agony as she saw the tall figure of Leverous, his head averted, break away from the assembly and disappear quickly through the castle gate.

25

TOLEDO, SPAIN

The two-masted carrack had made a swift passage from Dingle. Staying far out in Biscay, it took full advantage of the northwesterlies and reached La Coruña in record time. Robert Walshe was relieved to stretch his cramped legs on firm ground again. The stench emanating from the cargo of hides and skins induced him to spend the days and nights huddled in a corner of the deck, politely declining the invitation of the Portuguese captain to share his quarters. The fresh air and the cleansing salt spray of the open deck were preferable to the malodorous atmosphere below.

After a brief respite in the hospitable house of the Earl of Desmond's chandler in the busy port, the chaplain felt refreshed and ready to face the second part of the journey. In the early morning he set out, with a guide and two mules, through the moist countryside of Galicia, on the long trek south to the royal court at Toledo.

Galicia, with its small rocky fields, streams that hurried through narrow valleys towards the Atlantic, the sides of its mountains covered with oak and furze, reminded Robert Walshe of the western parts of Ireland. Untouched by the Moorish influence to the south, the landscape retained much of its Celtic origins, the stark stone crosses along the dusty roads, symbols of its later Christian conversion.

From the slate walls of Lugo they journeyed southwards through the meseta and its flat wheatlands, towards the forbidding city of Zamora and into the province of Castile. Crossing the Duero, they followed a well-worn track, busy with traffic, which led them down the steep incline towards the university city of Salamanca.

Dazzled by the golden aura radiating from the stones of the ancient city, Robert Walshe stopped to absorb the familiar sight, his mind bathed in remembrances of youth and the fervent promises he had made to professors and friends to return. But he had not done so until now. Life had taken him to many places but until now not to Salamanca. The view was as he remembered it: the great Roman bridge, punctuated by twenty-six arches, the terraced rows of houses topped by the spires, turrets and domes of the cathedral.

His guide led him through the wide Patio de las Escuelas, dominated by the imposing façade of the university, with an elaborately carved medallion of Ferdinand and Isabella, for whom, with thousands of his fellow scholars, he had lustily cheered on the occasion of a royal visit to the university. The memories intensified as they neared the Plaza de Anaya and the hostel of Santo Tomás, home to some of the multitude of foreign students, including himself. He dismounted stiffly, his tiredness dispelled by the warmth of the welcome, in his native tongue, from the lips of Richard White from Waterford, friend of his student days and now professor of theology at Salamanca.

The remaining daylight hours and a long part of the night he spent in the hospitable professor's rooms, appeasing his friend's hunger for news from Ireland. White was the Earl of Desmond's contact with the Spanish court and had been involved in the earl's previous intrigues with the emperor. He was familiar with the protocol and immediately dispatched the earl's letter by courier to Toledo.

Two days later, fully rested and replenished with food and information, Robert Walshe set out on the final stage of his journey, which led him across arid boulder-strewn hills towards Avila. From there he and his guide traversed the desolate sierras and moved down through red, rolling plains which gave him his first glimpse of the imperial and crowned city of Toledo, seated majestically on a plateau above the Tagus.

Robert Walshe and his companion entered the city through the Puerto del Sol, and made their way through a tortuous network of narrow, cobbled streets, where Christian, Muslim and Jew had once lived together. Long since the burning fires of the Inquisition, with its dual motivation of material greed and religious fanaticism, had suppressed the non-Christian population and with them Toledo's intellectual and commercial greatness. Yet, even now, the place with its tall houses, guarded by iron-worked doors, silent and menacing relics of its rich heritage, clung tenaciously, despite its commercial decline, to its status as Spain's royal city.

They emerged from a web of dark alleys into the sunshine of Plaza de Zocodover, once a Moorish souk and still Toledo's principal trading area. Rising high above the stalls and booths of the market, were the forbidding walls of the royal palace of the Alcazar, his journey's end.

He found lodgings in a street off the plaza and set off for the Alcazar to meet White's agent, a low-sized, rotund Catalan Dominican. The friar promised to expedite his summons to the court and advised him to return to his lodgings and await word from the court.

The summons came two days later, not from the emperor but from the emperor's influential minister, Cardinal Tavera, Archbishop of Toledo. Robert Walshe was received by the slightly built churchman in a dark panelled library, over-looking the reddish waters of the Tagus. The cardinal greeted him coolly, his English stilted, his eyes disdainful. On a heavily ornate gilt table lay the Earl of Desmond's dispatch, which Tavera, with pursed lips, perused in silence.

Robert Walshe looked with curiosity at the aristocratic

churchman, scion of the noble house of Mendoza. Next to the emperor Cardinal Tavera was the most powerful man in Spain. His reputation as a virulent opponent of the Reformation and as the prime mover in rekindling the fires of the new Inquisition, made the cardinal, as Robert White had warned, both feared and hated throughout Spain. No one was safe from the impenetrable secrecy and insidious accusations on which the fires of the Inquisition fed. Instead of Jew and Moor as in the earlier inquisitions this Inquisition was directed against those tainted by the new reforms. As with the previous persecutions, the full force of the Inquisition was directed against the wealthy and those filling high judicial or municipal offices, whose demise would be most rewarding in confiscated property and wealth. A network of spies and informers kept the inquisitors supplied with information, while the cardinal provided the emperor with dubious evidence of heretical activity, extracted under torture, as a way of encouraging him to join the pope's crusade against the king of England.

Without lifting his eyes from the paper before him, Cardinal Tavera broke the oppressive silence.

'Before presenting your case to the emperor, a few formalities.' He spread his hands wide on the table. 'Are we to understand that the Conde of Desmond seeks the emperor's assistance to fight a crusade in Ireland?' The calculating eyes bore into the Irishman.

Robert Walshe cleared his throat. 'That is correct, your eminence.'

'Then are we also to understand that the heresy of Luther is practised in Ireland?'

The Irish chaplain knew he must answer with care. He was being examined by the ultimate inquisitor, before whom many more able than he had fallen.

'My lord cardinal, the king of England has commenced the dissolution of the Irish monasteries. Confiscation of church lands, properties, benefices – '

The cardinal waved his hand impatiently.

'*Si, si*, Frao Walshe. But heretics. What of Irish heretics? The crusade of the Holy Empire is directed against those who have broken faith with God, who refuse to abide by the doctrines of our Mother Church.' His voice rose sharply. 'What methods are employed in Ireland to save God's faith from blasphemy, heretic souls from damnation. The *auto-da-fé* perhaps?'

The Inquisition in Ireland? Robert Walshe blanched visibly. The burning of human flesh in atonement for religious deviation. It was impossible to imagine such a penalty being executed in a country where the punishment for murder was merely an *eric*. If Irish law did not countenance the taking of life as a punishment for murder, roasting a sinner to death for a breach of religious dogma would, in Ireland, be considered preposterous.

'With respect, my Lord, the *auto-da-fé* of which you speak is not known in Ireland, where all are of the faith of Christ.'

'Then,' the cardinal pounced on his reply, 'the Conde of Desmond perhaps seeks the emperor's assistance for material gain? Ours is a crusade, Frao Walshe,' the cold voice admonished, 'not a *conquista*, as in Mexico or Peru. Surely you are not heathens in Ireland?' His smile was condescending.

'No, my lord. But neither are we able to resist those who would wish to make us heretics.'

The cardinal showed no reaction. He pointed to Desmond's letter with a long elegant finger on which a large ruby glowed.

'This Geraldine. If he is the leader of the Irish, why is it the Conde of Desmond who petitions his majesty?'

'The Geraldine is yet a minor,' Walshe explained. 'Until he is of age, the Earl of Desmond leads the league in his name, to protect him from the English king, who seeks to kill him, as he killed his father and his family.'

'*Si, si*, it is very sad.' There was little emotion in the cold voice. The cardinal raised an elegant shoulder. 'But hardly a matter for the emperor.'

Robert Walshe persisted. 'The Holy Father sent dispatches to the Irish lords urging them to form the league. He promised the Irish lords help from the emperor and the king of France.'

A look of distaste flashed across the aristocratic features. 'Be under no illusion, my good Frao,' the cold voice rebuked him. 'It is Spain and the glorious empire on which the success of this crusade depends. It is Spain who will remove the godless darkness that plagues Europe. France will hem and haw and seek to gain political advantage. We have little faith in her promises of assistance. She makes loud protestations of support to the Holy Father, but is hand in glove with the Antichrist in England. But Spain's motivation is one of faith.' His eyes dropped to the letter on the table. 'And frankly, Frao Walshe, I am not satisfied that Ireland's motivation is the same.'

The dispassionate eyes looked at him. If Spanish assistance for the league rested on the recommendation of this aloof, unfriendly intermediary, Robert Walshe thought that the hope of it was doomed.

'But,' the cardinal added with false humility, 'I merely serve the emperor. He will tell you personally of his decision.'

The cardinal rose quickly and made to leave. He turned sharply at the door. A languid smile flitted across the finely shaped features.

'We celebrate an *auto-da -fé* at the Alcazar at noon tomorrow. The emperor will see you after the ceremony. It may be instructive for you to see how we advance the work of God in Spain. Perhaps a lesson to take back to Ireland. *Si.*' With a slight inclination of his head, he disappeared through a door camouflaged in the wall panelling.

A servant ushered Robert Walshe outside into the warm sunshine, a welcome contrast to the chill of the cheerless fortress. He wandered aimlessly through the warren of streets, jostled by the afternoon crowds as they hurried along, his eyes dazzled by the contrast between the darkness of the alleys and the brightness of the plazas into which they led. His mind hardly registered the exotic architecture that surrounded him, a mix of Muslim and Christian, the sumptuous detail of church, mosque and synagogue, artistic reminders of Toledo's chequered history. They passed the ornate exterior of the monastery of San Juan de los Reyes, the paean of triumph to Spain's great rulers, Isabella and Ferdinand, rich with exuberant artistry, the spirit of the age of discovery, exploration and expansion, the positive side of the great monarchs' legacy. On the western wall were iron manacles of Christians rescued from the Moors during the Granada campaigns, silent symbols of man's inhumanity to his fellow man. Walshe thought of the countless wrists and ankles shackled in dank prisons, lost to the living world. Tomorrow he would witness the dark obverse of Ferdinand and Isabella's legacy to Spain: the fires of religious intolerance and human avarice.

He slept fitfully through the night, his rest disturbed by images of fire, dark prisons and skeletal beings. Next morning he arrived at the Alcazar fatigued in mind and body, unable to shake off the sense of grim foreboding which the nightmares had left in their wake. The claustrophobic atmosphere, the noise and heat of the city, made him long for the fresh, open spaces of Ireland. After his audience with the emperor, he resolved to shake the dust of Toledo from his feet without delay.

The Dominican friar waited to conduct him through the grim, endless passageways of the fortress and into a wide courtyard, bounded on three sides by the high apartments of the palace and, on the remaining side, by the Tagus. Tiered seats were arranged on three sides facing the centre, where a large crucifix towered above a raised wooden platform. Before it was a smaller platform with a stake protruding from the centre; alongside lay a mound of faggots.

The friar showed him to a seat on the left side of the square. The spaces beside him quickly filled with tonsured friars and monks. Across from him, a door in the outer wall opened to admit a crowd of chattering citizens, who scrambled to secure the most advantageous view. In the section which faced the centre, sumptuously attired nobles and their ladies leisurely took their places, chatting and laughing, as if they had come to see a play or a pageant. Behind them on a raised terrace, decorated with silken banners, with colourful tapestries draped across the carved balcony, stood an empty throne.

Loud trumpet blasts heralded the arrival of the emperor and his entourage and the crowd rose to its feet. From the distance Robert Walshe could discern a tall, bearded figure on the terrace. As the crowd resumed their seats, a procession slowly emerged from within the fortress. Silken-fringed banners, borne aloft by six noblemen of the royal court, escorted Cardinal Tavera, Inquisitor General of Castile, bedecked in the purple colours of his office, towards the raised platform in the centre of the square. They were followed by a concourse of ecclesiastics in sacerdotal robes who formed in a crescent behind the crucifix. A murmur of anticipation greeted the arrival of the heretics, disgorged from the dungeons beneath, where they had been incarcerated and tortured, some for as long as two years. Their yellow sack-like smocks, falling from neck to knee, were embroidered with a crimson cross and liberally garnished with emblems of devils and leaping flames. Pale and emaciated, they blinked in the unfamiliar light and dragged themselves along as best their injuries and disabilities allowed. As they passed close by him, one of the prisoners lifted his head and for a moment a pair of eyes mirrored the horrors already endured and the naked dread of the ultimate torment ahead. In helpless shame, the Irishman shut his eyes to the agonised look of the victim.

Silence descended on the attentive crowd as the inquisitor-general rose to his feet. From a parchment he read the list of heretical activities of which each prisoner stood accused. Six were taken from the group and returned under guard to the dungeons, condemned to be reconciled with the church through a further period of incarceration, confiscation of property and denial of secular privileges. The two remaining were adjudged to have insufficient defence for the charges brought against them and were, as the cardinal-inquisitor intoned, 'to be purified by fire and faggot'. His verdict concluded, the business of the Church complete, the inquisitor-general and his escort departed in procession, leaving the sentence to be carried out by the secular authorities.

The two prisoners were hustled towards the stake and bound firmly hand and foot. The faggots were piled high around them until only their heads and shoulders were visible. A flaming torch was applied. Mesmerised, Walshe watched the flames creep towards the two figures straining ineffectually at the ropes that bound them. Then the first screams of agony assailed his ears. The acrid stench of burning flesh stung his nostrils. He felt the bile surge in his stomach and ran from his seat into the passage by which he had come.

'It seems the Irish have little stomach for the work of God.' The spare figure of Cardinal Tavera confronted him, a supercilious smile on his face. 'You will follow me.'

White-faced and enfeebled by the spectacle, the chaplain stumbled after the cardinal. The corridors which they traversed were hung with silken tapestries. Soft rugs littered the floor. Barely aware of the munificence of his surroundings, Robert Walshe followed the light steps of the cardinal into a long narrow chamber. A babble of voices momentarily ceased, as the cardinal entered the room. Tavera indicated to Robert Walshe to wait and knocked on a door at the end of the chamber and disappeared within.

The Irish chaplain surveyed the chamber, his eyes dazzled

by a veritable palette of colour. The room seemed to shimmer with satin and silk, to glisten with gold and precious stones on the encrusted raiment and jewellery of noble and cleric. He had accompanied the Earl of Kildare to the English Court, to Hampton and Richmond, but he had never seen such a lavish and animated display of riches. Like proud peacocks, in high pleated ruffs of the snowiest white, the haughty scions of the aristocratic dynasties of Spain preened and flaunted themselves. Gold crosses and diamond pendants gleamed on silk-covered chests, pearl-encrusted doublets brushed against slashed satin pantaloons. Rubies, emeralds, sapphires and diamonds adorned fingers and dagger hilts. The scene was one throbbing prism, shooting rays of colour in every direction. It seemed to him that all the fabled treasures of the new world of the *conquistadores* must surely be on display.

The cardinal reappeared and beckoned him within. The door closed noiselessly behind them. Seated on a raised throne, heavy with ivory inlay, sat a fair-haired man of middle years. His long sensitive face was partly hidden by a curled beard. A moustache covered his upper lip. The chaplain felt the cardinal's grip tighten on his arm, preventing him from moving forward. The emperor was reading intently the Earl of Desmond's dispatch. In contrast to the sheer opulence of his court outside, the emperor's dress was the epitome of restraint. A short, loose coat of soft velvet, trimmed with ermine, was relieved by a silver cross which reflected against the black taffeta of a finely worked slashed doublet.

The Irish chaplain felt his knees buckle slightly, overcome momentarily with the realisation that he was in the presence of the most powerful man in the world, the Holy Roman Emperor, King of the Hapsburgs, the Lowlands, ruler of Burgundy, Naples, Sicily, Spain and inestimable kingdoms in the New World.

After what seemed an age, the emperor raised his head and beckoned the Irish chaplain closer. The cardinal removed his hand from his arm and Robert Walshe went forward, bowing low and in that position waited for the emperor to speak. The guttural tones at first surprised him, but he remembered that this grandson of Isabella and Ferdinand was a native of the German states.

'The Conde de Desmond's envoy is welcome, as ever, to Our court,' he began. 'We are mindful of his loyalty to Us in the past and that We share a common faith. Ireland, like Spain, is a devoted daughter of the Holy Church.' The parchment rustled in his hand. 'But my Lord Cardinal tells Us that God has happily protected Ireland from the wicked heresies that assail us here.' The emperor waited for Walshe's response.

Robert Walshe straightened his back and faced the figure above him. 'That is so, your majesty.'

'And you have no need of the *auto-de-fé*, praise be to God,' the Emperor added with sincerity.

Robert Walshe felt comforted that another shared his revulsion. By reputation Charles was no supporter of the papacy. He had spared neither the pope nor Rome when defending his secular privileges in the past. Only if the proposed crusade was to the emperor's advantage, regardless of his cardinal's exhortations, would the wily emperor be lured into defending the Church of Rome. And from his attitude it appeared to Robert Walshe that, as yet, Charles was far from being committed.

'The Earl of Desmond begs to ask your favour and support in the war he is to wage on the king of England,' the chaplain said quickly, expecting to hear the cardinal interrupt. 'With your majesty's assistance, he will serve to maintain Ireland as an ally of the Most Holy Roman Emperor, an enemy to your enemies.'

The emperor looked keenly at the Irishman, as if balancing his argument against another. The plausible voice of the cardinal intervened.

'Your majesty's commitments are many, your resources

already stretched. Ireland is far distant, the country unknown. The leader of the Irish lords is but a boy of eleven.' A hint of colour tinged the sallow complexion, as if the aristocratic prelate felt humiliated that his advice was being undermined by a lowly Irish cleric.

There was a lengthy silence. The emperor rose from his seat and moved in a leisurely manner to the window. His voice was as unhurried as his movements. A man not prone to act in haste, Robert Walshe reckoned.

'There is much to decide before We commit ourselves against the heretics; much negotiation before the first bolt is loosened. Where there are many parties to a plot, there are of necessity many perils.' He smiled kindly at the Irish chaplain. 'It is said that we Spanish are of the one blood with you Irish. From the time of Milesius, thousands of years ago. A few more months will not deter our reunion.'

Robert Walshe bowed low before the emperor. He must know the emperor's mind regarding the real intent of his own mission, to hear his answer to judge for himself how sincerely it was meant.

'And the Geraldine, your majesty,' he persisted, 'the young son of the Earl of Kildare. The king of England seeks to kill him. He is in need of sanctuary until the threat subsides.'

A look passed between the emperor and his minister, which told Robert Walshe what he wanted to find out. There would be no help forthcoming for Gerald, he knew, even before he heard the evasive response.

'If what the Conde of Desmond says is true – that the Irish are united in the boy's defence – then the boy has little to fear from my uncle. Is it not so?' Charles smiled brightly towards the Irishman and read again from Desmond's letter in his hand.

It was as he had expected, Walshe consoled himself. Despite his overt condemnation of the Reformation, cruelly manifested by the Inquisition, Charles was still in the political marketplace, where loyalty and allegiance were negotiable. While he might make pretence of being about to espouse the mantle of Defender of the Faith, relinquished by his uncle in England, the emperor was as active as his rival François in negotiating with Henry. Perhaps an alliance with Henry might prove more advantageous for Charles than leadership of an holy alliance against him. Whatever alliances would emerge from the intrigue and subterfuge, one thing was certain: there would be no Spanish succour forthcoming to the Geraldine heir until the emperor decided which side he should favour.

'This Irish league,' the emperor broke the silence and addressed his cardinal, 'could yet become a link in a chain that might serve to stretch our enemies to their limit. In Our empire of Germany for instance.'

The cardinal coughed affectedly behind his hand. 'With respect, your majesty, I fail to see your point.'

'As a distraction, my dear cardinal, as a distraction.' Charles smiled knowingly to himself. 'No matter. It is merely speculation. But Ireland presents a tantalising prospect for the future. And perhaps deserves some consideration in her present difficulties.'

Robert Walshe felt his heartbeat accelerate. Was Desmond to get his arms and men after all? The emperor motioned to a scrivener who sat unobtrusively at a slanted desk in the corner and in a quiet precise tone dictated his reply to the Earl of Desmond.

'To the illustrious Conde de Desmond. Your letter and envoy reached Us at Toledo. Your good intent for Our health and the well-being of the glorious crusade on which We shall soon embark fills Us with joy. That We can depend on the loyalty of you and the Catholic lords of your country is a blessed boon to Our cause.

'Touching your requests for Our assistance in your war, We are mindful of your needs in this and will not be found wanting. We will send you further messages when We are more in readiness to send you the assistance that you seek of

Us and of which We send you now a token.

'Until that happy time, I leave you to the protection of God.'

It was the reply of a politician, skilled in diplomacy and expediency, the twin essentials of his office. It offered nothing, but held out the promise of much. To a recipient like Desmond, however, who merely played games with the emperor, as the emperor played with him, it would be hardly enough to elicit support from such dubious and reluctant allies as O'Neill or the lords of the Pale.

To Robert Walshe it confirmed with certainty, as he watched the emperor dip the quill in the silver inkpot, that Christ's teaching had as little relevance to the pope's crusade as it had to the Geraldine League. Power was the common goal of all: pope, emperor, François, Desmond, even Henry Tudor. Where secular and clerical ambition overlapped, the struggle for secular power was hidden behind a screen of religion. Silently Walshe thanked God that the brand of religion espoused in Spain had not reached Ireland. Despite its laxity and disarray, the Irish church had not perpetrated such atrocities as he had witnessed here in the name of God. It seemed to him that Catholic Spain had more in common with the practices of the heretic king of England whom it plotted to depose.

The smell of molten wax filled the room and the emperor pressed a small gold seal into the molten blob.

The scrivener handed the Irish priest the parchment. With a deep bow to the tall figure on the throne, Robert Walshe was ushered out. The eyes of the milling courtiers and emissaries eyed him without interest as he walked from the stifling atmosphere of the Alcazar into the bright sunlight outside.

26

Kilkenny Castle,
Lordship of Ormond

High in her lofty eerie in the south tower, the Countess of Ormond eased her weight in the chair. Since daybreak she had worked on the leather-bound ledgers, turning the parchment pages and, with a fine goose quill, writing her observations on the entries in a clear hand. She felt an inner glow of satisfaction when the long columns of figures, rents, payments in kind – from a bushel of wheat to four score kine, from one groat to a hundred marks – were entered correctly against the name and the amount owing, then totted and reconciled. Inaccurate figurework on the part of her clerks she treated with severity. They knew better than to present for her inspection anything less than excellent. She had been tutored by the best administrator in the business and received from others what he had demanded from her.

She looked out from her turret window over the fertile countryside that surrounded the castle and the city below. The ledgers at Maynooth had been splendid, red morocco-bound vellum she remembered, with the wild boar Kildare crest embossed in gold on the cover. The Great Earl had them specially brought in from Cadiz. Twice yearly, May day and Michaelmas, her father, with some ceremony, removed them from the great iron chest and laid them on the table at the oriel window in his study. There for the space of a month, she painstakingly checked the amounts received against the charges levied on each of her father's liege lords and tenants. The entries ran to hundreds. Her father's *maor* collected the rents and dues from his lesser dependants, while the greater lords and chieftains paid their dues twice yearly to the earl in person. But she entered each payment with equal care, from the most powerful lord to the lowliest tenant.

The Great Earl would come to inspect her work, carefully perusing her neat entries, making random spot-checks on each page, while she held her breath in trepidation, lest he should find a mistake. But he never did. Sometimes in his jovial way he pretended to and would laugh at her dismay. But the admiration, the fulsome praise with which he extolled her talents to her family, to his retainers, was all she wanted in reward. When the last entry was entered and checked, together they closed the heavy ledgers and ceremonially returned them to the iron chest. She would then turn the key in the iron lock and hand it to him.

'Safe as Strongbow's tomb.'

His customary saying rang in her head as she looked down on the walled city below. She pushed aside the sentimentality that had caught her offguard. While her father had finally turned from her, the talents he had nurtured within her had survived her painful dismissal. Ambition, fearlessness in adversity, shrewd judgement of people and events, combined with the requisite subterfuge, needed to manipulate and motivate, were the attributes she had acquired from the Great Earl and which she had since cultivated and tuned to a fine art in pursuit of her own ends.

And with no little success, she thought proudly, looking out over the compact city of Kilkenny, with its high walls and snug rows of tiled houses. Kilkenny was the heartland of the lordship of Ormond. Its great castle rose up from the banks of the Nore in a solid four-sided phalanx of towers with crenellated curtain walls and battlements. It dominated the busy market town that had grown around it. A deep, sloping moat encircled its thick buttress walls.

The countess had put her individual stamp on her husband's city and lordship. The rents and tributes were now properly accounted for. To protect and strengthen the borders of the extensive lordship, she had embarked on a programme of building and restoration of the border castles. She had appointed a marshal to oversee the proper billeting and cessing of troops throughout the lordship, so that she would have a well-equipped force to defend it from attack. It was because of her foresight that she could now provide the king of England with an army greater and better equipped than his own and sustain Grey's soldiers when they arrived from Dublin. Yes, she thought with satisfaction, she had transformed the lordship of Ormond into a well-managed modern state, to the bewilderment of her inept husband and, had he lived, to the certain admiration of her father.

As befitted the daughter of such a renaissance figure, the countess had been mindful not to overlook the cultural life of her city. Beside St Canice's cathedral, she had established the first school in the lordship, for the children of the townspeople. Her castle boasted a library to rival her father's at Maynooth. Indeed, she contemplated with satisfaction, some of the volumes that had adorned the shelves in Maynooth now reposed in her library, salvaged from the ignorant hands of the English soldiers who had paid for their ale in the taverns of Dublin with priceless tomes plundered from Maynooth. Within the castle grounds, the Flemish artisans and craftsmen she had lured from the looms of the Low Countries produced the finest woven carpets and tapestries. Within the bustling, well-appointed streets of the city, silversmiths, brewers, candlemakers, pewterers, innkeepers and shopkeepers plied their trade, safe from pillage or attack. The streets were neatly paved and sheltered under the pillars and arches of the grey, marbled houses of the citizens. Orchards and gardens surrounded the city walls and stretched down towards the swiftly flowing river. The air was fresh and wholesome. Yes, she thought proudly, her city could compare favourably with any in Christendom.

A clatter of hooves on the roadway drew her to the narrow window. Four horsemen dismounted at the bastion which guarded the drawbridge across the moat. She recognised the squat figure of Brabazon. Grey must have shifted himself at last from Dublin, she thought.

A knock sounded simultaneously on the door and Bessie Blount entered, curtseying before her.

'The harper, my lady. He is returned and asks to speak with you.' The Englishwoman's nose twitched with disgust.

The countess glanced out of the window and saw Brabazon lead his horse over the drawbridge.

'Send Master Brabazon to me first. We can hardly expect such an important personage to give place to a mere minstrel,' she added with sarcasm. Her maid noiselessly withdrew.

The countess returned to her seat by the large table. Grey was late for their rendezvous at Leighlinbridge. She had expected as much. Doubtless he had sent Brabazon to present his excuses rather than face her himself. They were so transparent, these men on whom the destiny of lives, kingdoms and civilisations rested. They blustered and blew, inflated with the verbosity, boastfulness and assumed importance of their mission, a screen for the paucity of their abilities. She could read them like a book. All of them: her brothers, husband, Brabazon, the king, Cromwell, even her father, all lacked the female intuition, which if combined with male strength and confidence would make a complete and unconquerable being. But God in his wisdom had apportioned his talents between the sexes and endowed the female with the instinct he denied her male counterpart. For a woman astute enough to have been blessed with the talents of both, the world was her oyster. And for her, for the moment, the world of which she longed to be mistress was Ireland.

The door opened and Mistress Blount ushered Brabazon into her presence. In a quick glance the countess observed the grime and sweaty appearance of the usually fastidious Englishman. It was high time, she thought, that the would-be conqueror experience the discomfort of campaigning in the country he sought to conquer. It all seemed so easy, so clear-cut, when viewed from the comfort of quarters in Dublin. Time indeed that the arrogant Englishman became acquainted with the dusty tracks, the mountain passes, the smoking campfires, the beds on hard rock beneath the dripping rain.

'Pardon my appearance, my lady,' Brabazon gestured with distaste towards his dust-covered doublet, hose and boots. The usually pristine ruff at his neck, she noted, was limp and soiled. 'Your servant insisted that I should attend you immediately.' His voice held a whine of protest.

'I presume that your master's message is more urgent than your appearance.'

'The deputy will reach Leighlinbridge on the morrow. He will await you there.'

She sneered openly in his face. 'My scouts informed me of that fact yesterday, Master Brabazon. I have had your progress since you quit Dublin, or lack thereof, observed. And so it appears that the travail you have suffered in bringing me these riveting tidings is of no account.' Her eyes swept over his dishevelment with unconcealed satis-faction.

'Nay, my lady! My coming hither was to convey tidings that might be to your advantage before your meeting with the deputy.' Brabazon could not conceal his delight at scoring a point over her.

Her eyebrows shot upwards in anticipation. She watched him withdraw a folded piece of white linen from inside his doublet. He leaned over the desk and shook it free from its fold. Two withered petals fluttered on to the open ledger before her. She glanced at them with no especial interest

274

and raised her eyes towards Brabazon awaiting his explanation.

'My lord deputy has recently added a new enemy to the growing list. The Bishop of Dublin, publicly reprimanded by him in front of the entire citizenry, as he went about his duty as minister of the Reformed church.'

'If Grey wishes to stick another dagger in his own back, I certainly will not stop him. What are these?' She gestured impatiently towards the petals.

'Rose petals. Found by the bishop in his cathedral, after he observed a most intriguing meeting there.'

The countess lifted one of the petals from the desk. 'Withered rose petals. Hardly instruments of intrigue or treason.'

'*White* rose petals.'

Something stirred in her brain and impatiently she urged Brabazon to continue. He looked longingly at a chair which stood empty near the table, but the countess gave no indication that he could be seated. Wearily he shifted his weight from one foot to the other.

'The bishop recently had two unlikely converts in his cathedral. Grey and O'Donel, the new chieftain of Tirconel, once your father's hostage, I believe.'

The countess's brow creased in vague recollection of the youth at Maynooth. His precocious personality had amused her father, who had been solicitous of him, treated him as a foster-son rather than a hostage. She had been of an age to curb the youth's obvious forwardness and she had kept him in check easily enough. He had played on the affections of her younger sister, Eleanor, much to the displeasure of Leverous, she seemed to recall. She had found the tutor and O'Donel on more than one occasion brawling like common kern in the dark corridors at Maynooth. Both had often appeared at dinner in the great hall sporting a thickened lip or blackened eye. She had never bothered to investigate their differences, presuming them to be no more than the petty squabbling that afflicted growing boys. O'Donel had gone from Maynooth abruptly with her father to the English court and out of memory.

'Since leaving Ireland, O'Donel has become something of a knight errant, it seems, in England, France, Italy. He is recently returned to assume the chieftaincy of Tirconel. But he did not return empty-handed. He brought a message from the king's cousin, Reginald Pole, to his cousin, my lord deputy Grey . . .' Brabazon's voice cut across her thoughts, 'together with a reminder to the deputy of their common ancestry.' He nodded towards the petals on the table.

The countess's pulse quickened. She picked up a petal and held it between her finger and thumb. A faint scent of perfume came from the velvety texture. She looked expectantly at Brabazon.

'And to seek his assistance in a crusade. Against the king.'

'Crusade.' She laughed hollowly. 'Don't be absurd, Brabazon. Grey's interest in religion is as feeble as his desire to capture my nephew.'

'But put both together, my lady,' Brabazon persisted, 'and it becomes more plausible.'

'You speak in riddles.'

Brabazon sighed and continued. 'To assist the crusade being plotted on the Continent against the king, Pole proposes to set the Geraldine heir up as king in Ireland, Grey to rule in the boy's place until he is of age.'

Her laugh echoed mirthlessly around the room. 'By the Holy Virgin, the absurdity of English thinking on Ireland never ceases to amaze.' She looked witheringly at Brabazon. 'You have no conception of this country, its customs, traditions, its laws. The Irish chieftains would never accept Grey as their leader, no matter how closely connected in blood to the Geraldine or how much it might antagonise the king. For Grey lacks the single essential element, power. With barely enough forces to protect the Pale, Grey would never command the allegiance of lords like Desmond,

276

O'Neill, O'Brien, MacWilliam and the rest. Without my help he is not strong enough even to take on MacCarthy.'

But, she thought silently to herself, Grey's treasonable contact with Pole, allied to his reluctance to capture the Geraldine, would further damn him in the eyes of the king. His majesty must be told of these developments immediately. But she could not leave for England now, not when the Geraldine was within her grasp. She could afford no mistake this time, no vexatious intervention by her sister and her son. Nor by Grey, she vowed. If she sent Brabazon to the king, she would not trust him not to steal a march on her. Besides she needed him to watch Grey. There was only one option. She would have to induce her reluctant husband to undertake the sea crossing to England again.

She sought to throw Brabazon off the scent. 'The likelihood of Grey becoming high king of Ireland borders on the absurd,' she said dismissively. 'His reluctance to capture the Geraldine is sufficient to destroy him.'

Brabazon opened his mouth to protest, but she cut him short. 'Tell Grey I will meet him at Leighlinbridge in two days.'

Brabazon looked at the petals on the desk and made as if to retrieve them. But something in the countess's look stayed his hand and with a curt bow he left.

She toyed with the petals a moment before replacing them carefully within the folds of the linen cloth.

The door opened and Bessie Blount brought in the second visitor of the day, standing as far away from him as the narrow confines of the doorway allowed. The countess dismissed her servant and examined the unkempt figure before her.

The harper's eyes glistened wildly in anticipation of the news he was about to impart.

'You found the Geraldine in Carbury then?'

He shook his unkempt locks. 'No, my lady. In Desmond.'

The countess rose quickly from her seat behind the desk and circled her timorous victim.

'Desmond?' The word cracked like a whip.

MacGrath turned like a scarecrow in the wind to face his inquisitor.

'Aye, my lady. The Geraldine was brought from Carbury by the Lady MacCarthy and the boy's tutor to Desmond, where he remains.'

Desmond. She had not anticipated such a move by her sister and Leverous. Why should they seek Desmond's assistance? Either Carbury had proved an unwelcome refuge or something more sinister was afoot. Brabazon's revelations about the Pale lords and his more recent revelations about Grey and Pole flashed across her mind. The harper hesitantly interrupted her thoughts.

'May it please you, my lady. There is more. The Earl of Desmond has formed a league of all the chieftains and lords of Ireland. They came, one and all, to his castle of Askeaton and swore to save the Geraldine from the English king. Aye and make him king of Ireland.'

The countess grabbed the harper by his shaggy mantle. Her voice hissed into his face.

'Who attended Desmond's meeting? Names. Give me the names.'

Eyes wide with fear, the harper spluttered the names in a veritable litany.

'O'Neill, O'Connor, MacWilliam, O'Brien, MacCarthy, O'Connor, Lords Dunsany, Howth, Baltinglass and others of the Pale lords. MacMurrough, O'Connor Faly, the new O'Donel . . . There were more, but 'tis hard to remember, my lady,' he pleaded to the hard eyes that held his.

She released her hold on his mantle. Her ponderous bosom heaved with anger. She had heard enough to know some untoward and far-reaching plot was afoot, of which she was ignorant. Her fingers drummed the table in an increasing tempo. In light of Brabazon's information, the stink of a conspiracy rose higher and higher. Pole, Grey, Desmond and the common binding factor, the Geraldine.

The harper shuffled his feet on the dry rushes. She flicked her eyes in his direction. Hesitantly he spoke, fearing that his words might provoke a further rage in this formidable woman.

'The Earl of Desmond sent your brother's chaplain to Spain, to the court of the emperor.'

She slammed a fist into the open palm of her other hand. Her brother had left too many loose strings behind him. Leverous and now his chaplain, Robert Walshe. She must cut them off before they could endanger her plans further.

'The Lady MacCarthy, is she still in Desmond?'

'Until she removes to Tirconel, for her marriage with the new O'Donel, my lady.'

The harper's revelation for a moment caught the countess offguard. Her jaw fell in surprise. Her sister to marry with O'Donel? It was as unnatural a union as had been her own. Even if her sister could not endure another year in an empty bed, marriage to the object of her youthful aversion seemed preposterous.

'You are certain of this?'

'I heard the Earl of Desmond announce the news with my own ears.'

The marriage plans of her sister stretched the conspiracy wider. North, south, east and west, even the Pale, under the very nose of Grey, were implicated in a fantastic plot which, if it succeeded, could be fatal to her plans. For if her nephew, supported by the chieftains and Grey, became king of Ireland, it would extinguish her own ambition. What inducements could Desmond possibly offer, she wondered, to make O'Neill sit with O'Donel, MacCarthy with Desmond? And her brother's chaplain dispatched to the court of the emperor. If Charles chose to ally with François, what better way of attacking Henry than through the weakest chink in his armour, Ireland.

The conspirators had chosen the best time to strike at the king. Henry was totally preoccupied by the manoeuvres of his enemies on the Continent, his forces and coffers were already overstretched by the uprising of the northern lords in England and the need for protecting his border with Scotland. Without her support, he was powerless in Ireland. Yes, she thought, with satisfaction, her dispatch to the king would make startling reading. His Irish deputy at the centre of an international conspiracy against him, the Geraldine fugitive still at large, the usually divided Irish chieftains about to unite and ally with his enemies abroad. It was a nightmare that must sound the alarm bells even for Henry Tudor. And to whom must his grace turn to in Ireland? Whom could he trust? There was only one possible answer.

The herper's voice penetrated her speculation.

'The harp, my lady. You promised, when I brought you news of the Geraldine.'

'And so I did. And will, when you have completed your task. Not before.' Her voice was inflexible. 'Return to Desmond. You will take a message to the new O'Donel chieftain. It is time we renewed acquaintances, particularly now that we are to become related. Wait outside.'

She dismissed him curtly with her hand. He shuffled slowly towards the door and looked forlornly back at the large figure at the desk, hoping in vain that she might change her mind. She raised her head and the adamantine look in her eyes made him realise the futility of his hope.

As the door closed behind him, the countess was already bent over a sheet of parchment which was rapidly filling with the strokes and flourishes of her industrious hand.

27

GREENWICH PALACE, ENGLAND

The sun shone down on the king and his entourage, protected from its rays under the arbour of honeysuckle and climbing roses. The pink buds peeped through the summer greenery. The drone of bees mingled with the strains of a lute, the notes dropping softly like water from a fountain, at once soothing and refreshing. The music ceased abruptly. With a grimace of pain, the king carefully stretched his ulcerated leg. The pain, which had become a constant torment, seemed to find some relief in the sun's heat. He laid the lute on the grass beside him and rested his bulk against the tree trunk.

Amid the splendour of the privy garden, for a moment, Henry basked like a great golden cat. He had a special fondness for Greenwich. He had been born here and had spent the carefree days of his youth on the river, which flowed past the palace on its way to the high seas of his fantasies. In the tiltyard, beyond the garden walls, he had first learned to break a lance. In his adult years he continued to associate Greenwich with pleasant summer interludes, an escape from the stench of London and from the turmoil and intrigues of state. But this year's early sojourn at the riverside palace had a more urgent cause. The plague again stalked the streets of London and he had fled downriver with his queen to the wholesome air of Greenwich.

The lighthearted chatter of his queen and her companions sounded pleasant to his ear. With eyes half-closed under white eyelashes, he watched their womanly gestures. Silver needles held in lithe fingers flashed in the sunshine, as Jane and her ladies tended their needlepoint, stopping now and then, heads close together, to whisper and giggle, darting anxious looks at his reclining form for fear their chatter might disturb him.

He looked fondly at the pale winsome face of his queen. He had been attracted to her even before Anne had ceased to please him. The differences between his two wives were multiple. Where Anne pouted and teased, concealing her deviousness beneath a veil of provocativeness, Jane was, as she appeared, serene and kindly. Too kindly, he mused, recalling her recent intervention on behalf of his daughter, Mary, in her obstinate refusal to swear the oath of allegiance to him as head of the Church. To his angry reproach that his daughter would be the natural enemy of her expected child, Jane had merely smiled in her enigmatic way.

Jane was his antithesis, he thought. Her quiet presence radiated a tranquillity that, as he grew older, he needed more and more. She was his refuge from the secrets and plots which darkened his mind. She reminded him of himself, before the heavy crown of kingship had been foisted on his youthful head. Then he too had seen only good in everyone, and wished ill to no man. Experience had smashed the fragile innocence of youth and had taught him to be as ruthless as those who sought to destroy him. But Jane would never suffer the metamorphosis that he had undergone; he did not wish her to. For her innocence and goodness would serve as his mirror-image of what he had once been but would never be again.

He noted with satisfaction the evidence of her advancing pregnancy beneath the unlaced bodice of her gown. The son that she would bear him would inherit some of her qualities, he hoped, to balance his Tudor ruthlessness. And this time he *must* have a son. The years were fast receding and the fruit of his loins as yet had been disappointing. Sullen pope-loving Mary had her mother's obstinate streak and Spanish blood. Should she succeed him, she would fire the flames of inquisition throughout the realm. Anne's red-headed daughter Elizabeth he had recently bastardised and so extinguished her right of succession. A son by Jane, a son to train in the tiltyard and tennis court, to teach the craft of kingship, a son to assure the Tudor dynasty – the need gnawed an insatiable void within him.

He would bequeath his son a more secure throne than he had inherited from his father. That he had vowed to do, by fair means or foul. He had sacrificed much to have this son: disposed of Catherine, Anne, More, Fisher; procured murder, execution, confiscation; reversed universal religious belief, perhaps to the damnation of his soul; defied princes and popes; pushed his people to the limits of their loyalty, all in pursuit of his desire for a male heir.

He sighed with contentment. Norfolk had all but suppressed the northern uprising. The earl's speed and application to the task had surprised him. But fear and self-preservation made for effective spurs, Henry knew. The ruthless retribution he had exacted from Doncaster to Berwick against lord and commoner suspected of aiding or abetting the Pilgrimage of Grace had removed almost every vestige of support for the rebels. The ringleaders were safely incarcerated in the Tower and, one by one, were beginning to pay the ultimate penalty on the scaffold at Tyburn or in the fires of Smithfield.

Jane's eye caught his and a blush slowly tinted her face. What lay behind that demure countenance, that pleasing manner, he wondered. He had scarcely noticed her when she had arrived at court to attend Anne. It was at her father's house in Wiltshire that she had first come to his attention and even, before Anne's demise on the block, he was captivated enough to distract his mind from the fate he had meted out to his second queen. His desire for Jane had not waned during her pregnancy. Unlike the duration of Anne's confinement, when he had not hesitated to find an outlet elsewhere for his passions, the celibacy he had enforced upon himself during Jane's pregnancy was undertaken as a penance he secretly offered for the safe deliverance of the son he craved, rather than out of any consideration for his queen.

With his eyes still upon her he sang softly the verse she had inspired when he had first noticed her, and to which his minstrel had set the music. Her ladies-in-waiting clapped politely at his somewhat tremulous rendition and Jane flashed him a fond look and lowered her head to her needlepoint.

'Methinks, ladies, the singer scarce does justice to the tune.'

A chorus of protest greeted his words.

'Your grace's song has even made the birds listen,' Lady Exeter insisted.

A shrill whistle greeted her remarks and they laughed merrily, as a peacock, resplendent in his array of forest green, sapphire blue and deep gold plumage, strutted by them.

'Not it seems yonder exotic bird from the New World.' Henry joined in their laughter. 'Nor this bird of ill omen,' he added, as the black-robed figure of Cromwell descended the terrace steps and advanced towards them through the lime trees, closely followed by the spare figure of the Earl of Ormond.

The king's good humour evaporated and with anger written across his heavy features, he rose to his feet, bowed to the queen and her ladies and moved away from the bower to prohibit Cromwell from coming closer. He had expressly told his secretary to deny access to anyone from London, lest any breath of the accursed plague should contaminate the air in Greenwich. Something of great urgency must have arisen for Cromwell to have risked his anger to permit Ormond an audience.

Cromwell motioned Ormond to wait and hurried towards

the king as fast as his bulk would allow. He saw the anger on the royal visage and bowed low before him.

'Your grace, I would not dare to have brought him to you, if the news did not warrant it.'

Henry looked to where Ormond waited uneasily.

'Did Ormond come from London?' Behind the softly-spoken question, a dam of anger waited to be unleashed.

'Nay, your grace,' Cromwell quickly assured him. 'My Lord of Ormond heard of the plague in London and stopped at Richmond.'

'By God's blood, Cromwell, 'tis as well for you and for him,' the king whispered through his teeth. 'What brings him here?'

'He brings tidings from his wife. The news from Ireland is disturbing, your grace. I thought it best that you should hear of it forthwith.'

Henry knew that Cromwell was not given to exaggeration. It was one of his valued traits. Without replying, he walked briskly towards the waiting earl, who doffed his velvet cap at his approach and in a wide arc swept the ground before him. Henry feigned a disarming pleasantness and greeted Ormond jovially.

'Ah, my lord of Ormond. We did not think to have the pleasure of your company so soon again. How goes it with your lady wife?'

'Ever about your grace's business,' Ormond replied, a trifle nervously.

'Not so much that she neglects her duty to her husband We hope. You look somewhat peaked, my good lord. We poor men need the comforts of a woman's touch. Or are Irishmen made of sterner stuff?' Henry laughed loudly and clapped the older man on his thin shoulders.

Ormond tottered under the blow, but balanced himself in time.

'As your grace says. What would we do without them?'

Perhaps in your case much better, Henry thought,

remembering the redoubtable countess. He motioned Cromwell to join them.

'Our Lord Privy Seal informs Us that you bear news of urgency from Ireland.'

Ormond looked at Cromwell, who handed the king a parchment square.

'Let us walk some way, gentlemen,' Henry said and started down the gravel path that led to an ornamental pond. In the centre an elaborately carved fountain in the shape of a dolphin spouted a jet of water. Henry paused and opened the countess's letter. Without comment, he looked at the two faded rose petals. His small mouth tightened as he read the neat concise hand. He felt the heat rise within him, smothering him in a speechless rage. He crumpled the parchment.

'The twin leaves of treason.' He held the rose petals aloft and cast them angrily into the pond. 'Plantagenet and Geraldine.' A vein throbbed on his broad temple.

Cromwell moved hesitantly forward. 'Your grace's ambassador at the Spanish Court confirms the visit of Kildare's chaplain and,' he added knowingly, 'he was received in audience by the emperor.'

Henry turned to Ormond. 'This league the countess writes of . . . do many of the Irish lords support it?'

Ormond shook his head. 'It is impossible to know, your grace. My wife learned only of the principal names. All the strongest lords in Ireland – and the Pale,' he emphasised, 'attended at Desmond's castle.'

'It would be most grievous, at this time, should the Irish lords find unity in any cause, especially in that of the Geraldine,' Cromwell intervened.

For a moment the words of his late chancellor, Wolsey, flashed through the king's mind. He could still hear the hissed hatred in the voice of Wolsey as he warned him against Kildare and his treachery in Ireland. 'For the Irish would prefer a Geraldine to come among them rather than God

Himself.'

Henry's leg ached agonisingly and he moved a few steps away from the two men to conceal his discomfort.

His policy towards Ireland had always been one of containment. Divide and conquer, rely on the Irish propensity for tribal warfare to wipe each other out and prevent any one of them from challenging his sovereignty. 'Put an Irishman on the spit and you'll get two others to turn him' was the proverb which had guided his policy towards his other kingdom.

It had been easier to tolerate Ireland's disloyalty and barbarous ways than to try and overpower her by force – at least until the time was ripe to crush her into submission. But that time never seemed to come. There were always more urgent matters. Kildare's treason and his son's rebellion had brought the whole question of Ireland's unstable state into sharper focus and it was a Kildare now once again who forced his hand. Ireland unified under the banner of Kildare, aided by one or other of his conniving continental enemies, or both, was a nightmarish prospect. The Geraldine must be captured without delay. It was obvious that his Irish deputy could no longer be trusted; his Yorkist blood had blinded him to his duty.

But he could spare no army for Ireland. There were rumblings still in the north and the sack and closure of the monasteries had evoked more unrest among the common people than he had expected. Most of it had been directed at Cromwell, as he had intended but for how long? Scotland was stirring again, while developments on the Continent required all his resources to be at the ready should Charles and François decide to ally against him. In the meantime, the dangers in Ireland had to be contained until he could expend the substantial outlay required to subdue it once and for all.

He looked at the Irish earl standing at a respectful distance and beckoned him closer.

'The countess writes of enticing an O'Donel chieftain to abet her endeavours against the league. What is known of him?'

'Little enough in Ireland, Your Grace. As a youth he was hostage to Kildare who brought him to court.'

'Yes, yes, We seem to recall, the Irish Don Juan.' Henry conjured an image from the past of Kildare's brazen ward with his overfondness for English finery and English ladies. Catherine, with her lack of humour and her intolerance of boudoir frolics, especially among her ladies, had complained of the Irish youth to him, he remembered. 'He disappeared at the time of Kildare's impeachment and imprisonment, We recall.'

'To France and thence to Italy, it is thought, your grace,' Ormond said, 'but 'tis not certain. O'Donel is something of a phantom, flitting hither and thither. He returned to Ireland on the death of his father, whom he is to succeed to the lordship of Tirconel, in Ulster.'

'From Don Juan to pope's crusader: an unlikely progress.' The king's brow furrowed in thought. Perhaps, as the countess recommended, O'Donel was a likely target for bribery. 'Your wife thinks he might be usefully employed to break this conspiracy against us in Ireland. What say you, my lord?'

Ormond's eyes darted uneasily, as if he was unused to having his opinion sought. Ormond on his own, Henry knew, would prove no match for a combination of his peers in Ireland. His wife was another matter. She had the strength and motivation that could release him from this predicament in Ireland and crush the conspiracy there before it got out of hand. What reward would she seek in lieu? The lands of Kildare, the deputyship of Ireland? He had learned his lesson with her father and brother and, despite her avowed loyalty now, she was contaminated with the same blood. The Countess of Ormond would serve his purpose, and no more. Henry folded her letter carefully and handed it to Cromwell.

'It appears so, sire.' Ormond's hesitant response vaguely registered in Henry's mind.

'Has Grey left Dublin to pursue the Geraldine?'

'At my leaving, your grace, he was preparing to rendezvous with my wife in Ormond. But the lord deputy, we fear, will make excuse that he has your grace's writ to invade only Carbury. The Geraldine fugitive is now in the lordship of the Earl of Desmond.'

'Desmond, that cursed imposter.' Henry looked sharply at Cromwell. 'Have We not ammunition here at court to fire in his direction?'

'Indeed, your grace,' his secretary smiled smugly, 'one who is most anxious to be of service against his cousin.'

'See to it. The sooner the Geraldine heir is caught, the sooner this base conspiracy against Us in Ireland will fall asunder.'

Both Cromwell and Ormond indicated their agreement.

'Very well. Prepare a writ for Grey. Command him to press on against Desmond, without delay, mark you. Ormond here will take over the ammunition we speak of by which to ensure Desmond's downfall quicker than whatever force We could send against him.' The King's small eyes narrowed. 'Should Desmond agree to disperse this league and abandon his treasonable intrigues with Our enemies abroad, he is to be allowed to continue as earl. 'Tis too costly to dislodge him now. And it matters not to Us who be the Earl of Desmond, provided he be Our loyal servant.'

'And Grey?' Cromwell asked softly.

The King's small eyes were calculating and cold. He would have Grey's head, but not yet.

'The countess considers that my Lord Grey is the Earl of Kildare newly born again.' He lifted his broad shoulders. 'As yet the evidence against him is slight. We will give him more rope, perhaps, to hang himself.' He turned to Ormond. 'The countess has Our leave to press Our case as she thinks fit. To lure O'Donel to Our cause or not. Now, my Lord, what bait do you suggest We use to lure that fine bird to Our net?'

'Power over his rival O'Neill in Ulster,' Ormond answered without hesitation. ''Twill kill two birds, for O'Neill is long suspected of collusion with your grace's enemy, the king of Scotland.'

'God's blood. What a hornet's nest We have in Ireland.' The king shook his head and placed a friendly hand on the earl's shoulder. 'But We are grateful to you and your wife for your watchfulness there on Our behalf. It will not go unrewarded.'

The elderly nobleman drew himself up to his full height and with a deep breath bowed his thanks low before the king.

'Give your countess Our special greeting and blessings in her noble work . God speed you back to Ireland on the morrow.' The king's tone conveyed the urgency he intended.

Ormond bowed low once more and withdrew slowly, facing the king as was customary. Henry motioned to Cromwell to see him on his way.

The peaceful humour of the day being shattered, Henry turned away from the queen's bower and made towards the far end of the garden, through the leafy shade of the arboretum.

He would make his choice immediately between François and the emperor. The uncertainty was conducive to the hatching of such grievous plots against him. He could not continue much longer to play one against the other. Between them, he could well fall foul of the pope's attempts to lure both into a crusade against him. Of the two, Charles was the most likely to be entrapped in the pope's scheme. The fires of the Inquisition might fan his Catholic tendencies. Cromwell's spies reported from the court at Toledo that the arch-fanatic, Cardinal Tavera, was actively encouraging his emperor along the road to Rome. The emperor's audience with the emissary of the conspirators in Ireland was but the beginning. His antagonism towards Henry regarding his treatment of Catherine might still rankle, even now, after her death and Anne's execution.

If Henry allied with Charles, he would automatically alienate François, whom he suspected would then renew the old alliance with Scotland. But it was a risk he would have to take. France and Scotland were now less a threat than an alliance – of the pope, the emperor and Ireland, unified and rebellious once more under the banner of the Geraldines. With its religious undertones, such an alliance would assuredly attract the opponents of Henry's religious reforms within England, with the horrendous result of a return to civil war, a reopening of the barely healed wounds of the white and red roses, a reversal of all he and his father had achieved, and a wretched inheritance to bequeath his son.

Henry turned abruptly and strode towards the palace. He would not allow the security of England to be sacrificed by the lust for power of either Charles or the pope, hidden beneath the veneer of religious dogma. His son would inherit a strong, prosperous and unified kingdom and become, after him, the absolute ruler of England and of her dark shadow to the west. He would allow no Geraldine brat in Ireland to diminish his son's inheritance.

The king hurried along the cool halls towards the privy chamber. Until one or other of the parties to the unholy alliance could be neutralised, the way ahead, the only way now, was to declare for Charles.

28

DINGLE, LORDSHIP OF DESMOND

It was with ill-concealed resentment that Desmond allowed
Leverous to go to Tralee and thence thirty miles westward,
to the harbour of Dingle. But for the intervention of
Eleanor's son, Leverous might well have found himself
confined to the dungeons in Askeaton Castle. At first the
earl had ordered that he was to remain in Askeaton, and
Leverous had seen him ominously motion to his gallowglass
captain, MacSheehy. MacCarthy had quickly intervened and
the earl had reluctantly acquiesced. MacCarthy lightly shrugged
off Leverous's thanks as they fell in with one another for the
long journey to the westernmost stronghold of the Desmond
lordship.

As soon as he had received the word that his ship had
been sighted off the Blasket islands, the earl had wasted no
time. With his principal urraghs and a well-appointed army,
he set out immediately for Dingle. Desmond's force was
handpicked to impress the Spanish reinforcements. Six score
gallowglass in gleaming chainmail were followed by rows of
kern, about one hundred in all. A score of arquebusiers, with
their cumbersome weapons slung over each shoulder and
flasks of powder at each waist, marched at the rear. At the
head of his army, Desmond sat astride a chestnut stallion,
its smooth coat, mane and tail combed to a silken sheen. A

score of his principal urraghs, five abreast, followed. A train of empty wagons brought up the rear, raising clouds of dust on the dry dirt track. It was apparent that Desmond expected his ship to contain more than the customary Spanish sack.

Leverous rode alongside MacCarthy to the rear. They had spoken little since leaving Askeaton. Occasionally Leverous felt the eyes of the young chieftain looking towards him, but except for a few pleasantries MacCarthy remained silent. Leverous was as well pleased. He did not feel inclined to converse with anyone, and especially with MacCarthy. He simply had no idea what to say, for he could scarcely trust himself to speak of the subject he knew was the source of the embarrassment between them. The startling announcement of Eleanor's betrothal had affected more than his relationship with her; it had placed an impediment between him and her son. He felt that Cormac suspected that he and his mother shared something more tangible than memories of Maynooth. Perhaps, in an unguarded moment, he had let slip that there may have been more between them than they either dared or cared to admit.

But if his mother's betrothal to O'Donel embarrassed her son, it tormented Leverous. His body seemed to freeze in the courtyard when, trancelike, he had watched O'Donel take her hand and heard Desmond make public the unnatural betrothal. He felt no immediate pain or anger, just a feeling of emptiness, as if his heart had ceased to function. His stomach retched, his limbs were momentarily paralysed, unable to bear him away from the scene of his anguish and humiliation. He remembered stumbling through the gateway and crossing the bridge, and wandering aimlessly through the fair, being jostled and cursed at. Returning to the castle late in the evening, he had ridden out before nightfall to Limerick, where two weeks of his life evaporated in a haze of aqua vitae, low-roofed taverns and pot houses, and a brothel near the river.

Desmond's men had found him, dragged him from the

293

foul bed with jeers and sly winks and brought him back to Askeaton. In his absence, Gerald had refused to co-operate with his minders. Even Eleanor's pleadings had seemingly gone unheeded, as the boy steadfastly refused to leave his chamber. On his return Leverous found that Eleanor had already left for Carbury to put her affairs in order before her departure to her new home in Tirconel and her marriage to O'Donel. His mind still could not comprehend her transformation. A pain like a dagger thrust across his breast. His hand gripped the reins until the knuckles showed white. He had steeled his mind against thinking of her but an occasional lapse allowed the pain and humiliation to overwhelm him.

What had possessed her, he wondered. What devil cleverly concealed from him behind a façade of kindness, strength and loveliness, existed within her to effect such a profound reversal, to make her abandon whom she professed to love, and betray him for the avowed object of her revulsion? Betray their love that like a silken thread had bound them through the years of separation. To cast it off, without explanation, without remorse or elation. It was so much out of character that it smacked of sorcery, as if O'Donel had administered her some sinister potion that made her pliable to his lustful designs. But she had abandoned him before, Leverous reminded himself, and had kept her distance from him through the years of her marriage to MacCarthy: no letter, no message – nothing but a cold determined silence. Perhaps the ruthlessness of the Great Earl ran in the veins of more of his offspring than the Countess of Ormond.

And yet Eleanor had lain in his arms, murmured words of love in his ear, clung to him as if she could never leave him again, never exist without the love that had somehow survived their cruel separation. Her lips, her body had lied so well, he thought bitterly, for they had convinced him that she loved him. Was he so gullible, so desperate for fulfilment, he asked himself, not to suspect that she simply played with his emotions? He recalled her initial disquiet at his re-entrance into her life, her reluctance, the apprehensive glances in his direction before her reserve had faltered for that single night in his chamber at Askeaton. The night that had convinced him that his long apprenticeship to loneliness was over, for ever. He felt bitter, cheated and emotionally empty, an emptiness that no longer desired fulfilment. His physical needs could be adequately filled whenever he chose and without having to resort to the brothel, as in Limerick, where he had sought to obliterate every trace of her from his mind. He had been propositioned more often than he could recall by the wives and daughters of lord and chieftain, deserted or bored by their partners. No, he was determined, his quest for what had perhaps never existed was over.

'Desmond seems confident that the Spanish will be generous.'

At his side, MacCarthy's voice disturbed Leverous's bitter resolution. MacCarthy motioned in the direction of the carts which trundled noisily behind them.

'I do not share his optimism,' he continued. 'From experience I have ever found the Spaniard to be a wily trickster. He pays a groat to licence one boat to fish MacCarthy waters but brings three boats to fish on the one licence. Aye, we keep a careful eye on the Spaniard in Carbury. We have long experience of their ways and even longer memories.'

'Tis hard to trick the devil,' Leverous replied indifferently. 'I reckon Desmond can hold his own with the Spaniard in that regard.'

MacCarthy shook his head doubtfully. 'I fear he may be out of his depth in this one.'

Leverous felt disinclined to talk. It suited his mood at the moment. Yet he was fond of the young chieftain and could not blame him for his mother's betrayal, which seemed to have astounded her son as much as it had devastated him. Moreover, he had much to thank him for: his life. A life for a life. Perhaps that was the way she thought of it. Her debt to him for saving her from the river paid for by her son. Her own contribution to the debt paid that night in his chamber. Their account was now balanced and closed. The bitterness engulfed him again.

MacCarthy seemed anxious to converse.'Where lies the league if the Spanish help does not materialise?'

With an effort, Leverous concentrated on the question. 'It is hard to say. I cannot see O'Brien, MacWilliam, O'Carroll, O'Connor and the rest willing to risk their necks simply for Desmond's aggrandisement. And particularly not O'Neill. Power is the only way to be certain of their support, as Desmond well knows. Should he get his reinforcements from the emperor, it will make him unstoppable.'

'And where does Gerald fit into all this? If Desmond does not get help from Spain, then the league will collapse and there will be nothing between the Geraldine and the king.'

Leverous had asked himself the same question over and over. Eleanor's treachery and his own pathetic reaction had made him forget his promise to Garret. He had wallowed in self-pity and had relinquished Gerald's protection to others, whose motives he had every reason to suspect. Even Eleanor, he concluded, especially now in view of her marriage to O'Donel. His heart hardened. She had been instrumental in bringing Gerald to Desmond, he reminded himself, and had vowed to guarantee Desmond's intent. How could she fulfil her promise to him and to her nephew, by marriage to O'Donel and her removal to Tirconel, two hundred miles away?

The boy had reacted as one might expect from one too young to comprehend the intrigues which swirled around him. But it was Gerald who had roused Leverous from the stupor of self-pity. From the boy's eyes had radiated both relief and reprimand when he rode into Askeaton from

Limerick to resume his vigil by his side. At least the total dismal experience had made him alert to the danger that more than ever surrounded Gerald.

He had no answer to MacCarthy's question. Here at the edge of the world, surrounded by strangers, whose allegiance was based on expediency, the name of Kildare might not have survived Garret's memory and might not exact loyalty to his son, should Desmond's league fail. Then the way would be clear for the Countess of Ormond, backed however reluctantly by Grey, to persuade or compel Desmond to deliver Gerald to the king.

Leverous searched for a reply, not wishing MacCarthy to take his silence as an affront, but the young chieftain spoke first.

'Should Desmond's league collapse, you and Gerald are welcome to return to Carbury.'

Leverous looked at him in surprise. 'But your people's opposition to the Geraldines, your uncle?' he asked, recalling Eleanor's reason for removing Gerald from Carbury in the first instance.

MacCarthy smiled reassuringly. 'My mother's marriage to my father more than managed to heal that bitterness. My uncle likes to appear occasionally from behind my shadow to let us know he still exists, but he is of no serious threat. A blow-hole for hot air.'

So Gerald's presence in Carbury had never threatened her son's position after all. How well Eleanor had deceived him, Leverous thought bitterly. As if he read his thoughts, he heard MacCarthy continue. 'Whatever differences are between you and my mother, I hope it will not come between us. I wanted you to know that before I return to Carbury.' He paused before continuing. 'I will not be attending my mother's marriage in Tirconel.'

Leverous looked in gratitude at the young chieftain, whose quiet assurance and maturity had impressed him from their first encounter in the snow at Colaughtrim forest. He

297

had enjoyed their subsequent companionship at Carbury and Askeaton. MacCarthy was his own man. Even the Earl of Desmond's claim of suzerainty over him seemed tenuous, dependent on MacCarthy's acceptance, rather than on the earl's ability to enforce it. He was someone Leverous had found it easy to confide in and admire. Eleanor had borne her husband an able and a likeable successor.

'I appreciate your offer, Cormac. I know it is sincere. But I have not quite run out of ideas of my own.'

Leverous spoke with the assurance he did not feel. He might be glad to accept MacCarthy's offer yet. But he must speak alone with Robert Walshe before Desmond spirited him away again, to ascertain where exactly his loyalty lay. It was for that reason he had insisted on making the journey to Dingle.

He scarcely noticed the majestic splendour of the mountain ranges they were skirting. Awesome and aloof, clothed in a summer mantle of the faintest blue, the peaks soared above into an azure sky, dotted with white cumulus clouds that sailed lazily by like great sheep fleeces. To their right, giant Atlantic breakers rolled in white frothed sheets on a sandy shore, which stretched away into the distance. The sun shone warmly between the clouds, occasionally throwing its shadow on the sand below. Out in the ocean, islands, browsing like great whales, lured them onwards to the edge.

The murmur of talk among the soldiers and horsemen increased as they rounded a bend in the track. Far below, in a fertile valley which ran towards the sea, a walled town lay, protected to the north by the highest mountain Leverous had ever seen.

'Dingle,' MacCarthy said.

In a sheltered bay, a two-masted ship lay at anchor. Leverous felt his pulse quicken, while around him men spoke excitedly. The pace increased as the journey's end beckoned.

The gates of the tower to the east of the town were open

to receive them. Looking every inch its overlord, Desmond led his army through the gate. A dirt track ran between a row of stone thatched houses, with outbuildings and stores. Along the route it seemed that every man, woman and child waited to see their overlord and his impressive following. Faint cheers of 'Desmond aboo' rose now and then from the crowd but, for the greater part, they looked on in silence as the rows of armed soldiers passed by. Desmond was a taxing overlord, feared rather than loved. The smell of fish and hides mingled with the fresh salt smell of the sea. Rows of wooden barrels were piled house high in great stacks. From within the open doors of the stores, firkins of salt gleamed among the mounds of black cattle hides that awaited curing.

Without drawing rein, Desmond led his force towards the harbour. Expectation and excitement grew among the massed ranks behind him. The cavalcade rounded the last corner and the jetty came into view. Desmond raised his hand and the cavalcade halted. There was silence, save for the noise of the carts, as they drew to a stop. All eyes stared in disbelief. There were no lines of Spanish soldiers, no mounds of weapons and supplies. Except for the citizens who clustered along by the walls or sat on the small currachs and clinker-built single-masted fishing boats drawn up on the grey shingle, the harbour was deserted. All eyes looked out towards the bay, to where the bare masts of the caraval swayed in the swell. From the starboard, a long boat was being launched.

In silence, as if mesmerised by the oars that dipped and flashed, Leverous watched the boat being propelled closer. He could see the slight figure of Robert Walshe seated in the bows. The Earl of Desmond, flanked by some of his urraghs, rode down to the jetty and waited for the boat to tie up. Unnoticed, Leverous dismounted and followed behind. Robert Walshe was being helped ashore. The chaplain scanned the faces on the jetty before he located Leverous. His look vindicated Leverous's insistence on

299

coming to Dingle. Robert Walshe, he felt certain, had tidings to divulge to him other than those he was about to impart to the Earl of Desmond.

The earl dismounted and, taking the chaplain by the arm, led him aside. He inclined his head as he listened intently to Robert Walshe's information, lifting his sharp eyes occasionally to scrutinise the chaplain's face as he digested the outcome of his mission to Spain. Leverous saw Walshe hand the earl a parchment from which a large seal, attached by a crimson cord, adhered. The earl broke open the seal and read the contents. He murmured something to the chaplain, who pointed to the longboat which had returned to the caravel and was being loaded with cargo from the larger vessel. The earl retraced his steps and faced his silent urraghs. He brandished the parchment high over his head.

'The Emperor of the Holy Roman Empire supports us in our fight against the heretic king of England,' he shouted in his croaking voice. There was a muted shout of approval from the ranks of his followers.

'The Geraldine League is to be a part of the glorious crusade which the emperor raises against England.

There was another even less enthusiastic response from the crowd.

'But the Spanish soldiers, the weapons?' one of Desmond's urraghs prompted impatiently.

Desmond hesitated for an instant before pointing towards the caravel in the bay from whence the long boat was to be seen returning.

'The emperor's token of his confidence in our league.'

The crowd watched impassively as the longboat tied up at the jetty and the barefooted sailors nimbly discharged its meagre cargo.

A dozen arquebuses, with powder flasks, a hundred or so Toledo blades, some demi-lances and Moorish pikes, were piled on the jetty. A murmur of disappointment rose from the earl's followers at the emperor's paltry investment in the league. Around him, Leverous heard the half-muted curses of dismay and ridicule. How would the wily earl placate his allies in the league, he wondered, with this miserly display of Spanish assistance?

'It is but a sample, a forerunner of the army and weapons on their way from the emperor.' Desmond's voice sounded strained. His urraghs seemed unconvinced and moved disconsolately away to converse in groups around the harbour. The earl motioned to his marshal who gave orders for the arms to be loaded into the carts.

'There is sack aplenty for all to drink the emperor's health and to the success of his crusade and of the Geraldine league.'

This offer got the warmest response of the day. It had been a long, thirsty trek, throats were dry and expectation deflated. Desmond knew best how to revive lagging spirits. His bonnaghts were dismissed to eat and drink their fill at the townspeople's expense.

Leverous felt a hand on his arm and turned to see the chaplain at his side. Silently, Robert Walshe gestured towards a single-masted galley which lay beached on the sloping shingle and, like a shadow, disappeared into the crowd.

Leverous made his way quickly through the soldiers and townspeople who still milled in front of the harbour watching the Spanish weapons being loaded into carts. He crouched down behind the wooden hull of the galley to avoid the vigilant eye of the Earl of Desmond. Idly he wondered if Garret's chaplain, like his sister, had deserted Gerald, lured from him by Desmond's vain promises of some rich benefice perhaps. Was Gerald's safety still Robert Walshe's priority as it had seemed to be, before he embarked on the earl's business to Spain? Like a bowstring, Leverous's instinct, in the light of Eleanor's duplicity, was taut with suspicion of everyone who proffered help to Gerald.

Robert Walshe came around the high bow of the galley, greeted Leverous tersely and crouched down beside him. Leverous noticed that his thin features were more prominent

301

and his eyes were encircled by dark rings of fatigue. His voice sounded tired and flat.

'All is not as it appears, as you probably realised.'

Leverous nodded in acknowledgement.

'The emperor bides his time, before declaring his preference. My own guess is that it will be for Henry. His hatred of François runs too deep to be patched over by the thin tissue of a religious crusade.'

'And Desmond's league?' Leverous prompted him, his heart racing in anticipation.

'What king turns away any offer of assistance, no matter how insignificant? The emperor realises better than anyone what opportunities Ireland could offer, as a back door to England, should England prove Spain's enemy. And remember, my friend, Charles can now use the earl and his league as an added lever to deter Henry from assisting François. This miserly contribution,' he pointed towards the jetty, 'is rather a warning to Henry than a gesture of support for Desmond.'

'And Gerald? Where does all of this leave him?' Leverous looked directly at the priest, to see if his face should reveal any hint of duplicity. There was none that he could detect and Walshe's answer placated him.

'Our brief from the Earl of Kildare stands. In fact, if anything, it is reinforced in light of what I learned in Spain. It is essential that you and I have a plan in hand to spirit the Geraldine to safety, as soon as Charles declares for Henry and France becomes a safe sanctuary for Gerald again.'

Robert Walshe noticed the shadow of disquiet on his companion's face and smiled reassuringly.

'The king and Cromwell have their spies everywhere. You can be certain that news of my audience with the emperor has already reached the king in England. Do not doubt it. But, my friend, we must bide our time here and hope that Desmond can keep the league together until France declares openly against Henry. It is only a matter of time, Thomas. I am certain of that.'

'Time may not be on our side. Much has happened since your departure to Spain.'

Leverous related about the attempt on his life and, in as detached a tone as he could muster, Eleanor's betrothal to O'Donel.

The chaplain heard the news in silence. His keen eyes searched Leverous's face, as if to discern how both events had affected him.

'I am sorry for you, Thomas,' he said softly. Leverous could not tell to which incident he referred, but by the tone of his voice he suspected that it was to the latter.

''Tis merely a way for O'Donel to spite O'Neill,' he said gently. 'Another knot in the long rope of their feud.'

'And other feuds besides.' Leverous could not keep the bitterness from his voice. The priest looked at him with sympathy and laid his hand comfortingly on his shoulder.

'Aye, O'Donel carries the heavy hump of rancour on his back. It makes him an unstable ally in Gerald's cause. You are right: it is time we thought of getting Gerald to safety before the league falls or is ripped apart by the king and his Irish supporters.'

Leverous inclined his head in agreement. Apart from Gerald's safety and his promise to Garret, he wanted nothing so badly as to shake the dust of Ireland from his boots for ever.

'Desmond will try to make more of this paltry cargo,' Robert Walshe said. 'And I have deliberately fed his hopes of additional help from Spain to encourage him to hold the league together and give us time to plan Gerald's escape. What do you think?'

'There seems little alternative.'

'There is always O'Neill.'

Leverous looked sharply at the chaplain. 'He will be hardly inclined to help, now that Gerald's aunt is to marry with his most bitter enemy.'

'They are not married yet, Thomas,' the chaplain gently reprimanded him. 'Now is not the time to despair. Let us keep our hope and wits about us for another while yet.' He rose slowly from his position behind the galley.

'Are you to return with us to Askeaton?'

'The earl is anxious that I should return to Spain with another dispatch to the emperor.'

Leverous felt his unease rise. He needed Robert Walshe's support and counsel, particularly now in view of Eleanor's defection and Cormac's imminent return to Carbury. There would be only himself to stand between Gerald and his enemies, both known and unknown.

'And will you?'

The chaplain's voice had a weary ring. 'I told the earl I would consider it. But in truth, I have no desire to return to Spain. For I tell you, Thomas, my faith in God would not survive a second visit.'

Leverous looked in puzzlement at his companion. But the chaplain seemed disinclined to enlighten him and seemed lost in his own thoughts.

'As you, my friend, I serve only one cause,' he said finally: 'the Geraldine.'

29

LORDSHIP OF ORMOND

It had been, as Grey had expected, an acrimonious journey. From the moment the countess had met him at Leighlin-bridge on the border of Ormond, they had been at logger-heads. His meagre army of two hundred paled in comparison to her force of cavalry, kern and gallowglass, over five hundred, he reckoned, . The bickering had started immedi-ately and had continued unabated. Orders given by one were countermanded by the other. On the question of the most suitable route south, he had let her have her way, considering that she was more familiar with the terrain. But in the matter of command of the combined forces, he was adamant. Taking their cue from their leaders' animosity, the two armies viewed each other with suspicion.

The weather was ideal for a campaign which involved the transport of so much equipment: war carts with the ordnance, arquebuses and two light culverins, wagons laden with rations of biscuit and beer and to carry back the hoped-for booty, the essential bonus of war. The expectation of prey was intense among the English soldiers, desperate to snatch some recompense for their service in lieu of pay. Grey greatly feared a mutiny in his ranks should the expedition against MacCarthy fail to fulfil their expectations.

They had made considerable headway. The ground was

305

dry and the great rivers that barred the way south were low and easily forded. At the insistence of the countess, they skirted O'Connor Faly's country lest the foolhardy chieftain, the fosterer of Kildare's son, and custom-bound to protect him, might harry them from the shelter of the woods and marshes and thereby slow their progress. Grey almost hoped that he would: anything to delay the nightmare prospect that awaited in Carbury.

The countess well realised that without the king's stinging reprimand Grey would never have embarked on his mission to Carbury. She watched his every move like a hawk, questioned his every command. In the infrequent lulls from her strident voice at his shoulder and in his sleepless nights, bivouacked under the open sky, the objective of this sortie into MacCarthy's country tortured his mind. What must happen at MacCarthy's castle he dreaded to contemplate, when, as the king's deputy, he would have no alternative but to do the duty he had so far evaded: to take prisoner his own nephew, Elizabeth's son, a mere child, and send him into the voracious maw of the Tudor dragon. Unlike his capture of Silken Thomas, Grey knew he did not have the excuse of ignorance as to the fate that lay in store for his nephew. He would send the boy to a certain death, just as assuredly as if he pulled the rope or swung the executioner's axe.

It was late evening and they were deep in Ormond territory. The sun was a red ball of fire low to the west. The next stop within the vast lordship was to have been at the castle of Kiltinan, seat of the Baron of Dunboyne, a cadet branch of the House of Ormond. But the baron had met them at the border of his territory and pleaded inability to cess both armies. After much argument, it was agreed that the Countess of Ormond's forces would be cessed at the baron's town of Kiltinan and that Grey's army would be quartered further on at the town of Cashel. Although anxious to keep the countess under observation, Grey was relieved to be rid of her exasperating presence, if only for a few days. He mistrusted her more in her home territory, with the obvious advantage it gave her over him. Moreover, he had noticed a reticence in her, singularly out of character, as if she nursed some plot to which he was not privy. He knew that her spies were in place within his army as well as in his own administration. But on this campaign he had taken a lesson from her book of stratagems. For the next few days, though out of his sight, she would be under his observation. One of the few chinks, he had discovered, in the armour of the armadillo was her voracious appetite. The Breton cook whom she had lured from his kitchen at Thomas Court had been more than willing to supplement the stinginess of his new mistress, by some additional work for his former master.

The train reached a divide in the rutted track, the countess raised her hand and the combined force drew to a halt. 'The road to Cashel.' She pointed ahead. 'We will regroup there in three days from now.'

Grey raised his hand briefly in acknowledgement and led his army westwards.

Grey's army moved on through rich, undulating pasturelands, on which herds of black cattle grazed, interspersed with enclosed fields of ripening corn. Scattered groves of oak, ash and birch threw long shadows in their path. The country was as fertile as the best in England, Grey acknowledged, not without surprise. And how much more lay beyond the dark line of forest and mountain towards the west? It was incredible to believe that, while the king claimed suzerainty over all this, he, the king's deputy, did not possess a single accurate map of it. Even now, in his journey through the heartland of Ireland, he had to rely on native direction. But it would change. Of that he had no doubt. The age of exploration and discovery had arrived and Ireland would yet prove a more accessible option than the distant Americas to satisfy his fellow-countrymen's lust for land.

'Land fit to kill for, my lord.' Brabazon's voice interrupted his reverie. Grey scowled, annoyed that his very thoughts seemed to have been read by his under-treasurer.

'Or die in the taking,' he brusquely replied.

Brabazon's laugh was condescending. 'Forsooth, my lord. A few committed Englishmen, a well-equipped army. Enough to cower the natives and topple their leaders from their paper pedestals.' Brabazon noisily inhaled the sweetly scented summer air. 'An elixir to embolden even the most fainthearted.'

Grey ignored the taunt. They were passing close to a wide river which wound away to the left to lose itself among the dark shadow of the distant forest. Beyond the forest lay the lordship of Desmond and the hinterland of the Irish world. Ireland, Grey mused, would never be conquered until her secrets, hidden and protected by this natural curtain of primeval forests, unforded rivers, lakes and marshes, were uncovered. The conquest of Ireland would be hastened more by map and roadway than by force of arms. He made a mental note to requisition the services of a cartographer and a surveyor from the king, so that he might better know the country he was expected to conquer.

As they rounded a sharp bend, his gaze was arrested by a spectacular sight. Before him, a rocky outcrop of limestone rose majestically above the surrounding plain, crowned by a striking cluster of buildings and towers, with steeply pitched roofs. The slanting rays of the setting sun threw spangles of rose gold onto the dark mass of buildings astride the mound, making the entire structure seem enveloped in flames.

'*Caiseal Mumhan*,' the Irish guide pointed dramatically towards the vision.

Grey heard only the word *caiseal*. He beckoned to Crowley who, as a native, might know something of the striking settlement.

'The rock of Cashel, my lord; palace of the ancient kings of Munster, now a monastic settlement.'

'Not for long, my lord,' Brabazon assured him. 'I recall it

is listed among the settlements to be suppressed.'

'Thankfully for you, Mr Brabazon; it is as yet in the business of hospitality. You will not refuse a bed and board, tonight I dare say, even from a monk.'

The under-treasurer glowered in response.

Grey led his weary army towards the rocky fortification. He directed his captains to make camp at its base beside the little village that lay beneath its shadow. With Brabazon and Crowley, he rode up the rocky pathway and entered the main courtyard. A cowled monk bowed before him and silently showed him up steep stairs to a spartan room, with a roughly hewn wooden bed. A sturdy table, a chair and a wooden chest were the only other furniture. His servant brought him water and a napkin and with relief, Grey washed away the dust of the journey.

He chose to dine alone in his room and, despite the hardness of the bed, fell into a restless sleep, waking as the dawn pierced the lancet window above his head. He opened a door which led outside to a narrow wall-walk, commanding a fine view of the surrounding plain.

Wisps of morning mist wafted like spectres about the clustered rooftops and towers. Part of the church lay in ruin, its walls blackened by fire. He turned from the grey buildings and looked out over the walls. Below him the countryside lay silent and remote in the early morning haze. The air was fresh and sweet. A dew lay heavy on the pastureland, that like a verdant carpet swept upwards from the plain to envelop the rocky outcrop where he stood. Towards the village, columns of smoke rose lazily from the thatched roofs. Down in the courtyard, a door creaked loudly on its hinges and disturbed the silence.

Grey was about to return to his chamber when he caught sight of Brabazon and Crowley entering the courtyard directly below him. He moved behind the wall, not wishing to be seen. Their voices carried easily in the still of the morning.

'She can raise another five hundred if need be,' he heard Brabazon say. 'Unless he is an utter fool, Desmond will think carefully before taking on the countess and Grey combined.'

'Aye,' Crowley agreed with his companion, 'with the culverins to smash his castles about his head and the countess's special surprise to topple him from his throne. There will not be room for two Earls of Desmond.'

''Twill be easy talk to the imposter then,' Brabazon replied.

'When does she propose to let Grey know the new destination?'

Brabazon's sarcastic laugh wafted towards Grey in the stillness. 'Not until they rendezvous again. She trusts him even less than does the king. But then she trusts no one. Not even us. Remember that, Crowley.'

Their voices faded as they entered the stables on the far side of the courtyard. Grey watched them emerge and ride out down the steep path towards the camp below.

For a moment he crouched where he was, unable to comprehend what he had overheard. His anger at being tricked was replaced by a disturbing premonition. So the lordship of Desmond was their true destination. The countess had more ammunition in her formidable arsenal than the king's writ. Concealed somewhere in her following was Desmond's competitor, the king's earl.

Grey's ignorance of the changes in plan was proof beyond doubt that the king's suspicions of him ran deeper than he suspected. So deep that the king no longer trusted him with matters pertaining to his office. His under-treasurer, God's blood, Grey swore softly, his very clerk, knew more of the destination of the king's army than did the king's deputy. His Yorkist blood and relationship to the young Geraldine, linked to his reluctance to pursue his nephew, had been brewed into a damning potion, stirred by the able hand of the countess. But if the king was so distrustful of him, why had he not been recalled or suspended from office? But perhaps he understood the king better than the Irish countess. He had first-hand knowledge of Henry's propensity to use his subjects until such time as they had outlived their usefulness. Despite her cunning, the countess was no more than a tool in the hands of the wily Tudor, who would never again entrust Ireland to Irish hands. For the king had learned a sharp lesson with Kildare and, Grey knew from experience, the Tudors had very long memories indeed.

Grey's mind wheeled at the dilemma the unexpected revelations posed for him. It was more imperative now than ever, he realised, that his nephew and his tutor should not be captured, lest his assistance in their flight from Donore should be revealed. It would confirm what was yet but suspected. And if the boy and his tutor evaded the countess this time, it would make his failure to capture them before appear less damning in the eyes of the king. If only the boy could be spirited away to the Continent, to Scotland or even to Ulster. But how was he to alert the boy's tutor to the impending invasion of Desmond? His nephew must have been either forced or lured to Desmond, perhaps as part of the crazy plan in which that peacock O'Donel had sought to involve him in St Patrick's.

By some stratagem, the countess had discovered that the boy had been moved from Carbury. She must have persuaded the king to invade Desmond and keep him in ignorance until the last moment. Well, Grey thought, let her think that she had succeeded. He had never met the elusive *de facto* Earl of Desmond. Stories of his ruthlessness and cunning had been much talked of at court and his blatant collusion with the emperor was well known. The stories were further embellished by the supposedly rightful claimant to the earldom, James FitzGerald. Tolerated at court, indigent and powerless, with no part to play in the king's expedient policy towards Ireland, FitzGerald clung to a fast-receding dream of restoration. The time had come, it seemed, for the king's Earl of Desmond to pay for his dinner.

Grey returned to his room and hurriedly dressed. He ordered his sergeant-at-arms to make ready an escort of a dozen riders, armed and mailed. As he had hoped there was an entrance to the monastery from the west. Brabazon and Crowley had ridden eastwards towards the camp. Grey knew he must make it from the monastery to the fringes of the forest without being detected by them. He had no desire for their company, especially in the unofficial and premature incursion he planned to make into the lordship of Desmond.

All was still as he left the sprawling monastery by the west gate. The horses clambered down the sloping pathway, their breath laboured in the stillness. The sun had not yet broken through the dense morning haze. Grey spoke low to the Irish guide, riding by his side. The guide had little English but enough knowledge of Latin to understand him.

'What direction is Desmond's castle?'

The Irishman looked quizzically at him from under his long glib as if the question was meant in jest.

'Which castle? Askeaton, New Castle, Shanid, Castlemaine, Castleisland, Kilmallock, Dingle . . .'

Grey held up his hand to stem the litany. 'The nearest.'

'Kilmallock.' The guide pointed south-westwards. 'A distance of two days.'

Too far, Grey thought. He must be back in Cashel before nightfall, before suspicions were aroused. But he must make contact with one of Desmond's people. The plan he had hatched depended on it.

'The nearest settlement?' he asked the guide, who nodded his understanding and led them towards the dark line of the forest.

The reached the fringe of the forest and were soon enveloped within its dense foliage. Grey could discern no visible pathway through the undergrowth, but the guide, with unerring instinct, rode unhesitantly forward through the trees.

What the merchants and entrepreneurs of London would

give to own the fortune that surrounded them, Grey thought, as he rode through the virgin forest of mighty oak, yew and ash, which formed a green awning over the subsidiary layer of rowan, hazel and holly. English forests, once as serried and widespread, had long fallen to the woodsman's axe for firewood, to build towns and villages and the great ships that plied the high seas in search of new worlds to conquer. Bluebells, wild orchids and soft mosses carpeted the clearings between the trees and mingled with the smell of earth and decaying undergrowth. Every sound seemed magnified in the enclosed stillness. A raucous cry of a rook made a horse rear, and the rider's curses profaned the silence.

They had travelled about an hour when the guide pointed to a well-trodden track which disappeared northwards through the trees. They followed this for some hours, stopping at a stream to water the horses and rest. The track followed the course of the stream as it wound its way through the undergrowth. No human being crossed their path, although it would not have surprised Grey if from behind each tree, shrub and moss-covered rock, a myriad eyes watched their every movement. His soldiers were getting restive. They preferred the open countryside. Within the oppressive confines of the forest, they were vulnerable to an ambush. He was about to order the guide to turn back, when the sound of rushing water and voices reached his ears. Grey gave a low order and from behind him there was a rasp of swords being drawn from scabbards.

They rounded a sharp bend which opened into a large clearing. A stone barn and a few thatched stables and cabins stood beside the stream which gushed in a whirlpool around a great wooden millwheel. A wagon stood before one of the stables, propped up on one side by an oak beam, one wheel missing. Beside it were piled oak chests and numerous wooden boxes. Four horses grazed peacefully in the clearing. One raised its head and neighed softly as the horsemen broke from the cover of the forest. From within one of the stables,

313

the sound of a smithy's hammer resounded.

A woman emerged from one of the cabins, a pitcher in her hand. She observed them silently before darting back inside to reappear, accompanied by four men. From out of the stable a burly figure emerged, the iron tongs and hammer of his trade in his hands.

Grey signalled to his Irish guide and, with a word to his men, nudged his horse further into the clearing and drew rein near the group. Their eyes took in every detail of his appearance, from the flat-topped hat on his head to the silver spurs on his boots. One of the men muttered something to his guide.

'What did he say?' Grey asked, without taking his eyes from the faces before him.

'He asks if you are Gall.'

'Tell him we are, but that we come in peace.'

The guide spoke rapidly in Gaelic and simultaneously the four men snatched their short swords from the belts around their waists and, pushing the woman behind them, made threatening moves towards him.

'Ask them are they of the Earl of Desmond's men.'

The question stopped them in their tracks and one of them spat derisively on the ground before replying. The guide translated, disbelief in his intonation.

'They say they are MacCarthy's men. From Carbury.'

'You think they lie?' Grey asked the guide.

'They do not lie,' a woman's clear voice replied in English.

From out of a cabin came a woman of striking appearance followed by two peasant women. Her demeanour and dress made Grey realise that he was in the presence of a woman of some standing. Her dark hair was braided and coiled around her head. Her russet dress, low-cut at the front, fell in straight folds to the ground. A row of gilt buttons adorned the bodice. A scarf of primrose silk caught around her neck was folded over her breasts and held in place by a gold pin. She showed neither fear nor anger at their intrusion, just a quiet curiosity.

314

Grey dismounted and bowed before her. The hazel eyes watched him with a not unfriendly stare. There was something familiar about her features, he thought.

'Madam, you speak English. Perhaps you might advise me how best I might get a message to the Earl of Desmond.'

She held his gaze for a moment before replying.

'Perhaps I could be the bearer of your message. I am on the road to the earl's castle. And would be there sooner had a broken axle not delayed our passage.' She indicated the wagon as she spoke.

'You are English.' She said it as a statement. Her eyes looked beyond Grey to the drawn swords of his men. 'Here we treat visitors with welcome and good cheer. The sword we reserve for our enemies.'

Grey looked around the clearing. Apart from the four men still with swords drawn, the smith and some women, there was nobody else to be seen. He motioned to his men to sheath their weapons.

'Whom do I have the honour to address?'

She hesitated before replying. Those finely drawn features, the attractive hazel eyes, English fluent, enunciation clear, by dress and demeanour a lady – yet they could hardly have met before. Grey had never set foot inside Desmond before this moment.

'I am widow of The MacCarthy of Carbury, Eleanor FitzGerald. And you?'

The explanation dawned on him before she had finished. The familiar features recalled his brother-in-law, her brother. So this was the daughter of the Great Earl, who had been spirited away to marry with the chieftain of Carbury, whose territory he had set out to attack. Perhaps his nephew was with her here. The coincidence made his heart race in anticipation.

He spoke quickly and low. 'My lady, 'tis imperative that I speak with you. In private.'

The urgency in his voice dispelled the reluctance he saw

flash across her eyes. He had not answered her question and preferred to be silent until they could speak alone.

She spoke in Gaelic to the smith who showed them to a low-set cabin. Inside, Grey's eyes took a moment to adjust to the darkness. She stood before him, a perplexed look on her face.

'You have not told me who you are,' she reminded him quietly.

'Leonard, Lord Grey.'

He heard her intake of breath. She darted him a look of fear and loathing and made to leave.

'Hear me out, my lady, I beg you, for your nephew's sake, if nothing else.'

She stopped at the door, her back towards him.

'I intend the boy no harm. I am his uncle.'

'You are the deputy of the murderer of my kin.' Her voice sounded harsh in the quietness of the cabin.

'I have already risked much, my office, perhaps my life, to protect my nephew. *Our* nephew. Perhaps his tutor told you. I am hardly likely to do him ill now.'

'Then why are you here? As deputy or uncle?' She turned towards him, her eyes searching his face.

'As both, but no less committed to my nephew's safety. I pledge my oath on that.'

'As you pledged your oath to Silken Thomas and my brothers,' she replied bitterly. 'Their trust in you caused them to perish at Tyburn. Why should I heed you?'

'Because, madam,' he answered her shortly, 'you have simply no option, if you wish to save your nephew's life.'

She stood before him, uncertain whether to go or hear him out. He pressed home the slim advantage of her indecision.

'Your sister, the Countess of Ormond, has the king's writ to invade Desmond, capture the boy, and break up this league formed in his defence. An army lies this moment in Ormond.'

She showed no reaction. 'The Earl of Desmond can match your army and more besides. His urraghs alone can muster more than the king or my sister.'

'But can their loyalty be assured, when the Countess of Ormond produces her thunderbolt before their very eyes?'

She looked at him uncomprehendingly.

'James FitzGerald. Some would say, the rightful Earl of Desmond.'

By her reaction he knew she understood the effect the return of the claimant to the Desmond earldom would have on the legion of urraghs now bound by fear and dependence to the present earl. It would, as the king had astutely surmised: divide loyalties and sow the seeds of dissension among them. Above all, it would put paid to Desmond's ambition of becoming undisputed leader of the Irish chieftains.

'Where do you stand on this?'

He sighed deeply and smiled ruefully. 'I wish I knew,' he said truthfully. 'Because of your sister, the king suspects that I drag my heels about capturing my nephew. And he is right. But he has no hard evidence and I do not intend to provide him with any.'

'Then you are with my sister.'

He raised his hand. 'My lady, listen to me. There is little time. Yes, I intend to serve the king's interest in Ireland. I'll not deny that I view Desmond's league with alarm and will do my utmost to break it and sever its connection with the enemies of England. But the king's irrational fear, which lusts for the blood of an eleven-year-old child, my nephew – that I cannot condone. To my mind, the Kildares have paid in full the penalty for their disloyalty.'

'Then it seems to me, my lord, that to do your duty, you must sacrifice your nephew or your head,' she said with some pity.

'Not necessarily. The boy must be taken out of Desmond forthwith, to a safe place out of your sister's reach. To Ulster

317

or to Connacht perhaps. I will then arrange for him to be taken out of Ireland, to someone who is trusted, both by you and by the boy's tutor. Someone who will give him the sanctuary your brother intended. But I must have your help if my plan is to have any chance.'

His appeal, he saw, caught her by surprise. He continued.

'With the boy removed from Ireland, Desmond's league will fall asunder and the threat to the king in Ireland will be removed. The boy will be saved and I will have done my duty.'

'Desmond will never agree to disband the league or to let the boy go.'

'Have little care on that score, my lady. Desmond will be most desirous of doing the king's bidding, for your sister holds the key to his change of heart.'

She looked at him suspiciously.

'Who is this go-between of whom you speak?'

'Reginald Pole.'

The name seemed to allay somewhat the look of suspicion on her face.

'The boy might be taken by ship to Brittany perhaps, where the cardinal could arrange for his protection. Even if François is by that time allied with Henry, he will be loath to attack a papal legate. It would be more than his crown is worth. The old religion is still powerful in France.'

Eleanor weighed up his proposal in silence, her eyes searching his face.

'How do I know what you propose is simply not a trick to trap my nephew and send him to the king? As you did his uncles and brother?'

He sighed. 'I had hoped you would trust me, but perhaps expected that you would not. I will have a letter with the seal and signature of Reginald Pole on the ship as proof of my goodwill. You will keep the letter until such time as news of the boy's safe arrival in France is brought to you. If anything goes amiss, you are at liberty to send the letter to

318

the king as proof of my treason.'

She thought about his proposal for some time, before giving a reluctant nod of her head.

'How will we know the time and place of arrival of the ship?'

'That, I'm afraid, must rest with you. You must nominate some person on the western coasts where the ship might land. Someone you can trust.'

He could see the struggle that raged within her and prayed that the logic of his proposal would outweigh her doubts.

'Send the ship to Dubhdara O'Malley, in Mayo.'

'The pirate?' he replied, surprised at her choice.

'A friend,' she replied simply and turned to go, but stopped abruptly to look back at him.

'I will let Thomas Leverous know of your plan. I fear I may be of little use in its implementation. I am to marry soon,' she said quietly.

He bowed low towards her. 'My good wishes to you and your intended spouse. Do I know his name?'

She hesitated before answering 'Manus O'Donel, lord of Tirconel,' she said, as she disappeared through the door and into the bright sunlight of the day.

A cold shiver of apprehension ran down Grey's spine.

30

KILTINAN CASTLE,
LORDSHIP OF ORMOND

The countess had personally supervised every detail, choosing the food, overseeing the laying of the table, instructing Dunboyne's reluctant steward to set it with his master's finest silver goblets and plate. She had requisitioned the baron's private chambers on the top floor of the castle for the duration of her stay. To Dunboyne's hesitant enquiry about the identity of her expected guest, she had given an evasive answer. But to ensure that his curiosity did not jeopardise her plan, she dispatched him, on the pretext of delivering a message to Brabazon at Grey's camp at Cashel. She wanted no curious eyes or loose talk that might reveal the identity of her guest and imperil her plan.

She had left nothing to chance in her efforts to impress him, to lure him to her cause. She knew that he was not the usual Irish warlord, unrefined in manner and unsophisticated in taste. O'Donel had flown far and high in his short career. Further than herself but not as high, she consoled herself. His tastes had been cultivated and refined in France, Italy and at the English court. While mutton joints and *uisce beatha* might suffice to whet the appetite of another, O'Donel's palate required more careful cultivation. Her cook, lured from Grey at Thomas Court, had responded to her challenge and had conjured a feast of such subtlety to tantalise even the most refined taste. With obvious first-hand knowledge, Dunboyne had assured her that the young woman installed in the bedchamber above would satisfy the appetite and expectation of even the most experienced profligate.

Her ploy to be rid of Grey for the duration of O'Donel's visit had worked. Dunboyne had said his lines according to cue. It was becoming increasingly easy to hoodwink Grey, she thought with some satisfaction. He seemed to have lost both his nerve and his authority. Brabazon and Crowley now openly looked to her for direction and she could yet manipulate, to Grey's further discredit, the craving for booty rampant among his unpaid soldiers. However she thought, as she moved the oak chair for her guest so that it faced the evening light, further control of Grey might not be necessary. If O'Donel, as she planned, agreed to conspire with her, Grey's days were numbered. Proof of his deliberate obstruct-ion of the king's command regarding the capture of her nephew would assuredly be extracted from Leverous or the boy by the rack and thumbscrew in the Tower and copper-fastened by O'Donel's testimony of Grey's conspiracy with Reginald Pole and the Geraldine League.

Still she would have to play her cards more shrewdly than she had ever done. O'Donel was no gullible backwoods chieftain. He had lived under the roof of the Great Earl, she reminded herself, at the courts of Henry Tudor and of François and in the country of Machiavelli. Within such climates of subterfuge and cunning, the ambitious chieftain undoubtedly had been well schooled. Drawing him within her orbit was necessary to enable her to fulfil her promise to the king and to realise her ambition. Where her father had extended his power by ties of matrimony and dependence, she preferred to extend hers through reward and punishment. Later O'Donel would be the perfect foil to diminish the influence of O'Neill in Ulster and neutralise him as a threat to her ambition to rule all Ireland. Her ties with O'Donel might be of a more personal nature, if the harper's story of his impending marriage to her sister was true. Nevertheless whether through matrimony or reward, she must convince O'Donel that his destiny lay with her and entice him from the conspiracy to protect the Geraldine heir.

From the kitchen attached to the baron's private apartments, the aroma of cooking aroused her craving. She moved down the short passageway separating the kitchen from the chamber. Her stomach for food was her one foible. It began as a consolation for the alienation of her youth and had developed into an addiction. As others craved sexual satisfaction or maternal fulfilment, her mouth was the receptacle of her pleasure.

Her cook respectfully stood aside as she examined the result of his craft: mutton stuffed with garlic, venison done in a feather-light pastry and coated with sugared mustard, roast wood-pigeon with pickled cabbage, pink salmon, garnished with fresh watercress, quail and woodcock. She tasted and picked and nodded in appreciation. He was worth the extra angels it had cost her to entice him from Grey, whose taste buds, if Brabazon was to be believed, were well dulled by his indulgence in *uisce beatha*. She issued her instructions for the serving of the feast and accompanying beverages and then climbed the short flight of stairs to the bedchamber.

She stood for a moment at the door, observing the baron's seductive nymph who reclined under the tester on the silk counterpane. The nymph looked up at her entrance and resumed the combing of her honey-coloured tresses with languid ease. The baron had praised her talents effusively, although the countess doubted if his sexual preferences were as exacting as O'Donel's were reputed to be. At least she was young and comely, she thought, as she closed the door and returned to the chamber to await the arrival of her guest.

Nearing the door, she heard the strains of a harp being

inexpertly plucked within. Her brow furrowed with anger. She had expressly told Dunboyne that his household was prohibited from entering this wing of the castle during her tenure. She flung the door open in anticipation of a confrontation. Seated in the deep window embrasure, a figure, with the hood of a mantle covering his head, continued unperturbed to strum a small harp. She felt her anger mount. MacGrath was meant to conduct O'Donel only as far as the castle courtyard. How had the knave managed to evade her guards at the entrance? And where was O'Donel, she wondered, her anger giving way to unease?

In one sudden movement she swept the harp from his hands and sent it crashing to the floor. The figure stooped to retrieve it and a mocking voice reprimanded. 'My music does not meet with my lady's approval? Tch, tch. Then ''tis just as well that I earn my bread by other means.'

The countess was taken aback by the cultured tones. The figure stood up and shook the hood from his head. Blue eyes mocked her incomprehension. With a flourish he flicked the cloak aside to reveal the tattered rags of the lowliest kern.

'Forsooth, madam, could you not dress your harper better?' he indicated his tattered trews and worn jerkin. 'By my oath, you must value his music as lowly as you do mine. He has got the better of the exchange, I assure you.'

Relief slowly dispelled her anger. O'Donel had hardly changed in appearance since the days in Maynooth. The same youthful golden looks, the same irritatingly confident manner.

'The harper was to guide you to Ormond.'

'I am touched by your concern for my welfare, Lady Margaret,' O'Donel said with sarcasm. 'But having negotiated my way safely from England to Italy, I dare say I can find my way to Ormond. As for your harper, he lies at Askeaton, in better apparel than when he found me.'

With an effort she ignored his insolence.

'I thought instead to become a harper, for a day, as a penance for my excesses,' he whispered suggestively. 'But the apparel suits me little, and my harping, it appears, pleases even less.'

How could her sister have fallen for such a jackanape, she wondered? She smiled frostily and bade O'Donel be seated, forcing herself to be cordial. Jackanape or no, he was the kernel of her plan.

'Your choice of disguise is as inventive as I would have expected from one of your reputation,' she concurred, as she rested her bulk in the chair opposite him. 'We have heard snatches of your life since Maynooth and have often envied you. As free to roam the world as we have been tied to duty here.'

'Not without reward, my lady,' O'Donel countered suavely. 'As I hear, you command as much power as did once the Great Earl your father, while I have yet to make my start.'

'Come, come, O'Donel, modesty ill becomes you. The lordship of Tirconel is no mean platform on which to build your ambition.'

'Perhaps my marriage with your sister will benefit Tirconel, as yours did Ormond.'

Her violet eyes looked at him speculatively. ''Tis strange, I never thought your youthful attraction to my sister would be reciprocated.'

A smile flashed across O'Donel's handsome features, without touching his eyes. 'Time alters circumstances and feelings. Once I was deemed an unsuitable suitor for her hand; now she is a willing recipient of my proposal.'

His impertinence fed her annoyance. With an effort she forced herself to ignore it. She needed the services of the knave. And one day he might soar too high and she would enjoy his fall all the greater.

'Forsooth, O'Donel, your prospects hardly depend on your marriage to my sister. Indeed, if it were so, I would fear for your success. The Geraldine name no longer bears the same prestige in Ireland. It is tainted with rebellion and conspiracy.'

'Then perhaps I should seek to make my mark on the backs of the Geraldines,' O'Donel slyly replied.

'The certain way to the hangman's knot, more likely. The cause of the Geraldines is lost. Their dream of power in Ireland belongs in the past. The present is what concerns me.'

'The future is more my concern.' He was watching her like a cat.

'I am glad to hear it. Perhaps I can offer you a more profitable one than that which you now contemplate. I hear that neither the pope nor Desmond has a reputation for largesse.'

He looked sharply at her. The air of sardonic bantering disappeared. She rose abruptly.

'Perhaps we can gauge how close our ambitions lie over supper.'

She rapped the table loudly and her cook carried the first of the succulent plates shoulder high into the chamber.

It was a pleasure, she thought, to see the trouble she had expended appreciated by one whose tastes were as highly developed as her own. They spoke little but concentrated on the delights placed before them.

'My lady,' O'Donel finally sat back in his chair and wiped his mouth with a linen napkin, 'I can say with certainty that the table of neither king nor pope could surpass this repast.' He lifted the silver goblet. '*Sláinte 'gus saol agat!*'

'*Sláinte,*' she replied and rose from from the table. She indicated him to the chair facing the window where the evening light shone on her guest and would allow her to scrutinise his reaction to her proposal more closely.

Dressed in the ragged clothes of the harper, O'Donel still cut an elegant figure, but behind the carefree exterior, she knew, he waited attentively to hear what was behind her invitation.

Without a word, she lay two withered white rose petals on the table between them and felt a moment of elation to see his smug composure momentarily ruffled.

'Withered, alack,' she said with false apology, 'but then they have travelled far. From Paris to Dublin and from there to me,' she lied. For the petals given to her by Brabazon she had sent to the king. The ones that lay now on the table she had picked in her garden in Kilkenny. But it mattered little. They had produced the desired effect.

O'Donel immediately regained his composure. 'Had I known that there was such a scarcity of fresh roses in Ormond, I would have brought you a posy from Desmond.'

His reaction was as she had anticipated. O'Donel would continue to dance around the issue until she pinned him down.

'Let us dispense with this charade. I hardly asked you here to bandy words of foolishness.'

'Nor to sample the excellence of your cuisine.'

'The king knows of your intrigues with the pope and Reginald Pole, and your part in this ill-fated league of Desmond.' She frowned in puzzlement. 'I find your efforts to establish Geraldine dominance in Ireland strange, to say the least. As I recall, you have little to thank the Geraldines for, even less than me.'

O'Donel stretched his elegant legs and sipped from the goblet. His carefree blue eyes were clouded with animosity. The bantering tone had disappeared.

'We cannot always choose the star we are to follow. The choices presented are few.'

She leaned towards him. 'Then allow me to present you with a choice. The star you have chosen is no more than a meteor which, mark me, will come crashing down to earth. The pope, my friend, is a fickle ally. He struggles for power now with the king of England as he did recently with the emperor, whom he now seeks as his crusading knight. But you as well as I know the real issues in Ireland. Can you imagine O'Connor, O'Carroll, MacWilliam, O'Brien and the rest risking their necks behind the banner of the pope?' She paused. 'Can you imagine O'Neill doing so?'

The blue eyes narrowed and the handsome face was distorted by a scowl. She knew she had struck the vulnerable spot in O'Donel's armour and quickly pressed home her advantage.

'Remove the Geraldine heir and Desmond's league falls apart. No matter how much the pope in Rome or Reginald Pole exhort, the Irish chieftains will be guided by the only star they know – survival and how best to win advantage over a rival. MacWilliam against Clanrickard, Kildare against Ormond,' she paused, 'O'Donel against O'Neill, as it has always been and ever will be in Ireland.'

The pale eyes looked coldly in her direction. 'What do you offer that is any different?'

'Victory,' she simply replied. 'For you, at the expense of O'Neill.'

'And for you?'

She paused, reluctant to voice the ambition she had nursed and buried deep within her, concealed from everyone, from her husband, from Brabazon, from the king. The blue eyes willed her to disclose it and somehow she knew that if she did, O'Donel would be hers.

'Victory at the expense of Grey.'

O'Donel whistled through his teeth and a sardonic smile spread slowly across his features, that made her want to stretch out her hand and lash his face. She held herself in check.

'My humble pardon, for ever doubting that the Great Earl's ambition was less likely to be found in his daughter than in his puny grandchild.' He filled her goblet with red wine and then his own and raised it in a toast. 'O'Neill and Grey against Ormond and O'Donel.' He clinked his goblet against hers. 'I tell you now, my lady, it is no contest . . . but a slaughter.'

The countess felt a glow of satisfaction. She had accomplished what she had set out to do by getting O'Donel to take her bait. Once again tipping her goblet against his with a flourish, she began to outline the plot in which he was to play such a crucial role.

31

ASKEATON CASTLE

Eleanor emerged from the gloom of Clonish forest into the brightness of the open countryside. With a shiver of relief she felt the warmth of the sun melt the chill from her body. The residual feeling of confinement, the result of endless miles of trekking through the densely wooded cover, gradually vanished. Until her fortuitous meeting with Grey, the long journey from Carbury had been uneventful. She had said a sad farewell to the members of her household in Kilbritin, who were shocked by her unexpected departure. She had never thought of leaving Kilbritin and certainly never to marry Manus O'Donel. The panic of what lay before her almost compelled her to flee back to the safety of the familiar surroundings. With an effort she tried to control the sense of fear and entrapment which threatened to overwhelm her.

She cursed the allurement that drew O'Donel to her. If she could identify the intangible attraction, she would happily efface it. There was no one with whom she could share the burden of her guilt and the shameful price she had to pay. To confide meant disclosure of the reason that forced her to marry O'Donel. Cormac and Leverous, the two people in the world closest to her, from whom in any other circumstance she would have sought consolation, were particularly

329

excluded. To protect Cormac's identity, she must abandon happiness, surrender her honour and lose the love and respect of the only man she could love.

His face that day in the courtyard at Askeaton Castle, when Desmond made public her unnatural betrothal, had tormented her every waking moment since. The look of painful disbelief, of betrayal that lay naked upon his face, struck her like a dart, spiked with double barbs of shame and anger. In desperation she ran through the milling throng who crowded round her, hands extended in congratulations. But Leverous had disappeared and did not return. She knew she must meet him once more to tell him of Grey's startling proposal. She dreaded the moment.

She loved Leverous, of that she had no longer any doubt. With that awareness came the realisation that her love for Donal had been but a comforting substitute for the passionate longing that had waited to be revived within her. With Leverous, love had been, as she had expected, a fusion of bodies and minds. It was as if their feelings for each other had been suspended, locked away secure, waiting for the moment of reawakening. In the darkness of his chamber at Askeaton she realised she had at last arrived at her emotional destiny. But the fruit of their love, which should have been the proud declaration of their union, had become an instrument of deceit and blackmail, primed to wrench them apart again. She closed her eyes in agony at her cruel fate.

Her escort chatted among themselves, relieved that the end of the journey was in sight. But as the grim walls of Askeaton Castle loomed before her, it seemed that every step forward carried her towards a hideous destiny she could not avoid, as if she was entrapped in an endless nightmare. O'Donel had made his intention clear of leaving for Tirconel as soon as they had signed the marriage contracts. Desmond had offered the services of his brehons to negotiate on her behalf. To their indignation and O'Donel's annoyance, she had invoked her right by brehon law and had instructed them to include a clause ensuring that the marriage was to be of one year's duration. It was a paltry concession, an insignificant indulgence from the hell that lay before her.

Her extraordinary meeting with Grey had served to distract her mind from her troubles. The anger she had initially felt towards the king's deputy had almost clouded her evaluation of his strange offer. Memories of her brothers, of Silken Thomas, made her curt, and suspicious of him. It was too late when she realised the enormity of the risk he was taking to save Gerald from a similar fate which the king had meted out to the boy's uncles and stepbrother at Tyburn. Grey had put his very life on the line to save her nephew. For should the king, through her sister, discover his collusion, Grey would follow her nephew and brothers down the road to Tyburn. She did not underestimate her sister's capacity for evil and sincerely hoped that neither did Grey.

In the distance she saw a rider on a small hob gallop in her direction from the castle gate. As he drew nearer, he waved an arm excitedly. She smiled in acknowledgement of Gerald's shouted greeting, distorted by the distance between them. She had grown attached to him over the months they had been together, since his rescue from her sister and their long confinement at Kilbritin and Askeaton. It was good to have a child to care for again. Although Cormac was but eight years older, it seemed a lifetime since he had been like Gerald in the indecisive period between boy and man. She had seen more of Gerald than she had seen of her own son at that age. Cormac had been in fosterage for most of his growing years, as Gerald would have been, had not such disasters occurred to mar and change the course of his young life. She had seen the naked terror in his eyes on her departure to Carbury and the disbelief at her assurances that she would return. Leverous had disappeared without trace and the boy feared that the last frail bastion of his insecure world would crumble.

He galloped madly towards her now, bareback and

331

without stirrups, jumping expertly to the ground as Desmond's men had taught him. His face was flushed with excitement as he walked beside her horse, embarrassed in his boyish way to reveal his happiness and embrace her before her escort. Affectionately, she tousled his hair, the same auburn curling locks as his father's.

'Leverous has come back.' His first words snatched her back from the meagre moment of happiness at seeing him. 'My Lord of Desmond's men found him in Limerick. He is going to stay this time,' he added with certainty.

'I'm sure he never intended to stay away for long,' she said quietly.

'I think he did.' The honest eyes looked up at her. 'I think he thought we no longer needed him.'

Eleanor felt the prick of tears behind her eyes.

'He is my only friend,' Gerald continued. 'Except you,' he added and smiled bashfully. He remounted his horse and rode beside her. 'My Lord of Desmond got chests full of swords and arquebuses from Spain. They came in a ship to Dingle. He brought them in wagons to Askeaton this morning. I saw them. They are in the guard house.'

'And the Spanish soldiers?'

Gerald shook his head. 'I did not see any soldiers.' Perhaps Desmond had left them at Dingle or Tralee, Eleanor thought, to produce them later as a conjuror to impress his allies in the league.

They crossed the bridge over the Deel and entered the great courtyard of Askeaton. A steward ran to help her dismount and gave her hob to a waiting horseboy.

'Mother.'

She turned and saw Cormac emerge from the darkness of the stables, closely followed by Leverous, who stopped abruptly in the doorway. 'We expected you yesterday,' she heard her son say.

Eleanor stood uncomprehendingly before him, her gaze looking beyond him to Leverous, whose eyes held hers for a fleeting moment before turning from her towards Gerald.

'An axle broke,' she heard herself reply as if from a distance. 'We made a detour to a smithy; then came on with all speed. I have news of great urgency for Desmond and for you, Thomas,' she said softly to Leverous. 'Can we speak?'

He nodded curtly without reply. His face showed neither gladness nor regret at seeing her, just an impassive indifference.

'Perhaps in the garden,' she said. 'we are less likely to be overheard.'

Cormac sensed the atmosphere between them and placed his arm about Gerald's shoulders. 'Come, Gerald, let's have a look at the Spanish blades.'

Eleanor and Thomas crossed the courtyard without speaking and entered the walled garden. The air was as heavy as the silence that lay between them. They walked a little way along the gravelled path, ablaze with pink roses, mad red poppies and vivid yellow and blue pansies. Eleanor's mind groped for an opening line that might break the tension. But anything that occurred to her seemed trivial and demeaning. She stopped short and faced him.

'I must speak my mind, Thomas. In God's name, we cannot part like this, with such bitterness between us. As before, only now it matters so much more.'

He stood motionless before her, his dark blue eyes as cold as a sword blade. He would not make it easy for her. But even as she tried to speak, she knew she could not reveal the reason why she must betray him, cast away their love for a hideous parody. To speak her mind was to speak the truth, to reveal the dark secret that perhaps might make him hate her more. She felt suddenly weary, felt her guard of resolve slipping away to reveal her naked weakness. She held her hands to her face, to block out his look of studied lack of interest, as if whatever she might say was no longer of concern to him.

'Do not look at me so, my dearest, I beg you,' she

whispered through her fingers. 'I cannot bear it. Desmond had no right to make the announcement as he did. I knew nothing of it.'

'It matters little,' his voice was harsh. 'You are still to marry O'Donel. He boasts of nothing else, rubs it in like salt in a wound every time I have the misfortune to cross his path.'

'Please believe me, Thomas, it is not my choosing.'

He looked incredulous. 'God's sweet life, Eleanor, credit me for not being an utter fool. You paid your dues in full, as the daughter of the Great Earl of Kildare, nineteen years past. This time you are free to choose as you will.'

'Would that I were.' Her voice trembled with the emotion that surged within her. 'Believe me, Thomas, I am more a captive of circumstances now than ever I was then. How can you above anyone believe that I could marry that contemptible charlatan? How could one I found so repulsive as a girl be acceptable now that I am free to choose? Surely, my love, you know me better than that?'

'God's blood, if the truth be known, I know you not at all,' he shouted in exasperation. 'Only as a memory, a phantom of my dreams, of my desires, of my . . . of my love.' His voice sounded strangled. He struggled for control and turned away from her. 'Tell me then what or who forces you to marry this time.' His voice was heavy with sarcasm.

She looked at him in silent agony.

How she longed to say the words aloud which echoed within her – 'Our son' – so that he might hear and understand. Her heart cried out, craving his understanding. The burden of their guilt was becoming too heavy for her to bear alone. She steeled herself against the compulsion that made her want to tell him the secret that both bound and divided them.

A rumble of thunder to the south broke the silence. He turned and, seeing she would not answer, with an impatient shrug of his shoulders made to leave. Her hand reached out to detain him.

334

'I have a message from Leonard Grey. He lies in Ormond with my sister, with an army, ready to invade Desmond to seek out Gerald for the king.' She saw him start. 'Grey gave warning to move Gerald west or north. Desmond will be attacked within three days.'

'How did you hear this?' His eyes looked at her with suspicion.

She told him briefly of her meeting with Grey.

'Only a fool would take the battle to Desmond in his own patch. He will match anything your sister or Grey can send against him.'

'But not the surprise my sister has in tow.'

Curiosity replaced the look of indifference on his face.

'James FitzGerald, the court earl. His return will divide the loyalty of Desmond's urraghs for certain.'

Leverous swore softly. 'Not to mention the effect on Desmond's allies in the league. Compounded by the fact that the emperor has not been as generous as Desmond led them to believe.'

Briefly he told her about the emperor's response to Desmond's request for support for the league and how the earl sought to keep it from his allies, until he could persuade Robert Walshe to return to plead his cause again with Charles. The tension gradually eased between them, united again in the cause of Gerald's safety.

'Grey begs that we do not divulge his part in this. I am to tell Desmond that the warning comes from a friend within Ormond.'

Leverous nodded in agreement. 'Grey has put his head in the noose this time. God's mercy on him should your sister suspect his complicity.'

Eleanor paused before imparting the rest of Grey's offer, uncertain as to how Leverous would react.

'Grey offers to procure safe passage for Gerald to France.'

Leverous looked at her incredulously. 'The king's own deputy offers to commit open treason against him! Grey must be mad or so sickened of life to contemplate such a death wish.' He eyed her with suspicion. 'It stinks of treachery. Perhaps a convenient way for Grey to capture the boy, instead of having to hunt for him around the country?'

'He says his concern is to break Desmond's league and that the only way to do it is by removing Gerald from Ireland. He offers a bond on his word.'

He listened with interest as she told him of Grey's proposition regarding the letter from Reginald Pole.

'Reginald Pole.' Leverous said the name with reverence. She saw his resistance wane.

'That would make the cardinal doubly involved in having Gerald brought to France.' He stood silent for a while before her, his hand to his forehead, as if he balanced her tidings against something he already knew. 'Robert Walshe is certain that the emperor will ally with Henry against François. He has withheld this from Desmond, so that the league remains intact until Cardinal Pole sends for Gerald to come to France. But now, with his rival on his doorstep, Desmond will use the league to bargain with Grey, to disband it in exchange for his title. The pieces begin to fall into place. Perhaps Grey is right. If he succeeds and gets Pole's consent, perhaps it is best that Gerald leaves Ireland. And the sooner the better.'

'Where will Gerald find sanctuary until then?'

'We must . . .' he stopped and looked at her, '*I* must,' he corrected himself softly, 'hasten away with him. Perhaps to O'Brien in Thomond.'

'Further,' she advised him. 'The Shannon will not erase the scent; my sister will resume the hunt for Gerald with greater effort now that there is no league to protect him. O'Neill might be inclined to help now that the league is no more. You could send him word. Choose someone you can trust. Gerald's life depends on it.'

'I only know two such people: Cormac and Robert Walshe.'

She felt a stab of pain at the slight, and renewed

apprehension at his choice. Always Cormac, she thought. He saw her hesitation.

'You do not agree?

'Of course.'

Another roll of thunder heralded the approaching storm. They walked slowly back along the path. Their last steps together, she thought in panic. And she had no words to say, to tell him of her love, and her dread of being without him. She felt his eyes on her and, turning, saw that a look of sadness had replaced his earlier indifference.

'I imagined it all so differently,' he said softly. 'That together we would take Gerald to safety. Leave this blighted country. Go to France, to Italy perhaps, to the scenes of my student days in Padua; to Florence.' He reached for her hand and held it tightly in his. She saw him struggle with the thoughts he was trying to enunciate, when a familiar sardonic voice cut across his words.

'I ask you, my lord, what is a poor besotted lover to think, when he finds his betrothed ignores him for another?'

Leverous quickly dropped her hand and they turned to see O'Donel and the Earl of Desmond approach. Eleanor saw O'Donel's face harden, as he shifted his gaze from her to Leverous. She felt a shiver of fear. There was malice in O'Donel's eyes.

'I heard you had returned, my lady,' Desmond said curtly. 'Your escort informs me that you encountered an English force inside Desmond.' His voice was accusing.

'I was on the point of bringing you the news, my lord.'

'But you thought to share it with others first, it seems,' O'Donel accused her.

She felt Leverous bristle at O'Donel's rough tone. Even Desmond looked at him askance.

'Come now, O'Donel, you have but recently returned yourself,' the earl admonished him. 'Doubtless Lady Eleanor looked for you and could not find you.'

Eleanor ignored O'Donel and turned to the earl. She

337

related the warning given by the leader of the English group, deliberately omitting Grey's name, as she had promised. At the mention of James FitzGerald, Desmond's narrow face froze in a tapestry of alarm and loathing.

'*Marbhfháisce air*!' he cursed harshly, his face creased in worry. 'How many are there?'

'Two armies: Grey's and the Countess of Ormond's. Some seven hundred all told.'

Desmond swore again. 'The accursed Ormonds. Since Kildare's fall, they have not ceased to swell their numbers at every opportunity.'

'"Tis my nephew they seek,' Eleanor told him. 'If he were to be taken to shelter elsewhere, to Connacht or to O'Neill in Ulster, Grey might be less inclined to – '

'O'Neill?' O'Donel spat out the word as if it were poison. 'O'Neill seemed little inclined to help your nephew before.' He turned to Desmond. 'I will take the boy to Tirconel, until the danger is passed. He will feel at home there, now that his aunt will be there to keep him company.'

Eleanor felt her heart beat with apprehension. She dared not direct a glance at Leverous lest it be intercepted by O'Donel.

'What is there to stop Grey or the Countess of Ormond from pursuing Gerald into Tirconel?' Leverous protested. 'Your forces would stand even less chance against theirs.'

O'Donel threw Leverous a look of contempt. Eleanor saw a crimson flush of anger spread across Thomas's face. The hatred between the men was palpable.

'Listen to the Gall,' O'Donel sneered, 'who speaks without knowing of what he speaks. My lordship is protected by something greater than whatever force the Countess of Ormond or anyone else can send against it. Mother nature has been generous to us in Tirconel. Rock, bog, mountain and river are worth more than a host of gallowglass or English hirelings. Send an army of two thousand across the Curlews and I promise you it will take no more than two hundred of my kern to decimate them.'

'Yes, yes,' Desmond interrupted him impatiently. His black eyes darting nervously. 'Leave with the boy as soon as possible. It is best. I shall have to deal with Grey.' His face was worried, the habitual look of arrogant control pierced by uncertainty and vulnerability in the face of Eleanor's disclosures. The threat presented by the presence of his competitor overcame his ambition. 'Are you to accompany the boy?' he asked Leverous.

Eleanor held her breath, part of her crying out that he would come, the other willing him to stay.

Leverous's eyes challenged O'Donel. 'Yes.'

Desmond nodded and made to move away. Without taking his eyes from Leverous, O'Donel called after the earl, 'Lady MacCarthy's marriage contract, my lord.'

'H'm, yes, it is best that we see to it now. I have little time to waste. My lady, if you would.' Desmond waited impatiently for her.

Eleanor glanced at Leverous, but his head was averted from her. O'Donel took her arm. With a shudder of revulsion, she shook his hand away and followed the hurrying figure of the earl down the path.

32

LORDSHIP OF DESMOND

Despite the strength of the combined forces, both armies moved forward uneasily. The Ormond soldiers knew that they were in the territory of their traditional enemy. They were born and bred to fear and hate their Desmond neighbours and knew instinctively that their feelings were reciprocated. Preceded by the standard-bearers, the English cavalry and infantry darted anxious eyes around at the unfamiliar landscape, disturbingly distant from the protection of the Pale.

They had skirted the dark mass of Clonish forest, so that they were approaching Kilmallock from the south. The dense forest posed an insurmountable barrier for such numbers and it was thought better to travel the additional distance around it. Their numbers and strength would have counted for nothing against the Desmond wood-kern, flitting like shadows among the trees, hounding and harrying.

The Countess of Ormond had long experience of Irish battle tactics: ambush, sudden attack and retreat, regrouping for lightning strikes again and again. She had used them to her advantage on many occasions. Such tactics in such terrain could demoralise the best army in the world. But against their superior numbers and weapons, in the open field, Desmond's kern and gallowglass would stand little chance.

And if the sound of cannonballs against the wall of his castle did not bring Desmond running, the presence of his rival was bound to make the vain earl more amenable to handing over the Geraldine and disbanding the futile league he had formed to protect him.

The countess glanced with little interest at the court earl, riding alongside her husband. He cut an impressive figure in his English garb, but she reckoned his chances of acceptance in Desmond as slight. The present earl had an iron grip on the vast lordship that would be impossible to prise open. Like the king, she cared little about the validity or otherwise of his claim to the title and lordship. His usefulness was merely as a threat to make the present earl desist from protecting her nephew and from intriguing with the king's enemies abroad.

As she expected, Grey had procrastinated about the change of destination and refused to cross into Desmond until she had produced the king's writ and the court earl. Once satisfied, he had little option but to bow to the inevitable. To smash Desmond's league, she suspected, was the extent of his ambition. It was well she had made alternative plans with O'Donel, to ensure the capture of the Geraldine heir. Despite the king's explicit command, she expected little co-operation from Grey on that account but, she consoled herself, obstinacy had an easy knack of being interpreted as treason. Grey would pay the penalty as assuredly as had her brothers at Tyburn. She wanted him far away when she took custody of her nephew. There must be no mishaps, no warnings or sudden rescues, as before. She would personally accompany the boy to London. The arrangements had been made and everything was in readiness. The king's words of praise and gratitude already sounded in her ears; the sword of state rested in her hand. Once she was in control, the ambitions of her father might be realised by the daughter he had discarded.

She eased her weight on the pillion. She had invested

much to attain her ambition and now the end of the lengthy struggle was near. All the components of her elaborate plan were in place. Desmond was but the cloak of her real target. She looked impassively at the figure of Grey. Clad in his surcoat of chainmail, the hilt of his sword protruding at his thigh, he rode straight in the saddle, the epitome of a professional soldier whose natural habitat was in the field. He had proved a disappointing rival, as predictable as the inappropriate military tactics he doggedly employed in Ireland to the amusement of the Irish, who led him a dance though the wilderness and laughed, hidden deep in the undergrowth, as he and his heavy-set army floundered in the quaking bogs. This elaborate display of power and arms, the well-ordered lines of mailclad horsemen, pikemen, arquebusiers, and halberdiers, little impressed the Irish, who simply disappeared, driving their herds before them and leaving a denuded countryside to their pursuers. With little to sustain them, the pursuers soon became the pursued, the target of ambush and hunger and were glad to retreat to the protection of the nearest town. To rule Ireland, one had to adapt to the peculiarities of terrain, as much as to the prevailing customs. Her father had built his power on that basis, as she intended to do.

The scouts returned and indicated that Desmond's castle of Kilmallock seemed deserted.

'The village has gone booleying.' One pointed westwards. 'All but for a few *cailleachs*.'

'Booleying,' the countess echoed in derision, as she nudged her horse forward. 'Fools, Desmond has merely driven his cattle and everything else besides into the mountains before our coming.' She raised her voice on purpose so that Grey's soldiers could hear. 'He has picked the country clean.'

Cries of disappointment erupted from the ranks. Grey shot her a damning look. 'How many guard the castle?' he asked the scouts.

The taller of the two passed a hand across his glib and looked towards his companion for confirmation.

'The constable and the castle guard, about a score in all, no more.'

'And Desmond?'

The scout shrugged his shoulders. 'The *cailleachs* would not say.'

'Press on,' Grey ordered.

The army set in motion again, the wagons bumping over the uneven ground. The turrets of Desmond's castle loomed in the distance. It was a small but solid pile, situated alongside a river which drained the fertile pasturelands around it. Crenellated curtain walls, about twenty feet high, enclosed the bawn. A small barbican, with a projecting parapet above, guarded the entrance.

The army halted some distance from the walls. All was silent, except for the raucous cawing of the rooks nesting high above.

Grey rode towards the castle. 'Open, in the name of the king.' His words rebounded aimlessly off the silent walls.

'It appears deserted,' the Earl of Ormond rather needlessly called, relief evident in his voice. 'Perhaps we should make camp,' he offered hopefully, but was silenced with a look by his countess.

'It is time we tested Desmond's hospitality and eased our bones on something softer than the rocks.'

Her words were greeted with approval by the soldiers, already sniffing the scent of prey from the castle and the deserted village that lay within its shadow.

'Doubtless Desmond has given you the key,' her husband said, as he dismounted and stretched his legs.

Her husband was becoming a liability, the countess thought. Advancing age had dented his ambition and had made him content – a certain recipe for defeat. She was relieved that she had kept him in ignorance about her arrangement with O'Donel.

'My lord deputy holds the key to Kilmallock,' she replied. Grey looked suspiciously at her.

'The sound of cannonballs against his walls will bring Desmond scurrying from his den.'

'And give him warning of how the king deals with traitors,' Brabazon added.

'The king's writ does not empower me to enter a castle, unless provoked,' Grey crossly reprimanded his under-treasurer.

'Provoked?' the countess laughed scornfully. 'And what is this, pray. A castle barred against the king's deputy, by a traitor, an imposter.'

Grey hesitated, undecided.

From the direction of the village, angry shouts and curses erupted, accompanied by women's screams. A section of the Ormond forces had broken ranks and had set about ransacking the cabins surrounding the castle. Before they could be stopped, some of Grey's troops ran to join them and fought like dogs in the dust over the meagre loot. Some ancient women, their faces lined with the wrinkles of their years, cried a stream of curses and abuse at the looters. At the door of a cabin a younger woman struggled to free herself from the frenzied clutches of a soldier, her long smock torn about her breasts.

Wearily, Grey motioned to Brabazon to intervene and turned his attention once more to the castle.

'Well?' the countess asked impatiently. 'It will hardly open of its own accord.'

Grey shouted an order and two war carts were driven forward. The sacking was removed to reveal the square snouts of the breach-loading cannon.

It took some twenty men to haul the heavy brass ordnance into position. The gunner lit a match and held it close to the loading breach.

As Grey lifted his hand to give the signal, a rider galloped into the line of fire and slowly advanced towards them. The countess recognised Conor O'Brien, chieftain of Thomond. O'Brien's eyes flickered uneasily towards the cannon but he continued to advance. She heard Grey speak to the gunner, who extinguished the match. The eyes of the chieftain searched the faces of those before him. His gaze alighted in recognition on the countess before settling on the court earl. He spoke in Gaelic.

'The Earl of Desmond sends me. He regrets that he is unable to be here to welcome you to Desmond, but requests the honour of meeting you.'

Grey signalled to Crowley, who translated the chieftain's message. The lord deputy inclined his head but before he could reply, a figure pushed forward.

'There is only one Earl of Desmond and it is I,' the court earl interrupted, his voice shaking with indignation.

Grey motioned to the countess, who laid a hand firmly on the court earl's arm. Her eyes warned him to silence. Grey smiled pleasantly at O'Brien, who did not seem to understand what the court earl had said.

'We are always happy to meet loyal subjects of the king. But why does my Lord of Desmond not come himself?'

O'Brien's eyes glanced over the mass of armed men, before coming to rest on the cannons. 'He was uncertain whether you come in peace or in war.'

'The king's subjects have nothing to fear from his army, if they are truly loyal and loving subjects,' Grey intoned.

O'Brien digested his words and eventually replied. 'The Earl of Desmond awaits,' he pointed upriver, 'one mile hence with his army. To avoid bloodshed, in a gesture of goodwill to your lordship, he offers to meet you halfway, alone save for an escort.'

Grey did not answer immediately. He glanced towards the countess, as if he feared she would countermand whatever he decided.

The fool, she thought; she had masterminded the entire situation. She knew that he would accept Desmond's offer to negotiate rather than risk a battle, which, even if he should win, would result in little advantage to the crown. Grey could not remain in Desmond indefinitely and had not sufficient forces to garrison the sprawling lordship. Perhaps his hesitation stemmed from fear that Desmond might sacrifice the Geraldine heir to save his neck and position. But if her plan had worked, the boy was well on his journey northwards with O'Donel, towards the place where they had arranged to meet.

'Very well,' Grey decided. 'In one hour, with an escort of no more than ten. Tell the Lord of Desmond what forces and what ammunition,' he pointed to the court earl, 'we bring with us, so that he might not forget his word.'

Crowley translated Grey's words. O'Brien indicated his understanding and galloped out of sight. A rumble of disquiet rose from the ranks of Grey's soldiers, as they saw their chance of booty fade again.

Within the hour, after much bitter haranguing, the countess compelled Grey to include her in the party to meet Desmond. It was decided that the court earl would remain behind with the army, for fear an ambush might eliminate the trump card that seemed likely to ensure Desmond's co-operation. O'Brien would have confirmed his rival's presence to the earl and there was little need to antagonise him further, at least until they had heard what Desmond had to offer.

They met in open countryside, with the river Maigue between them. Desmond's trust of the English was cond-itional, the countess noted cynically. She looked at the slight figure astride a black stallion which pawed the ground nervously. The earl's dark eyes scanned the faces of Grey's escort for a glimpse of his rival. She had never met the ruler of the neighbouring lordship, despite the incessant attacks and reprisals they had waged on each other's territory. Even her father, she recalled, had been cautious when dealing with his powerful but sensitive kinsman.

Desmond's English, spoken with an Irish brogue, was

deliberate and hesitant.

'We are sorely grieved that you invade Desmond,' the earl's croaking voice complained. 'We have given no reason.'

'On the contrary, my lord,' Grey replied. 'The king has heard of your intrigue with his enemies abroad. Inviting them to Ireland. Making conspiracy against him.'

Desmond considered his reply. 'We understood in Ireland that the emperor and the king were friends. That France was the enemy of England.'

The Countess of Ormond smiled to herself at the old man's cunning. Grey could hardly demur, since the outcome of Henry's secret negotiations with both Charles and François still remained unresolved.

Grey tried another tack.

'This league that you lead flies in the face of the king's authority in his lordship of Ireland. It makes him think that you plot with his enemies against him.'

'Tell me the enemies of the king, so that I may know them.'

She saw Grey's colour rise at Desmond's impertinence.

'I have enough ammunition to unseat you, my lord, not only from your charger there, but from your seat in Desmond. Your title is in doubt. Your cousin swears that he is the rightful earl.'

Desmond did not reply at once, but his quick eyes swept the party to try to locate his rival.

'Then my cousin is a liar, an imposter.'

Grey had hit the Earl where it most hurt him and sought to press home the advantage. 'The king has no wish to wage war on you, my lord. He is content that you retain your title, so long as you cease to conspire with his enemies and abandon this ill-conceived league.'

'And that you deliver up the son of the Earl of Kildare,' the Countess of Ormond cut across Grey's sonorous tones.

In angry undertones, Grey bid her be silent.

'I need no Ormond to tell me my duty,' Desmond's angry

347

voice carried across the river. 'The boy merely passed through Desmond and is long since gone.'

'Gone where?' Grey asked.

'To O'Neill in Ulster.'

The countess felt a warm glow of satisfaction. O'Donel had done his work well.

'O'Neill is now the head of the league,' the earl continued. A sly smile spread over his narrow features. 'It seems, my lord, that the king has more to fear in Ulster than in Desmond.'

The countess listened with delight to the exchange between Grey and Desmond. Her plan was working to perfection. Grey must now attack O'Neill. It was part of her bargain with O'Donel and it would also serve to keep Grey distracted and give her the opportunity to take the boy to London and claim her reward.

'It seems we waste our time here,' she said in low tones to Grey. ''Twould be better that we divide our forces. I will keep Desmond under observation and you take on O'Neill.'

'With three hundred men?' Grey replied scornfully.

'Then let us continue against O'Neill together.'

Grey looked at her suspiciously.

'The men grow restive without some source of booty,' Brabazon reinforced her argument. 'If we are not to attack Desmond, then let it be O'Neill. I tell you they will mutiny for lack of spoil.'

Grey moved away from them and faced Desmond on his own. 'In whose charge was the Geraldine taken to Ulster?'

The countess held her breath.

'The boy's aunt, the Lady MacCarthy, and his tutor, Thomas Leverous.'

The countess breathed more easily once more. Grey seemed satisfied with Desmond's answer.

'My lord, we will leave you in peace and look on your recent folly but as a temporary lapse of loyalty. Should you persist in your treasonable schemes, your lordship will be wasted and your cousin installed in your place. And from what I hear, there are many within your dominion that consider him more lawfully entitled than you. Beware, my lord. The king watches your every move.'

Without a word, Desmond wheeled his horse around. They watched him ride away with his followers until the gently sloping hills swallowed them from view.

The confrontation had gone better than could be hoped for, the countess thought. She would break away from Grey when she neared the place where she had arranged to meet O'Donel and finally take custody of the Geraldine.

33

LORDSHIP OF TYRONE

'Twenty beeves and forty marks.'

'Thirty beeves and fifty marks,' the brehon bargained.

O'Neill sighed loudly in exasperation. Magennis seemed determined to continue the haggling. O'Neill's stomach rumbled in protest as the aroma of boiled mutton and newly baked griddle cakes wafted towards him. The shadows had begun to creep across the fern and the long grass, as the warm August day drew to a close. Summer lingered into autumn but tomorrow he must reluctantly give the word to strike camp. It was well time to drive the herds back to the lowlands, return to Dungannon and prepare for the long winter. This year's booley had been both successful and enjoyable. The herds had had good grazing, their numbers increased by the new crop of calves, made sturdy and strong on the fertile upland pastures. O'Neill had hunted the red deer and wild boar throughout the summer and had seldom returned to camp empty-handed. The sun had helped his wounded leg and the pain seemed like a memory. He had good reason to be reluctant to leave the pleasurable tranquility of the uplands.

With a slight movement of his head, O'Neill indicated to his brehon that he should increase the offer to Magennis. The bargaining ritual had gone on long enough. The evening was for relaxation and feasting, for lovemaking and slumber. Yet he was careful to uphold the traditional proprieties pertaining to the ceremony less he offend his urragh, particularly when Clandeboy had tried to entice Magennis to purchase his slantyaght from him. O'Neill had to make certain that Magennis was his, so that the strategic pass into the Pale at Newry would remain in friendly hands.

'Thirty beeves and fifty marks . . . and,' the brehon withdrew a linen parcel from under the board, as O'Neill had instructed him, 'the O'Neill's *tuarastal.*'

Magennis looked doubtfully at the parcel which the brehon unwrapped from the linen folds to reveal a leather quilted jack and a heavy mailshirt. The brehon held them before Magennis. O'Neill saw him hesitate, knowing that to accept the gift would bind him doubly to O'Neill, by honour as well as by tribute.

Magennis bit his underlip. 'Thirty beeves and forty marks.'

O'Neill allowed a smile to escape across his face. The scriveners on both sides of the table, goose quills suspended above parchment, sensed that the long bargaining was at an end and waited his order to record it. He gave it. Magennis took the proffered gifts. With relief, O'Neill rose from the table and shook Magennis's extended hand. It was important to allow his urragh the last word so that he might not lose face before his followers.

Declining his invitation to remain for the night, Magennis paid O'Neill's *maor* the forty marks, arranged with him for the beeves to be driven to Dungannon before the feast of All Hallows and departed for his lordship with his party. Magennis seemed pleased with the outcome of his slantyaght and O'Neill hoped it would serve to deter Clandeboy and his English *agents provocateurs* from further interference with his urragh.

He gave the order to begin preparations for the evening meal and made towards the stream. His sons and their foster-brothers played noisily around the cluster of buildings that served as communal shelters during the period of the booley. They were rudely constructed with stone and wattle, windowless, with a single door and were used only when necessary, for in summer every daylight hour was spent under the sky. Depending on the weather, O'Neill preferred to spend the nights in the open, with his liegemen and captains, their legs stretched towards the warm campfire, recounting blow by blow raid and counter-raid, the exaggerated deeds of fighting men. Only the urge for his concubine or the inclemency of the weather induced him to sleep within the claustrophobic atmosphere of the bothy.

From the surrounding foothills of the Sperrins, he saw the creaghts and their dogs making their way towards the camp. Sentries would take their place for the night to protect the herds of small black cattle, which dotted the sides of the undulating hills all around, from the ravages of the wolf packs which roamed the isolated uplands.

O'Neill washed quickly in the cold mountain stream, shaking the droplets from his glib and beard. The mild breeze dried his skin. Loud reports of gunshots punctured the evening silence. Leisurely he made his way from the stream to a nearby hollow between two hills where his bodyguards practised with the arquebuses. Devlin, his captain, came to meet him. Together they watched the men, stripped to the waist, fix the cumbersome weapons on tripods and fire at an empty beer cask a hundred paces distant. The heavy thud of the ball as it struck its target confirmed that his kern were becoming accomplished shots, as Devlin had predicted.

'They need practice against moving targets,' O'Neill told Devlin. 'O'Donel or the English will hardly sit as patiently as the casks yonder.'

Devlin thought for a moment. 'Perhaps a boar hunt?'

O'Neill nodded his agreement. 'Arrange it. Soon. We might well have need of them, sooner than I had planned. This league of Desmond's fills me with foreboding. It is trouble which might well spill over into Ulster.'

'It can brook no good if O'Donel has a hand in it,' Devlin agreed.

Without answering O'Neill retraced his steps towards the camp. From the start he expected that O'Donel's interest in the league was motivated by something more sinister than protection of the Geraldine heir. It was strange that one who had been taken hostage by the Great Earl should go to such lengths to protect his grandson. But O'Neill had too long experience of O'Donel treachery to lower his guard against him, and his surveillance had paid dividends. O'Donel was in league with the Countess of Ormond and the English king. His disguise as an itinerant harper had not fooled the spies O'Neill had left behind him at Askeaton to monitor his every move. He knew of O'Donel's secret meeting with the countess in Ormond. What transpired between them he could but guess, yet it had convinced him beyond all doubt that Desmond's league, regardless of the help he might extract from Spain, was doomed by conspiracy from within its own ranks.

He felt a twinge of sympathy for his young cousin. Even the boy's aunt had thrown in her lot with O'Donel, if the intelligence he received was to be believed. It had surprised him, since he had long viewed his cousin Eleanor with favour: a woman of intellect and honour, he thought, one who viewed O'Donel with hostility. Why she should have undergone such a change of heart he could not fathom. But, he shrugged, women were as unpredictable as the weather; after three wives and numerous concubines, he understood that better than most. Perhaps being too long alone without a bedmate had made his cousin susceptible to O'Donel's advances. He would have asked her himself, if he had known she wished to marry again. For as certain as the great river beyond flowed into Lough Neagh, by marrying the Great Earl's daughter, O'Donel sought advantage over him in Ulster. O'Neill cursed his cousin for her lack of judgement and himself for a missed opportunity.

Under a solitary rowan tree his servants dressed the long board for supper. O'Neill leaned against the trunk under the berry-laden branches. In the verdant valley below, a lake glistened like beaten gold in the light of the evening sun. The lowing of cattle and the sharp barking of the creaght's dogs, sounded distant in the stillness. A breeze sighed through the drying leaves above his head. Here O'Neill felt at peace, part of a tapestry of timeless continuity, of life and death, of ancestry and custom, the custodian of some priceless gem inherited from his ancestors, lost in time, when his ancestral gods had fashioned the valley. Three thousand years ago, perhaps a remote ancestor, during a summer booley, had looked down on the selfsame valley and had felt the weight of responsibility as he did now. He was part of something greater than himself, above any transitory quest for personal power, the guardian of a sacred inheritance, honour-bound to pass it on intact to his successor.

The sound of approaching hoofbeats disturbed his contemplation. He remained motionless under the tree and watched his sentries escort two riders into the clearing before the bothies. The peace of the moment was shattered by this intrusive reminder of the world outside. He recognised Robert Walshe, the Earl of Kildare's chaplain and the young MacCarthy chieftain of Carbury, son of his cousin, the woman who was to marry with his enemy. Apprehension spiced his curiosity as to the reason for their unexpected arrival.

They walked towards him but, taken aback by his reserve, stopped short some paces away. The chaplain broke the silence.

'My Lord O'Neill. Forgive our intrusion. But it is a matter of the utmost urgency.'

'Aye,' O'Neill replied coolly, 'we usually smell trouble on the breath of visitors to Tyrone.' Their travel-weary faces made him relent. He motioned towards the table. '*Is túisce deoch ná scéal.* You will sup with us.'

A steward brought them water to wash away the dust of the journey, while horseboys attended their horses.

The evening sun was low in the west when O'Neill and his party finally sat down at the board under the tree. O'Neill sat in the centre, flanked by Devlin and his chaplain. He gestured the visitors to their places opposite. They sat on cushions of heather covered with brightly-coloured rugs. The table was set with wooden platters and meaders. O'Neill's chaplain intoned the Latin words of Grace.

A makeshift cooking pot had been constructed from a calfskin, secured by three stout staves forked at the top which were slung over a fire of wood. The mutton in herb-flavoured juices was served in joints on large wooden trenchers, together with mounds of freshly baked bread. From large earthenware flagons, O'Neill's steward poured the Spanish sack into the wooden meaders. Around them, members of his extended family and household occupied smaller tables set up outside the bothies. Among the boulders and bushes on the periphery, the campfires of his kern and gallowglass glowed intermittently. On his signal, a harper took his seat nearby and the tinkling strains warmed the dwindling twilight. Around them hunting hounds and cattle dogs competed for the bones flung towards them. The food was good, the wine had the tang of the oaken casks that had carried it over the sea from Spain. The night was calm. The great canopy above them shone with a myriad stars. But for the intrusion from outside, O'Neill contemplated sourly, everything was conducive to his utter contentment.

'How fared you with the Spanish king?' he asked Robert Walshe. 'Was he as generous as Desmond would have us believe?'

The chaplain shook his head. 'I fear, my lord, that Ireland and the Geraldine league do not occupy a prominent place in the emperor's plans. He did send a token gesture, some shot, blades, a few score pikes.'

O'Neill smiled wanly. 'No eager Spanish hordes, hell-bent on freeing Ireland from the Gall. Ah yes, Desmond's hopes are as foolish as his ambition.' He pushed the platter away from him and cleaned his soiled hands on some dried grass. He filled the meaders of his guests to the brim and reclined on his elbow on the heather cushion. 'What instructions does the Lord of Desmond send his allies now?'

Kildare's chaplain answered him. 'I fear we bring ill-tidings, my Lord.' He looked at the young MacCarthy before continuing. 'From Thomas Leverous and the Lady MacCarthy, who ask for your help.'

'The Lady MacCarthy?' O'Neill looked with some amusement from one to the other. 'From what I know, the Lady MacCarthy has little need of my help.' His voice hardened. 'She has O'Donel to protect her now.'

A look of surprise and embarrassment passed between the chaplain and his companion.

'My mother's concern, my lord, is for the safety of the Geraldine,' MacCarthy said sharply. 'Have little doubt on that score.' He lowered his head over his meader. 'I will not deny that my mother's decision to marry O'Donel took me, took those around her, by surprise. But I believe there is something more behind it. For it is as if O'Donel forces her with some hidden threat to buy his support for the league.'

'The league!' O'Neill answered him with a dismissive wave of his hand. 'It was doomed from the start. Its very essence runs contrary to Irish nature. It asks me to ally with an enemy who, when my back is turned, would gladly stick a dagger in me. It asks me to dismiss my heritage and my obligations as The O'Neill, to forget a history of treachery and bloodshed. It asks me to sell my birthright for Spanish gold, as once MacMurrough sold his honour to the Gall. For as MacMurrough brought in the Gall to Ireland, Desmond and his league would bring in the Spaniard, to be a new plague amongst us for another four hundred years.' O'Neill lapsed into silence. The breeze rustled the leaves above his head. 'But then Desmond is a Gall too,' he muttered and drank deeply from his meader.

'As we all are,' MacCarthy reminded him softly. 'In part at least. You, as well as me, O'Neill.'

Much as he wished to, O'Neill knew that he could not deny it. By marriage and by the sword, the Great Earl had ensured that Geraldine blood was fused with the royal blood of Ireland, so that the Geraldine ambition to rule Ireland might be more acceptable when it was seen that the blood of both Gael and Gall were mingled in their veins.

O'Neill looked at MacCarthy. 'I'm afraid it is of little relevance now. For there is more behind O'Donel's pretended adherence to the league.'

'Pretended?' Robert Walshe repeated, alarm evident on his thin face.

'O'Donel left Askeaton to keep an unlikely appointment with very strange company.' They waited for him to continue, puzzlement evident on their faces. 'With the Countess of Ormond.'

Puzzlement gave way to foreboding at his disclosure. MacCarthy banged the board before him with a clenched fist. 'The traitorous swine.' A wooden meader fell and rolled off the table onto the fern beneath.

'But he is the pope's envoy. Trusted by Cardinal Pole. The principal initiator of the league,' Robert Walshe protested.

'To further his ambitions in Ulster, most likely at my expense,' O'Neill said.

'My mother's future husband.' MacCarthy sounded astounded.

'But O'Donel has taken the Geraldine to Tirconel, for safety from the countess.' Robert Walshe added, still unable to comprehend O'Neill's revelations.

'Tirconel? But the boy was to stay with Desmond, I understood.' O'Neill felt the prick of disquiet raise the hair on his neck.

357

MacCarthy shook his head. 'Three days ago, O'Donel left Askeaton with my mother and the boy.'

O'Neill slowly rose from the board. The smell of treachery was becoming stronger by the second and it wafted towards Tyrone.

'Grey and the Countess of Ormond combined their armies and were at the borders of Desmond ready to pounce,' Robert Walshe explained. 'We all were agreed that it was the only option in the circumstances; even Leverous, who bears no love for O'Donel and trusts him even less.'

'How convenient that the countess should first give O'Donel time to take the boy away,' O'Neill said

'We had no knowledge then of O'Donel's meeting with her.' The chaplain's face was white and strained in the semi-gloom.

'Mark me, the boy will never see Tirconel. O'Donel has made some pact with the countess, on that you can be certain. The Geraldine in exchange for . . .

O'Neill's forehead creased in thought and he rose and stood by the rowan tree where an hour previously he had basked in contentment. He gazed across the darkening valley, westwards beyond the dim outline of the Sperrins, towards where the winding arm of the Foyle divided Tyrone from Tirconel. Once he could be certain that whatever threatened Tyrone would come out of the west, from O'Donel's country. Now, new enemies threatened from the east. From their coastal enclaves and stench-filled towns, the English sowed the seeds of unrest among his urraghs, like Clandeboy, Magennis, just as O'Donel had tried with O'Hagan, to sap his strength and authority. This new O'Donel had been taught by the Gall to play the game by their rules. What juicy award had the countess or the English king dangled before him in exchange for the Geraldine? O'Neill could only surmise, but instinct and experience told him that O'Donel's reward would be at his expense.

'The Geraldine in exchange for Ulster.'

The answer sped towards him from the distant mountains fanned by the westerly breeze. With English help, O'Donel would be strong enough to lure his urraghs from him and so replace him as overlord in Ulster.

He had suspected that Desmond's grandiose scheme, wrapped in its illusion of unity and in the chimerical expectation of foreign succour, would evaporate when faced by the grim reality of Irish politics. For behind the façade of the Geraldine League lurked the individual lust for power over an enemy, over a neighbour, of each individual who shouted approval and roared loyalty to the Geraldine that night under the oak beams of Desmond's castle. Responding to the raw emotion of the night, they had agreed to something against their very natures – to relinquish their individual powers and privileges. In the cold reality of day, the Irish chieftains had time to reflect more soberly on their commitment and the price they would have to pay should the league fail. Their doubts would have been strengthened by Desmond's failure to fulfil his promise of Spanish aid, a failure they would regard as releasing them from their commitment.

Desmond's experiment would leave in its wake merely what it had tried to replace: the jostling for power and protection by the chieftains and liegemen, amidst the ebb and flow of the political tide. It would allow him, in his capacity as The O'Neill to continue his obligation to his people, to his heritage, to open a new chapter of hostility with O'Donel. Suddenly O'Neill felt the burden of aggrievement lift from his shoulders, as the natural purpose of his life, temporarily suspended by his flirtation with the league, was restored.

He turned towards the chaplain and MacCarthy, who were watching him anxiously. Now was as good a time as any to make a start, he thought.

'If you believe that Lady MacCarthy acts with the Geraldine's interests at heart, that her proposed marriage to

O'Donel is merely a smokescreen.' He heard their words of affirmation. 'Very well. We intercept O'Donel. The Geraldine is yours to take where you will. O'Donel is mine. *Marbhfháisce air.*'

AUTUMN

34

HAMPTON COURT, ENGLAND

It was now six hours since the birth pains began. Lady Essex announced the news. Bustling down the corridors from the queen's apartments, through the Guard and Presence chambers, she burst into the privy chamber, despite Cromwell's best efforts to forestall her entry, her excitement temporarily making her forget formality. The king was engrossed with the Archbishop of Canterbury, hearing Cranmer's plans for the distribution of the newly printed English Bible in Wales. There was little problem ensuring its availability in churches throughout England, but Henry was anxious that it would be translated quickly into Welsh, to speed the spread of the new reforms in the land of his ancestors. There was no going back he realised. All the bridges between England and Rome were down; he had thrown his gauntlet at Clement's feet.

'Your grace, the queen is in labour!' Bowing low before the king, Lady Essex breathlessly delivered herself of the news.

Henry hardly saw her, as she lingered expectantly for his reaction to the event that had kept the entire court in a state of animated suspense over the past weeks. He had waited for this moment in dread anticipation, his joy tempered by memories of Catherine's deliveries of stillborn and diseased children, of Anne's defiance, both of his desire for a male child and of the astrologers' assertion that her child would fulfil his long-desired hope. This time his need for a son was so desperate that Lady Essex's news renewed the nagging doubts of his ability to produce a male heir. The confidence that had grown within him over the past months that Jane indeed carried his son, receded once more.

Accompanied by Cromwell and Cranmer, he hurried to the queen's apartments on the east side of Cloister Green Court. From a lowering grey sky, an autumn squall dashed the rain against the window mullions as he traversed the corridors of the new royal apartments, designed and constructed under his personal supervision. With fleeting satisfaction he noted that the work of superimposing Jane's initials over Anne's on the elaborately plastered ceilings had been completed. There must be no reminders of his past failures at Hampton Court.

The bedchamber was already crowded with the royal physicians, the queen's chaplain and her personal attendants. Like a scythe with a swathe, the king cut a passage through them to the great bed, adorned with silk hangings and cloth of gold. The curtains were pulled back and, deep within the high-banked pillows, Jane's face, flushed with the pain and exertion of her travail, looked feverishly in his direction.

He took her small clenched hand in his and felt the tremors that tore through her body. He murmured some words of comfort and tenderness. She did not respond, but glanced briefly at him with a mixture of anger and pain. He moved away from her bed and beckoned to her personal physician.

'There is nothing to be concerned about, your grace,' Brode assured him. 'The queen's pains are taking their course. It will be some time yet before nature's work is done.'

'And I will have a son,' Henry whispered, more to himself than to the physician.

'With God's grace, your majesty.

364

'We are to be informed immediately the birth is imminent.' He must be present at the very moment of delivery, the moment of vindication.

In the outside chamber Henry exchanged brief pleasantries with the Seymours who had come to Hampton Court in anticipation of their daughter's delivery. He did not tarry long with them. He had other matters on his mind. Followed by Cranmer and Cromwell, he retraced his steps along the tapestry-hung walls, through the long gallery, towards the Chapel Royal.

Kneeling on the royal pew under the ornate moulded ceiling, he offered prayers for Jane's safe deliverance of a son. Surely God would hear his plea this time? It was England's security rather than any masculine vanity on his part that made him kneel in humble supplication. But God also knew the dark deeds he had committed, the momentous rejection of doctrine which the world had ever accepted to be God's truth, administered by God's vicar on earth, whose role he had usurped. God knew of his part in the execution of Fisher and More, in Anne's downfall, in Catherine's degradation, in the humiliation of his daughters, in the horrific cruelties of Tyburn and Smithfield.

But whatever he had done, God also knew that it had been carried out in observance of his divine duty as king, protector of England and her people. God knew also of the ravages England had endured through dynastic quarrels and weak monarchs in the past. God must know that England needed strong continuous leadership, which could be achieved only through a male heir. He *must* have a son. He bowed his head and prayed in the old way his nurse had taught him as a child when belief was uncomplicated and sincere, shutting his eyes in deep concentration. For if he did not have a son, his daughter would succeed him. He shivered in dread, for England would be even worse served by a woman, as had been proved during the unhappy reign of the last female ruler, Queen Mathilde. No, God would understand that what he had done, the lives he had expended, the sacrifices he had made, had been for the common weal of England, in his God-given duty as her divinely ordained king.

With difficulty, Henry arose from his knees. The ulcer on his leg had opened again and the pain was as bad as it had been in the spring. He bowed his head towards the altar, where the sanctuary lamp glowed before the sacred host, and went out into the corridor.

'My lord archbishop, We expect you to be too occupied with prayers for the safe deliverance of the queen to continue Our discussion further today.'

Cranmer took his meaning and, bowing, left them.

'Well?' Henry asked his chief minister. 'Have you located the crone?'

'She awaits your grace's pleasure, in the Horn Room.'

Cromwell made to accompany him, but Henry dismissed him. It was enough that he had to confide in his minister to find the woman without making him privy to what must transpire between them. Idly he wondered if his inclination towards the supernatural and the mystical emanated from his Celtic blood. In times of uncertainty he found himself irresistibly drawn to the mist-filled land of Merlin, that lay beyond the Marches to the west, last bastion of the other world. If his predilection for such pagan hocus-pocus became common knowledge, he thought, it would rest uneasily alongside his recent denunciation and prohibition of the superstitious and idolatrous practices of the Church of Rome.

Henry entered the Great Hall and walked quickly along its length, under the magnificent hammer beam roof, the wondrous affirmation to the craftsmanship of the English artisans whom he had personally chosen and supervised to build it. The more acceptable face of the supernatural had failed abysmally in Anne's case, he recalled. This time he had abandoned the astrologers to return to the sorcery of his Celtic origins.

She was waiting for him in a corner of the Horn Room. Her bright blue eyes observed him calmly from a ruddy face, encircled by a deep hood. He had expected a shrivelled hag, but she was more like a farmer's wife. She curtsied and waited for him to speak. Her presence made him uncomfortable, uncustomarily beholden, vulnerable in his need of the singular powers she possessed.

'The queen is in labour.' His words sounded unintentionally harsh. 'I must know the outcome.'

She nodded pleasantly as if he had asked her for a bagful of apples. From within the folds of her cloak, she removed a leather pouch, held closed at the top with a thong. She knelt on the ground and spilled the contents on to the flags. Henry watched in silence as intently she examined the pattern of small sticks and pebbles at his feet. She murmured quietly to herself, her head moving from side to side, her body rocking back and forth. At one stage, he heard her take a short gasp, as if something sinister had revealed itself to her. He felt a quiver of fear.

'It will be a son,' she said at last. Her words were delivered with such certainty that at once he believed them. He felt the first rush of relief course through his body.

'Will he live?' he asked her hoarsely.

She did not answer him immediately, but moved her hands over the twigs and pebbles before her. One hand, he thought, seemed to hover uncertainly for a moment before continuing the weaving movement of the other.

'He will live,' she said and quickly gathered up the twigs and pebbles and replaced them in her pouch.

Without a word he left the gold angels on the table beside her, walked quickly from the Horn Room and retraced his steps through the Great Hall. The joy that welled within him seemed as if it would burst forth from within and erupt in loud exclamation of the news that he must keep buried within him for a little longer.

He hurried towards Wolsey's closet and closed the door

firmly behind him. He wished for no company at this time, no fawning courtier or official, spouting their reverential words of empty encouragement. Perhaps he would have welcomed the presence of a brother or a friend to stay the vigil with him, but he had neither. His brother Arthur, in whom the dynastic hopes of his father had been so firmly vested, Henry hardly remembered. Arthur had died as a youth, less than five months after his brother's marriage to Catherine. Their father's ambitions had been transferred to him. His duty was plain and simple: to continue the Tudor line as kings of England. And to this day, Henry thought bitterly, he had failed.

Friendship he had found to be an equally elusive aspiration. In boyhood he had had many friends before the burden of kingship had been foisted on his shoulders. Then friendship had become a liability, a weakness open to exploitation. Although he made merry with companions, both noble and common, hunted, jousted and played tennis, caroused with carefree abandon, his kingly office denied him the right to friendship as much as it allowed him the prerogative to choose whom he might favour with his company.

His eyes were drawn upwards, towards Wolsey's mural and the distorted likeness of the Earl of Kildare. He could imagine having such a man as a friend to share both joy and tribulation. A man, he remembered, with a heart as brave as his own, courageous, even reckless in valour, intelligent, a true disciple of the renaissance. And, he mused, had he made him a friend, instead of listening to the petty begrudgery of others, might Kildare have responded to his friendship and not have fallen into disloyalty? He knew the answer. For as kingship had been bred into his blood, Kildare's blood had bred him to rebel.

A short knock on the door concentrated his mind.

'Enter,' he called, annoyed at the intrusion.

His annoyance immediately turned to apprehension, as

Andrew Brode cautiously made his way inside. Henry rose, as if by meeting the ill-tidings on his feet he might be better able to ward them away.

'There is no cause for alarm, your grace,' Brode said hurriedly, noticing the king's look of grim foreboding.

The physician's open face for a moment assuaged Henry's dread.

Brode hesitated choosing his words with care. 'The child is ready to be delivered, but the queen . . .' he hesitated again, '. . . her body cannot accommodate the birth as nature intended.'

'What are you saying?' Henry felt the blood rush to his head. His small eyes snapped. Was he to be denied again?

'She must be delivered by the knife, your grace. It is the only way.'

In one swift movement, the king was beside the physician and shook him roughly by the shoulders. 'The risk to the child?' he shouted.

Unruffled by the king's outburst, Brode stood his ground and calmy replied. 'To the child, little. To the queen . . .' he lifted his shoulders; 'there is always the possibility of infection.'

'The child must be saved, do you understand?' The king's small eyes stared at Brode.

'Then I have your grace's permission to operate on the queen?'

With a curt jerk of his head, the king gave his assent. 'When?'

The physician bowed his acknowledgement. 'Immediately, your grace. Do you wish to witness it?'

Henry quickly shook his head. 'Later,' he told him dully and watched the door close behind him.

The cursed witch had seen more in her twigs than she had revealed. Henry pounded the panel beside him with a clenched fist. A plague on her. He would have her roasted alive at Smithfield. God could not deny him, he reasoned,

369

not now when he had resolved the problems that had threatened his son's birthright and made his kingdom strong and secure. The last of the leaders of the northern rebellion had been executed on Tower Hill and at York. He had spared no one, not even Lady Bulmer or Robert Aske, despite the pardon he had promised them. He had not shirked his duty to ensure that rebellion would never stalk the land again. His secret deliberations with Charles seemed ever more likely to succeed, leaving the threat of a religious crusade against England a mere fantasy in the bitter mind of Clement in Rome, chaffing at his lost supremacy and revenue.

He glanced again at the mural. The only threat remaining was in Ireland – that malingering shadow at his back. But with Spain on his side, the Irish would find Charles a fainthearted ally, while he had every faith that the Countess of Ormond would fulfil her promise to deliver up the root cause of disaffection there, the Geraldine heir. He arose and for a moment contemplated the mural which depicted Wolsey's Kildare. A death for a life. Kildare's son to safeguard the life of his son and the future safety of England.

He could wait no longer. Quickly he retraced his steps along the corridors towards the queen's apartments. Around every corner, groups of his household retainers and retinue whispered in huddled groups, falling to their knees as he passed.

As he entered the privy chamber, cries of pain which reminded him of a snared animal sounded from within the queen's bedchamber and made him flinch. There was little relief from the torment of a Caesarean delivery. As he approached the door, the cries suddenly were mingled with those of another, a lighter but shriller cry. The door opened before him and the stench of blood, the sickly sweetness of the perfumes of those crowded into the room, mixed with the scent from the flowers strewn on the floor, made him want to retch. Around the bed the physicians looked approvingly as the midwife emerged from behind the curtained bed and wrapped a blood-streaked object in a cloth.

Brode approached him, smiling and pointing to the bundle in the midwife's arms. 'Your son, your grace. May God bless him.'

The precious words were lost in the murmur of assent which rose from the company in the chamber. Henry felt giddy, unsteady on his feet, as if he had drunk deep from some inebriant. He looked at the wrinkled face, the tiny fingers of one hand clutching convulsively at the edges of the cloth. They placed the bundle in his arms. It felt weightless and fragile and he held it carefully at a distance from his jewel-encrusted doublet, lest a ruby or a pearl should mark the face that looked unfocusingly up at him. He felt elated and strangely humbled.

'We have a son. England has an heir,' he whispered in wonderment to himself. He glanced across to where the earl marshal stood with other members of the household. 'Let the world know We have an heir.'

The earl marshal departed and soon the sound of cannon from the tiltyard proclaimed the news that the Tudor dynasty was at last assured.

35

FOOTHILLS OF OX MOUNTAINS,
PROVINCE OF CONNACHT

The premonition weighed on Leverous like a black cloud.
The feeling intensified as they left O'Connor's castle at
Ballymote. There was no tangible reason to justify his sense
of unease. Their journey from Desmond had been without
incident or mishap. The earl's escort had brought them to
Portumna above the watery expanse of Lough Derg, where
boatmen waited to ferry them across the Shannon in small
hide-covered river boats. They had been met on the other
side by Felim O'Connor, with horses and supplies and an
escort of some two score men. Unaware that the league had
collapsed or of the failure of Spanish support, O'Connor
imagined that he was fulfilling his commitment to the league
to protect the Geraldine heir and bring him safely through
his lordship across the wide plains of the Maghery of
Connacht.

Some nights they spent with one of O'Connor's urraghs
or within the walls of a monastery, but for the most part
they avoided human settlements and kept to the hills and
woods. At his sprawling castle of Ballymote, O'Connor
relinquished responsibility for the Geraldine to O'Donel, as
he had agreed with the Earl of Desmond.

Surrounded now by O'Donel's followers, Leverous had

been on edge. His suspicions were further aroused by Eleanor's whispered revelation that one of the kern in O'Donel's party seemed familiar. That night around the camp fire, the kern withdrew a small willow harp from his saddle bag and made to play it. Without apparent reason, O'Donel snatched the harp from his hands and cuffed him about the head.

The incident revived Eleanor's memory.

'The kern is the itinerant harper I saw playing at the *aonach* at Askeaton,' she confided to Leverous, further fuelling his disquiet.

But there was something more; some vague intuition pricked Leverous into a state of constant alertness. Perhaps it was O'Donel's uncharacteristic agreeableness and his curiously benign toleration of Leverous's hushed conversations with Eleanor throughout the long trek.

By day, Leverous rode close to Gerald and, at night when they rested around the campfire, wrapped in their mantles, Gerald lay by his side. Since leaving O'Connor's castle, every nerve in Leverous's body had been taut, alert to every sound and movement in the night, his eyes watchful and mistrustful of O'Donel. He knew that if MacCarthy and Robert Walshe were to make contact with them, it would have to be soon. Once inside Tirconel they would be at O'Donel's mercy and too far north to alert O'Malley. From the conversation of the kern, Leverous had deduced that they were but a few days' ride from Tirconel. He made up his mind. If after one more day Cormac and Robert Walshe had failed to find them, he would make a break with Gerald and take their chances.

O'Donel rode at the head of the escort. Eleanor, Gerald and Leverous were together in the centre. Leverous's conversations with her were terse and guarded, not necessarily because of what lay between them but because of their common suspicion of O'Donel.

'Whose country is this?' he whispered to her in English.

She turned her head. They had fallen into a somewhat strained congeniality – a mask for their emotions but it made communication bearable.

'I am not familiar with these western parts. O'Malley's and MacWilliam's country lie somewhere towards the west. Towards the sea.'

'This is O'Hara's country,' Gerald piped up between them. They both looked enquiringly at him. 'I heard a kern say it this morning.'

'Well done, Gerald,' Leverous said.

Gerald was aware of the air of tension and seemed at ease only in their company, Leverous noted. The weeks they had spent together in close proximity at Kilbritin had encouraged the boy to think of Eleanor, Leverous and himself as a family. Their abandonment of him at Askeaton, Leverous to nurse his rejection in Limerick and Eleanor to return to Kilbritin, had made the boy more possessive and dependent on them since their return. From the start of the journey from Desmond, Gerald sensed their antagonism towards O'Donel and in turn had become reticent with the Northern chieftain and his men. Despite O'Donel's patent efforts to win favour with the boy during the journey from Desmond, Gerald maintained his distance, his brown eyes expressing his dislike. O'Donel ignored the boy's obvious antipathy and continued to try to ingratiate himself with him.

'How long must we stay in Tirconel, Leverous?' Gerald asked suddenly.

Leverous exchanged a look with Eleanor. 'Until we are certain it is safe.'

'Then where will we go? To Kilbritin?' His face lit up in anticipation.

'Perhaps.' Leverous saw the doubt spread across the boy's face at his unconvincing reply.

'Why must we always move? First Dangan, then Donore,' he ticked the places off on his fingers, 'then Kilbritin, Askeaton and now Tirconel. Why can't we stay in one place?

Like Kilbritin. I want to go hunting or cattle raiding with Cormac. Why?' His voice rose audibly.

'There will be plenty to hunt in Tirconel, my lad.' O'Donel swung around in the saddle. 'Plenty of O'Neill deer and cattle await you.'

O'Donel's men guffawed. Gerald scowled at O'Donel and reverted to silence.

Ignoring O'Donel's remark, Leverous sought to reassure the boy. 'Because, Gerald, there are some people who wish you no good . . .'

'Who want to kill me?' Gerald asked, more curious than afraid.

The directness of his query, Leverous knew, left no room for evasive platitudes.

'I'm afraid so. But your friends will make sure you are safe.'

'That's true, *a stór*,' Eleanor said reassuringly, as she noted the apprehensive look on her nephew's face. 'Leverous and I will . . .'

Before she could finish, O'Donel jerked his horse suddenly around to face them. Their own horses shied away in fright, almost throwing them.

'Leverous and I will do what?' O'Donel's handsome features were distorted with ill-temper, as Leverous remembered him so often before in Maynooth, when the thin veneer of charm O'Donel assumed had been drawn back to reveal the viciousness that lay behind.

The escort halted and suddenly Eleanor, Gerald and Leverous were isolated in the centre, encircled by O'Donel's men. It was as if the move had been planned in advance. Fear, like a clasp of a mailed gauntlet, clutched at Leverous. There was something afoot and it had little to do with Eleanor's remark or the distance she had purposely maintained from her prospective husband on the journey from Desmond.

'But then I have to remind myself, my dear,' O'Donnel's

375

eyes filled with such loathing that Leverous visibly recoiled as if O'Donel had struck him, 'that you share more than just a friendship with your Englishman, more than you have shared so far with me, and certainly more than you shared with your senile fool husband.'

Even as he dug the spurs into the sides of his horse, Leverous knew that his reaction was as O'Donel intended. He was being goaded into a readymade trap. Dimly he heard Eleanor urging him to stop his headlong charge. The jar as they collided almost threw Leverous over the horse's head, but he twisted sideways out of the saddle and flung himself at O'Donel. They hit the ground with a thud that for a moment left them both stunned on the grass. O'Donel was first to his feet, sword already in his hand, before Leverous could scramble from the ground and unsheath his.

'Look out, Leverous. Look out.'

Gerald's thin shout of warning made him roll away inches from where O'Donel's smooth blade, with a serpent's hiss, slashed the grass beside his head. He scrambled to his feet and, with his sword free, faced O'Donel's next thrust.

Like two fighting cocks they circled one another. O'Donel made a pretence of lunging towards him and Leverous jumped back out of range of the long blade.

'You picked the wrong game to impress the lady, Leverous,' O'Donel sneered. ''Twere better that you kept to books and ledgers than to cross swords with your betters. Watch the woman and the boy,' he shouted to his men. 'Each has a master to answer to.'

O'Donel lunged at Leverous again, engaging him in a violent exchange which, with difficulty, Leverous parried, falling back near the line of bushes that led towards the woodland beyond. O'Donel gave him little respite before launching another fearsome attack. Leverous parried the blows as best he could, his breath beginning to sound strained as he sucked the air into his lungs. A swift lunge by O'Donel got through his guard and Leverous felt the warm blood flow down his arm. The hilt of his sword felt slippery in his grasp, as the blood trickled through his fingers. Sensing his advantage, O'Donel stepped up the tempo. The clash of the steel blades echoed in the stillness of the evening. With shouts of encouragement from his men, O'Donel moved in for the kill. Leverous retreated under the barrage, his sword arm unable to do anything but parry the onslaught. Their blades became entangled, locked above their heads, and they grappled with each other with their free hand. Leverous felt O'Donel claw at his face, his fingers searching for his eyes. Summoning all his energy, he heaved him away and O'Donel fell to the ground. For a moment Leverous had the advantage and hesitated. The moment was lost and, like a cat, O'Donel regained his feet.

'Fool. Luck gives few chances. You had yours and, I promise you, you'll have no more.' O'Donel's words had a deadly intent.

His attack came strong and rapid. His blade rose and fell with the speed of hail, raining blow after blow. Leverous felt his remaining strength ebb away like the blood which seeped from under the sleeve of his tunic. His spur became entangled in a briar and he crashed to the ground.

'Eleanor, Gerald, run.' His shout sounded weak and hoarse.

Contemptuously O'Donel kicked the sword from his senseless fingers and with eyes cold and pitiless raised his own above his head.

'They have nowhere to run, except to where they are destined. One to me, the other to the king, and you, my friend, to your maker.'

Mesmerised, Leverous watched the sword swing in a wide arc. At the highest point the blade caught the rays of the evening sun and turned a blood red. But when the blow came it was not from the blade but from O'Donel's shoulder, as he crashed down on top of him, the sword falling from his fingers. Leverous raised his head, as a stockily built man,

377

astride a horse, lowered his bow and joined in the mêlée which raged around him. O'Donel's men were being attacked from all sides with savage determination. Leverous pushed O'Donel's body aside and got shakily to his feet, dodging the sword and javelin thrusts of the combatants. He looked frantically around for Eleanor and Gerald and finally found them.

She ran towards him, arms outstretched, her face pale with relief. There was no pretence or reticence in the warmth of her embrace. He held her close for a moment, to still the tremors he felt run through her body.

'Quickly, now is our chance.' He released her arms from around his neck. He pushed Gerald forward through the bushes, pulling Eleanor with him. From behind, the sounds of fighting had all but ceased. Leverous knew they must make the cover of the wood if they were to have any chance of escape. Freedom lay so tantalisingly close but from behind he heard shouts and the sound of pursuit.

'Run on,' he shouted at Gerald, who was covering the ground like a swift hind and, putting Eleanor behind him, Leverous turned to face their pursuers sword in hand. There were two and they bore down on him on horseback.

'Hold hard, Leverous,' one called out, removing his iron morion. It was Cormac. Behind him was Robert Walshe.

Leverous sank to his knees, weakened more from relief than from the loss of blood that was oozing from his arm. With whoops of relief, Gerald came running back, followed by Eleanor, who embraced her son.

Robert Walshe handed Leverous a flask. He felt the warmth-inducing *uisce beatha* restore his senses. Eleanor knelt on the ground beside him and tore away the slit sleeve of his tunic, revealing a deep gash on his forearm. Cormac held his arm fast and quickly doused the wound with some *uisce beatha* from the flask. The pain shot through him.

''Tis better to be safe,' Cormac consoled him, as Eleanor wrapped his arm with a piece of linen torn from his shirt.

'O'Donel?' Leverous asked Cormac.

'Dead.'

Leverous felt lightheaded with relief.

'O'Neill's constable, MacMahon, had his name on the arrow that killed him. There'll be many a dry eye in Tyrone at O'Donel's passing,' Cormac added sardonically.

'And many an O'Donel sword to avenge it.'

They looked around as the spare figure of O'Neill rode into their company. Behind him, his kern were laying the bodies of O'Donel's company side by side on the grass.

O'Neill looked down at Leverous. 'It is your good fortune that O'Donel's life was forfeited to MacMahon, my best shot. His father's soul can rest in peace and a traitor has been removed from the Geraldine camp.'

Leverous looked up uncomprehendingly at O'Neill.

'O'Donel was in league with the Countess of Ormond,' Robert Walshe explained. 'He was leading you into a trap.'

'Did Desmond know?' Eleanor asked.

O'Neill shrugged. 'It is doubtful if he knew the full extent of O'Donel's treachery.' O'Neill gave Eleanor a long hard look. 'But did you know, cousin?'

The colour rose in her face. 'O'Donel's treachery spared no one, believe me.'

There was an awkward silence, as O'Neill waited for Eleanor's explanation. None was forthcoming. Leverous felt aggrieved. Her silence invited suspicion, her agreement to marry O'Donel implied knowledge of the treachery he was contemplating against Gerald. But despite her evasive reply to O'Neill's accusation, Leverous instinctively knew that she was ignorant of what O'Donel had planned.

'But O'Donel must have had an accomplice, if only to make contact with the countess,' Robert Walshe said.

'The bard,' Leverous said, and told O'Neill what Eleanor suspected.

They helped Leverous to his feet and he followed the others to examine the faces of the dead kern. The body of the bard was not among them.

'Then we must assume that he escaped and will make his way to the countess,' the chaplain said.

The sound of approaching hoofbeats brought swords again from scabbards. O'Neill's kern crouched low, holding their iron-tipped darts aloft in anticipation. Leverous grasped his sword.

Two horsemen galloped into view and made straight for O'Neill, shouting their message in Gaelic.

'The Gall. The army of the Gall make ready to cross the Erne.'

'The Erne?' Cormac echoed everyone's disbelief.

'How many?' O'Neill asked his scouts without a trace of emotion.

'Near a thousand. Well-appointed and armed. With machines of war.'

'The army of Grey and my sister,' Eleanor said. 'But they were to attack Desmond!'

'Someone pointed them instead to Ulster.' O'Neill cursed low under his breath.

He barked orders to his men, who remounted in silence and awaited their chieftain's command. O'Neill swung into the pillion. The silver harness jingled in the quiet, as his horse tossed its head impatiently. He turned towards them, his eyes raking over each one of them before coming to rest on Gerald.

'Whatever assistance I gave was to save your life and to thwart the ambitions of my enemy. That is all I know or wish to know. The Geraldine League was doomed from the minute it was conceived in Desmond's ambitious head. For this,' he indicated the bodies on the ground, 'is the only cause I follow. My cause is Ulster, just as Desmond's is Munster, and so it will be until we are conquered by someone stronger. Who that may be only time will reveal. But it is of no concern to me. So long as I live, I will not be ruled by anyone, Gael or Gall.'

O'Neill leaned down and beckoned Gerald. Leverous felt the boy hesitate. O'Neill cut an intimidating figure, his face fierce and aloof under the rim of his iron morion. Leverous gently nudged Gerald forward until he stood before the chieftain. O'Neill regarded his young kinsman in silence.

'For one foolish moment, I allowed myself to think that once more under the saltire of Kildare, I might find common purpose with O'Donel. But even the Great Earl, aye, and your father, faltered under the burden.'

Gerald stared unblinkingly up at his cousin.

'The days of the high kings are no more in Ireland. I know because I am of them. The only cause worth fighting for is survival.' O'Neill extended his hand to Gerald. The boy hesitated for a second before stretching out his. O'Neill shook it solemnly, with a certain ceremony. 'God go with you, cousin Kildare. May foreign princes treat you better than your own.'

Wrapped in his shaggy mantle, O'Neill disappeared, followed by his warriors on their hardy ponies clad in their chainmail jacks of bygone wars. His barelegged kern in saffron shirts and brief tunics, armed with outmoded weapons, loped by his side, willing to face the might of armour, arquebus and cannon to defend their master.

It seemed to Leverous that he was witnessing a scene from another world, from another time, when heroes rather than mere mortals walked the earth. A heroic time, like like that of Troy, when Hector, Achilles and the rest might well have appeared as O'Neill. But that age had long been overtaken by scientific discovery, by new philosophies which released man from the bondage of the past and encouraged him to look beyond the narrow confines of his patch into the wider world outside. Here in the Irish hinterland it still lingered, an anachronism in the renaissance world. O'Neill was a prisoner of his heritage and his unassailable courage was wasted on a lesser ideal than his talents deserved. His role as protector of a *status quo*, championing the dated conception of a ruler above the concept of a state, blurred his vision and made his neighbour, O'Donel, seem as much an enemy as the king of England. As O'Neill had disclosed in his words to Gerald, Ireland was not yet able to make a king who would rule for the good of all.

'Who is the Lord O'Neill to fight next?' Gerald asked.

Leverous looked down at the young face. Your uncle and your aunt, he thought, but aloud said simply, 'The English.'

'We had better make a run for O'Malley's country,' MacCarthy said. 'If the harper gets to the countess, we'll need wings to outrun her.'

Remembering his own precipitous flight from Donore, Leverous nodded and walked over to where his horse grazed, the reins trailing the ground. Robert Walshe was saying Latin words over the bodies of O'Donel's men. As Leverous passed by the line of slain, the blue eyes of O'Donel stared sightlessly towards the faded autumn sky. Leverous knelt down to close them. The handsome face was in repose, as if asleep. Leverous felt no personal sense of triumph, just relief.

As he rose, he caught Eleanor's gaze. Her eyes fell to O'Donel's body. What thoughts lay behind the calm composure, Leverous wondered? What plans did she envisage now that O'Donel was no more? He steeled himself from contemplating. He had been through the speculation before.

36

ENGLISH CAMP, LOUGH ERNE,
BORDER OF TYRONE

The mist wafted in from the lake and seeped under the door of the cabin, touching everything with a clammy breath. The bolster and the woollen coverlet, even the down mattress the countess had brought with her from Kilkenny, felt damp to the touch. But she was scarcely aware of the discomfort and the squalor. Physical comforts mattered little. Her endurance was unlimited if the result was worthwhile, and the deputyship of Ireland was worth whatever affliction nature and Grey's ineptitude placed in her path. In any event, she had a soldier's training and a stamina to match. She had requisitioned the miserable cabin as soon as she had laid eyes on it. Grey had raised no objection, deeming it, in his crusty courteous way, a concession to her sex.

But her designs on the lowly hovel, which stood in isolation at a distance from the lakeshore, were motivated by reasons other than propriety. It enjoyed one important advantage over a tent in the open camp. Under its sodden thatch and behind its mud walls she could converse undisturbed with O'Donel's messenger, out of sight and hearing of Grey, her husband, and all inquisitive eyes and ears.

O'Donel was already two days behind their agreed schedule, she thought anxiously, and now nature had decided to conspire against her and delay Grey's advance into Tyrone against O'Neill. Her eyes narrowed in concentration. Perhaps that was the reason for O'Donel's failure to contact her? Did he think that she had reneged on her part of their arrangement? She had expected that by now Grey would be well on the way to Tyrone and she, pleading the inability of one of her sex to continue, would be on her way to keep her appointment with O'Donel and to take custody of her nephew. A quick dash to Ormond and thence to England, and the gratitude and reward of the king.

But the hostile expanse of water that stretched before them, barring the way north, was a deterrent that no one had expected. In vain might Grey angrily berate his Irish scouts for leading him into such an impasse, but, as they protested, they were as much strangers as the deputy to the territory and knew nothing of the watery barrier stretching, it seemed, into infinity, north and south. After much discussion and recrimination, Grey elected to march parallel to the lake, southwards, in the hope that it narrowed at some point where it could be forded. It had taken three days to find the place where the lake became an isthmus. It would take yet another day to finish the construction of the wooden ford to ferry the army across.

The countess had refrained from informing Grey of her intention to return to Ormond. She expected him to have no objection, remembering his strenuous efforts to dissuade her from coming on the campaign in the first place. For the hundredth time she paced the confines of the cabin, between the crude bedstead and the door. Where was O'Donel's messenger? He must contact her, to arrange where they were to meet to exchange her nephew for the information he required.

She had expected O'Donel to demand something less predictable than a chance to strike against his enemy O'Neill: money perhaps, land, or a position in her administration in Dublin Castle when she became deputy. But it was ever the same in Ireland: the opportunity to gain advantage over a rival was the only reward that mattered. Even O'Donel, for all his wordly-wise ways, succumbed to the Irish malaise. When and where Grey was to attack O'Neill, so that he might know when to make his own assault on Tyrone, was the price he demanded for betraying the Geraldine.

A stealthy footfall sounded outside the cabin. The countess took a small dagger from under the bolster and listened attentively. Someone whispered a reprimand and, simultaneously, a low knock sounded on the door.

'Who goes?'

'MacSweeney.'

She drew the wooden bolt. The captain of the Ormond gallowglass loomed out of the swirling fog, fanned by a chill wind that blew in from the lake.

'My lady, this *bodach*,' he gestured contemptuously towards a shadowy figure behind him, 'claims that you will see him.'

The figure moved closer, a harp clutched beneath his arm.

Curtly she beckoned MacGrath inside and dismissed the captain. She closed the door with a bang and rounded on the harper, her frustration at the delay spilling out in anger.

'God's blood, what delayed you? What game does O'Donel play?'

'O'Donel is dead.'

The stark words froze her anger into bleak dismay. The plan she had so diligently plotted, the route to the power she craved, the compensation for a lifetime's rejection, lay smashed in pieces by the harper's announcement. She leaned on the roughly hewn bedpost.

'What did you say?'

MacGrath licked his cracked lips, terror shining like sweat on his face.

'O'Donel is dead,' he whispered. He fidgeted with the fringe of his mantle. 'We came to the place where it was

385

planned that O'Donel would kill the Geraldine's tutor. They fought. The tutor put up a fight but O'Donel got the upper hand. As he was about to dispatch him, we were attacked by O'Neill.'

'O'Neill?' the countess exclaimed.

The harper nodded his dishevelled head. 'An arrow got O'Donel. All the rest were slaughtered. I hid in the bushes and then fled through the woods and made my way here. That is all, my lady.'

'I smell treachery,' she hissed and eyed the harper, who backed away.

'Not me, my lady. I swear it. I did all you asked.'

His fear was so patent that she was inclined to believe him.

'Should I find out that you lie to me, MacGrath, not only will I smash your harp into a thousand pieces but the fingers that pluck the strings as well.'

He swallowed convulsively, knowing that she did not threaten idly.

'O'Neill rode with the Earl of Kildare's chaplain and your nephew.'

'My nephew?'

'The MacCarthy chieftain.'

Robert Walshe, MacCarthy and O'Neill. The plot was as thick as the fog outside.

'Where is the Geraldine?'

'When O'Neill heard that you were on his border, he left to gather his army. The Geraldine went west with your sister, the tutor, MacCarthy and the chaplain.'

'Where?' she barked, her eyes widened in anticipation.

'I heard them say O'Malley's country, in the west.'

'The pirate?' She digested the harper's information. The answer, like a blinding light, revealed itself immediately.

'The sea,' she breathed.

The last remaining escape for her nephew and his protectors. She was certain now there was a plot afoot in opposition to her own. But who had alerted them to her arrangement with O'Donel? He had come in disguise to Kiltinan, so well disguised, she reflected, that he had duped her. Some tongue had wagged. But it was irrelevant now. O'Donel could not deliver what he had promised. She would have to rely on her own devices once again.

'When did they leave for O'Malley's country?'

'The same time I left to come here, my lady.'

'Wait outside.'

MacGrath hesitated, shivering with indecision. 'The harp, my lady,' he whined.

'Outside,' she barked, pointing to the door.

Minutes later, she drew on a mantle, pulling the high-fringed collar around her neck, and let herself out of the cabin. The harper hunkered by the cabin wall, like a pile of rags, his head sunk on his chest. Without a glance in his direction, she set off purposefully.

The fog lay in great banks over the mirror water of the lake. It swirled in vapoury wisps around the countess as she walked through the camp. Bleary-eyed soldiers, huddled around smoking campfires, looked up sullenly at her approach. Others, still resting on the waterlogged ground, jerked into alertness in consternation, as her figure loomed terrifyingly before them out of the mist. Their curses followed her in the eerie silence. They were near mutiny, especially Grey's English bands, who had received no pay since spring. Their supplies had long run out and they were left to forage for food as best they could in the surrounding countryside. Many were sick with the ague and others had deserted. Their unkempt camp women clustered around pots hanging from tripods and blew the reluctant flames to life.

But the countess gave the camp scant attention. A new scheme was already fermenting in her head to rectify the reversal to her plan. She had it devised by the time she reached the tent for the morning parley.

Her husband and Brabazon were already there. She joined

them to await the arrival of the deputy.

'This cursed fog will play havoc with the crossing,' her husband complained. 'God's truth, you can barely see your hand, never mind O'Neill.'

'No more than he will be able to see us,' Brabazon smugly replied.

The Earl of Ormond looked at the Englishman with disdain. 'You are a fool to think so. Like a well-bred hound, O'Neill merely has to sniff the wind to know which way we go, while we flounder around in this pea soup. And in O'Neill's own territory. 'Tis madness, I say.'

The countess observed them in silence and wondered which of them might have betrayed her plan. Her husband was old and contrary, no longer able to stand the pace, his ambition long dented by age and contentment. Her husband for twenty years, the begetter of her son, he was still a stranger to her. She neither loved nor loathed him but tolerated him like an old hound, lame and diseased. She had already got what she wanted from him, the lordship of Ormond, the pitch from which to launch her ambition. Perhaps the Great Earl had chosen well for her, she mused. Perhaps he knew then what she was to discover later for herself, that a union based on affection was not for her who could neither give nor receive. Ormond had taken his pleasure elsewhere, while she had taken hers in stealth and in stratagem.

She shifted her gaze to Brabazon. He had too much to gain from the capture of her nephew to jeopardise his chances for advancement by colluding against her. The lands and riches of Kildare lay waiting disposal by a grateful king to those who had contributed to the capture of the lawful heir and would ensure Brabazon the estate and position he craved. Yes, she thought, Brabazon's greed was so patent and predictable as to eliminate him from suspicion.

That left Grey, the blinkered military mule. She doubted his capacity for intrigue, yet his success might well have sprung from nothing more devious than a desire to save his nephew from the Tower. Grey's lack of political acumen might well have blinded him to the dire consequences of his meddling but one way or another he would pay dearly for his role in the Geraldine débâcle. For even though O'Donel was dead, their meeting in St Patrick's had been overheard by another, one whom Grey had made into an implacable foe. The testimony of Bishop Brown, with the damning evidence of the white rose petals, would goad the king against his deputy and spur him to appoint another in his place.

The flap of the tent was drawn back and Grey entered.

'How do you propose to find O'Neill in that devil's brew?' Ormond accosted him.

Grey ignored the question and spread some papers on the rough board before him. 'We shall have to seek him further,' he said, a note of weariness in his voice.

They looked at him sharply.

'It appears O'Neill advances on the Pale, through the pass at Newry.' His hands gripped the edges of the board, his voice rising with suppressed anger, 'and because of this mad pursuit of vague conspiracies, he will find no resistance.'

The countess could scarcely control the mirth that rocked her body. While the king's army shivered and starved on the edge of this watery wilderness, O'Neill had nimbly out-manoeuvred them and, with blatant contempt, was attacking Grey in his own undefended backyard. A further indictment of the deputy's record, she thought with elation.

'By your leave, my lord,' Brabazon interjected, 'the Geraldine League is no vague conspiracy. I see it as an epidemic of such extent and force that if it is not stopped, it will serve to evict every last Englishman from Ireland.'

There was silence, as if Brabazon's foreboding was not considered by his listeners to be as serious as he seemed to think. The countess heard her husband sniff in derision, while Grey ignored Brabazon's remarks and continued to look intently at the papers before him.

'Perhaps O'Neill acts for the league. To divert us,' she offered.

Her husband glanced at her with suspicion. They both well knew that O'Neill simply acted in the native time-honoured way: to protect his own interest. To save his lordship from being pillaged by their army, he had brought the fight into the country of his enemy. The Pale would suffer the devastation intended on Tyrone, which would remain intact, its cattleherds, crops and settlements spared Grey's pillaging hoards. Both she and her husband appreciated O'Neill's strategy, while the Englishmen saw only the obvious. But now O'Neill was irrelevant to her plan. She must be rid of Grey so that she might pursue the Geraldine fugitive herself. Grey traced a line with his finger on a chart before him.

'It will mean a forced march, if we are to intercept him.'

'If the men do not mutiny first,' Brabazon murmured. Grey looked up sharply. 'They expected to have booty in Tyrone, as they did in Desmond.'

'Let it be known, by trumpet and by drum, that anyone who refuses to march today will swing by dusk.' Grey looked suspiciously at Brabazon. 'What is the latest muster?'

'Five hundred. Two hundred desertions since leaving Desmond,' Brabazon answered quickly.

'And all are English,' Ormond interjected pompously.

'Less my escort back to Ormond.'

The three men looked at the countess in surprise. She sighed deeply. 'I fear this rough living has sapped my energy. My husband will be better able to lead the Ormond companies.'

'Quite a change of heart, madam,' Grey said coldly. 'No reason could deter your coming.'

'Alack, my lord, the frailty of woman. We try to do more than our feeble bodies will permit us.'

They looked disbelievingly at her.

'How many horse?' Grey asked her.

'Twenty. Armed and provisioned.' She could afford no delays foraging for food among the natives on the road west.

Grey snorted like a bull. 'God's blood, madam. Have your wits gone soft in the fog? I can hardly spare two, let alone twenty. You will have to suffer with us.'

'They are Ormond horse, not yours.'

Grey's smile infuriated her further. 'But pledged to the king's service. Is that not so?'

Desperately she sought for a compromise. She could not be thwarted now in her final bid, and particularly not by Grey.

'Ten then. To be returned as soon as I reach Ormond.'

Grey fidgeted with the papers before him. It was a small price to be rid of her.

A plague on you, she thought, as she waited for his response. She expected him to be glad to see her go.

'Very well, madam. Since you seem determined to leave us.'

Without a word the countess gathered her mantle about her and disappeared into the fog outside.

37

KILLALA BAY, MAYO

'I think I hear the sea.'

Gerald was first to detect the unmistakable sound. Eleanor listened intently and smiled at Gerald in confirmation. She had spent too many years at the ocean's edge to mistake the hypnotic vibration that so often had lulled her to sleep in Kilbritin. The dull boom of the wave, followed by the rasp of the powerful undertow, sounded on the shoreline below them. She smelled the distinctive, cleansing tang of sea water, wafted towards them by the light autumn breeze.

Every mile of the trek across the mountains, every rut in the rough mountain track, had jolted the last ounce of stamina from her body. There had been little time to rest, to ease aching limbs, to appease hunger. The fear of pursuit was a sufficient spur to keep moving. The harper might well have alerted her sister who, like a cat with a mouse, would be loath to lose her prey.

Her life, she reflected, seemed to have dissolved into one long day of unending movement, through pastures, over mountains, past rivers and lakes, and nights of damp discomfort, huddled before the campfire, keeping at bay the darkness, the chill and, more lately, the remorse. Her life had altered beyond remembrance from what it had once been, safe and content at Kilbritin, before the news of the execution of her brothers at Tyburn, and the king's plot against her nephew, had propelled her on this unending odyssey. The inscrutable face of fate had hidden the web of deceit and intrigue in which she had become embroiled.

Would she have tried to escape if she had known that Leverous would enter her life again, save her life, befriend her son, that his love would reignite a passion which she had relegated to memory and disturb the grave of her deeply buried secret? Would she have run, if she had known that by the fall of a die, loaded by blackmail, she would agree to marry the tormentor of her youth, that she would inflame the rivalry between O'Donel and Leverous, watch in horror as O'Donel beat her lover to his knees, to lie defenceless before the death-blow, the lover to whom she must now show indifference to protect his son, their son; the man before whom the mask of her emotions had slipped to reveal her love, as cruelly as she had concealed it from him? Yes, she thought, perhaps it would have been better if she had taken flight, ignored the tug of honour and duty to her brothers' memory, her resolve to deny the Tudor king the opportunity to sate his bloodlust on the last of the Geraldines.

She was weary beyond belief. Every bone and muscle in her body cried out for respite from the constant motion, from the rock-hard ground that had become her bed, from the state of unending alertness that strained her ear to every rustle in the night, to every daylight sound which might signal capture. Deep within, her maternal impulse to protect her son vied with the blatant demands of her sexuality, to have the love of the man she desired. She had made enough sacrifices in her life to justify her right to love, but it seemed that even with O'Donel's death there was to be no release from the secret that both bound and divided her from Thomas Leverous.

Thomas, Cormac and Robert Walshe seemed disinclined to mention O'Donel's name. From their silence, she knew they were still puzzled about why she had agreed to marry the man whom she purported to despise and who had plotted the death of her nephew. Thomas had looked to her for some response after O'Donel's death, but she could not give it. For the obstacle by which O'Donel had taken advantage of her still remained. Thomas did not, could not understand, and had withdrawn from her again, resuming the air of concerned civility that he had adopted since the announcement of her betrothal to O'Donel in Askeaton.

The sun threw spangles of gold in their path as it descended towards the west. The fiery glow of autumn blazed everywhere around them, on the leaves, the burnished hedgerows, across the scorched grass. The vivid colours, like the false flush of the wasting sickness, camouflaged the decaying earth beneath. Red ochre, brown, amber and yellow leaves rustled from the sapless trees to join their companions on the ground. The landscape seemed at rest, hushed into a respectful silence, as it watched the year decline beneath a faded blue autumnal sky.

'The sea!' Gerald's triumphant shout disturbed the silence, as they emerged from the trees.

They drew rein and from the high cliff looked below at the blue expanse. Long languid waves rolled inward to toss their white-frothed burden on the shore and withdraw back into the deep. A remote silence hung over the sea and the high cliffs which sheltered the shingle beach below. Far out beyond the vast heaving mass, the setting sun threw darts of golden light on the waves. A cormorant, its great wings outspread, cast a black shadow as it skimmed low over the water.

From behind them, a shout made the horses shy. Hands slid quickly towards sword hilts and instinctively Eleanor moved close to Gerald. From behind a grassy hillock, two men emerged and observed them in silence. They seemed unarmed, save for a spear which the younger one held over his shoulder. The other, an elderly man, bowed down with age, his face weatherbeaten, carried three dead rabbits suspended from a thong in his hand. Both were dressed in coarse linen tunics, their legs encased in rough woollen hose.

'Ask them for directions,' Leverous whispered to Cormac.

Cormac nudged his horse forward. The two watched his approach warily.

'*Dia dhibh*. We are looking for O'Malley's country.'

'O'Malley?' The elder of the two repeated the name, as if surprised that they should know it.

'Dudara O'Malley,' Cormac added. 'Chieftain of Umhall.'

'Umhall? Back the west,' the old man jerked his thumb in the direction.

'How many days?'

The two looked at one another. 'By land is it?

Cormac nodded.

'I wouldn't know,' the old man replied. 'By sea, one day,' he said with certainty. 'Does O'Malley know ye?' The old man raised a quizzical eye beyond Cormac towards Leverous and then to where Eleanor and Gerald waited with Robert Walshe.

'Yes,' Eleanor moved her horse forward. 'Yes, he knows us.'

Taken aback at her intervention, Leverous moved aside to let her pass. She leaned down from the pillion towards the old man and showed him the seahorse emblem in the palm of her hand. The old man studied it in silence before raising shrewd eyes towards her.

'If ye have the seahorse, then ye know O'Malley.' He smiled at her in assurance. 'What do ye want us to do?'

'Take us to O'Malley,' Cormac said quietly.

The old man shook his head. 'I do not know the way by land. By sea,' he lifted his shoulders, 'my boat can carry only two.'

Cormac looked towards Leverous. 'Unless we send Gerald,' he said.

Eleanor saw Gerald's face crumple in dismay at the

prospect of being separated from them again.

'No,' she said firmly, 'let us stay together.'

The younger man whispered something to the other. The older one nodded and said slowly.

'We could bring The O'Malley to ye in one day.'

They looked at him in amazement.

'The beacon at Doonbriste,' the younger man explained and pointed towards a distant headland across the bay which protruded far out into the sea. 'O'Malley has a chain of beacons on the high points along the coast, right to his castle on Clare Island, to warn him of attack.'

'Aye, and for other reasons besides,' the old man said with a twinkle in his eyes.

Eleanor felt the first faint glimmer of hope stir in her breast.

'So you light the beacon at Doonbriste and the message is relayed to O'Malley, one beacon to the next.'

The old man nodded, delighting in her understanding of the age-old coastal alarm system. Leverous looked doubtfully towards the headland.

'Simple but effective,' Robert Walshe murmured. 'The only option, if we are to have any chance of getting to that ship,' he reminded Leverous.

'If there is a ship,' Leverous muttered.

Eleanor felt the anger rise within her. 'With O'Malley, Gerald will have some chance of escape, even if I have been duped by Grey.'

She saw Thomas wince at the coldness in her voice and silently grieved that events were driving them further and further apart. He rarely addressed her directly any more and his glances were cold and laced with suspicion. Her heart cried out within her at the injustice of it all. But as she looked at him, conferring in low tones with her son, she knew there was little she could do to lift the veil of distrust which now enveloped her, making him wary of her loyalty, despising whom once he had loved. How she longed to see the warm look of love dissolve the cold suspicion in his eyes.

'How soon can you light the beacon?' Robert Walshe asked.

'In one hour,' the old man said with certainty. 'We will make a start. For ye.' He held out the rabbits and Eleanor accepted them with thanks.

They watched them scramble down the cliff-face and emerge from a crevice in the rocks below, carrying a small hide-covered boat on their backs which they expertly propelled out into the bay. The oars flashed in unison, catching the last rays of the setting sun. The party watched from the cliff until the boat had disappeared.

They dismounted and made towards the wood. In a clearing they prepared to camp for the night.

Robert Walshe busied himself with a fire while Cormac and Leverous gutted and skinned the rabbits. Taking a small pewter flagon, Eleanor went with Gerald towards the nearby stream that scrambled through overhanging banks and rocks on its way to the sea.

'Will we be able to see the beacon from here?' Gerald asked.

Eleanor stopped and turned towards the sea, now barely visible in the twilight.

'Perhaps. But it is too soon yet. The men are still at sea.'

'I was never on the sea before. Were you, aunt?' he asked, swinging the flagon in a wide arc over his head.

'Yes. At Kilbritin. With Cormac and his father,' she said without thinking.

It was so natural that she could never think of them but as father and son. Donal and Cormac. She heard Gerald's voice.

'What did you say?'

'Are you to come on the ship with Leverous and me?'

Gerald voiced the question she dared not ask herself. Did she want to go? Did Leverous want her with them? He and Robert Walshe were Gerald's appointed guardians. She was but the guarantor of a chimerical plot that had failed abysmally, someone who was under suspicion of conniving with those seeking to take Gerald's life. It was neither necessary nor desirable that she should accompany them. She took the flagon from Gerald and dipped it into the clear water. He waited for her answer but she had none to give.

'Give that to Leverous,' she said, handing him the flagon. He looked at her, his brown eyes full of foreboding at her silence, and retraced his steps to where the campfire twinkled between the trees.

Eleanor watched him go, Garret's son and heir, the innocent target of a deadly conspiracy, the object of a king's vengeance, the catalyst of Ireland's doomed search for unity, the victim of her sister's unnatural lust, of O'Donel's revenge and of Desmond's vainglorious ambition.

She made her way slowly back through the brush towards the cliff. She sat on a tuft of grass and felt the tiredness ooze from her body. A cool breeze blew in from the sea. Eleanor pulled the woollen shawl over her head and tied it loosely at her waist. The afterglow of the sunset lingered, leaving a residual brightness over the water to the west. She heard a footfall behind her.

'Sit by me, Gerald, and we'll watch for the beacon.'

Eleanor turned to find Leverous beside her. His gaze was unwavering, as if he was trying to see inside her head. She felt his closeness and longed to rest against him to share the burden of her guilt and loneliness. He sat down beside her.

'I beg forgiveness for my ill-manners. I had no right to doubt that Grey's ship will arrive, to doubt you. No right at all.'

Eleanor drew the shawl close around her.

'It is nothing. It is a trying time for all of us. Even Gerald seems more tense.'

'Poor scamp,' Leverous said reflectively, looking out into the darkening abyss. 'It amazes me how well he has coped this far. Without you,' he said kindly, 'it would have been more difficult.'

She shook her head. 'He seemed happy and content enough with you.'

'Alone with his crusty old tutor? No, the boy needs something more, someone more sensitive to his moods and needs.'

'A mother substitute?'

He smiled. 'Whatever it is, I think it is the prerogative of a woman. You can not imagine how much at a loss I felt, in Donore and before, knowing he needed something more than I could give. An instinctive anticipation of his emotional needs, the right word to say at the right time. Just as I felt at his age, without a mother or father, family . . .' His voice trailed away into remembrance of the past.

'It did not seem to do you any harm,' she said softly.

'I was luckier than most. I was given a second family. Poor Gerald lost everything at once: mother, father, brother and foster family. But, like me, he was lucky enough to find a loving substitute,' he leaned towards her, 'and the final stage of his journey will be less frightening if he knows that you will be with him . . . with us.'

She heard his words as if from a distance, the words she thought she would never hear him say. Now that he had said them, she found herself at a loss to know how to respond. Did he speak for himself, as well as for Gerald? Were his words a proposal or a proposition? She looked at him, her mind in turmoil. His head was turned away from her. He offered her the opportunity to realise what her heart desired, the longing she had repressed for the sake of Donal, of Cormac, perhaps for no more exalted a reason than a shallow propriety to preserve her status. She was, after all, the Great Earl's daughter, schooled to fulfil a role in life that paid scant attention to the tugs and longings of the heart. And she had accepted that role, adapted to it so well that she had forced his love from her heart. She suddenly felt ashamed, undeserving. For, unlike her, he had given his love as he had given loyalty to her brother, unreservedly, without guile or ulterior motive. Her son, their son, still stood as the impediment between them, but O'Donel's blackmail had perished with him and her secret lay safely concealed within her again. For the first time in her life, neither duty nor devotion bound her against her will. She was free to choose her own way, unrestricted.

She tried to put words on the thoughts that danced in her head. Supposing she read too much into his proposal to go with him to France. Perhaps, as he said, his concern was for Gerald and nothing more, her presence merely a maternal cradle. Perhaps he intended her to return to Ireland, once they had Gerald safely in France.

He sensed her troubled look and turned to her. Below them the rise and fall of the waves beat a deep tattoo on the shingle. Slowly Leverous raised his hand to her face, as if uncertain of her reaction, and tentatively brushed away a strand of hair loosened by the wind.

'Now is our time, Eleanor,' he whispered softly. 'It will never come again. We have both danced until now to someone else's music. It is our time now, my dearest.' His fingers touched her lips and gently he raised her face towards his.

She tried to answer, but he placed a finger on her lips.

'I do not want to know what passed between you and O'Donel, what promise he made you.' He paused. 'Or what threat. For he is no more, like your father, your husband, like Garret. You know,' he said with a rueful smile, 'both of us stand accused of one sin. We have both lived our lives for others. Is it not time we started living for each other?' He held her gently from him, his hands grasping her arms. 'Look around you, feel, touch. We are alive; we are in love. There are no more barriers between us.' He drew her close and kissed her lightly but lingeringly, a kiss of introduction, of reacquaintance, of renewal. He drew her into his arms. 'No secrets, nothing more to keep us apart,' he murmured in her ear.

Across his shoulder, Eleanor saw Cormac standing at a distance and, behind him, Gerald came running from the camp.

'The beacon. The beacon,' he shouted as he ran, pointing towards the sea.

In the distance, a fiery glow lit the sky towards the west. Gerald came and sat between them on the dry bracken. Cormac, his arms folded on his chest, stood quietly a little to one side, looking out to sea.

'A flame of hope, of salvation.' Robert Walshe's words sounded like a prayer.

Eleanor looked up at her son, their son, with pride. He deserved his position as MacCarthy chieftain. He would make a responsible leader of his clan. Donal had taught him well and he had inherited Leverous's traits of character. The spontaneous affinity that had grown between Cormac and Leverous had tossed aside the barriers she had erected to keep them apart. The reasons she had kept Cormac's identity from Thomas were perhaps no longer valid. He was dedicated to fulfil his promise to Garret and that commitment seemed destined to take him away from Ireland. In her heart she knew him well enough to know that he would never harm their son. But would he be strong enough not to divulge his identity to Cormac, the youngung chieftain whom he thought of as a friend, but who was in truth his son? It was a cruel obligation to force on any father.

And how would such a revelation affect their relationship? He wanted her with him, to resume their long-postponed relationship, as if nothing but time had intervened. But how could she live a lie with Thomas by her side? And if she told him, would their love die in angry and bitter recrimination? Would he, as O'Donel had claimed, feel cheated, unable to forgive the ultimate and deepest wound she could have inflicted on him, that made him deny his own son?

Eleanor saw Leverous look at her as she observed her

son with an expression of quizzical supposition. She felt her heart turn over in apprehension, knowing she had no answer yet to give him.

'How long before O'Malley sees the beacon?' Gerald asked.

Leverous's eyes met hers over Gerald's head, and he smiled reassuringly as he took her hand in his.

'Not long now, Gerald,' he said.

38

NORTH MAYO

The Countess of Ormond was on the point of admitting defeat when Brabazon, who was one of the small group that had gone with her, spotted the fire out on the distant headland.

'Too great for a camp fire. Perhaps a churl's cabin,' he suggested, as they reined to a stop.

She stared hard at the orange light which cut through the darkness, like a beacon.

'A beacon,' she said aloud. 'What if it has been fired to signal some message?'

'In Cornwall, in the coastal parts, seafaring rogues, pirates, light fires in stormy weather to lure ships onto the rocks.'

Pirates, she thought, they must be near O'Malley's country.

To her relief, they had hardly sighted a living soul since leaving the camp on the Erne. While her mailclad, heavily armed escort was sufficient to ward off or outrun attack from the petty chieftains whose territories they crossed, she had skirted any sign of habitation to make certain they would not be delayed by parley or by skirmish. Time was not on her side if she was to find the fugitive band before they reached O'Malley. Not knowing that she was in pursuit might well have slowed their progress. But for each mile they moved closer to O'Malley's country, the greater the possibility that she might lose them.

'Well, there is no storm, Brabazon, so the beacon beyond was fired for some reason other than as a lure.'

Brabazon's eyes narrowed as he looked towards the glow of the fire. 'Perhaps to lure people,' he said softly.

The countess looked again in the direction of the headland. The fire did not seem to burn with the same intensity. It had to be a signal of some sort, but to whom?

'We will rest the horses.'

Brabazon conveyed her order to the men who, with creaking of leather and clank of arms, gratefully dismounted and stretched on the ground.

The countess withdrew to the shadow of a large boulder and leaned against the rock. Before her lay the dark outline of a wood; somewhere in the bracken-covered hills and mountain ranges to the west lay O'Malley's country and further off, the open sea. Somewhere in between, at rest or on their guard, were her sister, Leverous, Robert Walshe and the object of her ambition, the Geraldine. She had been thwarted at every step by plots and by circumstance. Even O'Donel, for all his boasting, had not been able to fulfil his promise. But this time she would personally oversee the end. There could be no mistakes because there would be no more opportunities. The boy must be taken, alive or dead – it hardly mattered now. At her meeting with the king in London, he had hinted at the latter. Memories of the inexplicable deaths of minors under royal custody in the Tower still rankled in England.

'If the boy should die, 'twould be better that it be done in Ireland,' Henry had told her.

Better for the king perhaps, but she was less certain. To realise the ambition which had spurred her to such lengths, she must be careful not to alienate those over whom she hoped to rule. It was one thing to achieve the power to rule all Ireland, but it was another matter entirely to exercise it, as Grey had found to his cost. To have the blood of the last Geraldine on her hands would serve only to alienate the supporters of the Geraldines in Ireland and make her task of governing them more difficult. If the boy died in the Tower, the blame would be laid squarely at the king's door. She knew this was her final chance to secure the power and estates of the Great Earl which, when allied to what she had built in Ormond, and to the deputyship, would make her more powerful than her father. The capture of her nephew would place the question of her loyalty to the king beyond doubt and demonstrate her ability to be his deputy, while concealing her ultimate ambition from him until she chose to divulge it. For her father had planted the seed of a Geraldine-ruled Ireland not only in her brother. She too was a Geraldine, albeit a woman, but a woman with the ambition of a man, and the only one left to fulfil the Great Earl's design. She smiled bitterly to herself. What would the Great Earl say if he knew that the seed of his ambition had germinated within the daughter he had so callously rejected?

Brabazon came towards her. His cloak swung with the movement of his swagger. The countess looked at him through narrowed eyes. She needed his sort, able and ruthless, to further her plans, but she would watch him closely, keep his wings clipped so that his ambition did not impinge on hers.

'This O'Malley – ' his high-pitched English voice grated in the night silence, ' – the men wonder about his forces, kern and gallowglass?'

She looked away from him. 'O'Malley,' she said dismissively, 'is a pirate, a sea-trader of sorts, more accustomed to fighting his battles by sea than by land. He has no gallowglass, though he ferries them in from Scotland for others greater than himself. You have little cause to worry. Should we encounter O'Malley, his kern stand little chance against our demi-lance and pike.'

'The party who protect the Geraldine,' Brabazon persisted, 'the tutor, the priest . . .' he paused, '. . . your sister. Are they to be taken with the Geraldine?'

She turned her back on him and made for her horse. 'Such a question no would-be conqueror should need to ask.

She beckoned to one of her men. 'Scout the wood before us. We will follow behind. Go quietly now.'

He touched his iron morion in response and walked his horse carefully towards the dark outline of the trees. She watched until his shadow merged with the darkness and then signalled to the rest to follow.

The wood was as dark and silent as a tomb. A path, barely discernible in the gloom, led through the dry undergrowth. There was no sound, except for the rustle of the dead leaves underfoot.

They had journeyed for an hour when the scout reappeared among the trees. He spoke in a whisper.

'There is a camp in the clearing, beyond a stream. I counted four people.'

She felt the anticipation mount within her, setting her senses alive.

'Four?' she frowned. 'What about a sentry?'

The soldier shook his head.

She gestured towards Brabazon. 'Have the men spread out.'

Soundlessly they did as she bade them and cautiously moved forward. The smell of smouldering wood drifted towards them on the breeze. A twig snapped in the silence. Suddenly like a woodcock from its nest, a figure sprang up from the undergrowth in front of them, with a shout that reverberated through the trees. The countess's horse reared up in terror.

'Attack, attack.'

A soldier nearest her stooped swiftly from his saddle and with the shaft of a halberd knocked the figure senseless to the ground. All around, the sound of swords being withdrawn from scabbards mingled with the noise of the horses crashing through the undergrowth.

The countess reined hard on her horse and cantered after her men through the bushes, regardless of the scratches and grazes from the outlying branches.

In the clearing beside the smoking remains of a fire, two men were being held at lance-point. She recognised Leverous and her MacCarthy nephew. Two figures covered by mantles lay asleep beside the fire. She felt exultant. She motioned to a soldier and watched with mounting anticipation as he bent forward and drew back the covers. Instead of the figures of the Geraldine and her sister, two pillions covered by a blanket lay before her.

Angrily she rounded on the prisoners.

'No basket to conceal my nephew so cleverly this time, Leverous. Where is he?'

'You have as much a notion as me,' Leverous replied evenly.

A soldier hit him across the mouth.

'I will ask one more time. And whatever about the Geraldine, remember you are expendable.'

The tutor stood his ground before her. His white shirt gleamed eerily in the dim light. The soldier raised his hand again.

'At the sound of alarm, he ran in terror into the woods,' MacCarthy answered her.

The countess fixed her eyes on her nephew. An insolent youth, she recalled from their previous encounter, and an able one, she remembered bitterly. If it had not been for his initial intervention at Colaughtrim forest, none of this charade, these outlandish plots and counterplots, this endless trek through the country, to attain the custody of a young boy, would have been necessary. He stared boldly at her with studied indifference.

'So, my brave nephew. It seems both your luck and your

mother have deserted you.'

She wheeled her horse to face her men.

'Spread out and search in all directions. Ten groats to the man who brings me the Geraldine,' she looked down at her nephew, 'Five for the Lady MacCarthy.'

Like hounds from the slips, her men tore off in every direction through the trees.

'There are cliffs here,' Brabazon shouted from the left.

She ordered her men to bind Leverous and MacCarthy, and joined Brabazon. In the dimness she saw that the ground petered out into sloping cliffs. She edged closer to the verge. The white crest of the waves were visible as they bore down on the shoreline below.

She froze as her ear detected a sound from the cliff-face further on. Silently she motioned Brabazon to follow her. They rode parallel to the edge for some distance, searching for any sign of movement, straining for the slightest sound. But there was nothing.

The sky was brightening towards the east. Soon it would be light and she would order a thorough check of the cliffs and the shore. The boy could hardly be far away and if by chance he had clambered down the cliff face, the sea would bar him from going further.

They retraced their steps to the clearing just as two of the searchers returned dragging a figure between them. The countess felt a small sense of triumph as her sister was flung to the ground before her. She looked down at the woman who had humiliated her at their last encounter, now barefoot, her hair in disarray, her dress soiled and torn.

'Well, sister, I expected you to be in mourning for your betrothed, O'Donel, that your keening would assail the heavens. Instead I find you traipsing the woods like a common campwoman with her paramour.' She saw Leverous strain at the rope that bound him. 'But then you never did set your sights too high. Where is our nephew?'

Her sister did not answer, but shook herself free from

the soldiers who held her.

'We found her on the far side of the stream, my lady. There was no sign of the boy.'

'Continue the search. It is nearly light. Bind her with the others.'

Eleanor pushed the soldier aside and faced her sister.

'For pity's sake, what twisted ambition drives you to sacrifice the life of a child, of your own blood? Is there no spark of humanity left within you to halt this madness, the ceaseless bloodletting of your family?'

The countess rounded on her in fury. 'Family? What family? I remember nothing but hurt and humiliation. My pride, my ambition, my son, tossed aside like dross in the interest of Kildare. Well let me tell you, sister,' she leaned down from the saddle until their faces almost touched, 'it is you and the rest of our family who made me what I am. Our father made me an image of himself, to think like him, to act like him, before he tired of the white crow he created and sold me off, a sop to his enemy, while my brother stole my place. And you,' her eyes flashed contemptuously over her sister, 'and the rest of his brood gloated at my fall. But I learned my lesson well, better than our father had intended; so well, in fact, that his ambition pales in comparison to mine.'

The countess panted from the exertion of her tirade. Around her, the soldiers stood motionless, eyes riveted on her, as if spellbound by her revelations.

'I pity you,' she heard her sister say softly.

The countess felt the bitterness and hatred rise like a wave within her, as of old, when her sister's condescending air served only to drive the thorn of isolation deeper.

''Tis you who must be pitied. You should know by experience that the king does not dismiss traitors lightly. Especially Geraldines,' she said, her voice once more in control.

From the bushes, two soldiers dragged a body into the clearing. Eleanor went to the motionless figure and turned it over.

'Ah, my brother's intrepid chaplain,' the countess taunted; "twere better that he stuck to his prayers than meddle in things that do not concern him.'

A groan came from the prostrate figure.

'Bind him with the rest,' the countess ordered, 'and her.' She pointed to her sister.

The soldiers dragged Robert Walshe towards where Leverous and MacCarthy were already fast bound beneath the tree. Eleanor was pushed roughly between Leverous and her son.

It was almost daylight. Out on the headland there was no trace of the beacon that had led them to their quarry.

'There is enough light to search the shoreline,' the countess said to Brabazon. 'Take three men on foot.'

Brabazon seemed to be about to remonstrate, but her look made him change his mind. There was no time for false dignity. The boy must be found before their presence was detected by some inquisitive locals, who might seek explanation for their activity. With a sullen countenance, Brabazon dismounted and led the men towards the cliff face.

The countess leaned against a tree a little way from the clearing. It would not be feasible to bring her sister, Leverous and the chaplain as prisoners back to Ormond. It would arouse suspicion and slow their progress. She had little option but to leave them for her men to dispatch and make it appear that they had been attacked by bandits. The countess was determined to bring the Geraldine alive to England. One more Geraldine stain on the king's hands would scarcely be noticed.

'My lady, I beg you. The Lady MacCarthy and her son. They have no cause to answer. It is by my entreaty solely that they became involved.'

It was as if Leverous had read her mind. She looked at him with ill-concealed dislike. Even a lowly tutor, a foreigner, she recalled, had been placed in preference above her in Maynooth, had received the affection that had been withheld from her.

'It seems that my sister fell victim to your entreaties before this, Leverous. The last time, I do recall, the Great Earl got her safely away to Carbury, before the result became too obvious to the eye.'

She saw her nephew lift his head and look from his mother to the tutor. 'Yes,' she told him, 'your mother and the tutor here shared more than a sibling friendship at Maynooth, or was it Thomas Court?'

'God's life, is there no depth to the evil within you?'

Eleanor's words were lost in the sound of movement from the cliff face. The countess swung around in anticipation. The three men who had gone to search with Brabazon were returning. Perhaps Brabazon had captured the boy on the shore below? She waited for them to speak, but they continued to walk towards her. They looked unfamiliar. One wore a gold earring in his ear. By the time she realised that they were not her men, a knife was against her throat. She could feel the blade through the silk partlet of her dress. Her arm was pinned behind her in a powerful grasp.

'One sound, one movement, and your mistress is no more.'

The voice was low and commanding as the man gave orders to his two companions, who silently gathered the weapons of the Ormond soldiers who were guarding the prisoners. From behind the tree a fourth man appeared, unbound the prisoners and silently motioned them towards the cliff. Eleanor glanced in her sister's direction as if she were about to say something, but Leverous hurried her on. In the morning stillness the sounds of the soldiers searching the wood could be heard. The countess thought to cry out but the pressure of the knife against her neck made it even difficult to swallow.

Using her body as a shield, her captor backed slowly towards the cliff. The countess looked in angry impotence at her men who stood in the clearing, uncertain whether to rush her attacker or remain. Minutes passed; she had no idea how long. She tried to shout them into action but her captor increased the pressure on her throat and her shout ended in a croak. From the shore below the sound of voices and the creak of oars could be clearly heard. Her captor suddenly removed the knife from her throat and at the same time pushed her violently from him to the ground. The impact knocked the breath from her body and for a moment she lay stunned on the grass. Her men ran towards her and helped her to her feet. Impatiently she shook them off and ran towards the cliff.

Clearly visible in the morning light, a galley, rowed with ten oars aside, made rapidly from the shore. Seated amidships, she saw her sister, Leverous and the chaplain. At the helm, a powerful figure whose booming voice echoed across the shore as he gave instructions to the crew. Beside him at the helm, the small figure of the Geraldine waved impudently to her.

The countess's cry of impotent rage echoed off the cliff face, the sound mocking her helplessness. Tears of anger welled in her eyes. With a rapid motion of her hand she brushed them away. The last tears she had cried had been over the still body of her son and she had no more to shed.

A movement on the beach below momentarily distracted her gaze from the galley which was moving lightly over the water, the oars rising and falling in unison. Brabazon, clad in shirt and hose and holding his bloody head, staggered into view, followed by his companions.

The countess reverted her gaze to the sea and watched as a sail was hoisted. The emblem of a horse unfurled and seemed to ride away over the waves with her dream.

39

BORDER OF THE PALE AND ULSTER

For two hours Grey followed the trail of destruction northwards. The moment he crossed over the wide ditch that separated the Pale from the Irish-held hinterland, the result of O'Neill's predatory incursion was evident all around. The Ulster chieftain had plundered the northern part of the enclave at will and, it appeared, had been offered little resistance by the inhabitants.

The neat dwellings and haggards of the tenants lay open to the sky. The sleeting rain hissed on the smoking ruins. The countryside around was stripped bare as if a cloud of locusts had devoured everything in its path. Before torching them, the invaders had picked clean every dwelling, taken every utensil, from pot to plough. The winter stores of wheat and corn had vanished. The outfields were denuded of the cattle herds which normally grazed within the enclosures. Among the smouldering ruins of the villages, an occasional body lay prostrate among the rubble. But most of the villagers had fled south before O'Neill, to the protection of the walled towns of Trim and Drogheda.

'God's blood, my lord; the Irish have no equals for plunder.' There was admiration in the voice of Grey's war-seasoned captain of horse, as he surveyed the scene of despoliation.

'O'Neill's greed will be his downfall. He will make little headway with so much spoil.'

'Are we to follow him, my lord. To Ulster?' the captain asked, as if they were to enter hell.

'When our reinforcements are in order.'

As soon as he had seen the first evidence of O'Neill's attack, Grey had sent messengers to the Pale lords summoning them to a hosting to drive against O'Neill into Ulster. It was a clear warning to them that they must now choose between loyalty to the king or be branded traitors. If the Countess of Ormond was to be believed, many of them had become entangled in Desmond's league. But the league was no more, and if the arrangements he had made were successful, the Geraldine might well be on the seas to France. Grey fervently hoped so, for with his nephew gone from Ireland, the shackles that restrained him from his duty were finally removed.

Against O'Neill, Grey was determined to demonstrate the full extent of his military prowess, frustrated for so long by political machinations. He felt the blood course with renewed energy through his veins at the prospect. Even the nagging pain in his belly had eased. The humiliation of past encounters with shadows in the mountains and glens of Wicklow, the aimless wandering, harangued by the Countess of Ormond, through Munster and the midlands were behind him. Here on the cultivated plains of the Pale he would demonstrate the full scope and power of his military expertise for which he had been trained and conditioned.

'What is the latest muster?' he asked his captain.

'At this morning's count, four hundred and sixty, my lord. Another twenty deserters since the last count.'

Grey swore under his breath. As well as putting pressure on the lords of the Pale for a clear indication of their loyalty, he was in sore need of their reinforcements. It would be suicidal to follow O'Neill into his lair, understrength and unprovisioned. For in the customary way, O'Neill had destroyed everything in his path, leaving nothing to succour his pursuers. Grey's troops were weary and mutinous after the fruitless trek. Desmond had needed little prodding to abandon the league other than the threat to his title posed by the presence of his cousin. The luckless claimant to the earldom of Desmond had returned to court to continue to plead his case for restoration with the king, a vain hope now that his rival had been brought to heel.

'Let the men know that when they beat O'Neill, all his booty is theirs.'

His captain raised a hand to his iron basinet and cantered back through the lines. Faint-hearted cheers erupted from the soldiers, as the captain spread the message through the ranks.

'By Christ's cross, Grey, you do not seriously consider pursuing O'Neill into Ulster?' the Earl of Ormond gasped at his shoulder. The earl's face looked blotched and miserable in the driving rain which had fallen incessantly since they had entered the Pale. 'You court disaster. There is no knowing what forces the devil has concealed in there.' He pointed vaguely northwards.

'It may not come to that, if we can turn him before he crosses into Ulster.'

'Even that is madness. The men are on their last legs, marched from pillar to post without reward, without food. We are in no condition to face O'Neill.'

A wry smile touched Grey's face. He felt some sympathy for the old warrior, not least because he was saddled with such a harpy for a wife. It was to the relief of both of them that she had returned to Ormond, her iron constitution eventually succumbing to the gruelling conditions of the field. Or was her indisposition just a feint to hide some ulterior motive? A needle of suspicion pricked at Grey. Had she heard some news about his nephew? He sighed resignedly. There was little more he could do to save the boy. If he had fallen into the clutches of the countess, then both he and his nephew were doomed. If not, then this pursuit of O'Neill gave him an opportunity to redeem the damage she had done his reputation with the king. A decisive victory over O'Neill – perhaps the enforced submission of such a prominent chieftain and an incisive foray into Tyrone for plunder to pay his troops – would go some way towards allaying the king's suspicion.

'By your leave, my lord, it looks as if we may be in a better position to take on O'Neill than you imagined.'

Grey pointed across Ormond towards the brow of a nearby hill, where a force of about one hundred horse appeared behind his messenger, who galloped towards him, the soft earth spraying in clods from under his horse's hooves.

'My Lords Dunsany, Howth, Slane, Fingal and Talbot, my lord,' he announced.

Grey felt a glow of satisfaction, not only at the prospect of additional troops, all horse, he noted, but at the clear signal that the ill-advised league had truly collapsed. O'Neill's devastation of their land had revived the loyalty of the Pale lords.

'God's blood,' he heard Ormond swear beside him. 'Is the king to be served by traitors?'

'Better than serving against him,' Grey said dismissively.

The straggling line of horsemen, footmen and the war wagons came to a halt in the muddy ground. All eyes watched the troop of horse who approached slowly, as if uncertain of their reception.

Dunsany and his companions doffed their hats in a gesture of submission and sat bareheaded in the rain before the king's deputy. Grey raised his hat briefly in acknowledgement. He felt sympathy for them. Some, like himself, related to the House of Kildare by ties of blood, had found the king's bloodlust against his nephew difficult to stomach. Apart from their traditional allegiance to the House of Kildare, the Pale lords had little in common with their Irish counterparts who still considered them, even after the passage of four hundred years since the Conquest, the usurpers of their lands. O'Neill's attack on their territory had brought them to their senses quicker than a thousand threats from Grey or the king.

'We are glad to have your company to avenge this dastardly attack on your territories,' he said kindly enough. He saw Dunsany's relief at his words; he had been expecting recrimination and abuse or worse.

'Though by God's blood you deserved it,' Ormond's anger boiled over, 'consorting with Desmond, in traitorous leagues and conspiracies against the king.'

'Come, come, my lord,' Grey interjected, 'nothing has been proven to implicate my Lord Dunsany and his companions with conspiracy. They are here to stand loyally with us against the real enemy. Is that not so, my lords?'

They murmured their assent.

'Then fall in and let us to it, before O'Neill slips through our fingers.'

Grey raised his arm and signalled the advance. The Pale lords fell in behind. With the rain streaming into their eyes, the army lumbered into motion and advanced northwards.

They reached the boundary of the Pale, facing MacMahon's territory of Oriel. The plains of the Pale merged into a landscape of low hills, interspaced with scrub, woodland and diminutive lakes fed by numerous streams and rivulets. The rain had eased into a light mist but the countryside seemed to be awash. Water oozed from the ground to meet what fell from the sky. Horses sank deep into the clinging mud. Grey had never seen such a waterlogged terrain and was glad he had left the cannon at Kells. The wagons would have stuck fast by the axles. He shivered within his armour, as the icy dampness chilled his bones. The heavy grey sky touched the tops of the surrounding hills, diminishing further the visibility of the short November day.

Despite the weather, the terrain and the fatigue of his

men, Grey was pleased with the progress. O'Neill would be reduced to a slow pace by the sheer quantity of his plunder, remnants of which littered the muddied track they followed.

Dunsany edged his horse nearer.

'What are your plans, my lord, when we come upon O'Neill?'

Grey glanced at the florid countenance beside him. It was imperative that he maintain the loyalty of the lords whose territory bordered the English enclave in Dublin. If he lost their support, it would leave the city without its protective hinterland, vulnerable to an Irish attack. And if Dublin fell, England could wave farewell to her Irish kingdom. The Vikings had realised the strategic importance of Dublin long before the English, Grey mused. The high walls and fortifications of the city still posed an insurmountable obstacle to the Irish, who had neither the equipment nor the expertise to take a castle. But ordnance and artillery were not the prerogative of England alone. The products of the latest design and expertise were to be freely bought in the Low Countries. And there was nothing to stop a powerful and ambitious lord, like Desmond or O'Neill, from acquiring some.

'When the scouts locate his position, methinks it would be better to head him off and turn him back towards the Pale.'

'With the cavalry?'

Grey nodded.

'Ours,' Dunsany gestured towards his companions, 'are fresh. We could more quickly get before him and head him back towards you.'

Grey thought for a moment. Another would think it rash to place such trust in those who but recently had conspired with O'Neill. He motioned to Dunsany to move a little forward, out of earshot of the others.

'Your intrigue with Desmond, my lord, was noted by those who bear illwill to the Geraldine.' Dunsany's head jerked sharply in his direction. 'A loyal gesture now might serve you well to right your account with the king.'

Dunsany nodded his understanding.

'Particularly now that the Geraldine is no longer in danger,' Grey added quietly, 'if you take my meaning.' Dunsany smiled his understanding.

'By my oath, my good lord, you will not find us wanting.'

Further discussion was cut short by the reappearance of the two scouts whom Grey had sent on ahead. They galloped towards him and reined their horses amid a cloud of steam.

'O'Neill has pitched camp not a mile off,' one announced excitedly.

'We saw his fires from the hill there,' the other pointed.

A ripple of anticipation ran through the lines.

'The devil take him. Let us attack before he vanishes into the wilderness of Ulster,' Ormond advised.

Grey looked upwards at the darkening sky. It would take another hour to cover the distance and to make preparations to attack O'Neill's camp. It would be almost dark by then. O'Neill had home advantage and allies in the surrounding countryside. Grey realised that he could not risk being drawn further inside Ulster than necessary – or engage in a drawn-out confrontation with O'Neill. He had supplies to sustain them for no more than a day. And they still must face the homeward journey to Dublin through a wasted countryside. He had to get in front of O'Neill's lines, to prevent him from fleeing deeper into Ulster, before he attacked.

'We shall rest until dawn. No fires. No cooking. Dry biscuit and water.' Grey heard the groans of dismay.

'We attack at dawn.' He signalled to Dunsany. 'We will hold the attack until we hear your alarm.'

Dunsany nodded.

'A plague on you, Grey.' The Earl of Ormond burst his way through the Pale lords. 'The king's work to be entrusted to traitors.'

The hands of the Pale lords slipped ominously towards

their sword hilts. Memories of the Kildare-Ormond feud still rankled.

'Talk sense, my lord,' Grey replied gruffly. 'My Lord Dunsany and his neighbours have good reason to avenge themselves on O'Neill. You saw their lands. 'Twas on *their* goods and chattels he preyed. But if you have doubts of their intention, perhaps your lordship might wish to accompany them?'

Grey's words took the wind from Ormond's bluster. His pale eyes shifted nervously under the rim of his flat-topped hat.

'I propose to stay with my army.'

'As you please.' Grey turned briskly towards Dunsany. 'Now, my lord, take half your force and skirt O'Neill's position. Attack as we agreed at dawn.'

Dunsany called out the names and with Lords Howth and Devlin led a group of cavalry towards the hills to the left. They were soon swallowed by the encroaching darkness.

Grey led the remainder of the horsemen to the shelter of a grove of birch and alder beside a swiftly flowing stream. The rest of the army sank to its rest, wherever it fell.

Grey's attendant unbuckled his master's plated armour, rubbed it dry and covered each piece with a sheepskin to keep it from tarnishing.

With his back to the rough bark and a blanket around his shoulders, Grey looked into the murky night. Did he ever imagine that his career would have sunk to such depths as this, he asked himself dourly? He thought of the battles in France, the glorious victory of the Battle of the Spurs, the French in full flight before them, the capture of Tournai and Therouanne. That was the warfare for which every professional soldier yearned, played according to accepted rules which both sides understood: the pre-battle tactics, the choice of terrain, the disciplined lines of armed men, armour and weapons burnished and ready, the valiant charge, the cut and thrust of the engagement, the thrill of hand-to-hand combat against a skilled opponent or a heart-stopping charge with lances drawn. But in this country, bereft of the skills of basic military strategy, no such proprieties existed. Unmanly skirmishing and cowardly ambuscade replaced the clean-cut battle he had been accustomed to. In Ireland his military skills were redundant against an enemy too cowardly to show his face, preferring to strike his opponent from behind the shelter of the forest or lure him to his death in a boggy morass.

A tremor shook Grey's body and he reached into his saddle-bag for the pewter flask. He tipped the nozzle to his lips and the familiar warmth coursed through his body and warmed his extremities. Perhaps this engagement with O'Neill was the start of a new chapter of his stewardship of Ireland, where he could demonstrate his talents as a soldier, concentrate on the military conquest of the country, avoid being sidetracked into the political mire. If his nephew had escaped to France, he would have a free rein to pursue the policies that would hasten the reconquest. His first priority would be a detailed map of the vast unknown regions outside Ormond and the Pale, the second to prise from the tight fist of the king a sufficient army.

He beckoned to his cavalry captain who was hunkering under the dripping branches nearby. It was a far cry from the silken-fringed tents of the generals in the English camp on the high ground above Therouanne, but the tactics for tomorrow's encounter with the Irish were as important now to him and the men he led as they had been against the French.

It was still dark when he heard the petty captains, in low voices, rouse their men. There were few protests from the huddled forms which rose from the sodden ground. A strange concentration descended on the army. Each soldier silently tested sword and bow or hoisted bill and pike over their shoulder. It was as if every man was lost in some personal contemplation, of inevitability in the face of death, reducing complaints and bickering to an eerie silence. Around Grey, the jingle of harness and spur sounded comforting in the darkness. The horses sensed the fear of the riders and shyed against saddle and harness.

Grey rose stiffly to his feet. His armourer buckled on his plated armour, leaving open the visor of his head-piece. His captains gathered around him for the final orders and returned to lead their companies into the designated positions. His horse was brought, fully harnessed for the fray.

'To victory.' he called out to Ormond, who struggled into his saddle, grunted in reply.

The army stood in battle array before the king's deputy, transformed overnight from the shambling lines of discontent and wretchedness into some semblance of a fighting force. Under the straitened circumstances, the captains had worked miracles. At the front, the banners of the English companies were hoisted aloft to mingle with a host of raised pikes, bills and spears. Grey ordered the English companies with some supporting cavalry to the flanks, with Ormond's Irish bands in the centre, headed by the remainder of the horse. The tactic he had gambled on depended on Dunsany's success to turn O'Neill back towards them.

At his order, the army shuffled to its feet. Grey led it across the low hills into the darkness. Beside him Ormond's horse stumbled in the dark, and the elderly nobleman cursed in irritation. Grey had bargained that a surprise attack might compensate for his lack of numbers and the condition of his travel-weary soldiers.

After they had marched for about an hour from the night camp, he brought the army to a halt. The rain had ceased and the air was alive with the coming dawn. A faint curtain of light slowly lifted on the horizon to the east. The landscape began to emerge from the shadowy sameness of the night into discernible features, trees, bushes, the hilly contours of the surrounding countryside. From a covering of rough gorse, a startled grouse shot into the air with a loud cry and disappeared in a hectic flap of wings. Silence settled over the army once more.

The sound was faint at first, so faint that it made Grey doubt that his ears relayed no more than the pounding of the blood in his veins. But then the sound became unmistakable and in the rapidly brightening light of daybreak, as if propelled by invisible hands, the Irish spilled over the hills into view. Grey lifted his sword high over his head and cantered towards them. A great shout erupted from the army behind him as the two flanks spread out like a falcon's wings to entrap the enemy.

O'Neill's kern were the first to meet the onslaught of Grey's cavalry. The Irish gallowglass and horse at the back were embattled with Dunsany's horse, who drove them into Grey's path as planned. Dart and short sword proved little match for bill and lance and the Irish kern fell like ninepins before the cavalry. Some fought their way to the flanks, but were cut down by English pike and halberd.

Grey cut his way through the Irish kern, who already were scattering, darting through whatever gap presented itself to escape the slaughter. O'Neill's cavalry pulled up before them and discharged a few desultory darts in their direction before galloping away to the left and to the right. Which of the horsemen was O'Neill? Of that Grey had no inkling. They all looked alike astride their small horses, long hair and mantle streaming behind them. O'Neill's gallowglass stood their ground to cover the kern's retreat, holding their own against the English horse and foot. The report of arquebus took Grey momentarily by surprise. He saw some of his men fall around him. A row of Irish arquebusiers lined the outline of a hill, their weapons on stands before them. The reports of the shot caused anxiety in his ranks. Grey had not expected that O'Neill's soldiers would be armed with the new weapon, still a rarity even in the king's army. In the lull that followed, O'Neill's gallowglass slipped away, while from the arquebusiers a new volley erupted to deter his men from pressing the advantage. When Grey looked again, the line of Irish arquebusiers had vanished from the hill.

Dunsany galloped towards him.

'Are we to pursue them?'

Grey looked around the scene of the battle. The Irish had scattered in all directions, into the fastness of wooded scrubland which surrounded them. In such terrain, ideal for their tactics of skirmish and ambush, the Irish could turn his victory into defeat.

Grey shook his head. 'Enough for one day. The booty?' he asked his captain.

'The cattle are corralled at O'Neill's camp. The rest is in the wagons and carts he abandoned.'

Grey nodded satisfied and gave orders that it be distributed as he had promised among the men, once they were inside the safety of the Pale.

'Summon the retreat,' he ordered.

It was a meagre victory, Grey thought, but sufficient to compensate for the wasted campaign against Desmond, and one which might perhaps convince the king that his deputy was on the right path towards the reconquest of Ireland.

For a moment his thoughts flashed to his nephew and he wondered if the victory he had gained over O'Neill would also be sufficient to wash away the smear of treason with which his attempt to save the Geraldine's life was tainted.

40

CLARE ISLAND,
LORDSHIP OF O'MALLEY

Leverous had never seen such an expanse of sky and sea. From their crowsnest perch atop the awesome cliff face, he felt strangely disorientated at the emptiness and the silence, humbled before the sheer majesty of the spectacle before him. Beside him Robert Walshe drew in his breath in mute astonishment. It was easy to feel close to the Almighty, confronted by such a vista of earth, sea and sky that made man feel insignificant, an unnecessary accessory amidst such infinite splendour. Below them, the lofty cliffs fell down to where white-crested waves battered the rocks. Gulls and guillemots wheeled on and off precarious perches on the cliff face, their raucous cries echoing in the vacuity below. A pair of choughs wheeled with nonchalant ease overhead.

Robert Walshe broke the silence. 'It is like peering over the very edge of the world, and, I tell you, Leverous, if Columbus and da Gama had not proven otherwise, I would be inclined to believe we are.'

Leverous nodded his agreement, still strangely moved, by the the starkness of the beauty which surrounded him. An almost painful sense of contentment enveloped him, that even in the contemplative days of his novitiate at Louvain he had not experienced with such intensity. It was as if he was witness to a sight unspoiled by the world's false adornments but which had remained as it had been created in the beginning.

'Did you ever wonder what might be beyond?' the chaplain pointed towards the horizon. 'The new worlds of the Americas. Pagan kings with palaces of gold, strange tribes of red-skinned men, silver mines, pearl-encrusted rocks...'

Leverous smiled at the elderly priest. It was out of character to hear Robert Walshe speculate about material riches. Ever since Leverous had known him, worldly goods seemed of little consequence in his frugal way of living. Rather, Leverous suspected, it was the lure of the unknown more than the fruits of conquest that stirred Garret's chaplain. Robert Walshe's life was one of perpetual movement, a modern day Mercury for the House of Kildare. His anxiety to embark on the next stage of their journey had been evident since O'Malley had brought them to his island. Every evening, the chaplain walked to this lofty vantage-point for sight of the ship that was to take them to France.

'After France, where next, Robert? The new worlds?' Leverous teased him.

'Nay, Thomas, I think my bones tell me what I am loath to admit. My days of travel draw to an end. My next journey will be to the next world.'

'You have seen more of this one than most,' Leverous consoled him. 'And if this ship of Grey's is not a mirage, you will see more yet. Me, I swear I do not care if I was stuck fast to the one spot for the rest of my days.'

Leverous stood up, his hand shading his eyes against the pale rays of the setting sun.

'Well, it looks as if we will have to wait another day,' he said, as his eyes swept the empty ocean.

They retraced their steps across the bracken.

'At least here we are safe from pursuit.'

'And what a sublime sanctuary,' Robert Walshe replied, sweeping his arm as if to embrace the splendour around them.

426

O'Malley's island was at the mouth of a bay which swept inwards towards the mainland in a giant horseshoe. Great mountain ranges bordered the bay on both sides, culminating in the conical peak of the mountain of St Patrick, its bare head thrusting spectacularly into the clouds. Windswept moorlands, punctuated by rocky headlands, swept upwards from the sea towards the foothills of the surrounding mountains. A myriad smaller islands, like bulwarks, sheltered the mainland from the ferocity of the Atlantic ocean.

O'Malley's lordship was confined to the area around the bay, including the inner islands and a string of others which defended the lordship seawards. A kingdom fit for a seafaring tribe, Leverous mused, and, if the stories about O'Malley were true, for a pirate of some notoriety. For without an intimate knowledge of the indented coastline, it would be impossible to locate O'Malley and his fleet of swift galleys and trading vessels in this maze of island and mountain. And, if this remote lordship had for centuries protected the O'Malleys, with luck it would provide the last sanctuary for the Geraldine in Ireland.

'I wonder what the earl would say if he knew that his son was still a fugitive in Ireland?' Robert Walshe asked.

They walked some way in silence, both men lost in their personal remembrances of all that had happened since the death of the Great Earl and conscious that their promise to him remained unfulfilled, a promise that now depended on the word of the one who had lured the earl's son and brothers to their execution at Tyburn.

It was a strange irony, Leverous mused, that Gerald's safety should depend ultimately on the deputy of his would-be executioner. But the Geraldine's erstwhile Irish allies, one by one, through fear and expediency, had melted away. Even relations, like Dunsany, Desmond and O'Neill, had abandoned him to safeguard their own positions. The Geraldine League had proved a shallow thing in the face of adversity.

But the most persistent threat to his son's life had come

from where Garret had least expected, from within his own family. Leverous would remember forever the spectacle of the Countess of Ormond, like some great bird of prey, its food snatched from its talons, on the cliff above them, her cloak flapping like wings around her, a malevolent colossus of hate, her scream of frustration echoing over the water as they pulled away from the shore.

But at least the obsessional hatred of one sister was balanced by Eleanor's undoubted affection and commitment to her nephew, a commitment blighted only by her inexplicable decision regarding O'Donel. Despite the joy of their reunion, the rediscovery of their love, her agreement to marry O'Donel, like a splinter under his skin, rankled yet. As yet, she seemed unwilling to divulge her reasons. Even now in the safety of O'Malley's island, on the brink of a new chapter in their life together, it stood an unspoken barrier to their happiness. She seemed happy to come with him, to share whatever life they might find in France, to face the undoubted danger that would follow them, so long as Henry Tudor lived. Leverous could not doubt her courage, her devotion to Gerald, her love for him. But whatever lay behind her brief dalliance with O'Donel, she seemed unwilling to divulge.

'It looks as if O'Malley's children have cured Gerald's fear of the sea.' Robert Walshe roused Leverous from his thoughts.

The goat track they were following wound its way downwards towards the harbour where, like a sentinel, O'Malley's stark castle stood brooding against the blue green sea. In the calm waters of the crescent harbour, beyond the boats and long galleys at anchor, three children in a coracle were engrossed at their play. Leverous and Walshe watched Gerald for a moment, with O'Malley's young son and daughter, from whom he had become inseparable.

'Where children belong, Thomas,' the chaplain said quietly. 'At play, not as pawns in the evil designs of their elders.'

A shout reverberated towards them as Gerald waved from the flimsy boat. They returned his salutation and continued down the track which ran into the sand of the sheltered beach. Around the castle, rows of empty barrels awaited the return of the fishing fleet. O'Malley had been gone four days to fish for herring near the great bank beyond the island to the west.

From the castle entrance, Leverous saw Eleanor emerge and draw a mantle over her head. The evening air carried the distinct chill of winter. Leverous felt the familiar deep-seated yearning and desire she aroused in him every time he saw her.

'Has the Lady Eleanor decided yet?'

Leverous looked quizzically at Robert Walshe.

'To come with us to France.'

For a moment Leverous hesitated. He had not broached the subject with Eleanor since they had talked on the cliff, but she had given him no reason since to doubt that she would sail with them.

'I believe that is her intent,' he replied guardedly.

Halfway across the sands they met, her eyes searching his as if to reassure herself that nothing had changed between them. The longing to sweep her into his arms, to hold her close to him, almost overcame his reserve. The elderly cleric exchanged a few pleasantries with them and continued alone towards the castle.

Leverous drew her to him and kissed her briefly. She sighed contentedly in his arms.

'Perhaps we should stay for ever,' he said softly. 'Forget about France. Look at Gerald; he has never been more content.'

'And I, my dearest, have never been happier,' she whispered.

He kissed the top of her head. 'Sadly for all of us, Ireland is too small to hide from the vengeance of your sister and the king. Even here on this remote paradise. For *Inis Cléire* will soon be discovered too. Even as the Americas. And besides, O'Malley tells me that when the sou'-westerlies blow in from the ocean, our island of peace becomes a howling cauldron.'

''Tis hard to believe.'

They walked towards the castle, leaving the imprint of their feet deep in the powder sand.

'Robert Walshe asked if you are to come with us to France?'

She lowered her head. 'If you still want me to come.' She seemed unsure.

He pressed his cheek to hers. 'My dearest heart, I never wanted anything more.'

Across her head he saw Cormac talking with Gerald and O'Malley's children, as they tied the coracle at the jetty. He would miss Cormac's company and his friendship.

'Have you told Cormac yet, about us, about leaving?'

She shook her head. 'There is no need. He seems to sense that we belong together. That we will be together.'

'He will miss you greatly.'

Her sigh was deep and troubled and Leverous felt the familiar anxiety rise within him.

'As I will him,' Eleanor eventually said. 'But he is anxious to return to Carbury. The O'Malley has promised to take him on the first wind. He is a good son, Thomas, and will make a fine chieftain.' Her eyes searched his face as if she wanted to say something more.

He drew her to him, that he might make her forget whatever troubled her. Did the spectre of O'Donel haunt her still, or perhaps she feared what lay before them, the uncertainty, the danger? As before, he thought bitterly, he had little to offer her, nothing but an uncertain and perilous future.

The wind was rising, whipping the sea with white streaks of foam and blowing the sand into their faces. He felt her shiver beside him and they hurried towards the castle.

Gerald came to meet them, holding a wicker basket. He was barefoot and dressed in a loose-fitting saffron shirt and worsted breeches in which he could have passed as the child of any kern or betagh. He held up two crawfish for their inspection.

'Look what I caught. Cormac said I can have them for supper.'

'Perhaps you should keep one for The O'Malley?' Leverous suggested.

'But he may not come tonight,' Gerald said, examining the wicked claws inside the basket.

'O'Malley will be here soon enough,' Cormac said with certainty, as he joined them. 'The wind is blowing up from the north. O'Malley will be making for landfall with the catch before the weather worsens.'

The light of the October evening was rapidly fading as they made their way towards the castle. Some of O'Malley's followers stood in groups around the entrance, awaiting their chieftain's return. They greeted them shyly, in their soft western brogue. Cormac and Gerald remained to talk with them.

Leverous and Eleanor entered the open forecourt of the castle and ascended the steps to the doorway. O'Malley's castle had little need of fortification. Its very isolation was its defence. Inside, a flickering torch lit their way past dark crevices from which nets, fishing pots and anchors protruded, up narrow steps and into a large chamber. A fire glowed brightly in a chimney-piece and torches threw shadows on the lime-washed walls. On a trestle table pewter plates were laid for supper.

Leverous crouched close to the fire. The wind moaned in the chimney-piece.

'It is a hard life, this seafaring. O'Malley has more powerful enemies even than Gerald.' He looked up at Eleanor, standing with her arms folded, her eyes fixed on the fire. 'You know, my love, I think I would prefer your sister and the king as enemies than the wind and sea.'

She did not reply. The light from the fire danced on her face as she continued to stare deep into the flames. She seemed somehow removed from him. That secret part of her that he could never seem to breach was perhaps why she had always held a fascination for him.

'My father was much in awe of O'Malley, I remember. They did some business once. He filled our childish heads with stories of O'Malley's exploits by sea, of storms and pirate raids.'

'It took someone special to gain the praise of the Great Earl.'

She leaned down beside him. He took her hand in his and their fingers intertwined instinctively.

'Imagine this, Thomas, after everything that has happened to us – Maynooth, Thomas Court . . .' she smiled softly in remembrance, '. . . Carbury, Askeaton, here on the ocean's edge, in a pirate's den, we are together at last. Out of harm's way. All of us. You, me, Gerald . . . Cormac. It is like a dream. I feel I will surely wake up and find myself at home, in Kilbritin.'

For a moment he felt a pang of jealousy. He chided himself. It was natural that she would refer to Kilbritin as her home. It had been for all the missing years. But how he longed to hear her say that home was with him. Maybe it would come in time, although he had no home to offer her. Perhaps when Gerald was safely settled in France with Cardinal Pole, they might return to Kilbritin. MacCarthy had said that he would be welcome.

He tried to console her. 'Perhaps one day we will both wake up and find ourselves at Kilbritin.'

He saw the reflective smile disappear from her face, as if his suggestion was repugnant. Hastily she stood up. His hand fell emptily to his side. What had he said that had made her withdraw from him? She leaned her arms heavily against the chimney breast, her head bowed.

He rose and went to her.

'What have I said to upset you? God's mercy, Eleanor, you know I love you. I would never do anything to harm you.' She did not answer him and he reached out and caught her by the shoulders, his hands less gentle. 'What is it?' he said roughly. 'What in God's name still stands between us. There is something. It was there the first day we met in Colaughtrim forest and it still remains. Share it with me, I beg you. Do not let it remain to fester between us.'

'We can never be together at Kilbritin,' she said, her voice dull and lethargic. 'Never, I tell you, never.'

He felt he was on the brink of the secret, the last remaining barrier that divided them, the reason for her initial antipathy towards him, perhaps the reason that had made her agree to marry O'Donel.

'Why?' he prompted her gently. 'What is it, my love? Whom do you protect? Is it Donal, Cormac?'

Her eyes widened with apprehension and, as she withdrew from his grasp, the sound of a tumult issued from below. Helplessly he stood looking at her, waiting for her reply, but she turned resolutely away.

Leverous jerked open the wooden shutter of the splayed window which overlooked the harbour. A galley was being fast tied to the jetty, while further out the single masted fishing boats were making their way to shore. O'Malley's powerful figure leapt on to the jetty with an air of urgency. He was followed by two strangers. All three made quickly for the castle.

'The O'Malley comes in haste. With strangers. There is something afoot,' Leverous told her.

Eleanor came and stood beside him at the window and touched his arm hesitantly. 'Thomas, forgive me. There is something that . . .'

Voices and footsteps sounded on the stairway and before she could continue, Gerald burst through the door of the chamber, closely followed by O'Malley, Cormac and the two strangers.

'The ship has come,' Gerald announced excitedly.

Leverous looked in puzzlement at O'Malley.

O'Malley placed a hand on Leverous's arm. 'They,' he said indicating the two strangers, 'are unfamiliar with our coast and put in at the Killary, a bay south of here. I came upon them as we returned home. They asked that they be brought to you without delay.'

The smaller of the two men stepped forward, doffed his cap and bowed to them. Short and stocky, his pleasant open face was lit by bright brown eyes.

'Captain Roger Allen, master of the *Étoile* out of St Malo.' He introduced himself in a heavily accented voice. 'You must excuse my delay, but we could not find O'Malley's harbour.' He turned to his companion. 'Permit me to introduce Monsieur Gaspard Gaucher, envoy of the Governor of St Malo.'

A small thin man, with an air of authority, stepped out of the shadows. He flicked disdainful eyes over the party before him.

'The Conte de Kildare?' he asked Leverous.

Leverous smiled, shaking his head, and pointed to Gerald. Both strangers looked askance at the Geraldine in his saffron shirt and rough hose, his hair tousled and damp from the sea.

'My message is for Thomas Leverous and Robert Walshe.' The envoy looked enquiringly around the group.

Leverous stepped forward. 'I am Thomas Leverous,' he said and, turning to Gerald, sent him in search of the chaplain.

'Also the Lady MacCarthy,' the Frenchman continued and looked at Eleanor, who nodded in acknowledgement. 'For you, madame.' He bowed stiffly before her and handed her a parchment.

She examined the seal and extended it to Leverous. Clearly imprinted on the red seal were the Plantagenet arms. She broke the seal and, after reading the contents, passed them to Leverous without comment.

Leverous recognised the hand of Reginald Pole. The contents were brief and to the point.

Greetings, my Lady
At the behest of my Lord Grey, I send this by the ship that,
God willing, he hopes will take his nephew, The Geraldine,
his tutor Leverous and the Earl's chaplain, Robert Walshe,
in safety to us in France. The King of France is now ready
to honour his promise to your brother.
I trust Lord Grey's intent, as I ask you to do. We will
contact you at St Malo and take your nephew and his
tutor under our protection.
Yours in God
Reginald Pole

Robert Walshe arrived with Gerald, and Leverous passed the cardinal's letter to him.

'You are satisfied,' Eleanor asked Leverous, 'it is the cardinal's hand?'

'I am satisfied.'

'It seems that Charles throws in his lot with England against France,' Robert Walshe observed

'And François finally keeps his promise to the earl.'

'After all,' Eleanor added in wonderment.

In a corner of the chamber, the French captain was speaking in urgent tones to O'Malley, who nodded his head and then turned towards them. His gold earring flashed in the torch light.

'My friends, the captain is anxious to set sail. The wind is fair set for a speedy passage south to France. Another day and it may turn contrary.'

'When?' Leverous asked.

Roger Allen spread his hands. 'Now, monsieur, as soon as you are ready. With the new alliance between England and the emperor, the ports of France have been placed on

435

alert. We must take advantage of the wind God has sent us or risk being boarded by English ships off France.'

Eleanor glanced apprehensively at Leverous. It was so sudden, so definite, after all the months of anguished speculation and waiting.

'Are we to go to France now, this very moment?' Gerald asked excitedly.

Roger Allen bowed and smiled encouragingly at him. 'With this wind, Monsieur Le Conte, you will be in St Malo in seven days. I promise you.'

'God willing,' Robert Walshe murmured.

Monsieur Gaucher stepped forward again and with some ceremony handed Leverous, Robert Walshe and Gerald each a page of parchment tied by a red ribbon from which hung a seal.

'Your pass into France. Guard it with your life. Without it you will not be allowed to disembark at St Malo. The authorities suspect all strangers. We expect to be at war within the month.'

'The Lady MacCarthy,' Leverous said, 'is also to sail with us.'

The French official gave a grimace of indifference. 'I was given but three passes, monsieur, which I have delivered to those named therein, as I was instructed. I know nothing of a pass for the Lady MacCarthy. I am sorry. But . . .' He shrugged.

'Then she will travel on my pass. I will take responsibility for her at St Malo.' Leverous felt a sense of dreadful foreboding.

'I am sorry, monsieur. That is impossible. The ship is the property of the Governor of St Malo. I may permit only those with official passes into France to sail on her. And should you insist that the lady sail with us, she will be refused entry on arrival and be put on an English merchantman to England.'

'This is madness,' Leverous protested. 'Lady MacCarthy

is the boy's aunt, his guardian . . .'

'According to the instructions received from Paris, Thomas Leverous and Robert Walshe are accredited guardians of the Conte de Kildare. No others were named.'

Leverous looked at the grim faces of Cormac, Robert Walshe and O'Malley before turning to Eleanor. But she had disappeared.

Sympathetically, O'Malley pointed to the short flight of stairs that led to the ramparts.

From the corner parapet which projected over the wall walk, Leverous found her, staring out to sea. She did not seem to see or hear him. She seemed aloof, untouchable, as at first in Maynooth, before their love had broken down the barriers between them. She was out of reach once more.

'My love.'

She turned to him. Her hazel eyes appraised him, as she might a friend, with affection, before dissolving into something more.

Slowly, almost resignedly, she came into his arms and with a sigh rested her head on his shoulder. They stood together, without speaking, their bodies close, their minds in harmony. Regardless of the chill of the northerly wind that buffeted them, they stood looking at the sea below, the green depths being churned to white by the freshening gusts.

'The Great Earl, the king of England, your sister and whatever else fate has seen to fling at us, have been unable to separate us. I swear, my dearest heart,' he whispered, 'where they have failed to part us, no petty port official will succeed. There are other ships that will take us to France. O'Malley's for instance.'

She lifted her head from his chest and reached up and gently touched his face. 'Without safe passes, or licence to land? Dearest Thomas, I have always asked too much of you and given so little in return. At Maynooth, remember, when my fear made you a mortal enemy of O'Donel. At Thomas

437

Court,' her eyes shone with tears that slowly tricked down her face, 'when my love compromised and deceived you. At Askeaton, when it condemned you to a false hope.' She shook her head. 'How can I let it compromise what is still intact. Your honour.'

'What are you saying?' His voice was rough and hoarse with emotion.

'Take Gerald to safety in France. Be the father to him as Garret begged you. As on your honour you swore to be. Gerald's need is greater than mine.'

'Than mine?' he asked brokenly.

'Even than yours, my dearest love, even than yours.' Her fingers interlocked with his and held fast, as if she sought to transfer to him her strength of purpose to overcome the pull of his emotions. 'Gerald is young, vulnerable, Thomas. He needs your guidance, your protection. The strangers who offer to assist him now, as happened before, may sacrifice him again, throw him to his enemies. Gerald needs you, Thomas, more than ever.'

He kissed her hand, then her cold lips, tasting the salt of her tears.

'More than you?'

'My love, the sea divided us before but never in our hearts,' she whispered, her words hypnotic in his ear. 'We will always be together. Every step you take, I will be with you, as I have been with you here. We are one, Thomas, you and I. Nothing can ever take you from me again.'

'You will forget me, as before. In your life of content at Kilbritin. You will love again, perhaps marry again. Bear some lord the children that should be mine, that should be ours. There is so much love I want to give you. To make up for all that has been wasted. God's sweet life, Eleanor, it is too much to ask!'

She held his face, forcing his eyes to look at her. He looked into their depths and felt he might drown in the agony of the emotion that drew him to her.

'Listen to me, my love. You have given me more than you know. Something that each day will remind me, should I forget, of your face, your love, of the promise I make you now, to wait for you, to come to you whenever and wherever you are. If you still want me.'

'I have given you nothing but my love.'

She nodded, unable to speak for the tears that were spilling down her face. Her eyes relayed some mute message that he desperately tried to decipher.

'And that is all I need.' He clasped her, afraid to look into her eyes, lest his resolve should crumble.

Gently she withdrew from him and turned from him to the sea. 'Bring Gerald to me, my dearest.'

Unable to trust himself to utter a single word, Leverous backed away and descended the stairs into the chamber.

Roger Allen strode towards him. 'I beg you, sir. For all our sakes, we must make the tide.'

'In a moment, captain,' Leverous said, and beckoned to Gerald.

Together they climbed the stairs. She was where he had left her and at their entrance turned and held out her hand to Gerald. She knelt beside him, her hand tousling his unruly hair.

'What a seafarer you've become,' she said with forced humour. 'And now off to France, no less. Upon my word, you will be as good as Christopher Columbus or St Brendan. You must tell me all about your adventures when next we meet.'

Gerald's face crumpled and he looked around at Leverous and back at Eleanor. 'Are you not to come with us?'

'Not this time, *a stór*. But I will wait for you,' she looked beyond Gerald to Leverous, 'for both of you, at Kilbritin.' Her voice shook. 'So do as Leverous tells you. Be guided by him as your father wished. Be proud, Gerald, of your family, your heritage. Remember always that you are a Geraldine of Ireland. Ireland is your home and will be soon again, I know.

You go to France, as you went to O'Connor, for fosterage. There is no difference. And you will come back to your home, to me, soon again.' She held him briefly to her. 'God protect you and keep you.'

She stood up, her hand resting on Gerald's shoulder, and wiped away the tears that welled in his eyes. 'Be brave. Like your father.'

He nodded and hugged her tightly.

Gently she pushed him towards Leverous. They stood in silence, Gerald between them. There was nothing more to say. She raised herself and kissed Leverous gently on the check.

'Look for me here when you sail,' she whispered, and turned away.

Helplessly Leverous stood watching her, transfixed, as if his feet were fast stuck to the ground. From the chamber below the voice of the French captain urged him to make haste and O'Malley came and gently took his arm.

On the jetty, the galley was made ready to take them out to the ship. Cormac lowered Gerald to O'Malley, who placed him in the bow beside Robert Walshe.

Leverous turned towards the young chieftain, his hand outstretched. Cormac grasped it firmly.

'I can never repay what you have done, for Gerald, for me. My life, your friendship.'

'Think nothing of it,' MacCarthy replied. 'My mother and I owe you more than you can ever realise. God go with you.'

They clasped each other in a brief embrace.

On a curt order from O'Malley, the anchor was raised, and the galley sprang over the waves, propelled by the long oars, that dipped and lifted in unison.

As they cleared the shelter of the harbour, Leverous looked up at her figure silhouetted high above them on the parapet against the darkening sky and felt his heart sink into the fathoms that lay beneath him. As he looked, she was joined by Cormac, who stood with his arm about her. And at that moment Leverous knew what bound them and his love sped across the water that separated him from Eleanor and his son.

EPILOGUE

The Geraldine Conspiracy is based on historical fact. The principal characters existed and, in the main, played the roles portrayed in the book. (Manus O'Donel did not die as depicted in the story but lived on as chieftain of Tirconel. The Geraldine had another brother, Edward FitzGerald.)

After the flight of the Geraldine to France, Ireland settled back into an uneasy peace. Henry VIII pressed home the political advantage in Ireland after the collapse of the Geraldine league. To discourage further conspiracy against him, Henry assumed the title King of Ireland, instead of Lord of Ireland, the title held by previous English monarchs, and resolved to tackle the unsettled political situation in Ireland. To this end, he introduced the 'surrender and re-grant' scheme, whereby the Irish chieftains were to acknowledge him as their king, nominally surrender their lands and Irish titles to him, rule their territories by English law and attend the parliament in Dublin. In return, he re-granted them their lands as gifts from the crown of England and conferred on them English titles. Many of the Irish chieftains accepted the king's offer, some by coercion, some by free choice, but most only for as long as it suited their purpose.

Henry finally aligned with the Emperor Charles against France. Through Thomas Cromwell, he continued to suppress the monasteries in England. Cromwell was eventually thrown to the wolves by his royal master and was beheaded on Tower Hill in 1540.

Henry's queen, Jane Seymour, lived only twelve days after

the birth of her son, who fulfilled Henry's ambition by succeeding him, as King Edward VI. But Edward's reign was of short duration and he died, aged fifteen, in 1553. Henry's daughter, Mary, by Catherine of Aragon, succeeded him and she in turn was succeeded by his daughter Elizabeth, the daughter of Anne Boleyn.

Sir Leonard Grey was recalled from service in Ireland and was replaced as lord deputy. On his return to England, Henry had him arrested and confined in the Tower on a charge of high treason. Grey was sentenced to be hanged, drawn and quartered; the sentence was commuted at the last moment to death by the axe on Tower Hill.

Conn Bacach O'Neill, chieftain of Tyrone, was eventually forced to accept the king's offer of surrender and re-grant and was created the first Earl of Tyrone. His grandson was destined to become leader of a further confederacy in Ireland against the crown during the reign of Henry's daughter, Elizabeth I.

Gerald FizGerald arrived safely at St Malo and was taken to Paris, where King François received him with great pomp and ceremony. After English agents had made several attempts to kill him, the Geraldine was secretly taken by Cardinal Pole to Rome. The Cardinal sent Gerald to Verona and Mantua to further his scholarship. Gerald joined the Knights of St John in an expedition against the Turks and the Moors, ending up on the coast of Barbary. He returned to Rome and was accepted into the service of Cosmo de Medici, Duke of Florence, as Master of Horse. On the death of Henry VIII in 1547, the Geraldine went to England and was eventually restored to the title and estates of his father by Queen Mary. He returned to Ireland in 1554 as the eleventh Earl of Kildare.

Robert Walshe accompanied the Geraldine and Leverous to France and on to Italy.

The Countess of Ormond never realised her ambition to be Lord Deputy of Ireland but continued to rule the lordship of Ormond with an iron hand until her death in 1542.

After her nephew's departure to St Malo, Eleanor FitzGerald MacCarthy returned to Carbury. She never remarried. She died at Kilbritin some time before the restoration of her nephew.

Thomas Leverous accompanied the Geraldine to France and onwards to Italy. Through the influence of Cardinal Pole, he entered the English College in Rome and was ordained a priest. On the Geraldine's restoration, he returned to Ireland and was appointed Bishop of Kildare. In 1559, having refused to take the oath of supremacy, acknowledging Elizabeth as head of the Church of England, he was deprived of his bishopric. Under the patronage of the then Earl and Countess of Desmond, he opened a grammar school in Adare, County Limerick, where he died in 1577.

448